OTHER BOOKS BY JEFFREY THOMAS

Novels

Monstrocity
Letters From Hades
Boneland
Everybody Scream!
A Nightmare on Elm Street: The Dream Dealers
Health Agent
Deadstock

Collections

Terror Incognita
Punktown
Aaaiiieee!!!
Honey is Sweeter Than Blood
Thirteen Specimens
Unholy Dimensions
Punktown: Shades of Grey (with Scott Thomas)
Doomsdays
Voices From Hades

As editor

Punktown: Third Eye

BLUE WAR

A PUNKTOWN NOVEL

JEFFREY THOMAS

SOLARIS

First published 2008 by Solaris
an imprint of BL Publishing
Games Workshop Ltd
Willow Road
Nottingham
NG7 2WS
UK

www.solarisbooks.com

ISBN-13: 978 1 84416 532 2
ISBN-10: 1 84416 532 9

A CIP catalogue record for this book is available from the
British Library.

Designed & typeset by BL Publishing

To Truong Thi Hong

The fuel they use for the locomotive is composed of mummies three thousand years old, purchased by the ton or by the graveyard for that purpose.
—Mark Twain, *The Innocents Abroad*

We could pave the whole country and put parking stripes on it and still be home by Christmas.
—Ronald Reagan, in 1965

Acknowledgements

Loving thanks to my wonderful autistic son Colin, for devising the name Dink Argosax. As always, much gratitude to Christian, Mark, George, and the rest of the Solaris crew, and to Stephan Martiniere for his stunning artwork. Thanks, too, to Truong Thi Hong, who became Hong Thomas somewhere in the midst of it all.

PROLOGUE
THE DREAMERS

CAPTAIN HIN YENGUN liked to joke to his men that he knew the jungle like he knew his wife's body. Both were beautiful. Both were blue. His wife's skin, and every frond and blade and leaf and vine of the jungle; ranging from pale robin's egg, to vivid sapphire, to midnight indigo. Stalks, stems, and tree trunks might vary from this monochromatic spectrum. They might be white as bone, black, or even bright purple. But the vegetation itself, the foliage—and the lizards that poised on glossy leaves large enough to wrap the bodies of the dead before they were carried into the tunnels dug for them beneath the forest floor, and the stained glass wings of the butterflies that drank the blood of blue-haired animals like a kind of long-legged anteater—all a shade of blue. Even the light from the twin, blue-white suns, and the steam that rose from the plants as last night's rain continued to evaporate. The very air itself, tinged with blue.

Yengun knew his men well, too. These six fellow scouts had accompanied him on many a patrol to

trace, to tease, the border of the no-man's-land called
the Neutral Zone, a thin strip of forest that separated the Ha Jiin's land from that of the Jin Haa, like
the cold space in a bed between estranged spouses.
The Jin Haa's country was very much smaller, so that
the Neutral Zone nearly encircled it like a castle
moat, except where it bordered the sea. In some
areas, stone walls had been erected on one or the
other side of the Neutral Zone. Or razor wire had
been strung, mines buried, booby-traps set. The Jin
Haa capital city of Di Noon had the best defense of
all: a base full of Colonial Forces soldiers sent here
from the Earth Colonies.

But there were stretches of jungle where no fence
marked the beginning of one nation's land or the
other's, where it all blended and blurred into the
blue-leaved limbo of the Neutral Zone. Even without
explicit demarcation, however, Captain Yengun
knew the boundaries as clearly as if the Neutral Zone
were color-coded gray against the blue of the Ha Jiin
land and the Jin Haa land in the distance were color-
coded orange. These boundaries had held for nearly
eleven years now, ever since the conflict the Earth
people had called the Blue War had ended. That
hated war, when the Jin Haa had won their autono-
my. How many good Ha Jiin soldiers, like these six
beside Yengun now, had he seen cut down all around
him in those days when the beautiful blue jungles
had nearly turned red with blood?

The mines and booby-traps, mostly leftovers from
the war, were an anachronism in a time when Yengun's own commander—overseeing the entire
boundary between the two lands—insured that a Ha
Jiin crime lord like Don Tengu could move black
market products and drugs in either direction across
the divide without being challenged. It more than
rankled Yengun, who had fought in the war for a

reason, for an ideal, and was still committed to his job even if his commander, and his leaders above him, had relaxed their sense of patriotism.

There was an eighth member of his patrol today, and she was not something with which Yengun was familiar, or comfortable. She was a woman of eighty or more, shrunken and withered, her blue skin gnarled like the bark of a tree trunk. Her white hair had thinned to show her scalp, thick purple veins bold against her temples. The old woman made her way slowly, and one of Yengun's men, Nha, held her arm like a doting grandson as they moved sometimes along a worn path, other times through thick brush that two of the men hacked with machetes. Impatient, Yengun wanted to scoop the woman up and sling her onto his back as he did his sons, but he had to show her respect. Not only because of her age, but because of her gifts. She was the witch of her village. Her dreams had come to the attention of the commander of border security. And if his boss took the witch's dreams seriously, no matter how Yengun felt about the man, then he must take them seriously, too.

It wasn't really so hard to believe her, though. Not with what was happening lately. Not since the advent of the Blue City. He figured the Blue City must be causing nightmares all throughout the Ha Jiin nation. The Jin Haa nation, he wouldn't doubt, too.

"Uh! Uh!" the witch grunted, pointing a trembling arm ahead, as if she couldn't speak the same language as these men. Her animal-like sounds made Yengun wonder if maybe she was an imbecile; sometimes the gods gifted such creatures. All Yengun himself had witnessed were monosyllables, but he reminded himself that she had related her troubling dreams to others. More likely she was just senile. Whatever the cause of them, her noises irritated him, but when Yengun looked at her he felt a touch of concern to see a dribble of blood from one of her nostrils.

"Yes," Nha whispered to her, the good foster grandson, "the city is just ahead."

Did Nha intuit her meaning, Yengun wondered, or was the witch speaking directly to his mind? Was that how she had articulated her dreams? In that case, Yengun would rather stick to her grunts and cries, than to have her palsied mental fingers kneading at his brain.

As Nha had stated, the Blue City was looming close at hand. One didn't need a witch to tell that. A faint mist between the trunks ahead was becoming a fog that would soon swallow up the trees altogether. And there was a sound like crackling fire, or perhaps raspy static turned to an intense volume. It became louder as the fog became denser.

This fog might have seemed natural to one who didn't know the jungles like Yengun did. He knew it was anything but natural. It became a white cell closing around them with shadowy trunks for bars. The crackling noise was now piercing. The old witch pressed her hands against her ears, grimacing.

Where they could see it, the jungle's flora started to take on a look of decay, plants wilted and leeched gray, until a little further along the denuded trunks of the trees themselves were blackened as if a fire had cut a swath through the forest, and these vapors were its smoke. The machetes hacked through brittle webs of sticks. At the same time, however, the forest floor turned marshy and wet as if soaked recently by torrential rains. This was the runoff from the Blue City. Yengun thought of it, bitterly, as the piss it gave back to the earth in return for all the nutrients it sucked from the soil and the life that rooted in it.

Yengun knew this charred-looking strip of jungle was almost geometrically straight, as if it marked a border on a map. The Blue City began here, on the Ha Jiin side of the Neutral Zone, and spanned the width of the Zone, extending into the land of the Jin Haa. Actually, though, it was the other way around. This cancer had begun on Jin Haa land, and extended across the Zone in this direction. Whichever the case, it was as though the city didn't care one iota about the boundaries written into a peace treaty over a decade earlier.

One moment the seven Ha Jiin commandos and their charge were squishing mud and matted dead leaves underfoot, the next moment their shoes were clacking upon pavement, as they emerged from the wasted vegetation.

Now that they had stepped into the open, the mist was not enough to cloak the city, the blue forest no longer camouflaging it. Through the fog, which rolled into the jungle behind them and steamed up into the air, Yengun could see how the Blue City rose against the blue, blue sky. He had seen the city from atop a mountain last week. It didn't just rise against the sky; it *soared*.

There was no other city of such size on the whole of the planet Sinan, not even the modern Di Noon. And until two months ago, there had been no Blue City at all.

"Uh," the old woman said, nodding vigorously and pointing the way again. This was not yet their destination. "Uh... uh!"

They continued onward. As they left the border of the pavement, the fog started to disperse, and gradually cleared altogether. So, too, did the deafening static recede behind them to a distant, less oppressive level. The fog and noise were signs of the Blue City's advance, the front line of its invasion.

"This is easier walking now, eh, auntie?" Nha tried to calm her agitation, but Yengun could imagine the young soldier was feeling anxiety of his own. Captain Yengun was feeling it himself. Some people had found the city exciting, had ventured into it with enthusiasm. He was far less enthusiastic about it, and his team was one of the patrols that had orders to keep such fools from their explorations.

At least he could understand how the scope of the city might tempt them. The sidewalk they had stepped onto was wide enough for a car to drive down, let alone the river-like expanse of the street itself. A latent instinct had moved them to the sidewalk, despite their inexperience with a city of this scale, and despite the fact that there wasn't so much as a single vehicle on the streets. And the buildings: not all of them were skyscrapers, but those that could be defined as such not only scraped the sky but lost their tops in haze; Yengun could imagine their summits crossing the boundary of the atmosphere into space itself.

There were skyscrapers with sides so featureless that one might think they were solid stone monuments in a graveyard for dead gods. Other buildings looked like they'd been pieced together from thousands of odd-matched parts salvaged from stripped factory machines. Buildings wearing an armor of riveted plates, like retired warships looming vertically with their sterns jammed into the street. Flat roofs upon which perched smaller buildings, symbiotically. Other structures tapering to needle points that seemed to etch the clouds upon the blue glass of the sky. Stacked apartments. Stacked businesses. Rows of smallish tenement buildings, with shop windows and shop signs at ground level.

Or at least, Yengun supposed they were meant to be shops. He couldn't be certain, because the windows were not clear. They were opaque. And the signs did not have words upon them. That was because every surface of every building in the Blue City was—blue. The same rich but bright shade of blue. And every surface, if seen closely, had a rough texture like pumice. The windowpanes were of this material. Even the sidewalk under their feet, the broad boulevards. No matter how heterogeneous the buildings, representing architectural styles from countless planets and seemingly constructed from a wide variety of materials, all were the same homogeneous color and texture.

Following the woman's quivering finger, they cut across an intersection, and Yengun paused at a street sign on the corner. Traffic signs that should have been video screens to direct the flow of vehicles were instead featureless blanks, but this sign had letters upon it, because it appeared to represent metal embossed with characters.

"What does it say?" asked Nha. Yengun had studied English back in the days of the Blue War. The basic language of his enemy. But Nha didn't know a word of it.

In a distant, distracted voice, the Ha Jiin officer replied, "Children Crossing." He turned, glanced around him, gestured at a nearby building with many opaque windows, broad but not too tall. "That must be a school."

"Uh!" the old woman barked, taking Nha by the arm and dragging him into motion again. The others followed along with her, as though she had become their leader.

Another of the commandos craned his neck to peer over the wall that surrounded the school across the street. "Shouldn't there be, what would you call it, athletic equipment? Gymnastic equipment?"

"You mean a playground?" Yengun said. Both talked in subdued voices, as if a hidden enemy, spying on them even now, might be listening. This was also why all of the men except Nha gripped their pistols or assault engines.

"Maybe it's a school for older children?"

"No. It's the same reason there are no vehicles. Those things are not a part of the city. The Blue City is like a statue modeled after a living person. But the statue doesn't wear the person's clothes and jewelry; it's just the body itself."

The soldier took in the blank windows all around them as though gazing back nervously at the unseeing orbs of a vast army of titan statues.

The woman dragged Nha into an alley between two office blocks, sizable but not towers. There was no trash heaped in the alley, no trash zapper to digest it, no derelicts slept on sheets of cardboard or under makeshift shelters. No graffiti slathered on the alley's walls. It was unnaturally clean. This was a well-kept necropolis.

When they emerged onto the next street, there was a sign of life so incongruous here that it startled them. A flock of large birds with metallic blue feathers had gathered on one building's high, flat roof, and the appearance of the scout party sent them bursting into flight with echoing squawks and the clapping of wings. These birds could be seen every day in their villages, scavenging for food. Here, they seemed like an ominous, alien species. Yengun himself nearly raised his gun to fire at them.

They probed further and further into the network of streets, some of them avenues so long that their ends were lost in haze like the tops of the skyscrapers. These towers cast such deep and pervasive shadows that the hot tropical air was actually cool, almost chilled Yengun's sweat-filmed skin. He looked back over his shoulder. He could no longer see even the tallest trees of the jungle. The Blue City surrounded him. Had swallowed them.

"Yes?" Nha said suddenly to the woman. "One more?"

Yengun looked at him, surprised. "What?"

"She told me it's one more street over."

"I didn't hear her."

Nha crumpled his face in confusion. "No?"

Yengun looked at the witch. The purple veins at her temples appeared fatter, darker. He thought he could even see them pulsating. She swiped her wrist across her nose to catch the blood oozing from it, only succeeding in smearing it on her cheek.

One of the team members motioned with his gun at a building across the next street. "Why do some of these places have all their windows open, but in most buildings they're all closed?"

Yengun had already spotted the rows of black holes gaping in the structure's rough blue face. He said, "That one would probably have energy fields instead of solid panes. Like the energy wall around the Colonial Forces base in Di Noon." He knew a lot about Di Noon because several years ago he had actually visited that city. There was a treaty, after all. But also, he had a computer in his home, and computers opened the universe and all its knowledge to him. Not to mention that another lifetime ago, he had fought as a guerilla in its streets.

"That's it," Nha told them, referring to the edifice with open windows. "That's the building she wants us to check."

Captain Yengun turned to meet Nha's gaze, then reappraised the building with fresh eyes.

"What are those on the roof?" asked the man with whom Yengun had shared the analogy about the Blue City being a statue.

The officer noted the antennae array atop the roof, like a cluster of thin blue spires. "I don't know. Transmitters, receivers. Maybe something to turn solar rays or radiation into energy. Not that any of it works."

"So those are part of the body? Not jewelry, so to speak?"

"Apparently," said Yengun.

He looked both ways before crossing the empty street; again, a latent urban instinct. The town where he lived with his beautiful wife and two young sons wasn't really all that greater than the village of shacks with corrugated tin roofs that the witch lived in.

As they reached the opposite sidewalk, Yengun obeyed another instinct—but much older and much more developed—and checked the status screen of his assault engine, a bulky but fairly lightweight weapon that could fire a number of different solid projectiles, from jacketed bullet to buckshot, and a ray beam besides, not to mention its grenade and rocket launcher features. It was a weapon the Ha Jiin military now bought from an Earth Colonies arms manufacturer. All safeties were in OFF mode.

"So what is it?" one of the men with machetes whispered, holding his pistol ready. "Offices? Apartments?"

"Who can say?" Yengun said. "Just a shell. Keep quiet now. Everyone alert."

"She told me they're sleeping," Nha said. "Not to worry... they're sleeping."

Yengun again gave his man a weighty look, then switched his attention to the elderly woman. She was staring into the nearest open window, almost quaking with fear or with the force of the impressions that bombarded her. Yengun nodded to the others, and the first scout climbed in over the window's sill.

They found themselves in a long hallway, lined with windows on one side and far-spaced closed doors on the other. Just like the building's exterior, the interior appeared as if it had been heavily coated in blue paint with a scratchy rough texture. No one spoke now; even the old woman seemed to have the good sense to keep quiet. She pointed down the left end of the hall, and they advanced. The specific door she indicated was second to last in the row. One could tell by looking at it that it was sealed shut. Yengun nodded to another man with an assault engine. This man lined up his weapon with the door's seam, and it emitted a bright white ray from one of its muzzles. A sizzling sound, then a thin black smoke started unraveling into the air. The others stepped back a bit. The scent reminded Yengun very much of an unpleasant smell from his war days. The smell of burning bone.

The hinges were fused shut, so the commando traced his beam along all four edges. When he was finished, another man stepped forward and stomped the door with his boot. A crunching sound of resistance. Several more stomps, and the door fell inward. A thick mist had been trapped in the windowless room beyond, and it flowed out of the doorway like spirits released from a tomb.

Right away, Yengun activated a flashlight on his gun, wading ahead of the others into the mist. He flicked the beam this way and that. The fog was so thick underfoot that he nearly dropped into a hole in the floor, but he caught himself and angled the light down sharply. It flashed back at him, reflected from the surface of a pool.

As the mist continued to disperse, Yengun made out three large holes in the floor of the sizable and otherwise featureless room. These holes did not look broken in the blue-colored floor so much as melted, perhaps, their edges rounded and grooved, giving them the appearance of organic orifices. The three cavities were filled with water. Or was it water? It had the biting acidic smell of the fluids that ran off from the Blue City into the jungle.

Yengun and the others inched closer, aimed their beams down directly into the pools. The old woman was babbling softly in agitation, hanging back and clinging to Nha's arm.

"What... dear gods, what is that?" one soldier asked, scrunching up his face in confusion, revulsion.

There was a shape in each of the liquid-filled pits, down deep in the earth below the thick crust of the floor. Threads like strands of web—or better, like veins—grew out of the edges of that blue rind. These hundreds or thousands of thin blue strands trailed down into the pools, connecting with the three dark shapes that the beams illuminated.

"Looks like a fossil," one man reported. The small figure, curled like a fetus, was entirely blue, rough as a statue carved out of pumice, and its outline was strangely distorted besides.

"This one's dead," a second man said, about a second figure. It was not a petrified thing, however. Its infant-sized body appeared soft, and yet horribly deformed, like a fruit rotted on the vine. The myriad blue veins seemed to pierce or at least grow directly into its flesh.

Yengun played his beam over the face of the relatively larger figure nestled at the bottom of the third flooded shaft. He could tell from subtle differences in its face that it was not a being native to this world of Sinan. But more obvious than that was the color of its naked skin. The skin was a whitish peach color, not blue like his own.

This third creature looked perfect in form. No distortions. No...

Yengun's breath caught in his throat. He heard the old witch mumbling, mumbling.

He had seen the eyeballs shifting back and forth under their thin lids, as the creature at the bottom of the third pool dreamed.

CHAPTER ONE
LOV 69

THE MEN AND women sheltering in the gloom of the Legion of Veterans' Post 69 ranged in age from early thirties to there-are-still-people-alive-from-that-war? The bartender was a veteran of the Red War, which had cost him an arm, replaced with a black prosthesis like something grafted on from a giant beetle. Watt was a Choom, one of the indigenous people of this planet, Oasis, though most of the Earth people in the colony city dubbed Punktown had been born here, too, as had their parents and even grandparents. To all appearances Watt was human, aside from the wide mouth carved back to his ears, giving his broad face a bit of a frog-like aspect. He was, however, rather more dangerous-looking than a frog.

Seated in the post were a couple of Punktown servicemen who had been deployed to the world of Echo, part of a raid on the colony city of Oracle. A group of Red Jihad extremists had captured and sabotaged the atmosphere control facilities there, resulting in the death of 37,000 colonists. One of these vets, named

Isaiah, cried a lot when he'd had a few Knickersons too many, recounting the numbers of suffocated children he had seen throughout the colony, strewn everywhere like placid-faced dolls.

There were the brothers Bobby and Wally, slouched over the bar in shiny blue jackets and faded baseball hats, all covered in glittering pins and embroidered patches indicating that they'd been crewmen aboard two military starcraft in the same fleet. They were withered and cantankerous and intent on claiming their explosive space battles made every other vet's war look like a picnic in the park. Gnome-like Bobby frequently came close to blows with younger vets, infantrymen bristling at the suggestion that their ground combat could be less hellish than what this old-timer had experienced from inside his massive warship. They always restrained themselves, however, having heard that his brother Wally had once smashed the jaw of a drunken vet twenty years younger than himself, in this very bar. Not to mention that Watt was quick to break up trouble, and that plastic beetle claw could grip you by the back of the neck good and hard on your way out the door.

Two black men with shaved skulls, a branded insignia on their foreheads and metallic silver bar code on the back of their necks, had been coming in to sit at one end of the bar for a few months now. No one knew what war or conflict they'd been in, and they didn't volunteer it. Maybe Watt knew, but he was discreet. They spoke to no one, not even each other, just sipped their Zubs and watched the big VT screens mounted on the walls. Their polished domes reflected the blue of a holographic sign that read: *"Zub... for a mellow buz!"*

Then there was Jeremy Stake. His engagement, known as the Blue War, had ended eleven years ago when he'd finished a four-year stint at the age of twenty-three. For whatever reasons others did not come here, and for whatever reasons he did, Stake was one of the few Blue War vets who favored this murky little post. "For a mellow buz," he murmured to himself, eyeing the two black men as he lifted his own beer of that brand. It was as good a reason as any, he supposed, for his presence here. *Buzz,* he thought. *It should say buzz.* But then, the beer would have to be called Zzub, wouldn't it? Such was the way he rested his mind, when taking a break from the more taxing puzzles his line of work entailed.

"Jer," Watt said to him, coming close.

Stake looked up at the Choom. "Heh?"

Watt tapped his forehead with the claws of his prosthesis.

Stake reached up to his own forehead, felt its flesh with his fingertips. Raised areas, like thick ridges of scar tissue. Like a raised, branded insignia. Like the insignia on the heads of the black vets he had been idly spying on. "Dung," he muttered, making sure he didn't look at them again. He had forgotten himself. It got away from him sometimes. The beer had made him *too* mellow. Well, the effect would pass, just like the buzz.

One VT, sound muted, was playing a game show wherein schoolgirls of Japanese descent, wearing nothing but mouse ears on their heads and painted-on whiskers, scurried through a giant maze while male contestants tried to shoot their quick naked bodies with paint guns. Stake loathed *GiggleMiceGo!*, but could seldom take his eyes off it when it was on. The other VT had its sound on, and was tuned as usual to an all-military channel. Currently a documentary on the training of troops for the Red War was playing. Trainees were marching along while their tough drill instructor kept pace. The soldiers were shouting a politically correct Colonial Forces chant:

"I respect all cultures, clans and creeds
But mess with me I'll make you bleed!
Sound off... sound *off!*
One, two, three, four
One, two—*three, four!*"

One branded black vet was watching *GiggleMiceGo!,* the other the documentary. Peripherally, despite his avoiding them now, Stake saw the two men turn their heads to face the door behind him. He saw Watt look that way, too. He swiveled on his stool.

Everyone was looking at the man who had just walked in, because he was in full Colonial Forces uniform. At LOV 69, uniforms were reserved for holiday parades. And funerals. Furthermore, the man was a captain. But it was Stake alone who recognized him, after his mellow brain sharpened up a bit.

Captain Rick Henderson seemed to be having a rougher time spotting Stake, though. He knew it was because he had unintentionally begun taking on the physical characteristics of one of the branded vets. He raised his hand to catch Henderson's attention. The tall man hesitated a moment, squinting into the cigarette haze, then smiled and approached the bar.

"I must be having a war flashback," Stake said, slipping off his stool to stand and shake the officer's hand.

"Tell me about it," grumbled another vet at the bar, hunched over an ashtray.

"What's this?" Rick asked, pointing to the raised symbol on Stake's forehead.

Stake tilted his head toward the two black vets, and Henderson gave them a look. "Ohh."

The Colonial Forces captain was familiar with Stake's gift. During the Blue War, when the captain had been a mere private and Stake had been a corporal, they had been part of a deep penetration team, venturing far behind enemy lines. Stake's ability to radically alter his features had come in handy then. Henderson knew he still utilized this ability in his current line of work as a hired investigator. But he also knew that Stake was a mutant, born to a mutant mother in the Punktown slum of Tin Town. It was not only a gift that Stake had never asked for, but one which could slip from his control if he let his guard down, and looked too long at another person's face. So Henderson well understood why his old friend's eyes darted only briefly to his own, ever in motion. Stake claimed this was why he seldom missed much about his surroundings. He claimed it was a trait that had kept him alive in dangerous situations, during the war and since.

They settled in together at the bar. Henderson asked, "Can you handle another round, or should we make it coffee? Or something stronger?" He was referring to the pills bartenders often stocked and sold to customers if they wanted to drive their helicar home instead of into the side of a building, these pills swiftly counteracting the effects of such intoxicating agents as alcohol and anodyne gas.

"Ahh… how about coffee?" Stake ventured.

"Sounds like a good idea." Henderson nodded to Watt.

"Wow, Rick," the investigator said, shaking his head. "I haven't seen you face-to-face in years."

"I still haven't seen your face yet," Henderson joked. He meant that his old friend's features still bore a fading resemblance to one of the black men, though his skin's pigmentation had not managed to darken to the same degree, despite a good try. When Stake's features did reshape themselves to what he called his "factory settings," his face would have an almost mask-like quality of blandness, blankness. This neutral state was not too broad or too thin in shape, too hard or too soft in its lines, too masculine or too feminine; deceptively solid, but a living veil of smoke over the bone beneath. Under close scrutiny in certain light one might discern the grainy look of his skin, smooth in texture though it might be, these grains being chromatophores that to a more subtle extent enabled his skin to alter its hue like the flesh of an octopus. In fact, Henderson had once seen a VT program about the Indo-Malayan mimic octopus, which could change not only its color patterns but configure its body to resemble a flatfish, or a poisonous lion fish, or a banded sea snake. It had right away put him in mind of Jeremy Stake.

Stake asked him, "How'd you find me here?"

"I remembered you hung out in a veterans' post, but I didn't know which one. I've just been to two others that are closer to your apartment."

"Yeah, I dunno, the number 69 appeals to me for some reason."

Henderson smiled. "That I can understand. Anyway, I've been trying to reach you since last night. Do you have your phones switched off?" He nodded his head at Stake's wrist comp.

"I like to rest my mind between cases."

"How are you supposed to get more cases if you don't pick up your calls?"

"Potential clients leave messages."

"I know; I've left a half dozen myself."

"So are you a potential client, Rick?"

"As a matter of fact, I guess you could say I am. Yeah."

Stake appraised the man with a sobering eye. "You stationed on Oasis now?"

"No. I came here just for you."

"It must be a hell of a case."

"Tell me about it," Henderson said, mimicking the drunk a few stools over. He sighed, and looked into the coffee Watt had just set down in front of him, as if searching through the rising steam for his reflection in the black surface.

"Are you serious, Rick?" Stake was making his own potion lighter and sweeter. "What's the problem? What can I do?"

"Shh," Henderson told him. "Can't you see I'm working through something here?"

"Working through what?"

"I'm wondering if I'm making a mistake coming to see you."

"Will you just tell me?"

Henderson blew out a long breath. It dispersed the occluding steam. "You know, when I was a kid I had a pet salamander named Brian. I guess you could call him a salamander, or a newt; he was a Tikkihotto amphibian. He had eyes just like them, in fact—all these little eye feelers. We had him a good five years, I think. Sometimes when it was quiet and I was doing my homework, or late at night, I'd hear this one tiny little *glub*. It was an air bubble rising from his mouth. It kind of reminded me that he wasn't just alive when I was looking at him; he was alive all the time. When he was alone in the house, in his aquarium, he was living his life. Do you know what I'm saying?"

"So far."

"You wouldn't think something like that would have a personality at all, let alone affection, but there was something strange. For whatever reason, Brian would never crawl into my hand, or my brother Paul's hand. Never do it. But my mom could do the same thing and he'd get right into her palm. And then he didn't want to leave; she had to practically dump him back into the water. Well, even though he wasn't as fond of me as he seemed to be of my mom, I cried the day we found him dead in his aquarium. Old, shriveled up."

"Hm," was all Stake could say. Waiting for more. Did his friend mean he, Stake, was the salamander? Still here in Punktown, alive, when Henderson was off involved in his own life? More than just some shadowy war memory?

"Ten years after Brian died," Henderson went on, "I shot a Ha Jiin man in the face with my pistol, from a few feet away. First man I killed, just a week after my nineteenth birthday. I'm the same person who loved a stupid little newt, and wept when he died. The same guy who shot a man in the face. And killed a lot of other people, after that day."

Stake didn't know exactly what Henderson was getting at, but he reassured him, "You're still that same person, Rick. That part of you didn't die in the war. I bet you'd cry again today, if you had a pet for five years and found it dead."

"I think you're right. But I'd also shoot a man in the face today, if he was pointing a gun at me."

"Okay, look, I really don't understand where you're going with this."

"I'm saying I hate to ask you to come back to Sinan with me. I know it did to you what it did to me. I know that's why you sit in this room, alone at this bar, with a beer in front of you and other ex-soldiers around you, close but not too close. Just like then, you don't want to get too close because you don't want to cry when they die. Maybe from old age now instead of a bullet, but it's still pretty much the—"

"Wait." Stake held a hand up. "Wait. You're asking me to go to Sinan with you?"

"Yes. That's where I'm stationed now. For the past two months."

Stake's expression became very grave. "Is this about Thi?"

"No, no—it doesn't have anything to do with her. Haven't you seen it on the news, Jer? Bluetown?"

"Bluetown. This is about Bluetown, then?"

"For starters, it is."

Stake had indeed seen it on the news. It would surprise no one who knew him—not that many did—that he should keenly follow any news about Sinan. Generally, there wasn't much to be seen in the popular media, however, because Sinan was more than just another planet. It was another planet in another dimension. It was, to date, the only extradimensional world that the Earth Colonies had ever engaged in war. And that was the other reason there wasn't much to be heard about it in the news. Old wars brought bad memories. What had needed to be done there was done, and most Earth colonists on their many far-flung worlds preferred to relegate Sinan to its unseen realm. Hadn't Stake tried to do the same? But again, at cross-purposes with himself, he always pricked up his ears at the merest mention of it. And the news about Bluetown was hard to miss.

"So is that why you were stationed there—to look into that?" Stake asked.

"Yes. I'll tell you what you may already know, and what you may not. A company called Bright Horizons has been working with the Jin Haa, creating little condo-type village complexes, in and around the city of Di Noon. Bright Horizons is a Punktown-based operation, owned by a David Bright. He's created similar complexes for dwelling and business on a good many colonized worlds. The process he uses for these projects was developed by a biotech team he acquired called Simulacrum Systems. They use a quasi-organic process, where the buildings are actually grown rather than built, according to a blueprint programmed right into the smart matter itself."

Stake had been nodding to urge Henderson along. He knew all this. It wasn't really anything new; there were even massive skyscrapers throughout Punktown grown from synthetic living material.

"Bright's approach is the best that's been developed. In the past, generally this kind of organic matter was grown over a metal skeleton, and that substructure would be covered in a mesh impregnated with current to induce the growth. Bright's buildings don't need to grow over any kind of framework, and they generate their own growth without need for current."

"Right. Bluetown is feeding off the jungle on Sinan. It digests cellulose and whatever other organic matter gets in the way. It's burning along like a forest fire."

"And almost as fast. Anyway, like in the older approach, this organism ends up solidifying into something like coral. Essentially it's only alive while it's growing—when the cells are reproducing. As the growth progresses, what it leaves in its wake is dead matter, like bone. And that's what people ultimately live inside: skeletons. Bright's stuff is smart, like I said. It's programmed to leave channels and openings in the walls for the integration of plumbing and cables, access panels for utility maintenance, and so on."

"But it's not so smart if it's running wild like this. Do they know what caused it to happen?"

"No, they don't. And it keeps on spreading. What should have been a little condo village for a few hundred people is turning into a whole fucking city. A lot of these structures are immense; two hundred floors and more. I couldn't believe the extent of it myself until I went out there and flew over it the first time."

"And all of it is blue because…?"

"It was just the color scheme Bright and his designers chose. The other Jin Haa condo units they've done were all in shades of orange; you know, the color of their flag. This one, being deep into the forest, he figured would be nice to do in blue. It's blue, all right. Crayon blue."

"Why retain the color but not the original blueprint? Did it start out as the village and move on to the city, or start out as the city from the onset?"

"The city."

"But is it inventing this city as it goes along? Where does it get the layout?"

"We thought it was, at first. We thought it was just randomly producing sample architecture that it had been exposed to through net transmissions it might have received, maybe through connection to the computer station that initially set the process in motion. But finally, one of our people recognized a particular building. It wasn't apparent, at first, because these things look so different in this coloration, and in this setting. But the building was distinctive."

"What was the building?"

Henderson paused to further the dramatic effect. "It's a library with two big statues out front, that serve as front columns. Art Deco-type women, holding twin globes that are supposed to be Earth and Oasis."

"Wait a minute—"

"Yeah. You know it, because you lived on Judas Street a few years back, didn't you? It's the library on Judas Street. Right here in Punktown."

"Are you saying this city is a copy of Paxton?"

"Yes. It's been confirmed. An amazingly detailed copy of Paxton. It isn't reproducing unlicensed, unregistered structures—such as homeless people and mutant gangs and so forth might put together, in between or on top of legally zoned buildings—but it's copying just about everything else. Occasionally a building here or there that should exist doesn't, and that might serve as a clue. It might indicate that there's a time stamp to the information it's accessing. It might be dated."

"My God. Punktown."

"The name we were using for the city before, in our internal communications, was Simulacra. Because of Simulacrum Systems. Of course, we weren't calling it that in the media, because giving the city a name implies that the thing is legitimate, here to stay, and that concept does not go over well with anybody, especially the locals. But anyway, since we figured out it's supposed to be Punktown, we've taken to calling it Bluetown. And that name *has* leaked out. That's why you've heard of it. But you didn't know what it referenced beyond the obvious."

"But, Jesus, Punktown... it's *huge*. It will overwhelm everything if it grows to full size. How much of that has it accomplished so far?"

"In two months, Bluetown has achieved an astonishing ninety-five square miles. That's astonishing because it's about a fifth of the four-hundred-seventy square miles the city of Punktown itself covers. And Punktown has an approximate population of sixteen million citizens. So Bluetown has already reproduced enough of itself to house over three million people. That's a lot of cellulose this monster is gobbling up. A lot of both Jin Haa and Ha Jiin forest consumed. But not just forest. Villages, farms. Temples. And now, it's closing in on the city of Di Noon itself. Its growth might be impeded by having buildings in its path instead of forest to nourish it, but we don't know exactly what will happen when the two cities collide. There might still be enough organic matter under the ground to push this thing on and on, bulldozing everything in its path. And if it does mean to reproduce Punktown in its entirety, then it will have to grind Di Noon out of existence. Take its place."

"Christ." Stake didn't know how long he'd been wagging his head. He turned his eyes toward one of the VT screens, watched the nude Giggle Mice as they scampered deliriously through their paint-splashed maze, like adorable giants rampaging through a psychedelic dollhouse city.

"And that's the start."

Stake faced Henderson again. "The start?"

"It's not what I want you there for. What I need you for—what I wanted to ask you to think about, I mean—is something we just found in Simulacra. It hasn't gone to the media yet, but it will leak out anytime now."

"Which is?"

"Something that was discovered two weeks ago by a Ha Jiin security patrol on their side of Bluetown. They did the right thing, and told our people about it so we could go in and investigate. Three cloned bodies, inside one of the buildings. Two dead, but one viable, and in the form of a child. A *human* child."

"You mean human as in Earth human, not Sinan human?"

"Yes. An Earth-type human."

"And three clones got into this building how?"

"They grew inside the building, apparently. Unless someone wired them up to the smart matter, it would seem the smart matter itself fostered the growth of the clones."

"What? You're saying this Simulacrum technique grew three human beings? How could it do that? That's a fuck-load lot more complex a structure to grow than the coral shell of some building."

"We don't know, but nevertheless, that seems to be the case. The programming of cellular reproduction that runs through the smart matter seems to have been communicated to these humans cells and led to their reproduction, as well, through some kind of connection Bluetown made with what we figure must have been human remains it encountered in its path."

Stake nodded. "Ohh... yeah. Human remains. MIAs, then."

"It would make sense. This matter is chewing its way across the countryside, sucking up its living fuel, and along the way it finds three Colonial Forces soldiers, forgotten there since the Blue War, either buried under forest refuse or buried by our guys or the enemy during the engagement. The city absorbs their remains and it sparks an odd reaction. Two clones come out dead—maybe because the remains were of men who'd been too badly mutilated, and the matter inadvertently let that fact influence it." Henderson snorted. "'Inadvertently,' like anything this stuff is doing can be called purposeful. Anyway, most remarkable of all, one of the clones is alive and awake and for some reason, a little boy of, say, five years old. I guess if the clone hadn't been disconnected from the smart matter, and grown to fruition, it would have been an adult."

"Is the child cognizant?"

"Yes, but with a mind like an infant."

"God, it's just amazing. I wonder if the clone had grown to adulthood, if enough of the brain plasticity would have been reproduced that it would have at least a few fragments of memory, enough to tell us who it is. Because, since you said you figure these are MIAs, I'm going to assume you haven't found any identification."

"Right, no dog tags or anything like that. But without a brain drip of long chain molecules, with the clone's original memories encoded in them, I'm afraid we wouldn't have gotten more than a shadow or two out of him even if he was allowed to mature before he was disconnected from the smart matter. We could continue his maturation ourselves, but to what end? Like I say, we'd get shadows at best. And of course, if allowed to continue aging in the natural way, the child will never have anything for memories of his original. His developing brain plasticity will be entirely unique as his life experiences differ."

"Whew," Stake said, and sipped his coffee for a taste of something more familiar.

"The connection I'm referring to, between the clones and the smart stuff, was a net of fine veins or roots that entered the flesh, but so minutely at their contact point that when the veins were severed, they left no wounds in the clones' skin—just these little nubs like the base of a stem, that atrophied and broke off the live child, leaving no trace."

Stake made an impatient brushing motion to get to another point. "But it doesn't make sense. If this city can make a human clone after it digests some remains in its path, why only these three? Considering the amount of land it already encompasses, shouldn't it have reproduced other clones, too? Okay, maybe not Ha Jiin or Jin Haa dead down in their burial tunnels, but what about other undiscovered war dead?"

"Who knows? Every building hasn't been explored yet."

"But not just people; why wouldn't this thing have reproduced about a gazillion dead animals by now? The earth has to be full of remains of all kinds of organisms. Why just these three?"

"That's all part of what's being investigated, Jeremy. By the CF, and Bright's Simulacrum Systems team, and some Ha Jiin and Jin Haa scientists too, for what that's worth."

"And so why me? What are you asking me to do, here, Rick?"

Henderson leaned his tall frame forward, as if the veterans' post might contain Colonial Forces spies, posing as nostalgic old drunks. "My commanding officer is Colonel Dominic Gale. My impression is that he's not exactly enamored of me. I think he sees me as an intrusion, or a threat. Maybe he takes my assignment as an indication that his superiors don't have confidence in his ability to sort this out and deal with it. Anyway, the fact is he's not friendly, and he's not cooperative. And his people are afraid of him, so they're loyal to him and all but useless to me."

"I see. So you're in need of a friend on Sinan."

"I'm in need of a guy who knows Sinan. And I'm in need of a talented investigator. And I know that you're both."

"But I'm not a scientist, Rick. You want me to figure out how the city pulled this off, and brought that kid to life?"

"No. I want you to tell me who this kid is. And the two clones that didn't make it. They've got to be MIAs, Jer. They've got families. People who need to know about what happened here."

"You said it's going to leak to the media?"

Henderson gave a little smile. "Yeah. I'll see to that."

"Huh. And why will you?"

The smile faded quickly. "I don't trust Gale. I'm afraid I don't trust the Colonial Forces at all, or the Earth Colonies embassy in Di Noon. If this didn't leak to the public, there's no telling what would become of that clone. Destroyed in the course of study, or as an inconvenient anomaly that can't be comfortably explained? Anyway, I didn't want to take chances. He's a person, Jer. He has loved ones out there. At least, his original did. If he ends up being unwanted by them, and if they want the clone destroyed—well, better that should be on them, than on me. I have to do as much as I can to at least give him that chance."

Stake grinned. "Why Rick—I think you've found yourself a new salamander after all."

Henderson lifted his black coffee. "Wipe my smile off your face."

"My...?"

"You're starting to look pretty ugly, my friend. You're starting to look like me, now."

"Dung," Stake said, flicking his eyes away. "I never learn."

But Henderson kept his eyes fixed on his friend. "What do you think, Jer? Again, I hate to ask you to come to Sinan. Then again, I hate to see you with a bar stool up your ass, sucking down the Zubs."

"You're right about that," Stake said. "There is no good place for me to be."

"I have a hotel room. I need to go back to my base tomorrow night. You have until then to think about it. If it's too much, believe me, I understand. *Believe* me."

"I am between cases," Stake said, as if speaking to himself.

"No, don't say anything now. Think about it tonight. I'll call you tomorrow. Just do me one favor?"

Stake hazarded a glance at his old friend. "Hm?"

"Turn your damn phones on, will ya?"

"Will do, sir." Stake gave the officer a salute.

Henderson looked embarrassed. At first, Stake thought it was about the salute, until Henderson explained, "You're right about the salamander, Jeremy. See how intuitive you are, even with some brews in you? I've given the kid a nickname."

"Brian," Stake completed for him.

CHAPTER TWO
THE CALL

WITHIN THE PAST year Jeremy Stake had had to move from his Forma Street apartment to one a mere block removed from the Choom ghetto called Phosnoor Village. Watt the bartender, when Stake had mentioned this to him, had suggested that Stake was a masochist. Hadn't Forma Street been a bad enough neighborhood? Stake had then asked Watt where he lived, in a penthouse in Beaumonde Square? This was Punktown, after all. For the most part, it didn't make all that much of a difference.

He had needed to relocate because of a case he had accepted, something rather out of the ordinary for him. A female of the Stem race had wanted to leave her husband and flee Oasis with two sisters. A radical undertaking indeed. It was the custom of the Stems not to allow those of other races to lay eyes upon their women. Supposedly it was due to their immeasurable beauty. After all, female Stems were voluptuously as thick around as a broom handle, white in color, with three lower limbs and three upper limbs, like immense walking stick insects. The males were taller at seven feet, with crimson-colored bodies thin as a pencil, but it was a mistake to underestimate them; they were renowned as warriors. By tradition, the males were required to punish those who inappropriately caught sight of their women—and the women themselves, if viewed—with death.

Rebellious modern women, these three. Stake had been successful in arranging transport for the Stem females to Earth. He had then picked them up in his hovercar and driven them to the teleportation center, had waited there until he saw them safely off the planet.

But the husband of the married sister, and their own two brothers, had found out that the women had hired an outsider to help them escape, and had managed to track Stake down. They had even come to his apartment on Forma Street, which doubled as his office, though he never accepted clients there in person. The result of this visit was that Stake had been hospitalized for an arm injury (now fully healed), and the two brothers had escaped alive. Stake's killing of the husband had been deemed self-defense.

Still, he had been receiving death threats ever since. He always met with potential clients in a public setting, such as a café or their place of business, and a few times he had suspected that a trap was being set for him and had declined to meet. He had recently turned down a job from a Kalian man. The gray-skinned Kalians were one of the few truly humanoid races, and thus not related to the Stems, except in that they treated their females in a similar way: a controlling abuse disguised as reverence. Stake wondered if he were becoming too paranoid now, suspecting that a Kalian might be aiding the Stem brothers in trying to lure him into an ambush.

Maybe it wasn't such a bad idea to get off Oasis for a little while, after all.

But of course, that wasn't his primary reason for contemplating Rick Henderson's offer. Stake wasn't about to kid himself. He knew it had more to do with Thi Gonh. The Earth Killer.

His current flat was a suite of rooms in a decommissioned destroyer, one of several space vessels transformed into apartment complexes in what had once been the Phosnoor Shipyard. Improvements in teleportation over the past few decades had made starcraft increasingly obsolete—obsolete like the vets Bobby and Wally, who rented rooms in this old beast themselves and had told Stake about it. Its outside still bristled with the dismantled remains of its guns and sensors. Inside, the walls bore rows of heavy rivets, the white enamel paint thick and cracked with age. Stake slept in a lower bunk, bolted to the floor, the upper mattress heaped with his clothes. Right now, first coffee of the day in hand, he paced in and out of his several connected rooms. He paused at a series of monitors set into a wall. One screen was black and dead, one whispered with static, but two were operational, giving him a view of the hall outside his flat and a view of the shipyard outside. It was gray and wet from last night's rain, the city skyline misted and phantasmal. He had read in a book once that on Earth, in centuries past, there had been reports of ghostly mirage cities as seen from places once known as Alaska, North Africa, Ohio, the Orkneys. He remembered that article when he looked at the city on days like this. The mirage cities had invariably been described as beautiful. Well, Stake thought even Punktown might be considered beautiful from a distance.

Airborne craft of various sizes moved through the sodden air like light-bejeweled deep-sea fish. One was more like a whale: a dirigible-shaped gas freighter with the word "ARGOS" in huge blue letters across its silvery flank, conveying a shipment from the company's sprawling refinery. Huh, Stake thought. Sinon gas, from the world Sinan. He saw these blimps all the time and thought little of them, but now this one seemed like the steely finger of God himself, prodding his mind.

As he watched, a helicar floated down into the shipyard's parking lot, its blowers sending up a spray from the rain puddles as it hovered. A young man with an umbrella and briefcase ran to the vehicle and hoisted himself inside, car-pooling to the office. Stake was reminded of larger helicraft he and other infantrymen had run to, hoping they wouldn't be shot as they broke cover, escaping one area of blue jungle so as to be deposited into another area of blue jungle.

Last night after coming home from LOV 69 he had fallen asleep on the sofa, going from watching VT to the VT watching him. He had dreamed of what Henderson had told him. In his dream, it was Stake and a team of Colonial Forces troops who had ventured into a strange blue building in a strange blue city. They had cut open a sealed door, and entered a room with three circular holes like huge organic orifices in the floor. Stake had got close to them, and looked down into the pools they contained. Three figures had been floating in the amniotic fluid: three adult men in blue camouflage uniforms. He'd recognized their faces. Three privates named LeDuc, Devereux, and Rick Henderson.

Stake had reached into one of the holes and dragged Henderson out onto the floor, bending over to resuscitate him. Two other men helped pull out LeDuc. They left Devereux in his odd womb, however, because he was dead, the pool dark red with his blood.

Stake had woken before Henderson and LeDuc could be revived. Before he could see if they were mere clones, mindless copies, or the actual men. Before he could see if they'd survive. But he understood the significance of the dream quite clearly.

Eleven years ago, those same three men had crouched in a forest clearing, away from the rest of the team, to take a brief rest from their advance. From their packs they had removed and examined personal possessions they'd recovered from the bodies of three of their fallen comrades, killed by a Ha Jiin sniper, belongings they hadn't had a chance to examine closely before that moment. There were cookies that one man's mother had sent him. It seemed that he had been saving them, too sentimental to actually eat them, but the three soldiers shared the cookies then as they began reading aloud to each other the letters that loved ones had sent to the three dead men. A letter from a mother, a letter from a wife, a letter from a child. As Henderson had related the story to Stake later, LeDuc had been the first to start weeping. But soon the other two followed suit.

It was their tears that saved them. For the entire time they were in the clearing, the same sniper who had killed the men they wept over had the Colonial Forces soldiers in her sights. But their brittle emotions, in that raw and vulnerable moment, had prevented her from pulling the trigger. This Ha Jiin woman was so accomplished a soldier, so skillful a sniper, that her own people had dubbed her the "Earth Killer." That ominous name had even found its way to the whispering lips of her enemy. She was said to be a tiny, hard-eyed killer, as beautiful as she was deadly, with a rifle as tall as herself.

But because she could not bring herself to kill those three enemy soldiers that day, her comrade reported her to their superiors. After the war she was tried for treason. Because of her exemplary record prior to that mystifying lapse in judgment, she was not punished, but she earned herself a new and more mocking moniker. Her people took to calling her the "Earth Lover".

The Earth Lover. Staring out into the gray morning, Stake smiled ironically. The nickname went beyond the mercy she had shown those three vulnerable soldiers in her crosshairs.

Her name was Thi Gonh. Stake learned this, because his team ended up capturing her and one comrade alive, and holding them prisoner inside a seized Ha Jiin monastery for a week, until Stake's crew could be met and joined by a unit of Advance Rangers. By this time, Corporal Jeremy Stake was the commanding officer. That was because the Earth Killer had previously picked off their lieutenant and sergeant—this sergeant being one of the men that Henderson and the other two had wept for.

Stake left the monitor, sipped his coffee as he resumed pacing his metal cell in the belly of this grounded leviathan. It was like sipping at his memories. Carefully, lest they burn him. Coffee both bitter and sweet, a blend of dark and light.

The young corporal had been bewitched by his prisoner immediately. She was beautiful like a blue-striped tiger, a blue-scaled cobra. And she had immediately been stunned to witness his chameleon-like abilities, as he unconsciously took on a semblance of her features. Stake couldn't speak much of her language, but Henderson had a translation chip in his skull. He'd told Stake that the woman was calling him Ga Noh. It was a Ha Jiin term for a kind of mythical entity: "a chimera or a shapeshifter," as Henderson explained it then. "A mystical kind of being; part human, part god. Maybe good, maybe evil."

They had been in awe of each other. Afraid, and attracted. Maybe attracted *because* they were afraid.

He had started out by protecting her from the other soldiers. He had ended up in bed with her, behind the closed door of her cell.

A single week, his lover. The Advance Rangers had rendezvoused, the prisoner had been transported away, and he and his team had carried on with their jungle fighting as if nothing exceptional had occurred. That was the last he had ever seen of the Earth Killer. At least, in the flesh.

Stake set his mug aside, leaned over his computer to see what messages might have come in while he slept. He was reminded of the last time he had seen Thi Gonh's face. It had been on this very screen, a year ago. With Henderson's help, he had finally learned of her current whereabouts. She told Stake that she had married, though she had been unable to conceive children, and she and her husband owned a farm.

Ten years of trying to forget her, and intermittently searching for her, only to have his heart ground under her heel in a call lasting a few short minutes. But then, it had only taken him a few minutes to be enraptured by her in the first place, hadn't it? And what a fool he'd been anyway. Pining for a woman who had killed his friends around him, a woman he had barely been able to converse with and had known for the span of a single week. Maybe, after that call, he'd have finally been able to forget her.

But at the time, Stake had been involved in a dangerous case, and had sustained a beating, and with her keen sniper's eye Thi Gonh had put this together during their call. Unknown to Stake, she had managed to concoct a lie to leave her husband, leave her world and dimension, to travel to Oasis. To Punktown, where she had never even been. She had stalked Stake like her quarry, never actually giving herself away. Afraid to disgrace her husband by drawing too close. Not trusting her prey, and apparently not herself. And when Stake's enemies had struck, she had struck too. She had killed two men before Stake could even blink. He'd been wounded by his enemies, had fallen into unconsciousness, and she had seen him to a hospital; in doing so, had touched his body while he was unaware. By the time he regained consciousness again she had already gone. Back to her far-flung world, her parallel realm of existence on the flip side of reality. As if she had never even been there; a figment of his delusion. But she had been there. She had risked her marriage and her life to come to his aid.

So she hadn't forgotten her Ga Noh either, after all these years. Just one short week a decade earlier, but their destinies had remained connected like the "entangled pairs" of atoms, as they were called, that made quantum teleportation possible across the multiverse.

He had not called her since, though. In the past year, she had not called him either. Were they waiting for the other to make that move? Or had her visit here to help him been a kind of closure, a coming to full circle, after he had protected her ten years before? A kind of ending?

If so, would it be a mistake for him to go back to Sinan now, and shatter that symmetry? Because he knew he could not possibly return to Sinan without seeing her. Rick Henderson had to know that as surely as he did.

Stake punched up his recorded calls. Some ads that he deleted, and one personal message. A face came onto his monitor. It was like a jack-o'-lantern's: empty triangular eyes, a single triangular nostril, gaping toothless mouth. It was the visage of a pencil-thin Stem, greatly magnified. Those macabre features in its rough, blood-red flesh did not move at all as its translated voice came through the speakers.

"Detective Stake," said one of the brother-in-laws of the Stem male he had killed, "you can hide with your changing face, like a moth against tree bark, but our people are born hunters, born warriors, and we will always find you. You should never have meddled in this affair. You had no right to interfere in our culture, our hallowed traditions. You had no business helping those three women. You have killed the honorable husband of a hateful wife who deserves a thousand deaths. Your people may have exonerated you for this crime, but you will find no such mercy from us. We will not rest until you have paid for your transgressions, Detective Stake. And you will find no rest, not here nor in the world beyond!"

The world beyond, Stake thought.

"You and all your arrogant kind are cursed, cursed, and you will know this on the day that a billion dead warriors feast on your soul in revenge!"

"Ouch," Stake said, "I hate when that happens." He cut the message off in mid-sentence and forwarded it to Punktown's police force, as he had been doing these past months.

He straightened and retrieved his coffee. It was cooling.

What did he have here now, aside from a couple of homicidal Stems—who if they were half as good as they bragged would have caught him already, but made every day a hazardous enterprise nonetheless? He had briefly been involved with someone last year but it hadn't worked out, due to his own lack of enthusiasm. The nearest he had to a close friend these days was probably Watt, and for all he could tell the man didn't have a lower body behind that bar. The only other person he might consider a close friend was, of course, Rick Henderson.

It might be nice, spending some time with an old friend like that. Doing him a favor. Making a little money. Sure. And avoiding the wrath of the Stem brothers and their billion hungry ancestors, besides.

Stake leaned over his computer again, and made a call of his own. It didn't surprise him that at this early hour the Colonial Forces captain was awake, showered, dressed in his handsome uniform. And apparently awaiting Stake's call.

"Congratulations," Stake told him. "You've become a recruiter."

CHAPTER THREE
THE WORLD BEYOND

THE QUEUE THAT lined up to board the pod was not a long one; mostly business types in expensive five-piece suits, and several blue-skinned Jin Haa who dressed and carried themselves with a similar aura of importance. This was, after all, the Theta Transport Station, not the Paxton Teleportation Center, where the crowd would have been very much larger. The difference being that at the latter institution, people teleported from one planet to another. At TTS, one could teleport to another dimension.

"Nervous?" asked Henderson, ahead of Stake in line.

"I'm wondering if people still get that nauseous feeling," Stake said.

Henderson smiled. "You may, Jer. That nauseous feeling was mostly about nerves, even back then."

As Stake watched, a bipedal beetle-like entity about five feet in height walked up the ramp ahead of the queue, so as to board the transdimensional pod before the passengers. An extradimensional being called a Coleopteroid.

"Our captain, so to speak?" Stake asked his friend.

"Probably just a technician. Or a consultant. Not like anyone actually pilots these things."

The extradimensional races the Earth Colonies had interacted with included the Antse, who wore over their own gray flesh the tightly fitting flayed skin of whale-like creatures called flukes, this skin a beautiful malachite blend of green and black. There were the putty-like L'lewed, who in this environment were required to spend most their time inside a small metal container which would be transported about for them on the back of a robot or hired aide. The Vlessi race—with a reputation even more ominous than that of the Stems—resembled thin white dogs walking on hoofed hind legs, but with heads shaped weirdly like a human pelvis. The towering Kodju people were capable of slipping from one plane of existence into another by a process that, while requiring great discipline, did not involve any technology.

But it was the Coleopteroids whose means of traveling from one dimension to another had proved most beneficial to the Earth colonies. As Paxton had become known as Punktown, and now Simulacra had been renamed Bluetown, so had the Coleopteroids earned themselves a more user-friendly nickname: the Bedbugs. Not that the Bedbugs were all that friendly. They mostly kept to themselves, and some of their activities in Punktown and in other Earth colonies had been controversial, if not occasionally alarming. But the enigmatic beings had been tolerated largely due to their cooperation in the advancement of quantum teleportation, in recent years making transportation to the known dimensions more accessible. Working in conjunction with the Earth colonies' Theta Agency—the government-funded scientific division responsible for extradimensional study and exploration—the Bedbugs had made it possible for Earth to discover the planet

Sinan in its alternate reality, seventeen years earlier. And thus, had made it possible for the Earth Colonies to send soldiers there two years later, and go to war.

The Bedbugs themselves utilized a different method to cross back and forth between their home dimension and others, and even before their cooperation with Theta researchers had operated a transportation terminal of their own here in Punktown. The conveyance they used to shuttle between dimensions was known as a tran. It looked rather like an ancient steam locomotive of black metal, and traveled along a complex series of tracks knotted into overlapping geometric configurations. As the tran accelerated, its rate of speed and the pattern it followed along this train bed determined which material plane the tran ended up disappearing into. As disturbing as Stake remembered traveling in a transdimensional pod to be, at least it didn't sound as dizzying as the technique the Bedbugs employed for their own needs.

A green twirling light came on above the ramp entrance, signifying that it was now okay to board the pod. The attendant began scanning each passenger as they advanced. Stake couldn't help but feel like he was nineteen years old again, carrying a simple rucksack of camouflage blue colors. Henderson passed through, turned, and waited for Stake to be scanned by the attendant, an attractive Choom woman with lipsticked lips wrapped halfway around her head. Stake tried on a much smaller sickly smile in return.

He followed Henderson forward. Neither carried any luggage; their one piece each had already been stored in a lesser chamber of the egg-like craft, hulking unseen beyond the end of the boarding ramp. Another attendant waited just inside the entrance, nodding at each passenger cordially. He was a Tikkihotto, fully human in appearance but for the striking difference that his visual organs were twin nests of clear tendrils that squirmed in the air with a life of their own. Stake remembered the pet newt, Brian, that Henderson had discussed, from the same planet and possessing a similar ocular arrangement. Tikkihottos could see colors that humans could not detect, could even discern the simple transdimensional life forms that ever floated in the air like plankton. Stake wondered if this ability was one of the reasons why a Tikkihotto might be hired to accompany a craft that would nose its way through the fabric of reality.

Henderson and Stake took their allotted seats in one of the forward-facing rows. This was the only real difference he saw between this commercial vessel and the troop ship he had last journeyed to Sinan in. In those old infantry pods, there had been two rows of seats facing each other, forcing the fresh recruits to see their fear mirrored in the faces of the soldiers opposite them. Stake remembered staring down at his boots instead. The guy across from him would be scared enough already without having to see his face literally reflected in that of the teenage Jeremy Stake.

The egg was sealed up, the last of the passengers having settled and the Tikkihotto having taken a seat by a monitor station near the door. Looking back at him, Stake could make no sense of the overlapping data that scrolled both horizontally and vertically across the monitor screens. Maybe only a Tikkihotto could grasp it.

"Prepare for initiation," said a voice from a speaker; surely not the voice of the Bedbug technician, wherever he was hidden aboard. As softly modulated as the voice was, Stake flinched a little at its unexpectedness; there had been no such cordial announcements in his experience. But what was there to prepare for, except psychologically? There would be no jarring movement. No actual movement at all, really, except for a thrumming vibration through one's soles and buttocks and back. The seats didn't even have safety belts. The craft did not employ locomotion in the conventional sense. It would stand still, in effect, and the multiverse would pivot around it until the pod was where it needed to be, and reality came to a halt once more.

The same voice began reciting a countdown. Stake turned to Henderson and joked shakily, "Nothing like milking the suspense. Do they *want* me to throw up, or what?"

Henderson patted his shoulder. "Hey, think of it as an interesting vacation. You're not going to war this time, Jer."

Going? In a way, Stake thought, had they ever fully returned from it? He couldn't speak for his friend, but sometimes it felt like some vital component of his being had been left behind him when he'd returned to his own dimension at the age of twenty-three. When you went to the Paxton Teleportation Center and had your body transmitted to another planet, that body was actually destroyed in the process, and what was reassembled on the other end was essentially a facsimile. A copy even more exact than a clone, but a copy nonetheless.

It had made Stake wonder what "me" was, if every teleportation was a death and a rebirth. There had even been criminals who, having attempted to flee via teleportation, tried to argue in court that they could not be found guilty for the misdeeds their previous incarnations had committed.

This line of defense had never proved successful. Just as Stake doubted that the families of the Ha Jiin he had killed, were they to capture him upon his return to Sinan, would ever find him unaccountable for his own killings.

A display at the front of the chamber indicated the pod's progress, a horizontal meter going from black to green. One might think they were in a bathysphere and the meter measured the depths to which they were submerging. The pod had no windows. If it did, Stake wondered what he would see outside them. Maybe only blackness. Or maybe the guts of space, time, and dimension, a vision so incalculably immense and complex that it would shatter his mind to take it in.

Only a few minutes had passed, but the display showed they were halfway there. Stake understood the *here* and *there* of it. It was what lay between that was so slippery, and frightening, to grasp.

The meter seemed to be reading the queasiness swelling inside him. He found himself trembling. Was the vibration he felt running through the pod, or himself?

Three-quarters of the progress meter had turned green now.

This was not so much a transdimensional pod, for him, as a time machine. Bringing him back to a place where people had tried to kill him, many more than just a couple of vengeful Stems. And where he had killed people. And fallen in love with a woman who to this day was still a stranger to him—but a stranger who moved on the periphery of his dreams, a stealthy sniper camouflaged in mottled patterns of memory and desire.

The meter was nearly full now.

"Prepare for arrival," said that same intercom voice, as bland and undistinguished as his own face.

Once more he thought, *prepare... how?*

The penetrating vibration simply stopped. Through the pod's body, at least.

Henderson patted himself jokingly and said, "Looks like we made it in one piece."

Every soldier knew of pods that had somehow been misaligned with their destination, ending up buried a hundred feet underground like a coffin, or merged with the side of a mountain like a fossil, with the crew all dead or—more horribly—still alive. And of course there were those pods that had just vanished, never to arrive anywhere, maybe hurtling through the infinite continua for all eternity.

But for these passengers, the voice came over the speaker one last time and said cheerlessly, "Welcome to Sinan."

SINCE DI NOON'S teleportation center was so much smaller than Punktown's, the terminal for the transdimensional pods was situated within the same complex. Stake and Henderson emerged into the main concourse, bags in hand, to be confronted with the most Sinanese people Stake had seen in one place in over a decade. There were enough Earther faces—and even some nonhuman ones—amongst the swarming crowd that he and the Colonial Forces officer did not draw all eyes, but they were definitely noticed.

They had first passed through a customs checkpoint where their bodies were scanned for weapons and their visas scanned for authenticity. The stern-faced young Jin Haa woman, grimly attractive in her military-style uniform, had looked up from Stake's face on her monitor to his face in the flesh. Stake had been nervous; had he begun taking on another person's appearance unconsciously? Could she detect some discrepancy between his visa image and himself? But a green light flashed to signify that he had been cleared, and he was admitted through to join Henderson. He had thanked the woman in her own language, one of the few words he remembered. She did not respond.

The two men had then been met by a pair of young CF military guards with blue camouflage uniforms, camouflage helmets, and cumbersome-looking but actually lightweight assault engines cradled in their arms. Henderson had explained, "There have been some violent protests, and even some terrorist-type activities, because of what's happening. When you see the scope of the problem, you may wonder why there hasn't been more violence."

"Why do you think that is?"

"They trust us that if we have the power to wreak such havoc, we have the power to make things right. A lot of them—the Jin Haa, if not the Ha Jiin—like what we do for them. And also, they're afraid of us. But fear and hate walk hand-in-hand. Things will get worse, believe me, unless Bluetown is stopped in its tracks real quick."

They waded through a sea of bobbing blue faces. Most of these were of a robin's egg hue, though others were an intense sky blue and some an even darker shade. Glossy obsidian hair that, when the light struck it just right, shimmered with a metallic red undertone. Eyes shaped by what was called, on Earthers of Asian lineage, the epicanthic fold. When these often beautiful, mask-like faces turned to regard Stake—with what? Curiosity? Distrust? Resentment?—their black eyes also caught the light just so and flashed an eerie red, glowing like the eyes of animals filmed at night in an infrared light, staring back at the camera. Perhaps dangerously.

Men and women both tended to be slight in stature and build, but tight-muscled and tough. Despite the mix of otherworldly visitors, the crowd was so much more homogeneous than any gathering of people Stake might encounter back home. All around him were the distinctive high cheekbones, the more or less slanted eyes, and that ebony hair with its hidden undercurrent of blood— worn short on the men, but usually long, so long, on the women. Everywhere, he saw what could have been sisters to Thi Gonh. He even swore he saw her, here and there, multiply cloned and blended into the congregation of travelers.

As the Jin Haa briefly returned his gaze, Stake believed what he was seeing in some of their faces was not just loathing, but self-loathing for their marriage of convenience with the colonists, self-disgust for their natural tendency to keep every unseemly emotion in restraint.

"Are you up for a flight over Bluetown, for a look?" Henderson asked him as they made their way toward the exits and the parking lots beyond, "or do you want to head straight to your quarters at the barracks?"

"I'd like to see it," Stake told him.

"Okay. You hear that, Aldo?" he said to one of the two security men. "We're heading out to Bluetown."

"Yessir."

They had just left Punktown, Stake thought. Now, in a way, they would be returning to it.

THE HELICAR THAT lifted high above the teleportation center was a military model known as a Harbinger, equipped with a variety of mounted guns and rocket launchers, such a craft tolerated because of the presence of the Colonial Forces base here in Di Noon, though Henderson had explained that as a civilian visitor, Stake himself would not be permitted to carry a weapon.

Outside the teleportation center, the air had closed around him steaming and hot, pressing the air from his lungs with its humid weight, but the interior of the Harbinger was cool. He leaned close to one window and peered down at the city below him as they rose yet higher.

The Jin Haa capital of Di Noon sprawled to every horizon, as if it might carpet the whole of the planet. Just as the crowd at the airport had lacked the wild diversity of Punktown's citizens, so did Di Noon's homogeneity contrast with the diverse architectural styles and influences Punktown had to offer. The majority of buildings, packed tightly flank-to-flank, were flat-roofed boxes with plaster walls, often painted white or in soft pastel shades. Most, however, were painted in shades of orange, from very pale to pumpkin to fluorescent. Orange was the color of the Jin Haa flag, the color of their independence from the Ha Jiin nation. Orange was the opposite of blue. A kind of defiance by pigment—though with their blue skins, Stake thought that their rejection of the Ha Jiin's blue flag and generally blue-painted buildings seemed almost like a rejection of themselves, in part. Another reason they were distressed at the nearing Punktown clone? Maybe Bright Horizons should have chosen orange for the project that had inadvertently spawned Bluetown, too.

Except for hotels, which were a few stories taller, not too many structures rose higher than three or four floors. The majority of streets were narrow, lined with shops at ground level, countless signs above countless little awnings. These streets and the broader avenues that cut through the city were absolutely thronged with bikes. There were wheeled bicycles and wheeled motorbikes, but most were hoverbikes that rode just above the pavement. The best hoverbikes were of Earth origin, a status symbol but increasingly accessible to Di Nooners. Like pretty beads offered to primitives, Stake thought. Like chewing gum for children.

Punktown's wider streets would have been packed mostly with hovercars, instead, and its sky would have been swarming with helicars. But here, Stake saw no other flying vehicles at all in the empty expanse of sky, made a pearly white by smog and humidity, through which blazed the blue-white glow of twin suns. Sky and city met in a kind of balanced flatness, broken only by a few scattered skyscrapers at Di Noon's center that crossed the border between earth and heaven.

But there was an intrusion into this yin-yang balance, now. It didn't take long for Stake to spot it.

Smog, humidity, and distance made the city beyond the city appear misted and ghost-like, an unfinished painting sketched in on the white glass of the sky. Here were the tall buildings that Di Noon lacked. The horizon was jagged with a profusion of soaring towers, like the lances of an advancing spectral army of giants.

"Simulacra," Henderson announced needlessly.

"Bluetown," Stake muttered against the glass.

The Harbinger hurtled toward it—despite its bristling weapons, quite unequipped to do battle with the phantom city's glacier-like approach.

STAKE THOUGHT OF the city of Pompeii, buried under volcanic ash. The hollows in the solidified ash that, when filled with plaster centuries later, proved to be molds in the shape of the citizens who had been smothered there. Bluetown reminded him of that. As if a city had been buried and then decayed, leaving a tremendous void in its place. The mold had been poured full of some blue substance like concrete, and this was what it looked like after it had been arduously excavated. A silent, unseeing facsimile, like those human figures in the poses they had lain in when they died.

"It's hard to take in, isn't it?" said Henderson.

Gliding above its doppelganger, Stake realized just how much he took Punktown's myriad architectural features for granted, overwhelmed as they were by the dazzle of neon and laser and holograph, billboards and graffiti, the wide-ranging colors that differentiated their surfaces, the teeming people and the vehicles that transported those people. Now, as they floated lower (dipping between two edifices so colossal they surged up past the helicar on either side), Stake could appreciate just how intricate was the detail Bluetown had reproduced.

Minarets, cupolas, porticos. Arched gothic windows. Art Nouveau facades with their organic, unpredictable curves. Art Deco. Neoclassical and Baroque towers. Columns with intricate plumed rattlesnakes inspired by Pre-Columbian stone pillars; pillars with leafy Corinthian capitals. Punktown's architects had copied these details from far earlier architects, and Bluetown had copied the copies. A skyscraper with its top three levels bearing mock pagoda roofs with upturned corners. Occurrences of the external wall decoration called an oculus, because it resembled an eye. Corrugated towers patterned after those at the ancient temple of Lingaraja, themselves mimicking phalluses, stabbing arrogantly at the sky—Punktown's skyscrapers built ever higher in their designers' penis envy. But it wasn't just Earth's history of architecture that was represented. Kalian onion domes. Huge, scalloped Tikkihotto temples. Smallish brick buildings that were remnants of the native Choom city that had preceded Punktown.

Overlapping elevated highways. Bridges for pedestrians or trams, linking one tower to another. Factories and adjacent dormitories for their laborers to live in (though with Punktown's economy, many of the original plants were just as desolate as these duplicates). There should have been metal support rods like bones buried in the concrete. There should have been actual rivets socketed into girders, instead of just a surface mimicry. And these buildings should have been erected over a span of many years, individually, not in a tide of organic concrescence. They had grown without grout, without welding, without the use of derricks and cranes, without drilling and the boring of heated penetrators.

Stake remembered reading of the so-called golden section, or golden ratio. An ancient geometric formula for designing and building, consisting of a circle divided into twenty-four parts of fifteen degrees each, a square inside the circle and four opposing triangles.

Even the human body could be broken down into these mathematical golden proportions, with an inverted triangle and overlapping circles. But where Stake envisioned bearded mystical types with rulers and compasses bending for hours over reams of inked parchment, this city was generating itself with a dreaming effortlessness. The sleepwalking of a god.

"Hey," Stake said suddenly, leaning his forehead against his window. "Did you see that? That was the Chrislamic Cathedral down there."

"Yeah?" said Henderson.

The jaggedly spired structure should have been made of black metal, with red stained-glass windows. More than that, it shouldn't have been there at all. "Red Jihad terrorists vaporized the Chrislamic Cathedral two years ago. It's gone now."

"Huh," said Henderson. "Well, I don't get back to Punktown much; guess I missed that. Like I told you, Simulacra here is copying Punktown, but it appears to be a dated Punktown. I don't know if they've pinned down the exact year yet." Looking out another window, he wagged his head as if seeing this surreal cityscape for the first time. "With all its crime, Punktown is one scary place. So it surprises me that it seems even scarier without any people at all. Then again, people you can kill. But this place..."

"But it's beautiful, too," Stake murmured close to the glass.

Peripherally, he saw Henderson turn to look at him.

Drifting above the city in the distance were a number of dark kites. No; parachutes, maybe, or large balloons, hanging in the air. But Stake had been to Sinan before, and he recognized them a moment later for what they were. "Benders," he said.

"Yeah," one of their two CF guards confirmed. "They seem to be drawn to this place."

"Just hunting birds and such, out here in the open," Henderson suggested. "Easy pickings."

Benders, as they had been nicknamed by the Blue War's soldiers, were extradimensional creatures that were able to pass into and out of Sinan's plane through some mysterious and apparently natural process. It was rare that they appeared in the plane Punktown existed in, though there had been occasional rumored sightings, including a few subway killings attributed to benders that were said to have taken to living down there. They closely resembled jellyfish—huge when adult—but jellyfish that floated in the air. As ethereal as they looked, Stake would always remember the kicking legs and screams of one of his comrades as he was lifted into the air by translucent blue tendrils, right beside him. The longer, blue tentacles paralyzed their prey, while shorter black tentacles administered flesh-dissolving enzymes. Stake remembered firing at the thing and it dropping the soldier, but too late. As he lay convulsing and liquefying, another soldier had had to shoot the young man to put him out of his agony. Before they had come to that wrenching decision, the man had stared past them and babbled about some strange place he was seeing. Maybe the poisons allowed him to look into the realm the benders came from. Maybe the sight of it had driven him mad.

"I guess so, sir," the guard responded to Henderson's speculation. "But we think they gather more around the place where those three bodies were found than anyplace else."

"Huh," said Stake, watching the distant hovering forms.

"We'll be over that soon," Henderson said. And a moment later, "Yeah, funny, it does look like the benders are lingering above the building, doesn't it?"

But as if they could tell the Harbinger was coming their way (and it was undetermined just how sentient they were), the benders drifted away before the craft could reach them, so that it didn't seem to get any closer to the creatures. Soon, however, the building in question was directly below the helicar. Their pilot swung them around for another pass.

The building wasn't all that large. Just five stories, but longish, with a flat roof. There was an antennae array atop the roof like a cluster of thin blue spires. "What are those?" Stake asked.

"Not sure," said Henderson.

"The windows are all open."

"It must have had energy barriers for windows." Henderson looked over at him. "You want to touch down for a peek inside?"

"Ahh..."

"No, no." Henderson waved the idea away immediately. "You've been through a lot for one day, taking the shift and all. You know your own pace. Let's get you to the base so you can get settled in for the night."

"Yeah, that's probably a good idea; thanks."

Henderson ordered the pilot to take them to the Colonial Forces compound back in Di Noon, and the Harbinger gained a greater altitude so that Bluetown took on something of the appearance of a holographic map. They cut along close to the edge of the forest briefly, though it was obscured by billowing mist that rose into the air like clouds being mass produced. A by-product of the city's self-assembly, like the plume of a locomotive that was dragging its great mass inexorably across the land.

CHAPTER FOUR
MAKING CONTACT

STAKE FELT GUILTY knowing that most of the men and women doing their stint at the Colonial Forces base slept in bunks, stacked like corpses in a morgue's drawers, but not so guilty that he wasn't grateful for having a room to himself, however small that room was. No windows to break up the monotony of the unadorned walls, but he soon had his comp unfolded and set up on a little table, its screen the closest thing he had to a view. After the vistas of Di Noon and Bluetown he had sailed above yesterday, he was feeling more than a little claustrophobic. Pouring his mind into the net made him feel more like he was flying again.

He had turned in early last night and slept like a rock; nine hours of unbroken slumber. How long had it been since he'd managed that without a pill? He recalled nothing of his dreams. How long had he managed *that* without a pill, too? Well, to be fair, his bouts with nightmares came and went, sometimes waning for months or even a couple of years before his phantasms regrouped for a fresh attack.

He had just returned from breakfast in the spacious mess hall, echoing with the chatter of hundreds of the base's personnel, most of them in blue camouflaged uniforms, just like the old days. Most of them were human. None of them were Sinanese. A young aide had come to where Stake was sitting alone, and politely introduced himself as an assistant to Colonel Gale, the outpost's commander. He had presented a bracelet in the form of a matte black band and said, "Captain Henderson has already processed your arrival, sir, except for this data bracelet. It's been programmed with your relevant information to serve as your ID, and it will allow your position to be traced should you run into any trouble when you're out on your own."

Stake had just stared at the bracelet in the young man's hand. "I'm a guest at this base, and I appreciate that. But I'm a tourist here, not personnel. Please tell your commanding officer that I'm flattered by his concern, but I'll be okay. I understand that tensions are high right now, and I'll exercise caution." Stake had then gone back to chewing his toast, leaving the kid squirming in his uniform like a schoolboy who'd forgotten the next half of his oral presentation.

"Sir? I think—"

"I'll talk to my friend Captain Henderson," Stake had said. "He'll square it with the colonel, don't worry."

And so the kid had staggered away, a short-circuited automaton. Stake was sure the colonel, whom he hadn't met yet, would be none too pleased, but Stake was none too pleased with the idea of having his every step monitored.

Now, back in his room again, refreshed from food and sleep, Stake bent to a private project before turning his attention to the matter he'd come to assist in.

Stake called up his comp's vidphone mode, and his address book. He scrolled down the column for G. *Gonh, Thi.*

Was that still her last name, or had she taken on the surname of her husband? He hadn't asked her, in the one brief exchange they had shared since he had last seen her face-to-face, eleven years ago. Back when she had been his prisoner.

Again, he had not contacted her in a year. Not since that single call, during which she had put it together that he'd been beaten in the course of a case. Not since the time she had managed to travel to Punktown to come to his aid, unbidden. But he'd never seen her there—elusive warrior that she was— despite her having fought on his behalf, and he hadn't seen her or heard from her in any way since the lone text message she had sent his computer while he was recovering from a gunshot wound sustained during the nasty confrontation she had aided him in.

And again, Stake had known all along that he could not return to her dimension and her world without some attempt to resume contact with her. To meet with her face-to-face, on civilian terms, as ill-advised as his guts told him that reunion would be. It was inevitable, wasn't it? As beyond his control as who he fell in love with.

Her number didn't ring through. A message came up on the screen. His system translated it as: SERVICE TO THIS NUMBER HAS BEEN DISCONTINUED.

So she had changed her number, then, sometime over the past year. Stake set about finding access to a local directory, hoping she had not taken on her husband's last name, or else he might never find her. He supposed he could have someone more familiar with the Jin Haa phone system or their version of the net help him hunt her up; Henderson, who after all had helped him locate Thi Gonh last year, after a decade gone by. But he was embarrassed to ask him, much as he knew his friend wouldn't be in the least bit surprised at his request. Not surprised, maybe, but not approving either, he feared. Especially since that was not what he was being paid for out of Rick Henderson's own pocket.

Before Stake went very far in searching for a directory, though, another thought came to him. In his mind, he saw again the sprawling expanse of Bluetown from the air. As their helicar was about to leave the eerie city behind, Stake had noticed black smoke curling out of a window in one of those buildings that had empty open windows instead of the crusted blue panes that most of the buildings evidenced, like eyes gone blind with cataracts. "Is that a fire in there?" he'd asked Henderson.

His friend had looked down and said, "Must be squatters. They keep a low profile, because of the security patrols of both the Ha Jiin and Jin Haa, but the patrols have been tolerant of them. Mostly they're on the lookout for troublemakers, vandals. More than that, really, I think it's just a gesture to make it look like they have some control over the situation. But a lot of people have been displaced already, farmers and people from small hamlets, and where do they have to go now?"

Farmers, Stake's mind echoed.

With her husband, Thi Gonh owned a farm. She had told him that herself during his call to her.

He didn't know where exactly her farm might be located in relation to the border between the Ha Jiin and Jin Haa lands. Where, in relation to Bluetown. Could it be, then, that her farm was one of those that had been swallowed up? Might she herself and her husband have been reduced to taking shelter inside one of the replicated structures of Bluetown, and that was the reason he couldn't get through to her now?

His vidphone beeped. For a moment, startled, Stake thought that maybe Thi Gonh's machine had alerted her to an attempt to access her former number, and she was calling him back. But it was Rick Henderson's face that appeared on the screen.

"Hey, buddy. Sleep well?"

"Yes, I did, in fact."

"I hear you declined the ID bracelet Gale had them make up for you."

"Sorry, Rick, but I'm not a wild animal to have a remote tracker clipped to its ear."

"I'll smooth it out, don't worry. Anyway, are you ready to have a look at the three bodies found in Bluetown? That is, the two bodies and the cloned child?"

"Sure."

"I'll be right there to get you, then."

Henderson signed off, and Stake put his comp into sleep mode. He would have to get back to his search for the Earth Killer later. His obligation right now lay elsewhere, and when he was on the job, Jeremy Stake was still a good soldier.

THE MILITARY BASE had a science department with a small staff, Henderson explained—as they navigated a series of bland corridors enlivened only by paintings and holoart created during hospital stays by Colonial Forces soldiers wounded in the Blue War—but the staff had been augmented since this Bluetown situation had begun. When they reached the Science Office, as it was designated, it was to find two guards gripping blocky Sturm AE-93 assault engines, forest-blue units that could fire solid projectiles (or plasma gel capsules), mini rockets, and ray bolts. Bulkier model AE-95s could also fire shotgun shells, plasma grenades, and several more types of beam. Stake was experienced with earlier models of both styles of weapon. The primal hunter in him got a testosterone rush just seeing them, and he almost asked one of the guards to hand over his weapon so he could have a look at it. He knew it was the location that made this feeling so intense. Memories experienced even by his hands.

The guards straightened up and gave Henderson a crisp nod in lieu of a salute. Henderson said, "Morning, boys. This is my friend from Punktown, Jeremy Stake. We're going to have a look at the Bluetown clones."

"Yessir. The colonel advised us as such."

One guard stepped aside to let Henderson approach a recognition scanner mounted by the side of the door. He leaned close to it, and a wave of green light rolled down his face and upper chest, reading his features and the ID badge clipped to his uniform. The lab door whooshed open, and the captain led Stake inside.

The head of the science department took note of their arrival; Stake figured she must have been given forewarning by Henderson. She came to meet the two men wearing an attractive little smile. "Captain."

"Ami, this is Jeremy Stake, my friend from Punktown and a former corporal in the CF. Jer, this is Ami Pattaya, our top lab rat."

"Mr. Stake." They shook hands. Where the guns had brought out the killer from his past, the science chief brought out the shy teenager. Ami Pattaya was small, brown-skinned, with vaguely Asian eyes in a striking face and a river of dark hair, her lab smock doing little to hide her compact curves or the short but shapely legs her miniskirt revealed. High heels arched her feet and made her calves look tensed and strong.

Henderson said, "We'd like to have a look at the Bluetown clones now, Ami; the two that didn't make it, and the one that did."

"Of course. I'll be right with you gentlemen." The science chief clicked across the room on her spikes to finish a bit of business with one of her technicians, a young black man they heard her address as "cutie." Stake seized the opportunity to widen his eyes at Henderson meaningfully.

"She must be popular with the boys stationed here," he said quietly.

"Definitely. And I've heard a few of the ladies lusting after her, too. She's a hermaphrodite."

"What?" Stake looked across the room at her with fresh eyes. "Wow. Surgical?"

"No; mutation. I shouldn't spread rumors but I hear she likes to party. You'd think most of these macho boys wouldn't go for a he-she, especially when there are plenty of female Jin Haa prosties out there, not to mention our female soldiers, but I think they like the down-and-dirtiness of it. Prison syndrome, sideshow kink, whatever. But she's been nice to me so it's rotten to talk behind her back like this."

"She's been nice to you?" Stake arched a brow.

"Hey, Jer, you better know I've never cheated on my wife. Here she comes. Time for us to pretend we're professional again."

"All right, gentlemen, if you'd walk this way."

"I'd walk that way if I was wearing stilettos," Stake whispered to his friend as they followed Ami into another series of hallways.

"And if you had an ass like that," Henderson whispered back.

"The wife, Rick, the wife."

Ami had stopped at a door, her smile knowing. Stake felt embarrassed and a touch guilty, but she seemed unperturbed as she opened the door and ushered the men into a small lab.

Two circular tanks rested atop a counter, the violet fluid in them burbling quietly. One tank contained what appeared to be a terribly deformed infant that looked like it had made it full term, at least, before expiring, though Stake knew better; that it had been grown in no human womb at all. Its disproportionately large head was bifurcated to such an extent that brain matter unraveled from the back of its open skull. Lidless black eyes gave Stake the disturbing feeling that the creature was studying him as he studied it. Its dead smile—both amphibian and cleft like a cat's muzzle—heightened the unsettling effect.

But the other dead clone was in an altogether different state. It seemed to be made all of the same blue smart matter as Bluetown's structures. Stake again thought of the ancient city of Pompeii, the molds of human figures. This creature looked more fossil than clone.

"Why is this one alone made of smart matter? Or, to what extent is it smart matter?"

"Here." Ami indicated a scanning display set into the edge of the counter at an angle. She touched keys, and a screen revealed the petrified clone's interior. A delicate skeleton, ribs as fine as a fish's, that the scan made appear red as if the bones were translucent and filled with glowing dye—or blood. "Maybe this MIA was only a skeleton, and the smart matter had to extrapolate the rest of the body, whereas the other two were in less of a state of decay. Or maybe it just got this one wrong, before it moved on to the next, and the next, more successful at cloning the remains each time. Honestly? I really can't account for the three different states of these remains any better than that."

"You can't tell if the bodies all died at the same time, or at different times, before they were buried or left at that spot?"

"No, I can't be sure."

"Has their DNA been cross-checked against the CF database?"

"Yes. There have been no matches."

"Is that because their DNA has been altered?"

"It could be. Though it doesn't read as unusual, in itself. It just isn't on file."

Stake put his hand on Henderson's arm and steered him aside, speaking softly. "What I'm thinking, Rick, is that these might have been deep penetration scouts, like me, purposely working without identification in case they were captured or died behind enemy lines, and needed to remain as shadows."

"But like you say, you were deep ops, and you were always on file, right? I know I was."

"Maybe they were even deeper penetration than us." Stake faced Ami again, was again struck by how fetching she was, those shining large eyes confidently accustomed to men drinking her in.

"Deep penetration?" she said. "Sounds like you guys had some fun during the war."

Stake chuckled nervously. "I wouldn't call it fun."

"Not even on leave? Hitting the bars in Di Noon?"

He thought of Thi Gonh. An enemy fighter, not an allied prostie. He changed the subject. "We're certain these are human beings from Earth, at least?"

"We are. You'll know it as soon as you see the living clone."

"Let's do that, then."

"He's being cared for in Health Services; I'll take you to meet him and our chief medical officer, Dr. Laloo."

As they headed toward the door, Stake had a thought and hesitated, looking back at the tanks of gurgling preserving solution. "The DNA doesn't match anybody on the MIA list, but how about soldiers who made it back alive? What if these clones were made from matter left by soldiers who didn't die? The DNA could have been there in blood or bits of flesh, after a firefight in which they were wounded. Who knows?"

"That might still prove to be true, that the originals are alive and not MIAs at all, though I'd say that's a less likely scenario. But in any case, their DNA has been cross-checked with all the data on file from all the Colonial Forces combatants who served in the Blue War, living and dead. Yourself included, I'm sure. Sorry, Mr. Stake; they don't match up with anyone living, either, at this point."

"Okay; just a thought. Well then, speaking of living, let me meet the clone that Bluetown got right."

"ARE THERE ALWAYS guards posted outside the science lab and the infirmary?" Stake asked, as two more soldiers with assault engines let the three of them pass through the door to the medical unit.

"No," Ami said. "But then we don't get specimens like these three clones every day."

The chief medical officer, Dr. Laloo, promptly appeared from a room labeled MORGUE, having been buzzed before their entrance that they were here to visit. His surgical gown was smeared with blood, and he still wore a hair covering and a mask over his lower face. For one terrible moment, Stake thought that they were too late; that the cloned child had been dissected in the course of examination, a fear Henderson had suggested to him.

"Was someone hurt, doctor?" Ami herself asked in concern.

"A local child was killed after stepping on a mine in the forest," the surgeon explained. When he lowered his mask, Stake could see from his ear-to-ear mouth that he was a Choom. "I've been doing an autopsy to determine whether it was one of ours, or

Ha Jiin or Jin Haa. Seems to be one of the latter two, fortunately."

"Not fortunately for the kid," Stake couldn't stop himself from speaking up.

The surgeon gave the stranger a frosty look. "What I mean is, both the Jin Haa and the Ha Jiin are not all that happy with us lately, and so what we don't need right now is another civilian killed by Earth ordnance left over from the war."

"This is Jeremy Stake, doctor," Henderson said. "I've brought him in to help us identify the three Bluetown clones."

"Mm," the Choom grunted dubiously.

"He'd like to see Brian," Henderson explained.

"Brian," Laloo echoed, not bothering much to hide his contempt that Henderson had deemed to give the clone a name. "Very well, then. This way."

Walking behind him down an off-branching hallway, Stake said, "Shouldn't you take off that bloody gown, doctor? It might frighten him." He was simply prodding the man now.

"He's got the mind of an infant. He doesn't know enough to be scared of blood," the surgeon groused.

A large tank with ventilation holes sat square in the middle of the room they entered. The eyes of cameras and scans were directed toward it, judging from the images on monitors arrayed with other equipment on work counters ringing the room. There was only one person in this room at present, and he sat on a mat within the specimen tank. A male human child of approximately five years old, wearing pajamas a Jin Haa or Ha Jiin child would wear; the best they could come up with right now, apparently. The child's back had been turned to them when they came in, but at the sound of their entrance he looked around, almost falling onto his back in the process. Badly coordinated. His expression was mild and good-natured but uncomprehending.

"What's with the terrarium?" Stake said.

"We're all out of cribs and playpens at the moment," Laloo said. "He's safe and comfortable, Mr.—what was the name again?"

"Stake. He's got the mind of an infant, you say? How soon will that change if he's left alone in a box like this?"

"Captain," Laloo complained to Henderson, "why do I have to put up with this right now? The clone is not being mistreated. It's not like I'm responsible for having brought it into existence, either."

"No one's accusing you of mistreating the clone, are we, Jeremy?"

"At least he's got VT to watch," Stake said, indicating one large monitor swiveled to face the child. A station geared toward preschool children currently played a bright and noisy cartoon.

"Oh, he gets interaction," Ami said, activating the top of the tank to slide open, and leaning over its rim to reach in for the child. He raised his arms to her, and she hefted him out with a grunt. "My poor back." The child sat on her hip like a chimp and burbled a laugh when she nuzzled her nose in his ear. "So cute."

"Even kids like her," Henderson joked to Stake.

The hired investigator stepped over to Ami, and rubbed his finger on the back of the child's hand as it gripped the scientist's smock. "Hey, Brian. What's your real name, huh?"

"See?" Ami said to him. "Definitely an Earth human."

Yes; a Caucasian boy with brunette hair and brown eyes, nothing to distinguish him from billions of other children—besides being grown by an organic city run rampant. Stake asked, "Is he perfectly formed? Nothing missing or defective?"

"It seems his vision is a bit weak, and his digestive system is a little underdeveloped, too," Laloo cut in, making sure Stake remembered who the doctor was here, "but nothing that couldn't be treated down the road. He's in excellent health, considering the manner in which he was formed. It's astonishing, the process not having been accomplished through technology."

"A pregnancy can certainly take place without the involvement of any technology," Stake said.

"Yes, you know, you're right. I'd entirely forgotten about that. If I ever need further consultation, I'll contact you, Dr. Stake."

"I live to serve."

"If you'll excuse me," Laloo said, huffing off to return to his autopsy, apparently preferring the corpse's company to Stake's.

"Jer," Henderson admonished him, but he was smiling, "remember that you may need to rely on the doctor in the future. We all want to cooperate here, right?"

Not taking his eyes off the child, Stake said, "Cooperate; right. So, Ami, as you analyze the two failed clones and Brian here, are you putting your head, together with the team from Simulacrum Systems, and the Ha Jiin and Jin Haa scientists?"

Ami seemed to fidget. "We're all sort of conducting our own independent investigations into Bluetown and the clones."

"That's surprising," Stake remarked, sarcastic.

"We'll get more angles this way."

"And no cohesion?"

"Oh Jesus!" Ami said.

Stake looked up at her, startled. Had he angered her?

"Your face... you..."

As much as Stake had felt his eyes gravitating to the stunning science chief, even after having learned of her mutation (*especially* after having learned of her mutation?), Stake had tried not to let his gaze linger lest he begin to take on her features. At first, he thought he had done so despite his precautions. But then he realized it wasn't that.

His face was acquiring the look of the child Ami held, instead. In a way, was the result an indication of what the clone would have looked like had it developed to maturity, assuming the process would have continued successfully? But Stake guessed his features still held an infantile quality that would be a lot less cute than the clone's, and a lot more creepy.

Stake smiled apologetically at Ami Pattaya. "I'm a shapeshifter," he explained. "A mutant." Like you, he almost added.

"You scared the hell out of me," she scolded him, still standing away from him a few steps and unconsciously clutching the contentedly gurgling child closer to her.

"Thanks a lot," Stake said, giving a pretend pout that made him all the more child-like.

"I guess we'll have to study *you* next, after we're done with the clones," she joked back, but she was regaining her composure and her eyes seemed to have an intrigued sheen to them.

Sideshow kink, Stake thought.

His inadvertent mimicry of Brian reminded Stake to check his wrist comp, a few moments later when he felt the science chief wouldn't notice. Sure enough, he had successfully captured still shots of her face, and the face of the Choom doctor Laloo, in the device's memory. He had taken the pictures of them surreptitiously, when pretending to scratch his jaw or adjust his collar. He made it a habit to add faces to his wrist comp's library, to keep on file. A shapeshifter could never own too many masks.

CHAPTER FIVE
SIMULACRA

THOUGH HE TRAVELED alone this time, Stake didn't need to rely on the helicar's navigation system or autopilot feature to find Bluetown again, not with the way the city-in-the-making stood out upon the horizon. And once he reached it, and lowered his craft down closer to the streets, he could still find his way around with relative ease. This was because—after he had got his bearings via a few landmarks, however transfigured they might be in this blue-colored replica—all he had to do was rely on his familiarity with his own corresponding hometown of Punktown.

He had insisted he go alone, so Henderson had arranged for him to have use of one of the base's helicars. Before Stake had left, the captain had looked at his friend gravely and said, "Be careful there, okay?" Still, despite this show of concern, Henderson had felt it was prudent to assign Stake a modified Harbinger, unequipped with guns and rockets.

He had plunged the helicar through effusions of mist that rose from the edge of the city, where it was alive and chewing. He switched on his external speakers and even from on high could hear the crackling static of its greedy consumption. Through gaps in the fog he saw pools that flashed back reflections of sky; the runoff of fluid from a process that spread like an apocalyptic, drowning flood advancing in slow motion.

He had noted an especially gargantuan building thrusting through the clouds—a mammoth of perhaps 1,500 feet, that stood up from a cluster of smaller buildings like a finger raised from a clenched fist—with one of its flanks still gaping open as its form solidified, so that it looked like an explosion had blown off that side. Fog steamed out like smoke from the blast, and from its interior of honeycombed floors came a waterfall of that fluid waste, which crashed down to the blue pavement below. A shorter structure next door, its levels tapering like those of a Mayan step pyramid, was forming more uniformly from the base up, and so its waste gushed down all its sides evenly like lava from a volcano.

But now he had the helicar riding almost as low as a hovercar above the network of streets, the fog and crunching sound left behind him, and in so doing he spotted signs that the city's staggering mimicry still had its limitations. Two examples of this were buildings that he knew were meant to be upheld on repulsor beams. One was the inverted pyramid of Synerluc Communications, which should have been floating massively above its point. Now it was like a child's top that had stopped spinning. Not only was the building no longer hovering, but it lay upon one of its three faces. Similarly, Stake recognized the exclusive sushi and karaoke bar called Floating World, which in Punktown was constantly following a loop that encompassed several city blocks, riding navigation beams as helicars did, high above the streets. The simulacrum of Floating World lay grounded in the middle of one broad avenue like an airship that had run out of fuel and come in for an impromptu landing.

Stake had a specific destination in mind, though, and so he tried not to be distracted by the particular details of how his hometown had been so wondrously and weirdly duplicated. He sped through the shadowed city canyons in the direction of the building where the three clones had been discovered. The only thing was, he would be crossing the now effaced border between the land of the Jin Haa and that of the Ha Jiin. Once, he had stolen into their land with Henderson and other young soldiers, stealthy as camouflaged leopards. Now, he was riding boldly into that same, paved-over land like a man on a Sunday drive.

Stake finally consulted his navigation system to determine when exactly he would be passing into Ha Jiin territory, if he hadn't already. He knew the vehicle's global positioning feature was programmed to mark that border more clearly than it was demarcated in its literal sense in these post-war days, as had been the case even before Bluetown had overrun the border.

He saw from the GP screen that he was already moving through the Neutral Zone between the two nations. A needless sort of buffer these days, perhaps, but he supposed it was a concession both countries had agreed upon to make them feel a little better than they would if they were lying fully cheek to jowl.

Just a little further to the land of his former enemies.

When he reached the border he realized he hadn't needed the GP screen, at least not on this street. Across its wide expanse a rope had been strung, and three evenly spaced flags hung down like laundry drying. All three were the blue flag of the Ha Jiin nation. Stake might have thought this was their government's official demarcation, but another feature seemed to indicate otherwise. Also hanging from the cord, spaced between the three vertical banners, were two crude effigies dressed in bright orange clothing. One scarecrow had a blue head, the other a pink head, and both had been shot full of holes out of which hung some of their dried grass stuffing. They were obviously meant to represent a Jin Haa and an Earth person, partnered in death. It wouldn't have been the most politically correct image for a government to present in this time of peace.

Stake had slowed to take in the display, but when he started forward again and drove under the dangling effigies he soon met those responsible for them.

He saw the black smoke of a cooking fire unfurling from a structure in which the windows yawned open, and then from the doorway two children peeked out. As Stake turned his head to look at them, something pinged off his windscreen. He glanced up to see an older boy, in his teens, in a third-story window extending a slingshot. He decided it was wise to accelerate somewhat, away from this group of Ha Jiin squatters. Stake had the irrational anxiety that they might recognize him as a soldier who a decade earlier had killed a parent, a grandparent.

Out of an alley, two men came running and stood on the sidewalk glaring as Stake continued along. One made some kind of angry, thrusting gesture of the type he recalled villagers had occasionally made when he and his fellow soldiers passed in a vehicle or on foot. Out of another doorway, cut open somehow to give the squatters access to the building's interior, another man appeared. He was holding a rifle in his hands. Stake accelerated again and swung around the next corner, expecting a shot to ring out. Perhaps if he'd lingered a little longer he'd have heard one. Maybe there was a shot, after all, but the weapon was silenced and he simply didn't hear it through his external speakers.

One family, or several from a village who had bonded together? Farmers, maybe. Sure, the city could provide them shelter, maybe even better shelter than they were accustomed to. But what about their food? Their livelihood?

The streets were soon desolate again. No angry faces in doorways and windows, like snapshots in some history book. No smoke, no flags. A ghost town once more.

A fairly pristine ghost town. No rubbish in the gutters, no rubbish walking the sidewalks. No assaultive advertisements—a visual and aural cacophony—such as holographic logos and mascots that tracked you like parasites until they eventually tired or you warded them off with anti-ad spray. No fault cracks in the buildings, no miasmic stench taking root in your forehead, no clamoring noise such as the beeping of countless horns echoing off the chasm walls. It was an improvement, in a way. It was as if Bluetown preceded Punktown: the optimistic model it had failed to live up to.

He had seen some slum areas of Punktown where weeds grew lush out of cracks in the sidewalks and trees sprouted from the rubble of collapsed houses. Despite the proximity of the jungle here, it was not the case in Bluetown with its immaculate blue floor. The mutant ghetto of Tin Town where he had been raised was more of a war zone than this city, which capped the battle-scarred Ha Jiin land like the lid of a vast sarcophagus.

It was too impressive to be wholly deplorable, and its width and breadth made it an inexorable force like a tidal wave, or the punishment of a god. Was this why the Ha Jiin and Jin Haa weren't stirred to outright rebellion in the streets at this catastrophe? Did it overwhelm them, render them helpless, fatalistic? After the long war, fresh in the memories of its survivors, were they too accustomed to the idea of being trampled, their lives crushed and reconfigured?

Thoughts of the slum dubbed Tin Town made Stake wonder what it would look like once the city had spread far enough to replicate that sector, too. He almost wished it would, so he could see re-created the tenement house where he had spent most of his boyhood. It would be less squalid, but perhaps more haunting.

These daydreams distracted him to the extent that he didn't see the other vehicle until it pulled out directly in his path, and he swerved a little to avoid it at the same time he worked to bring the Harbinger to a halt. Even before it had stopped, he saw soldiers leaping down off the back of their car, a big-wheeled Ha Jiin military vehicle that had seen a lot of use and perhaps dated back to the war itself.

Stake lifted his hands where they could be seen through his cockpit screen.

"Out, please!" one soldier commanded in English. He wasn't exactly pointing his weapon at Stake but he made a brusque motion with it.

Stake complied, with slow movements. Once out of the vehicle he kept his hands lowered, but away from his sides. He said hello in their language, one of the few words he remembered.

Two soldiers stood apart from him, to left and right. Stake took note of their assault engines; not Sturms like the CF men carried, but nearly as good, since they were obviously acquired from an Earth Colonies arms company. Whatever they might feel about their former enemies, that didn't mean the Ha Jiin military didn't want the best firearms they could get their hands on.

A third man stood between the other two, facing Stake without a weapon except for his holstered pistol. Stake could tell this man was a captain by the marks on his belt; a subdued display of rank to keep enemies from picking off officers too easily, something that might have saved more Colonial Forces officers from Ha Jiin snipers—such as Thi Gonh.

"Good morning, sir," the officer said in English, his face impassive.

"Good morning," Stake replied in his own language this time.

The Ha Jiin looked over Stake's sky blue Harbinger, despite its lack of armaments clearly marked as a Colonial Forces craft. Stake himself, however, did not wear anything like a Colonial Forces uniform. A short-sleeved buttoned white shirt, untucked and a tad wrinkly, baggy tan trousers, battered sneakers, and on his head the porkpie hat he favored. Whenever he felt like his face didn't know who he was, this little hat was like some kind of reminder, a humble chunk of identity.

"May I ask what your business is in this area, sir? Are you aware that you have entered the Ha Jiin nation?"

"Ah, yes, I am. My name's Jeremy Stake, and I'm a friend of Captain Henderson of the Colonial Forces base." Stake thought the Ha Jiin might know the officer's name but he showed no reaction to it. "He brought me in to help with the investigation into the clones that were found here, on your side of this... this city."

"I am Captain Yengun. I am the commander of the security patrol along this length of the Neutral Zone."

Stake was impressed with the man's English, but then the Ha Jiin had probably polished this last line in particular. Yengun was a small man with a light frame but muscles so tight they showed in his cheeks and jaw. Stake figured him to be a little older than himself. Again, old instincts awoke and he sized the man up for hand-to-hand combat. The Ha Jiin had their own martial arts techniques, but Stake felt his extensive deep penetration training might just give him the edge in a tangle. Still, he didn't want to underestimate the man; just because his tone was low-key didn't mean he couldn't make things very ugly very fast. Stake wasn't concerned about violence, really, but about being ordered to turn himself around and leave Ha Jiin land before he had a chance to view what he had come out here for.

"Captain, I was hoping to have a look at the building where these clones were found. I thought it might give me some insight into them—who they are and how they came to be there."

"You should know this is a dangerous place for someone to come looking around. There are wild animals, and refugees." Refugees. Stake would have thought to call them something like displaced people, but then he supposed refugees wasn't really off the mark.

"Yeah, I know—I passed some back at the border of your land. It looked like they wanted to string me up with their scarecrows."

Yengun frowned off into the distance. "Ah, I know them. I have moved them many times. That is the best we can do without arresting refugees, and we prefer not to arrest them. We chase them out of one building and they move on to another building. And another." He looked back to Stake.

"I don't mean to send you out looking for them. I can understand the situation they're in."

"You said this captain brought you in to investigate. Are you with the Colonial Forces?"

"No, I'm not. I'm an independent investigator. Well, I used to be a Colonial Forces man, back during the war." Stake shrugged, and then wondered why he had offered this information, especially when the captain stared at him for several long moments without saying anything. He had to have fought in the Blue War, given his age and his occupation. So, then, they had once served in opposing armies. Maybe even fired at each other somewhere along the course of the conflict.

Yengun finally said, "If you must examine this place, then my men and I will escort you."

Keep an eye on you is more like it, Stake thought. But he wasn't about to decline their escort, lest the officer deny him access out of caprice or spite. For want of a war, such an action might be the best a military man could do by way of flaunting his authority—particularly to an old adversary. So Stake said, "Thanks, captain, I appreciate that. Should I follow you in my vehicle?"

"Yes; it is not best to leave your vehicle unattended here. Refugees."

"I understand. All right, then, thanks. I'll stick close."

Stake returned to his helicar, and the soldiers clambered up into the open top of their own car. It turned and started off down the road, with Stake gliding along after them a few feet off a blue surface so even that one would have thought the jungle floor had been graded before it had been paved over.

He imagined that the advancing edge of the city plowed along a certain amount of large stones and other inorganic material it could not convert into its own matter or bury underneath it, but now he noted that not every feature of the jungle was willing to consent to transmutation even when the flood had washed over it. Not much farther ahead, several massive boulders broke the city's simulating effect by stubbornly holding their ground. One of these rested almost in the center of the street, the vehicles having to curve around it. The boulder might not have been broken down or submerged but the smart matter had at least managed to encapsulate it in a shell, so that it looked like a tumor bulging from the city's floor. A bit further along was an even larger mass of rock, half of it seeming to penetrate the flank of a building and the other half obviously on the building's interior. Again, its blue shell made it seem fused to the building like some malignant growth, though it was really the other way around.

They turned onto another street, then another, and so on. A few times Stake lost all sense of direction, as familiar with Punktown as he was. Punktown was simply too enormous for any one person to memorize in full, and Simulacra's strange approximation didn't help. At last, though, he saw the escorting vehicle pull over to the curb and park there neatly, as if to remain out of the way of traffic, should any miraculously appear. Stake floated in behind them, and his craft alighted just as neatly. The men reconvened between their two vehicles.

"That is the place." Captain Yengun pointed across the street. Then he started leading his party toward it.

Again, as from the air, Stake noted that the building wasn't all that large. Five stories, longish, with that spiky cluster of antennae atop its flat roof, looking like delicate stalagmites of blue mineral. This was one of those buildings in Bluetown, which—in its original form, apparently possessing barrier fields instead of solid panes—showed rows of open black windows that granted easy access to its interior.

When they reached the sidewalk, Yengun motioned for one of his two soldiers to go in first. As the man hoisted himself through a window, the captain unholstered his handgun and held it up ready by his face. He said something in an ominous tone. At first

Stake didn't recognize the Ha Jiin word, until he recalled that it was their name for the creature that in the old days the CF troops had called benders.

Apparently there were none of the jellyfish-like creatures within, or refugees either, because the man inside gave a signal and Yengun went in next. The other soldier nodded that Stake should follow, and he did. This last man remained posted outside, perhaps to watch over their vehicles.

"No weapon?" Yengun asked Stake casually once the three of them stood inside a hallway that spanned the front of the building, gloomy but with the glow of Sinan's twin suns beaming through a row of those gaping windows.

"No." Stake glanced up and down the corridor with apprehension. "Should I have one?"

"No, you should not. This way," the officer said, leading them down the left-hand side.

There were a number of widely spaced doors opposite the windows. The way Simulacra had fashioned them, the doors had been sealed shut, but they had all since been cut open with ray beams. Still, only one of the rooms beyond them had proved to house a mystery. Stake accompanied the other two men to this room, its door the second to last in the hallway.

Once inside the good-sized chamber, windowless and unfurnished, Yengun's soldier activated his assault engine's flashlight. Right away, he swept it across the room's floor, to better reveal the three large pits that yawned there. "Huh," Stake murmured. The two Ha Jiin men hung back as he stepped up to the lip of the nearest of them.

The hole didn't look broken in the blue-colored floor so much as melted, its edges rounded and grooved. For all Stake could tell, the pit might descend for miles; a bottomless well. He looked around at the soldier, and gestured for him to shine his light down there. The man edged closer to comply. The pit was not terribly deep after all. Below the thick blue layer of the floor, the surfaces of the pit itself were comprised of bare earth.

"The holes were filled with fluid... the fluid the smart matter sweats off as it multiplies," Stake said.

"Yes," Yengun replied, behind him. "It was drained away so the clones could be detached from their roots, and the pits examined."

The fluid's acidic, eye-burning stink was still in evidence, drained or not. "Smells like a bus terminal men's room," Stake said to himself. He knelt down and ran his fingers over the rim of the opening, where it formed a cross section of the floor. He felt the barest nubs remaining of the roots or veins that had sprouted forth from the smart matter to connect with the bodies resting at the bottom of the three cavities.

Stake was wagging his head. He didn't know how to assimilate any of this.

"This matter... it is alive," said Yengun.

"Yeah, sort of."

"And you call it smart. It has a kind of intelligence?"

"In a way."

"Sentience?"

Stake looked up at him. "I wouldn't call it that. The process starts with a computer hookup. The computer has sentience." He rose to his feet again. "But they disengaged the computer. The stuff keeps growing on its own momentum."

"We were the first to investigate this," the security officer said, moving his gaze to the next hole, and the next. "A team of my men and I."

"You were?" Stake looked at the man more closely; maybe there was something to learn from him, if not from the enigmatic voids themselves. "How did you find them in the first place? During a patrol, or did a refugee report it, or…"

"A witch. She had visions."

"A witch? You mean, someone with PSI ability?" Yengun paused, digesting the term, then said, "Yes. She told others about her dreams, and so we had her lead us here to see what she was going on about."

When Yengun returned his gaze to Stake, his expression grew subtly more disturbed. Stake broke their eye contact immediately. In looking too intently at the Ha Jiin, he had probably begun the barest overture of mimicry, not enough to be obvious but enough for Yengun to sense on a subconscious level. Stake had noted something unusual on Yengun's face, and he hoped he hadn't started to reproduce it. It was a scar on his right cheek. He knew that during the long war, many Ha Jiin soldiers had marked their faces for every family member killed by the Jin Haa and their Earth Colonies allies. These scars took the form of horizontal raised bars. Stake had seen the leader of the Ha Jiin people, Director Zee, on VT, and even his face bore several of these markings. But the single band on Yengun's prominent cheekbone was only half the length of what one of these scars would normally be. Could its shorter length mean that the lost loved one had been a mere child? Stake hoped not. He hoped the half-scar had been received in a wounding or accident instead.

Staring into the pit near his feet once more, the freelance investigator resumed, "So there have already been a lot of Earth Colonies people out here to look at these holes. Military people, science people, people from Simulacrum Systems."

"Yes."

"Do you think it might be a good idea," Stake prodded, "for your people to have these holes excavated, to look for more clues as to whose remains these were?"

"My commander already did have the holes excavated, after the fluid had been drained and the bodies removed. They have since been restored to the state they were found in."

"Really?" Stake reexamined the pits to gauge what they would have looked like before, and during, that process.

"Yes. I watched some of the work myself."

"I see. And was anything else found besides the clones? Bones of the original bodies the clones were grown from, or..."

"I saw the excavation team recover some scraps of clothing, and a few pieces of gear."

"You did? That's funny; my friend didn't tell me about that. And does your commander have these items now?"

"No. In the spirit of cooperation between our two governments, my commander turned over the gear and bits of clothing to the Colonial Forces commander, along with the clones themselves."

"Huh. And so, what did the clothing look like? Standard blue camouflage, like the Colonial Forces infantry wore during the Blue War?"

"No, actually. It did not really look like military uniforms. But I did not see it closely, and as I say, it was little more than rags."

"But not uniforms," Stake echoed thoughtfully.

"*Apparently* not uniforms. That I recognized, at least."

"You said gear. Can you describe it?"

"Not really. It was briefly, and from a distance. I suggest you talk to your people at the Colonial Forces base."

"Hm. Yeah, I definitely need to see that stuff, and I need to look into military records to find out which units of infantry fought through this section of your land."

Yengun nodded, watching the investigator. "You said you served in the war. For how long?"

"Four full years."

"A long time. And through which provinces, yourself? Vi Teng? Boa Hon? The Kae Ta Valley?"

"Boa Hon, yes. Other provinces. They moved me around a lot, in four years."

Yengun kept nodding. "I can imagine."

"Did you fight in any of those places?" Stake asked nonchalantly, but understanding why the Ha Jiin had asked.

"Yes. All of them. And my family lived in Vi Teng."

"I see. Well, that's one area I didn't fight in, at least."

"No?" Yengun ran a hand over the coarse, pumice-like texture of one of the room's walls. "Where does your family live, Mr. Stake?"

"We lived on the world Oasis, in the Earth colony Paxton. They call it Punktown. But my mother died when I was young, and my father—I don't know what became of him. He lost himself after my mother died. He was addicted to drugs. We were very poor, my family. We lived in a tough ghetto." This was all quite personal information, but Stake wanted the Ha Jiin to know that he hadn't had a breezy life, either.

"Do you have a wife?"

"Me? No, never."

"May I ask why?"

"Ah, I guess the standard reason. I never met the right woman." Stake didn't add that he'd never met a woman he could love who would also love a mutant with his unusual condition. And Thi Gonh? Had he really known her long enough to tell how they would have been if they'd met each other in a time of peace, different circumstances? "Are you married, captain?"

"Yes. And I have two sons."

"Congratulations. You're a lucky man."

Yengun smirked at him oddly. "Yes. Yes, I am. My sons are intelligent and strong. And my wife is very beautiful."

"I envy you," Stake said. He felt there was something wrong, however, something below the surface that Yengun might want him to know but which he couldn't decipher. Anyway, he averted his eyes from the man again, before his mimicry could engage itself. "So," he sighed. "I don't know what to make of what I'm seeing. At least I saw it. Like I said, my best bet now is to talk to someone at the base about the artifacts they found, and the units that came through here."

The three men retraced their steps into the hallway, and down to its end where they chose another window, this time, to climb through. The man they had left to cover them nodded in greeting, and they all started across the street toward their vehicles. Along the way, something Stake couldn't contain rose to his lips, now that the subject of wives, of beautiful Sinanese women, had come up.

"Captain Yengun, I've been looking for a woman named Thi Gonh, and I haven't been able to find her. I'm afraid she may have been displaced by the growth of this city. She and her husband own a farm. You may remember her, during the war, as the Earth Killer?"

Yengun stopped, halfway across the road, and looked again at Stake with a face almost as mysteriously blank as his own. "How do you know her? And what is it you want of that woman?"

Stake dared to hold his gaze for the moment; to hell with his ability. "During the war, I was the man who captured her."

Yengun's narrow eyes narrowed more. Just then, Stake felt certain he had earned the officer's hatred, and ensured that no more assistance from him would be forthcoming. In his dry tone, Yengun said, "You

were the soldier who protected her from your men,
who would have raped and killed her."

"Yes. That was me."

"They say it was because you fell in love with her."

Stake didn't tear his eyes away. "Yes."

"And they say you are a 'Ga Noh.' A..."

"Shapeshifter. Yes." So, the Ga Noh had become
part of the legend of the celebrated Earth Killer. The
disgraced Earth Lover. Stake couldn't help but feel a
thrill go ricocheting through his system like a bullet,
cutting swaths through organs and lodging in the very
center of him. In a way, in their legend, they had been
wed these past eleven years.

Yengun did something Stake did not expect at all. He
smiled. It wasn't much of a smile, but it was one. "And
you want to find her again."

"I just, uh, wanted to see how she's doing these days.
And I was worried, because of this." He waved his arm
around him, at Bluetown.

"I am sorry; I know of her, of course, but I do not
know her personally. And as you say, she is married
now. That much I am aware of."

"Well, thanks anyway, captain," Stake said, moving
toward his helicar. He had turned his eyes away once
more; not out of fear of transforming, this time, but
out of embarrassment. Or pain. "And thanks again for
helping me have a look inside there."

The Ha Jiin officer said nothing more. He just stood
in the middle of the empty road, pivoted his body and
tilted back his head to watch as Stake lifted the Harbinger high to take the easier way back to Di Noon, in
the Jin Haa nation, flying above haunted Bluetown
with its teeming population of ghosts.

CHAPTER SIX
MIGRATIONS

JEREMY STAKE WAS inside the little brown body of the CF base's science chief, Ami Pattaya, and it had happened as simply as this: she had called on him at his room to see how his trip to Bluetown had gone, having heard that he had borrowed a helicar for that purpose. She had told him he looked exhausted, and volunteered her skills as a masseuse. Stake had gone along with this transparent game—and why not? He was a man. Then again, so was she, in part. When she'd been astride his back and he'd heard her undoing her top, he'd felt her erection pressing against him through her clothes, and he'd rolled over to look up at her. They had started out that way, and ended up now with him atop her, both her legs resting across his forearms and spread in the air, her own engorged member flopping against her belly with his thrusts. Free of her padded bra, her breasts were as tiny as an adolescent's, but that was okay, and he felt her face was extraordinary. He couldn't help but stare down at it, and she grinned up at him, apparently delighted by her uncanny reflection there. Even his skin tone had darkened, and his breasts had swelled slightly, enough for her to want to squeeze them in her hands.

"Do you want me inside you?" she panted.

"First things first."

"It's up to you. Some guys like that—girls, too— but I prefer to be the woman, if you know what I mean."

"That's up to you, too."

"Do you ever change down there?"

"No, I can't pull that trick off."

"Good. I like that fine as it is."

When they were finished, Stake lay back on the bed wrung dry and watched her get up to pad naked about his room, chattering in her sunny, sweet voice and no doubt strutting her charms for him deliberately. Her hair fell down to her cute rounded bottom, and he complimented her on the hair, keeping his compliment on her bottom to himself.

"Thanks. If you had some acceleration gel you could grow your hair as long as mine and then you'd *really* look like me."

"At least my penis is longer than yours."

She stuck her tongue out at him.

"You remind me of a high school biology teacher I dated last year. You science types seem to find me an interesting specimen."

Near the bathroom door, she grinned at him. "Was she as beautiful as me?" she said with a charmingly innocent lack of modesty, throwing out one hip to pose. The movement made her softening member jiggle.

"No. And she didn't have a penis either."

"How boring," Ami said, before ducking into the bathroom. From within she called, "Come shower with me!"

"Let me get over my cardiac arrest first."

She poked her head out brightly to blow a kiss at him.

"You're terminally cute. Everybody on this base must be in love with you."

"I hope so! But I have to watch myself these days, because of Dom."

"Dom?"

"Dominic Gale! You know, the colonel?"

"You're dating the colonel?"

Another mischievous grin. "Shh. He doesn't like to share." She started to duck into the bathroom again, but Stake sat up to call her back.

"Ami, the Ha Jiin security captain I spoke to told me his people did some digging in the holes the clones were found in, and the remnants of clothing and gear were recovered. He said these were turned over to our people. Do you know anything about that?"

"Yes—well, not really. Dom told me, but he said they couldn't tell anything from it. Just a few shreds of uniform and a couple of pieces of equipment that could have belonged to any CF soldier."

"The Ha Jiin captain said it didn't look like scraps of Colonial Forces uniform."

"I don't know." She shrugged. "I didn't see it, but that's what Dom said." This time when she disappeared into the bathroom, he heard the shower come blasting on.

Stake had just swung his legs over the side of the mattress when his wrist comp on the bedside table beeped him that a call was coming in. He scooped it up, slipped it on. When he positioned his face over the device at a certain angle, its transmission engaged not only his eyes but his brain, so that its screen became a virtual one and filled the front of his mind. Thus, the familiar face he saw looking back at him had an extra potent effect. He sucked in his breath at the sight of it.

But his face was not so familiar to Thi Gonh, who looked confused as she stammered in imperfect English, "I am look for Jeremy Stake?"

"Dung," Stake muttered, knowing that he still retained much of Ami Pattaya's appearance, minus the sleek curtain of hair. "Thi," he told her, "it's me—Jeremy. I'm on an investigation, so I'm under disguise." He gestured awkwardly at his stolen countenance.

Now a grin came over her face. She didn't seem to make the connection between Stake's ability and the fact that the mask he wore was of a beautiful woman. "Hello, Ga Noh!" she said.

"Thi, I'm on Sinan, did you know that? I've been trying to reach you."

"Yes, I know, someone say that to Thi."

"Someone? Who was that?"

"His name is Hin Yengun. He is big Ha Jiin soldier."

"Yengun? He told me he didn't know you."

"Thi not know him. But soldier find Thi and say Ga Noh in Di Noon and look-look for Thi."

Now Stake smiled, too. "That son of a bitch."

The Ha Jiin woman's forehead rumpled. "You angry at him?"

"No. No, I'm glad he went to the trouble to do that!" Stake couldn't believe it. They were talking to each other at last, after all the imaginary conversations he had held with her. His grin wouldn't vanish. "Your English has gotten better," he said—though it had been better yet in the imaginary conversations.

"Sometime Thi's farm sell to people in Jin Haa, and Earth companies in Di Noon, so Thi study English more."

"That's great. But you have to stop referring to yourself by your name. You've got to say 'I,' 'me,' 'mine' instead. Okay?"

"Oh yes, yes. Sorry, Ga Noh. Thi means, 'I study English more.'"

He chuckled. "Very good."

One thing she hadn't referred to herself as was "ban ta." It meant "your lover," and it was what she had called herself in moments of passion during their brief time together. It was also how she had signed her last correspondence to him, the text message she had sent this wrist comp a year ago. Well, she was married, after all, wasn't she? Why should she call herself his lover now? Why should she be jealous to see him with this face on and his shirt off? At least her blue-skinned face truly appeared happy to be looking at his again, however altered it might be. Her smile made her eyes more slanted, dark and sparkling. He wasn't so used to her smiles. She had been more solemn as a prisoner.

"Ga Noh," she said, more slowly and carefully, "you want see me now?"

"See you? Yes. Yes, I'd like that." He swallowed involuntarily.

"But I have big problem, so big problem. Farm of mine... my farm... is all gone." She spread her hands out horizontally to left and right in a leveling motion. "Blue City make my farm dis-ap-pear. Nothing left." She wasn't smiling anymore.

"Ahh, Jesus, I'm so sorry to hear that, Thi. That's what I was afraid had happened. I've heard that's happening a lot."

"Yes, very bad, very hard for me. So if Ga Noh like to see me, come to town call Vein Rhi. Small town, where my family live. Daughter of my uncle."

"Your cousin?"

"Yes, cousin. Daughter, brother of my father. I and husband live with cousin and husband."

"That's nice, that she took you in. But Thi, your husband—he won't mind if I come see you there? He doesn't mind meeting me?"

"Oh no, no!" she said emphatically, and even glanced back as if someone might come in on her.

"Husband go to city Coo Lon today, talk to people owe him money. Need money very much now. If Ga Noh like to see me, hurry up come now, before husband back to Vein Rhi."

"I understand. So where is Vein Rhi?"

"Small town, very small, inside forest. Your car will show you?"

"Um, yeah, I'll see if I can find it on my car's system. If not, I'll download a map off the net; it's got to be there somewhere. I can always ask someone here at the base, too, if I need help."

"But hurry up soon, okay?"

"I'm on my way. Where will I meet you there?"

"Oh—soup bar name *Tah Vein Rhi*."

"Okay, great. I'll do my best, Thi. If you need to cancel before I get there, just call me."

She laughed brightly, startling him. He had never heard it. "Hurry up, Ga Noh look like me. Very like me."

Stake touched his cheek, which had stealthily rearranged its substance without his even sensing it, so intent had he been on his conversation. A high cheekbone under his fingertips, as if he were caressing her face. One lover's face exchanged for another's.

"I remember good," she said, grinning, and Stake thought he detected something extra contained within those words. Because it was while they had made love, of course, that he had gazed at her face most avidly, and mirrored her image most closely.

"I'm coming now," he said, grinning her own grin back at her. Then his smile faltered, as he heard sounds from the bathroom that indicated Ami Pattaya was about to emerge. "See you soon, Thi." He broke the connection before she could say more, and before Ami could speak and be heard over his wrist comp. Lowering his arm, he turned to see the science chief emerge from the bathroom naked. She stopped dead in her tracks at the sight of him.

"Jesus H. Christmas, will you stop scaring me?"

Stake touched his reconfigured cheekbone again. "Sorry," he stammered. "I was talking to someone on my wrist comp. Part of my investigation."

"You're so pretty, but I like me better." She started gathering up her things, bustling to be off quickly. "I'll try to come by tomorrow if I can get away."

"Mm," he grunted, noncommittal.

Wriggling into her tight little dress (at least it was a scientific white), Ami said, "What's the matter, do I make you nervous now? You seemed pretty intrigued half an hour ago. We're both special, and I appreciate your gifts. Why do you think I came here?"

"I do find you very intriguing, believe me," he reassured her. "Very exotic."

"Well, I'm finding you a little distant. I mean, your body is uninhibited but emotionally you're shy."

"I'm just distracted. Preoccupied." Now that Thi's face was imprinted on his mind, as if he had never disengaged from the wrist comp interface, he thought better of his entanglement with the science chief. "You know, I'm just thinking that if you're dating Colonel Gale, maybe it's not a good idea for us to be together like this."

"Why? Are you afraid?"

"Guarded."

She sighed. "He's guarded, too. See, this is why I can't settle on one person." The mutant pouted prettily. It looked like she practiced her charms in the mirror. "People think I must be complicated because I'm like this, but I really couldn't be simpler. I just want to be happy. You should try it sometime." With that, Ami crossed to his door looking like a child who'd been sent to bed without watching her favorite VT program. But before ducking out, she blew him another kiss.

The moment she was gone, Stake scrambled for his clothing so fast that one might have thought a jealous lover was on the way in.

FLYING OVER BLUETOWN, its shadows stretching long as afternoon advanced, Stake saw a caravan of Ha Jiin people traveling down one of the broad streets, moving deeper into the city like fish swimming upstream. They were about twenty in number; either an extended family or several joined together. A plodding draft animal pulled a wagon. Even the animal lifted its head to watch him as he coasted above. Even its gaze seemed reproachful.

There was something else moving along another avenue, and it took him a few moments to understand what he was seeing, even though he was well acquainted with carrion trees. The mangrove-like roots of these trees sucked up the decay of plants and animals from the forest floor, and when they required a more fertile ground for their feasting, they uprooted themselves and migrated as if on clusters of muscular tentacles. Carrion trees were the reason the Sinanese had taken to burying their dead in crypts beyond the reach of their hungry roots, but they had thrived during the Blue War. Stake recalled vividly the night he had ridden in the crown of one such tree as it waded through an extensive marsh system, when he had undertaken an infiltration operation ahead of the rest of his team. He remembered being surrounded by the tree's bruised fruit with its stink of rotting meat. What he was seeing now was three bushy heads of these carrion trees, as they crawled slowly along in a line. Unwisely, they had ventured into the city from its border, and unless they should turn back they had a very long way to travel across the paved-over soil to reach the next rich pocket of compost. But maybe they felt at home in Bluetown, since they essentially did the same thing it did. The Carrion City, they should call it, Stake thought.

He moved in the opposite direction of the wandering plants, leaving the edge of the city behind him.

He had found Vein Rhi fairly easily in the Harbinger's plotting system, and it was far enough into the forest to be safe from Bluetown's advance for a while longer. When it was time to come in low, however, Stake could barely see the road through the foliage. Descending through this was like submerging into a sea, great fronds and leaves and branches swiping and slapping at his windscreen like churning waves. Something like a blue-striped lemur with a parrot beak leaped onto his hood, shrieked, then bounded away again. "Sorry," he said.

Now gliding low and stirring up a golden cloud of dust in his wake, Stake followed a narrow, winding dirt road that was hemmed in tightly by black tree trunks strangled with sapphire lianas like veins. Deep within the territory of the people he had once battled, without a weapon, was probably not the best time for his mind to wander, but it did nonetheless.

As he had asked himself countless times, he was wondering why he had fallen in love with Thi Gonh, the Earth Killer.

Sometimes soldiers came to embrace the enemy. It was something like a child trying to befriend the school bully, but more complex. It had to do with trying to reconcile the hatred you had for the enemy, and the fear. Because it was uncomfortable to hate and fear. You were taught that these were bad things, that killing was a bad thing, and then one day you were taught the opposite. Sometimes the impulse to reconcile went beyond embracement to loving the enemy. How many times had Stake seen a Ha Jiin design tattooed on a vet's arm, a vet drinking Ha Jiin liquor, and he had even seen vets take a Jin Haa bride—not because she was of the allied race, he thought, but because she was as close to the enemy race as it was safe to lie. It was an intimate thing, having an enemy. In a war, you were as mated to them as your buddies. You needed each other, needed that relationship. And in time, this need could transmute into strange shapes.

Whenever Stake had seen a vet with a Jin Haa woman as his wife, he had envied him. He would acutely remember the smell and taste of his beloved enemy's blue skin, the satin of her hair under his palms, the slick warmth of her interior that—incompatible with him except as an accommodating space—killed the sperm that had so yearned to enter there.

Occasionally Stake even wondered if his attraction to this enemy person was a distorted extension of the adversarial frisson between the sexes, man's submerged terror of women as an alien species. The love/hate relationship with the mysterious, bleeding vagina. The delicious, intriguing fear of your female counterpart, like an alternate version of yourself, a creature from another dimension that you must face and try to merge with, make peace with instead of war.

Opposites attract. Worlds collide. The exhilarating confusion of it all; the precious pain, the delirium and depression.

Talk about a Blue War, thought Jeremy Stake.

CHAPTER SEVEN
EARTH KILLER

THE HAMLET OF Vein Rhi, where Thi was living with her cousin, was entirely surrounded by a wall of riveted metal panels, their bright surfaces extensively marred with patches of rust. At first these rust blotches might have seemed random, until one looked again and realized the stains formed pictures of people, animals, town and country life, and a great deal of religious symbolism. This "rust art" was accomplished by painting a caustic agent onto the metal, and letting it corrode over time. The practice had been inspired several centuries earlier by a truly accidental mottling of rust discovered on the metal wall surrounding a prominent village. The rust stain had been thought to be a spontaneous rendering of the great prophet Ben Bhi Ben. Thus, Ben Bhi Ben's image found its way into every instance of rust art. Especially fervid followers of Ben Bhi Ben's teachings would vigorously rub their hands across his rust-caked image, rasping their palms against the scaly red stains until blood flowed. If their wounds

became infected as a result, and their faces became
paralyzed with their mouths grimacing wide open,
this was considered a blessing; they were thought to
be "singing to the prophet"—despite the fact that
not much more than a gurgle could be uttered
through their locked-open jaws, and death soon followed.

Studying the wall around the hamlet as he climbed
out of his helicar, and remembering about scraped
palms and singing to the prophet, Stake snorted,
"Religion."

Every time he stepped out of an air-conditioned
room or vehicle on Sinan was like his first exposure
to its smothering heat, which he walked into like a
solid wall. It stole his breath. Or was that anxiety?
He started forward as if swimming through a boiling
liquid.

Approaching the wall, he took in one rust design in
particular. He recognized it as a group of monks, a
flock of birds rising from them as if released from
their raised arms. He knew that there were clerics
who had developed PSI abilities through arduous
training, and could even command animals to do
their bidding. During the war, captured Ha Jiin clerics had enticed birds through the windows of their
cells, filled their tiny minds with messages, and sent
them to seek out their brothers.

As he passed through the open gate to Vein Rhi—
and immediately drew the eyes of every person in his
vicinity—Stake half wished he had retained Thi
Gonh's Ha Jiin features, though without blue dye for
his skin and hair acceleration gel, it still would have
been an incomplete and ineffectual disguise. He tried
to appear to be staring straight ahead as he walked
along a central dirt road, but out of the corner of his
eyes he was scanning for a soup bar. Its sign would
no doubt be in Ha Jiin characters, so he hoped *Tah*

Vein Rhi was the only such institution in the little village.

Two little boys with wire-sharp crew cuts ran up to him and jogged alongside, chattering like monkeys. He gave them just a quick glance and smile. Nonchalant, like he came to Ha Jiin villages all the time. Like he belonged here.

The boys gave up on him after a bit and hung back, still jabbering. He saw people openly pointing at him. Faces appearing at windows. Men watched him with immobile resentment, maybe resenting themselves also for being too polite in this time of truce to curse at him, or worse. An old woman with a shriveled face stepped out almost in front of him, as if in challenge. He met her eyes and smiled but her expression remained dour. Had she lost a husband or son or daughter in the war? Further along, he spotted what appeared to be a bar, with two much younger women loitering outside. They were the first Ha Jiin to smile at him, but then he judged them to be bar girls, prostitutes. They wore snugly fitting white latex gloves, a look that Ha Jiin men found highly erotic. They were appraising him foot to head and he nodded at them, grateful for at least this much hospitality. One of them said something to him in her language but he pretended not to hear, walking onward.

There. An open-faced little restaurant, with cheap plastic tables and chairs facing out onto the street. Stake spotted Thi Gonh seated at one of these, watching for him. She'd seen him, too, and gave a shy wave. He suppressed a grin as he quickened his pace and stepped up onto the restaurant's raised floor. Thi didn't rise from her chair, but what did he expect—a hug?—especially here with all these eyes burning into him, apparently the first Earth man to set foot in Vein Rhi since peacetime?

"Ga Noh," she said, beaming. Again, it was disorienting to see her smile like this. Disorienting to be seeing her in the flesh after eleven years. The last time he had been this close to her, it had been to say goodbye before she was transported away as a Colonial Forces prisoner on an air cavalry craft.

"Hey," he said awkwardly, seating himself opposite her with his forearms on the sticky table. He noticed a hat with a floppy brim and a scarf on the table beside her. Ha Jiin women working in the field or riding hoverbikes in the city wore such scarves over their lower faces to protect themselves from dust, exhaust and the burning rays of the dual suns, though he knew Thi's accoutrements had more to do with having arrived at the restaurant incognito.

"Now I see Ga Noh's true face," she said.

"Such as it is."

"What is this?" She gestured at his little black porkpie hat with its gray pinstripes. "Is Ga Noh a cowman?"

"A… oh, a cowboy? No, this isn't a cowboy hat. I wouldn't be caught dead in a cowboy hat."

She reached across to him. He typically wore the hat tipped back on his head but she drew its brim down lower. "Gangboy hat?"

"Gangster hat? Okay; gangster I can handle." She hadn't touched his body, but just her adjusting his hat sent an electric charge through him. He recognized it as flirtation. "How about your hat?" He flicked it with a finger. "Is Thi a cowgirl?"

"Yes. I need new job now. Maybe new job, cowgirl."

She had been drinking tea—maybe a number of cups—while waiting for him, but now that he'd arrived she ordered them both a bowl of tah soup, a Ha Jiin staple, using her native tongue. As she did this, Stake took the opportunity to study her appearance. If she were to stand he knew she would only come to about his shoulder, and she wore a sleeveless yellow tunic and matching yellow pants, as comfortable looking as much-laundered pajamas. Her straight black hair was parted in the center, not falling to her waist as he recalled it but still down to her breasts, hanging in front as if to hide their shy smallness. The sleek hair shone a metallic red where the light shimmered on it. Her face had shed a little baby fat, but she had let her eyebrows fill out naturally, no longer plucking them into a finer shape, and he felt this gave her a more youthful look to compensate. He would put her in her mid-twenties if he didn't know she was thirty-four. Her lips seemed fuller, softer, less tight and hard than he remembered them, but at least the black mole under one corner of her mouth was unchanged. It was her. Thi Gonh. Right in front of him. He could touch her if he only dared.

Her flesh was robin's egg blue. Her eyes—large and almond-shaped indoors, but narrower in the sun or when she smiled—were intensely black but in certain light flashed laser red. They looked black now, however, like black holes in space from which no light, or no private investigator from another dimension, might escape. Now he remembered why he had fallen in love with her. It was embarrassingly simple, and it seemed shallow, but he found her incredibly beautiful.

He looked down at her hands, the little hands that had been so expert with a sniper rifle, but not so much to study them as to avoid stealing her features again. He didn't want to alarm the waitress as she set their soup in front of them, and also it just seemed too intimate an act for anyone but them to witness. His past imitation of her had occurred behind the closed door of the room in the captured monastery where she had been held prisoner; where the men under his command couldn't see what took place between them, much as they could guess it. They had resented him for it. Traitor, some of them had deemed him. Being manipulated by a prisoner who just wanted to save her own pretty skin.

But what did she have to gain from him now, then?

"Smells good," Stake said, inhaling the steam off the soup that Ha Jiin and Jin Haa alike never tired of for breakfast, lunch, or supper.

"Mm." She watched him expectantly. Expecting what? His first taste of the soup, transformation of his mannequin-plain features, or his reason for wanting to see her?

"Like I say, I'm so sorry to hear that your farm was ruined by this damn city coming in. I wouldn't blame this whole town for wanting to tear an Earth man like me limb from limb."

Thi finally looked less than cheerful. "My people very angry your people now. I not blame to your people, Ga Noh, but angry for Earth company that make Blue City happen. I have farm almost ten year!"

"I know, Thi; it's a tragedy for a lot of people. It must be very hard for you, after a decade of work. I can imagine your husband is furious." Probing her about him.

"My people talking maybe not let Jin Haa and Earth people come to Ha Jiin land again. And maybe we not going to Jin Haa land again."

"Hm. So they might want to enforce the border."

"Yes. People want money for farm and house and town bury by Blue City. Want money from Earth company. If Blue City can not be blow up and everything take away, people say they want to own land of Blue City where farm was before. Understand?"

"Yes; your displaced people would like to own that part of Bluetown that covers their property.

Though what they could do with it, I don't know. This is tough, tough material, and it might be hard to tear up or dissolve even the portion that covers your land, let alone blow up or tear down the whole city."

"I am afraid maybe new war is coming if Blue City not stop soon. New war by Ha Jiin and Jin Haa and Earth Colonies again."

"I hope to God things don't go that far. I hope something can be done about this quickly."

"This time if war, Ga Noh and I not fight each other, okay?" A little smile with her joke.

"Okay. Next war, you and I won't get involved in the fighting. I promise never to take you prisoner again."

"Ga Noh take care of me before. Protect me from your soldiers."

"And by the way, Thi, thank you for last year. Coming to Oasis, and following me around like that. That was pretty sneaky of you. You took down two of those bad guys who were trying to hurt me. You killed 'em real dead."

Thi showed a small, mysterious smile and her eyes were almost chilling. "I not know what Ga Noh talk about."

He chuckled. "If you say so. But thanks. I wish you could've stayed then, and seen me after I got out of the hospital."

"Okay now? I was worried, very worried."

"Oh, I'm fine now. I'm just sorry you had to lie to your husband about why you needed to go to Oasis. You told him it was business? Did he ever find out the real reason?"

"He was angry, know I am maybe lie to him. He understand, I think, about Ga Noh and I in war—fuck in bed together. Understand Ga Noh live on Oasis. He almost beat to me."

"Wait, wait, please don't say it like that. And you're saying he almost *beat* you? Oh Christ, Thi. I'm sorry."

"Nothing! No worry about me, okay?"

"Are you happy these days, Thi? I know you had a hard time after my people released you. Your people put you on trial for sparing the lives of the men you had in your gun sights. You were condemned for that, and all."

"No, no." She made a brushing motion. "I am okay now, okay. They make a joke—call me Earth Lover."

"I know, I heard that. And what about your husband, Thi? Are you, you know, happy with him?"

Her smile turned evasive, and was like a shrug. She looked into her soup. "We work hard together, work same-same many husband and wife."

"But is he good to you? You say he almost beat you."

"He is not smile a lot. Smile to men friends. Every day drink with men friends. Laugh to friends, not laugh to me. Many men are same-same."

"That doesn't make it okay. Is he gentle to you, at least? Affectionate?"

"He not kiss to me here." She touched her lips with her finger. "Never one time. And in bed we very hurry up." She slapped her palms together twice, and grinned shyly. "Sometime his milk come out before his baby go inside my baby!"

"What a waste of your baby," Stake remarked. Being a man, he couldn't help but feel immensely gratified by knowing this. But then he felt guilty for being smug. Should his ego be stroked by Thi having spent ten years with an unaffectionate husband?

Thi giggled. "Funny, hear Ga Noh talk about my baby!"

"Thi!" a voice called. They both turned sharply to see a woman approaching. She was as short as Thi but heavier, with a broad face and narrower eyes, and no hair on her head. As she came closer Stake saw her blue dome was scarred and textured like the globe of some planet. It was a condition he'd seen other Sinanese women afflicted with in the past, brought about by parasites. Despite this, the woman was grinning as she stepped up onto the restaurant's platform. "Thi, Chonh said he saw an Earth man walking in the town. Chonh is my older son," she explained to Stake. "Are you my cousin's friend?"

"Ah, yes," Stake said. "So you're her cousin. She told me you and your husband had taken her in. That was very kind of you."

"Well, my father lives in Vein Rhi, too, but he didn't have the room. My name is Nhot, by the way." She extended her hand for him to shake; hardly a Ha Jiin custom. Touching a woman in any way was considered rude, and could have dangerous consequences.

"I'm Jeremy Stake." As he shook her hand, he glanced at Thi and saw that her face had gone blank, unsmiling. She flicked her gaze at him and he tried to read it.

"Sorry to disturb you at your lunch, but my son was very excited and saw you coming down this way, so I thought I would investigate."

"Your English is excellent, Nhot."

"Why thank you!" Her cheeks were bunched round with that big grin. "I've been working through my computer the past few years; I'm lucky that I don't have to leave home to do my job. Sometimes I deal with your people on the net, so I've studied English quite a bit. I've helped my cousin with a few words, too, since she also has an interest in English. I've told her she should take the same net course I did."

Thi spoke to her cousin in their own language, her voice darker and tighter now, faster and more sure, but Nhot chided her, "Thi, it's rude not to talk in English in front of your friend." She turned back to Stake and said, "My cousin says you're here to investigate the spread of the Blue City."

"No, not exactly. Three life forms apparently cloned from Earth people were found in the city by a Ha Jiin security patrol. I'm looking into that, as an aide to the Colonial Forces."

"Oh yes, I see. We heard about that. So strange!"

"So did you grow up together, you two cousins?"

"Oh yes, though she's a few years older than me. A lot prettier than me, too, I know. I've heard everyone say it for years! Anyway, my father is her father's younger brother. My father was a captain in the war, did she ever tell you that?"

"No, I didn't realize."

"It's ironic. My father was an officer with many successes to his credit, but even after her trial for treason my cousin is still the one who is better remembered, for being the Earth Killer. I suppose it is her and not my father who will become a part of history. Who can guess these things?"

"My friend go back to Di Noon now," Thi spoke up. "Soon it is dark." She pointed upwards.

Nhot ignored her. "You were the soldier who caught my cousin during the war, right? The one who protected her from the other soldiers?"

"Yes. But you know, the war's over now, so it's great that we can all get together and share a meal this way."

"Yes, it's wonderful that my cousin and you can be such close friends. Have you met her husband yet?"

Stake's smile was strained. "No. Not yet."

"I see. He would be interested in meeting you, I'm sure."

"Well, it's been very interesting meeting you, Nhot, but I'm afraid your cousin is right; it will be evening soon and I'd better get back before it gets dark." He rose, and made an apologetic expression for Thi. "I don't have any of your money on me for the soup."

She waved away his concern. "My gift, Ga Noh."

"Ga Noh!" Nhot exclaimed. "That's right—we all heard about that! You can change your face like a chameleon! Is this your own face that we're seeing?"

"Yes. It happens involuntarily, a lot of times, so I'm trying not to look at either of you too long. Nothing personal."

"Oh, you wouldn't want to look like this." She patted her hairless scalp. "I'm sure you don't mind looking at my cousin, though. She's a very attractive woman."

"There are many beautiful Ha Jiin and Jin Haa women, yes. Your men are too lucky."

"Well, I don't think my husband is one of the lucky ones, but he still married me so I guess the lucky one is me. Are you married, Mr. Stake?"

"No, never. Maybe someday. Anyway, again, nice to meet you." He extended his hand to Thi this time. He wanted to make their goodbye look formal, but he also wanted to touch her flesh. Touching it in front of this other woman suddenly seemed like a satisfying thumbing of the nose. "It was nice to see you again, Thi. It was much better this time, now that the war is behind us." But it hadn't really been better, at least not for him. That made him feel guilty, too. Had it been better when she was a prisoner, threatened with rape and execution from the men under Stake's command?

"Thank you, Ga Noh," Thi said. Her smile hadn't returned. "Take care, take care yourself."

Stake turned from the women, stepped off the platform, and strode down the street. He hadn't given Nhot a look after Thi, because he hadn't wanted her face to be the last of the two he saw before he left. And he hadn't given Thi a further look because their little bubble of intimacy had been stolen from them, and the looks they exchanged could not be honest. He resented Nhot for that, and he resented her for the vitriol he had so clearly perceived behind her grinning mask.

He was bitter as he walked out of Vein Rhi, unsatisfied, confused, so he didn't raise his head to smile at the excited children who yapped around him like dogs. Maybe one of them was the son Nhot had mentioned. He reached the Harbinger, and was soon pointing it back the way he had come.

It was while he was in the air above Bluetown again, with Sinan's double blue-white suns lowering toward some gentle forested hills on the horizon, that Ami Pattaya called him. He put her through to the larger screen set into the helicar's console.

"Hey, shy guy," she said. "Question: did you find my ID badge in your room after I left?"

"Your ID badge? No, I didn't. Why?"

"I left in a hurry and I think I forgot it there. It probably fell off my lab coat."

"If I see it I'll let you know."

He had no specific use for her badge yet, but he collected such things when they came within grasp, just as he collected faces in his wrist comp. They were like tools added to a toolbox, disguises in an actor's make-up kit. He thought that maybe it wouldn't have been such a bad idea to bring hair acceleration gel, though he knew he would feel embarrassed to even briefly have long hair down to his ass, just as he knew his ass would never be as cute as that of the science chief.

But right now, it wasn't Ami's body—however intriguing and succulent—that he was remembering.

CHAPTER EIGHT
OUTRANKED

COLONEL DOMINIC GALE was younger than Stake would have imagined, muscular perhaps but still too lean for his six-foot-four height, with his skull fully shaved but wearing a strip of goatee from his lower lip to his chin. Though they often made good soldiers, Stake had never personally liked any man who tried to make his head look like a helmet or bullet. The beard looked like a patch of pubic hair he had torn off with his teeth. What did Ami Pattaya see in this man, except maybe the glittering Christmas decorations of his rank scattered across the blue camouflage of his uniform?

"Nice to meet you, colonel," Stake said pleasantly as he approached the room's oversized conference table of black Sinan wood.

"Park yourself, Mr. Stake," Gale growled. Stake couldn't place his accent, but then accents blended over time into new configurations. The closest thing he might call it was Australian. "You too, Henderson," he said to the captain, who had entered the room ahead of Stake.

"Mr. Bright," Henderson greeted one of the other men at the table, who wore an expensive five-piece suit. His hair was so immaculately cut and his face so perfect, probably through the aid of cosmetic surgery, that he looked even more android-like than Stake did in his "factory settings." Henderson swiveled in his chair to introduce this man and Stake to each other. "Jeremy, this is David Bright, owner of the Bright Horizons development company. Mr. Bright, this is Jeremy Stake, the freelancer I brought in to help us ID the clones that were discovered in Simulacra."

"Which is the reason I've brought you in here, if you've finished with the tea party chatter," Gale said, taking his place at the head of the table. "Now, I've been too busy giving hand-jobs to every screaming Jin Haa and Ha Jiin political and religious leader on this momfuck planet to spend the time meeting about this sooner, but I wanted to make it clear to everybody here that I'm not a happy soldier right now. I'm not at all happy, Henderson, that you brought in an outsider to look into these clones. You should have asked me first instead of doing this behind my back. How do you think it makes the CF look if we have to hire a blasting private dick to help us identify MIA remains?"

"I thought you had already made it clear you weren't happy about this," Henderson said calmly.

"So I'm making it clear again! I wanted to include your gumshoe friend, since you two are so damn close!"

"Gumshoe," Stake murmured, trying not to smile. Gale jerked his head his way, maybe having overheard him. Stake took off his porkpie hat belatedly and set it by his elbow.

"Dom," Henderson said, "look, you know I was brought in to help you tackle this Bluetown mess, and I'm just trying to use some imagination here. What's wrong with expanding our resources? Jeremy was a corporal in the Blue War; he has experience here. And I'm thinking maybe the Ha Jiin will be less intimidated talking to a civilian than to a Colonial Forcer."

"Oh, you're crafty, Rick, but make up your mind; is this guy a civilian or a soldier? You can't have it both ways. All right, look, Stake... this shit storm with the clones has leaked to the media somehow," he threw Henderson a suspicious look that almost could have set the man aflame, "and now it's in the public eye. So I'm going to let you stay here, just to show that the Colonial Forces uphold their commitment to locating and returning the remains of Blue War MIAs. People are keen on the living clone being returned to its family, like it's a little lost puppy or something instead of the anomaly it is. Beats me how civilians cloning themselves can be illegal, but everyone in our dimension wants to adopt this thing."

"I had some questions for Mr. Bright," Stake spoke up, "since he's here, and since the Bluetown matter pertains to the cloning matter."

"Bright's not here for your convenience, Stake; we just finished up another meeting before this one."

The owner of Bright Horizons held up a hand to Gale, then turned to the private investigator receptively. "Yes, Mr. Stake?"

"Sir, mainly I just wanted to know what your thinking is at this point on what's going on with your project. How a little condo village came to replicate Punktown, and how and why it whipped up those three clones."

"My thinking hasn't changed much since the beginning of this disaster, Mr. Stake, and that's why I'm open to any available resource at this point, myself. Where it still stands is that a virus, as yet unidentified, must have got into our computer system somehow, and the smart matter—instead of following the village blueprints—accessed a map or schematic of Punktown from another source instead. The media is saying a lot of irresponsible and hurtful things, like I'm doing this on purpose to develop Sinan to my advantage—but what advantage is that? Furious governments? Thousands of angry Ha Jiin and Jin Haa? What do I gain? Where's the fortune to be made? There's a fortune to be lost, that's all!" At least Bright's anxiety lessened the android look.

Gale cut in, "Mr. Bright is upset enough already with all this hell, Stake, for you to be agitating him more. He has his people from Simulacrum Systems looking into the Bluetown problem, and the clones. You stick to the clones yourself; better yet, stick to whatever remains the clones originated from. I'm telling you, I have enough shit underfoot to have you getting in my way by overstepping your boundaries."

"With all respect, colonel," Stake said, "Sinan has been opened to civilian colonization, commerce, and tourism. Unless I pose a direct risk to security here, I'm not subject to your command. I—"

Gale's six-foot-four, rocket-domed body shot up out of its chair. He bellowed, "You fucking well are subject to my command, unless you want me to deny you further access to Bluetown! I'll say this one more time: if you get into my hide, I'll not only kick you off this base, but off the planet and clear out of this godforsaken dimension—do you get me?"

Stake said mildly, "Sir, I appreciate that I'm being allowed to stay on the base and make use of base property."

Gale glared at Henderson. "Base property?"

"I'm letting him use a Harbinger. Without guns."

"Why don't you just let him sleep in my quarters, too, while you're at it? I'll bunk with the men," Gale said, reseating himself.

Stake thought again of Ami Pattaya, and smirked.

Gale sneered across the expanse of glossy table at the hired detective. "I know about you, Corporal Stake. Yeah. I know how you protected that Earth Killer bitch after she killed the two officers above you, and God knows how many other officers and infantry during the war. Just because she got all misty over pulling the trigger on Henderson here and two other guys when they had their guard down, you think she's Jesus Christ's kid sister. You kicked the shit out of a couple of your own men who you felt mistreated her."

"They *did* mistreat her."

"Poor thing. Poor fucking Ha Jiin sniper."

"Dom," Henderson said in a low but meaningful tone. "Please. We're getting personal here."

"Right. We wouldn't want to get personal, huh? Personal with the enemy, Corporal Stake?" He snorted. "Who got the worse case of Stockholm syndrome after you captured her—the woman, or you? I can smell the way you think. The Ha Jiin are more down-to-earth than us corrupt Earthers. They're better than us. Well here's a little history about me, since I already know a little of yours. Did you know I spent five months in a POW camp?"

"No, I did not."

"I was lucky it was at the end of the war, and they let us go with these dung-eating magnanimous smiles on their faces for the Earth Colonies media. But they sure weren't smiling when they held us in that camp. You try lying with your hands cuffed behind your back and leg irons on your ankles for weeks at a time, maybe blindfolded all the while, too. Try sitting shackled on a stool for three or four days straight, shitting in your breeches, and if you start to fall off you get a rifle butt in the ear."

"I'm sorry about all that, sir. And you're right, there were no saints. Never are."

"All I know is, your cute little Earth Killer friend never had it that bad, not even after she was out of your protection. You should remember whose side you were on, one of these days."

"Yes, sir. I'll try."

Gale made an abrupt, dismissing gesture that almost sent his coffee cup flying. "Get your buddy out of here, Henderson. I don't want to look at him."

"Let's go, Jer," Henderson mumbled, rising.

Stake nodded to David Bright on the way out. Bright just watched him with a pale, hopeless semblance of a face.

In the hallway outside, Henderson sighed and sagged back against the wall. "See what I have to deal with here, Jer? I think they clone guys like Gale at officer factories."

"So where did you come from, then? The gypsies left you on the doorstep of the factory?"

"I guess. Not that I don't understand what Gale went through as a POW."

"I know. I know."

"He's also getting a lot of heat about the virus that's going through both the Jin Haa and Ha Jiin lately."

"Not the computer virus Bright was talking about?"

"No, no—biological. A very potent STD. It sounds like something along the lines of mutstav six-seventy, and you know how bad that was in Punktown, and we had much better health services than these people do. Once it goes full-blown it has a one hundred percent death rate, turning a person's brain to mush like *spongiform encephalopathy.*"

"Like whatty-whatty?"

"Prion disease. Mad cow disease?" When he saw none of these names rang a bell, Henderson simply continued, "Anyway, you either die screaming in pain or laughing like a loony. It was putting tension in these people even before the Bluetown thing. Paranoia and resentment being at such heights, the widespread attitude is that Earth Colonies sex tourists brought it to Sinan, and now it's reached the general population."

"I'd heard there was a lot of disease rampant with the prosties, but I figured that was just business as usual. Didn't know it was anything like a plague."

"Getting very plague-like. So all things considered, you can see why these people on both sides are ready to jump out of their skins. And Gale, too."

"What he needs is a nice soothing massage. I'll see if I can talk to his girlfriend about it."

"Huh?"

Stake smiled and walked away, leaving his friend watching after him.

STAKE WASN'T JOKING about wanting to talk to Ami Pattaya, only lying about what he wanted to talk about. He thought he'd like another look at the cloned child Henderson had dubbed Brian, and he was working his way through the Colonial Forces base's maze of all but indistinguishable corridors when his wrist comp beeped him. He stepped to one side to let others pass as he took the call.

An unfamiliar Jin Haa or Ha Jiin man's face appeared on the tiny screen. Though they tended toward thinness and prominent cheekbones, this man's face was especially thin, his cheekbones especially pronounced. And his lips curled away in a snarl of crooked teeth.

"Fuck you!" the stranger roared. "Fuck you, asshole! You have your nose in my wife's ass like a dog, huh? You think you fuck my wife again, huh? She is my wife! My *wife*, asshole!"

Stake's heart started thudding hard. "Look, sir, we just had some lunch together."

"Lunch? You lunch on her hole, huh? You lunch on her hole?"

"Don't talk like that. We didn't do anything."

"You come here again, I kill you!"

"Okay, okay, I understand. You just don't hurt her, understand?"

"You don't tell me what to do! She is my wife—I do what I want! I already hurt her. Hurt the bitch good!"

Stake's heart suddenly stopped its thudding, came to a dead halt. "You did what?"

"You come here again, I kill both of you!"

"I asked you what you did to her."

"I do anything I want to her. Fuck you, okay? Fuck you!"

The stranger signed off. The screen went blank.

Stake lifted his head slowly. He felt so icy at the core that he seemed to be frozen there against the wall. But it was only a moment. And then he was moving.

CHAPTER NINE
BEATEN

HAVING ALREADY FOUND his way to Vein Rhi once before didn't make the return trip any easier for Stake, but it was the time that frustrated him and not the remoteness. More than frustration, he felt a kind of mental paralysis brought on by an overload of sorrow and concern. Because being here on Sinan opened up a floodgate of memories, he recalled a conversation he had had with another soldier in the last year of his four-year tour of duty. This man was a cloned soldier, one of many used during the Blue War, their units usually working independently of the "birther" units, as the clones called naturally born humans like Stake. Like all these soldiers, this one was bald, the skin of his head and face and entire body designed with blue camouflage like the uniforms they all wore. The clone's grin had shone white and mocking in this mottled mask as he said, "Your fatal flaw, corporal, is you care about things too much. It makes you vulnerable, and vulnerable makes you weak. It's one of the advantages I have over you—that is, besides greater strength and quicker reflexes, of course. My big advantage is I don't give a blast about anything."

Without actually mimicking him, Stake had returned a grin rather like the man's own. "I think you got that entirely backwards. If you don't care about anything, that means you not only don't care about killing the enemy, but you don't care all that much for the lives of your friends—if you even consider them friends—or your own life, either. But I think caring makes me more dangerous than you, not less, because I always have something to fight for. See? Something to inspire me, to motivate me."

The soldier's smile had turned cold then. "You saying that as a clone, I'm less than you?"

"No. It isn't just clones that feel the way you do. And I'm sure plenty of clones feel the way I do. It comes down to being human, however you got here. You either care about stuff or you don't. But if I care about something and you get in my way... well, then we'll see how weak I am, private."

Stake's progress was stalled even more at the town's rust-stained metal wall, as a group of men carrying poles with little hooks at the end prodded a group of slow moving yubos through the front gate. As a young soldier on Sinan, seeing yubos for the first time had made Stake think they were akin to the giraffe, with long necks drooping languidly amongst the foliage they fed on. But up close he had realized this long neck was too sinuous, and turned out to be a boneless appendage more like a single thick tentacle. The squarish head of the creature was actually rooted at the appendage's base. There was a kind of eight-fingered hand at the end of the limb, two sets of four fingers in opposition to each other, which plucked fistfuls of leaves to cram into the beast's mouth. Now Stake thought of the animals, which were used not only for labor but as a source of meat, as something more comparable to elephants. In addition to their other uses, the hands of slaughtered yubos were saved, sometimes hung inside houses as some kind of prosperity charm (plucking bounty from the heavens), and often seen pickled in big jars as a treat men liked to nibble on when drinking. Right at this moment, though, Stake was less interested in the animals as he was inclined to help the herdsmen by shoving the nose of the Harbinger into the rear quarters of the last yubo in line.

Finally they were all through, and Stake swerved his car around them to pass ahead. The men at the front of the line hadn't known he was back there, and he caught a glimpse of two of them turning their heads in surprise as he left them in his dust.

The first time he had come, Stake had left his vehicle outside the city wall to minimize any fanfare and walked to the restaurant *Tah Vein Rhi* on foot. This time, he boldly drove right up to its open-faced front, got out, and stepped onto its platform, unmindful of the children who were racing to catch up with his vehicle. He recognized the waitress who was setting bowls of steaming soup in front of a couple seated at one of the cheap plastic tables. Stake said to her, "I'm looking for Thi Gonh. She was here with me yesterday, remember? Thi Gonh?"

The woman was shaking her head in a seemingly universal gesture of incomprehension, or maybe she was telling him she wouldn't reveal where the woman was living, didn't want to become involved.

"Look, is there a hospital in town? A clinic? A doctor? Doctor?" He made a sewing motion on his wrist, hoping the waitress didn't send him to the local seamstress as a result.

"I show you doctor!" a voice chirped in English behind him. Stake turned to see that some children stood panting excitedly around his idling helicar. "I show you doctor!"

"Thanks. Get in," Stake said, opening a door for the child. The others moved forward as well but he blocked them. "Hey, hey, come on, I don't have time for this!" He lunged around to the pilot's side and slipped in, raised the vehicle above the dirt street again. "Point me the way."

"There!" the boy cried, ecstatic with this adventure. "Go that way!"

Stake glanced at the child as they took a turn onto another little street. For all he knew, this might be one of the children of Thi's cousin Nhot, whom she said had announced the Earther's presence the first time he had come to town. The boy's English made him wonder, as Nhot spoke it so fluently. Stake was no better at their language now than he had been during the war, and at times like this he envied Henderson for long ago having had a translation chip implanted, which enabled him to speak and understand their language, and many others, like a native.

"Go there!" his young passenger blurted again, pointing.

If Thi's husband had "hurt her good," Stake hoped that she had sought medical attention. If he couldn't find her in a physician's care, he'd try the police station next, such as there might be in this town, but he didn't want to attract the law's attention to himself if he could help it. His greatest fear was that Thi might be home, either too shamed or too badly injured to seek out a doctor. Or maybe her husband wouldn't permit it. Just imagining these scenarios caused Stake's teeth to clamp so tightly together they seemed on the verge of cracking.

Vein Rhi was far from the teeming bustle of Di Noon, but there were still enough hoverbikes, bicycles, leisurely pedestrians, and children running out in the street when they saw his vehicle coming to great-ly impede his progress. A diminutive mummy of an old woman shuffled across his path with such slow-ness and obliviousness to his presence that Stake hissed, "For the love of God!" He nearly made the decision to raise the Harbinger above the rooftops, but just after the woman had passed and he pushed onward again his miniature guide chirped, "Doctor over there, over there!"

Turning into the indicated street, Stake spotted a tiny clinic or doctor's office ahead. Like most of the homes and places of business in Ha Jiin and Jin Haa towns, its frontmost room was open to the street, with a collapsible metal gate that could be drawn across and locked for the night. Stake could tell it was a clinic by the front room, which in this case was a waiting area. It was packed with Ha Jiin sitting in chairs or leaning against the walls for lack of a seat. There were even a number of people waiting out in the street itself. Babies bawling miserably. Old people shaking and spiritless as if this might be their last day as mortals. A pretty woman holding the side of her face, which had puffed up apparently from an infect-ed, abscessed tooth. At first Stake thought she was Thi—her jaw swollen from a blow—and his heart leapt into his throat, but as he pulled the helicar up directly in front of the shabby little building he spot-ted her.

She would have been better off with a bulging jaw, like the other woman. Even from the street, as Stake scrambled out of the vehicle, he could see that her eyes were swollen with shiny reddish-purple bruises, one eye barely slitted and the other completely closed. As he strode toward the waiting room, the child fol-lowing along like a pet, he saw she had some bruises across her forehead, a bruise just under her chin, and a large especially dark bruise on her left upper arm that Stake knew could not be the result of a single blow. It was a place where she had been punched again, and again, and again.

The girl seated beside Thi was lovely, doe-eyed, tall for a Ha Jiin and thin; Stake figured her to be fifteen or sixteen. He also figured her to be accompanying Thi, a relative or neighbor, since she didn't appear ill herself and was sitting so close. The girl looked up at Stake first, as he stepped onto the waiting room's floor. All the other patients had looked up at him, too. Thi was the last, raising her head slowly as if drunken or half asleep.

"Ga Noh," she said softly. "Please go home. Please hurry go home."

"You're coming with me," Stake told her, voice tight. His heart had not only sunk back down from his throat but seemed to continue its descent, a bathysphere lowering steadily into cold darkness. "There's a good hospital in Di Noon. They have Earth technology and you won't have to sit all night before you get seen."

"No, please—I okay."

"I remember places like this. If you don't see the doctor by closing time, well tough luck and try again tomorrow." He extended his hand to her. "Come on."

"Oh," said Thi, alarmed, looking past him. "Oh no, oh no..."

Stake heard two things that caused him to turn around. One was the lumbering approach of a group of yubos, silent except for the rasp of their hides against each other and the heavy muffled thump of their steps, churning up a cloud of dust. The other sound was the cry of one of the men who was driving the animals along; Stake remembered glimpsing him on his way into Vein Rhi. The man tramped forward, leaving his companions behind, gripping his hook-tipped prodding stick. At last Stake recognized his sunken-cheeked face from the call on his wrist comp.

Stake stepped off the elevated floor of the waiting room and walked fast toward the man to meet him halfway, in the center of the unpaved street.

"Oh no... *no!*" Stake heard Thi wail behind him.

"I fucking kill you!" the man coming at Stake snarled, drawing back his stick to swing it at the Earther's head. "Kill both of you now!"

Stake caught the stick in his left hand. It stung badly, but he had hold of it, and jerked it downward and to his right. Thi's husband maintained his grip, so this redirected his momentum and threw him off balance. Stake grabbed the stick in his right hand now, instantly let go with his left. With his left arm freed, Stake smashed its elbow back into the Ha Jiin's face, impacting on one eye socket. This stunning blow caused the man to release the stick. It was Stake's, now.

Stake swiped the rod against the left side of the man's face. He could have hit him harder, but the sound of the wood across his cheekbone was still enough to make observers flinch. The man stumbled back, making an incoherent sound like a whimper, and Stake swung the stick lower and harder this time. It cracked the man across his left knee. He hit him on the knee again, and this time he went down.

Stake was kicking Thi's husband in the upper arm, in the same place again and again and again, when two of the other men herding the yubos came at him with their own sticks in hand. He swung around to face them, weapon held ready, but it was more the look on his face than the hook-tipped baton that caused them to stop in their tracks. One of the men was going gray, the other barely out of his teens. Neither looked like they wanted to follow through with coming to their companion's aid, but it was possible they still would out of a sense of obligation.

Peripherally, Stake took note of other Ha Jiin men in a half-circle behind him; mostly people who had been waiting to be seen by the clinic's lone doctor, or loved ones accompanying would-be patients. But were they waiting for an opportunity to lunge at the Earther who was beating one of their own kind, or merely spectators? Stake knew he was a skilled enough fighter to put down a lot of them before they could get their hands on him, but as small as Vein Rhi was, there were ultimately too many men who could come and oppose him. He felt a cold, almost detached certainty that unless he fought his way back inside the Harbinger soon, Vein Rhi would be the place he would die.

Thi's husband was curled in the dust, clutching his knee and shrieking obscenities and threats in his own tongue. He tried rolling onto all fours, but Stake planted a sharp kick in his ribs and he went onto his side again. The young yubo wrangler started forward a step, but Stake lurched at him one step in turn, and the Ha Jiin went into a crouch, holding his ground.

"Thi, get into my car! Go!" Stake bellowed.

"No, Ga Noh, please go home!" she sobbed behind him. "Please, please! It is worse now, more worse!"

"Go home," one of the male spectators echoed in English. Was it a threat, or said in concern for his safety?

"I'm not leaving you to this cowardly son of a bitch, Thi. You're coming with me."

The boy who had guided Stake here moved close to the helicar. "Come on, come on!"

A hoverbike pulled up a short distance away, and Stake saw that the man who dismounted from it wore a sweat-stained militia uniform. Great. Finding the Earther poised in an attitude of attack, the man slid his handgun from its holster and held it out at waist level. As he approached, he barked something in his own language. Stake let the rod drop close to his foot where he might retrieve it if need be, and straightened up a little, returning his wary gaze to the husband's two friends.

The militia man stopped a short distance away and demanded something or other from Stake, who shrugged and said, "English. Only English."

One of the male spectators moved forward to converse with the policeman, pointing animatedly toward the clinic, then at Thi's husband moaning in the road, then to Stake, and back at the clinic again. Stake had no idea whether the witness's report was in his favor or damned him.

Another vehicle turned the corner into the street, this one a big-wheeled Ha Jiin military vehicle that had seen a lot of use and perhaps dated back to the war itself. Stake recognized it even before it stopped and one of its three occupants jumped down to the ground and came toward him and the peace officer. Captain Hin Yengun looked grim as he took in the man lying in the dirt, the tense Earther so incongruous in this obscure village, and the militia man training his pistol on him. The policeman started speaking but after a moment the military officer held up a hand to cut him off.

"Mr. Stake," Yengun said, "what is happening here?"

"I'm glad to see you," Stake told him.

"I saw your craft in the air, and followed you here. I wanted to talk to you about something."

"What is that?"

"First explain to me what this is about. Why did you attack this man?"

"He's the husband of Thi Gonh, captain. And that's Thi Gonh over there." He swivelled around to point at the clinic, where Thi stood shakily, her arm supported by the beautiful teenager. "Though you might not recognize her."

Yengun stared at the woman's battered face for several long seconds before turning to Stake again. "Now I think I made a mistake telling her that you were looking for her."

"No, it was her husband who made the mistake, of thinking that she and I met to... to... we only got together to have something to eat and talk a little. And somehow he found out—I think I know who told him—and he did this to her."

"And so you did that to him. Did you come to Sinan still wanting to kill Ha Jiin people, Mr. Stake?"

"I should hope you'd know that isn't true, captain. You can see what this man did to his wife."

"It is a matter for us to handle." Yengun returned his attention to the militia man and gave some orders. This man in turn ordered the husband's two friends to pick up the injured farmer and carry him into the clinic. The husband had begun raging again but his voice faded inside the building. Yengun explained to Stake, "I gave instructions that the doctor is to tend to him, and then he is to be arrested for assaulting his wife."

"The doctor has to see her first—she might have a concussion."

Yengun called some more orders after the militia officer. Stake turned to see the man gesture for Thi to cut ahead of all the other waiting people. She entered a back room still assisted by the young girl. Stake thought he saw Thi glance back in his direction as she disappeared behind a curtain.

"Thanks," Stake said. "And now are you going to have me arrested, too? He came at me first, with this." Stake poked the hooked stick with his toe. "I was acting in self-defense."

"I am not going to arrest you, though there may be questions later when the militia officer makes his report. You are lucky that the townspeople did not attack you."

"I'm a bit surprised at that, myself."

"I imagine they can see that this man beat his wife very badly. And they know she is Thi Gonh, the Earth Killer. Despite the disgrace that came to her later, she is still thought of as a wartime hero, an inspiration for the common folk—that even a small, young peasant woman could rise up to oppose a greater enemy. I think some of my people even love her more because she became the Earth Lover. We are a romantic people, Mr. Stake, with poetic souls. Many were touched by the story of how this hardened soldier spared the life of three Earth men she could easily have killed. This is all why she was not sentenced as a traitor. There is even a folk song about her."

"Really? I never knew that. I'd like to hear it sometime." Stake wondered if he himself figured into that song in any way. He exhaled slowly and held his hands out in front of him, saw how they were shaking. Now that the confrontation had cooled and some semblance of order had descended, and Thi was being seen by a physician, he was finally experiencing the aftereffects of a potent adrenaline rush. "I can't believe that piece of scum would do that to her—a woman."

"Did you not kill Ha Jiin women during the war, Mr. Stake."

That brought Stake up short. Yes, in fact, he had. He knew for certain that he'd killed two young women who could have been Thi Gonh themselves. And then there were others he suspected he'd killed in various firefights. "That was different, captain. We were trying to kill each other. I was luckier."

"It was not appropriate for me to say that," Yengun muttered, as if more to himself than out of apology. He gazed toward the clinic uncomfortably. "In any case, there is the matter I wanted to discuss with you."

"What's that?"

"You recall that I told you a witch led me to the place where the three bodies were found, in the Blue City?"

"Yes?"

"Her dreams have not ended. I have been told she is still having strange nightmares. I thought that maybe these visions of hers might be illuminating to you in your investigation, somehow."

Before Yengun could relate what these dreams consisted of, Stake asked, "Do you think you could arrange for me to meet her in person?"

"She does not speak your language."

"If you were with me, you could translate for her."

Yengun grunted in assent. "Very well. Then I will arrange it. I will contact you."

"Thanks so much for this, captain. Thanks for thinking of me."

"For now, I think it is wise for you to leave this town immediately. These people may understand why you did what you did, but that does not mean they love Earth people, especially at this time."

"I hate leaving Thi Gonh here in her condition. I really wish I could take her with me to Di Noon."

"She is being seen to. Please spare the poor woman further humiliation, Mr. Stake. Leave her be, for now. Come—I will escort you safely out of Vein Rhi."

Stake nodded reluctantly, and sighed. "Thanks again, captain. For everything."

Yengun only grunted again, turned away, and climbed up into the wheeled vehicle with his two soldiers. Stake went back to his helicar, ruffling the bristly hair of the boy who had helped him before he slipped inside.

As he turned the craft around to follow the soldiers, Stake threw one more look at the clinic as if he expected to see Thi peeking out at him around the inner office's curtain. He realized his hands were still shaking at the Harbinger's controls. He hadn't yet expended all his bottled up energies—or emotions.

CHAPTER TEN
BRIGHT HORIZONS

DRIVING BACK ALONG the forest road, hovering close to the ground, Stake had to pause the car at an intersection with another road that was little more than a footpath in order to let a long string of people pass in front of him. Even before he saw what looked like a giant seedpod being carried on a litter, he knew from the incense and somber faces that this was a funeral procession on its way to one of the extensive burial tunnels that honeycombed the earth beneath the forests of both the Ha Jiin and Jin Haa lands. Customarily, the body was slathered with a bright yellow mineral solution that would crudely mummify it, then wrapped up in a single huge, blue leaf before being transported to one of these subterranean tomb systems. Down there, it would be unwrapped from its leaf coffin and slotted into one of countless cavities dug in the walls of the tunnels.

People in the procession turned their heads to look at his idling vehicle in surprise, curiosity, and disapproval, as if he had defiled their solemn rite. But in his day, Stake had done much more in the way of dishonoring the Ha Jiin dead. Then again, so had their own people. During the Blue War, both sides had taken their battle even beneath Sinan's surface. Ha Jiin guerillas would often station themselves in these catacombs, and so Colonial Forces units would go down in the tombs after them. But there was more in those labyrinths to attract the Colonial Forces than just enemy soldiers to be flushed out. There was the matter that had caused the Earth Colonies to become interested in distant Sinan in the first place.

Sinon gas.

In the tunnels, the gas might appear as a mere blue haze, or it might curl and billow so that one couldn't see more than a few feet ahead, an unpleasant prospect for a soldier on either side who was stealing through the grottos. The extent of the gas had a lot to do with the age of the corpses stocked in the tunnels—thin, attenuated mist if the remains were old, lusty and dense clouds if the more recently deceased were in residence—though very often, the dead were mixed together instead of segregated, families owning whole walls of niches so that they might bunk one day alongside their ancestors.

The blue gas was a by-product of the bodies' decomposition.

It had also been found to possess surprising properties. Earth Colonies researchers had discovered the gas could be used in excimer lasers, a wide variety of light bulbs, various medical applications such as general anesthesia, inertial confinement fusion, ion propulsion engines, and had proved particularly valuable in teleportation systems. This gas was not encountered in the decomposition of other animals or plants on Sinan, however, and it had been learned that it was the interaction of the yellow preserving agent on the interred dead bodies that provided the necessary reaction to produce the gas—which Earth Colonies research and developers had dubbed sinon.

To the Ha Jiin, though, these gases were the spirits of their ancestors, and were to be revered.

So it was that they had not taken kindly to the appearance of the first Earth Colonies researchers, and reacted violently to their intrusions. The hatred had only grown when the Earth Colonies turned to the nascent Jin Haa nation, to support them in their struggle for independence. In return for their help, the Jin Haa—more forward thinking, they boasted—allowed their allies to harvest sinon gas from their own burial tunnels, many of them now adopting the view that the gas was symbolic rather than the literal lingering souls of their dead.

But the Jin Haa nation was tiny compared to the Ha Jiin lands that surrounded it, and so it hadn't just been missions to search out and destroy the enemy that had sent Colonial Forces deep penetration operatives like Corporal Jeremy Stake into Ha Jiin territory. He had also frequently been sent down into the Ha Jiin burial catacombs, to set up small units that would siphon up the sinon gas and teleport it in measured quantities to a base that had been established in the city of Di Noon, where the gas would be refined and eventually teleported onward to Earth's own dimension. There was a symmetry to it all. Sinon gas made interdimensional teleportation more feasible, reliable, safe. And teleportation transported the gas out of the dimension in which it was to be found.

The Jin Haa had won their independence, and a bitter peace had existed for over a decade. The terms of peace, and pressure from numerous worlds within the Earth Colonies network, now prevented Colonial Forces units from stealing into Ha Jiin tombs to appropriate their gas. But despite their best efforts at negotiation, the Earth Colonies had still not persuaded the Ha Jiin to willingly let them harvest gas as the Jin Haa did. To the Ha Jiin, the blasphemous Jin Haa had literally sold their souls to their extradimensional allies. Thus, the Earth Colonies had only limited access to sinon gas—only that which the Jin Haa could provide, and the greatly dispersed quantities that could be extracted from the general atmosphere.

Stake's mind had stolen back in time and back down into the tunnels. He was remembering the faint odor of the gas and the stronger taint of incense that sought to cover the stench of the dead as much as pay tribute to them. He remembered the riddled and torn young Ha Jiin soldiers who had died amongst the rows of shelved mummies. He remembered the echoing screams of Colonial Forces buddies caught in booby-traps their enemies had rigged down there.

When he came back to himself he realized the procession had disappeared into the jungle like a train of ghosts. Disconcerted that he should zone out like that, he started the Harbinger forward again. As he gazed off to his right, he noticed a bluish fog in amongst the dense trees. The nearest entrance to the tunnels, and the one to which the procession was no doubt headed, was obviously close in that direction.

Stake's wrist comp alerted him to a call. He felt a jolt inside; news about Thi's condition? But when he saw the face of an Earth man on the screen he didn't recognize him, at first.

"Mr. Stake? It's David Bright. I got your number from Henderson."

Of course. Bright, of Bright Horizons. Stake had encountered him in Gale's meeting room briefly. "Hello, Mr. Bright. What can I do for you?"

"You can have dinner with me tonight at the hotel where I'm staying in Di Noon. Will you meet with me?"

"Yes. But can I ask what you want to talk about?"

"I'd rather not, over the net like this."

Stake could understand that. They settled on a time, and Bright told Stake he'd meet him in the dining room of Di Noon's most sophisticated hotel, the Cobalt Temple.

With the call finished, Stake lifted the helicar higher, higher above the jungle. He glanced at his rearview monitor. The little town of Vein Rhi was lost from view behind him.

THE COBALT TEMPLE was one of the tallest structures in Di Noon, a favorite of wealthy Earth Colonies tourists looking for an exotic and unconventional vacation they could boast about back home, and of businessmen who espied the investment opportunities Sinan had to offer. The many-floored building also rented out office space to some of these ventures, including the temporary base of operations Bright had established for his work here on Sinan. Perched at the very top of the cobalt-colored structure was a small traditional temple. It was the law that any building taller than ten stories—thus, taller than a legendary tree sacred to the local beliefs—had to have a temple at its summit in order to mediate between the material and spiritual worlds.

But when Stake had entered the hotel, he found that the Cobalt Temple also had a karaoke bar just off the lobby. He stood in the doorway a few moments, listening to a drunken mauling of an early Del Kahn hit, "Spirits on Wheels." Stake loved old music, though he thought a night in this bar might change that for him. Karaoke on Sinan. So the invasion had taken another, more insidious form.

His mustard-colored suit wasn't too rumpled from having been packed for the trip, and so a lovely Jin Haa hostess in a tight-fitting black dress invited him inside as if he might be some entrepreneur himself.

Stake declined, backed off, headed toward the entrance to the dining room instead. There, he accepted another alluring hostess's invitation and allowed her to escort him to the table where David Bright awaited him.

"Thanks for coming, Mr. Stake." Bright rose to shake his hand and both settled in at their table. "Let me order you a drink." Stake watched the man as he gestured to a waitress who could have been a sister to the two hostesses the detective had met. As at the meeting in the Colonial Forces base, Stake had the impression that the man was so filled with nervous anxiety that he was ready to explode out of his constricting five-piece suit.

"A Zub beer will be fine, if they have it."

"A man of humble tastes." Bright relayed the order to the young woman and she left them with menus. Neither man opened them.

"What can I do for you, Mr. Bright?"

Bright was watching the rear of the receding waitress as it moved within her tight sheath, maybe grateful for the distraction. "What's with the white rubber gloves a lot of these girls wear? For sanitary purposes? I hear there's a bad sickness going around, some kind of STD."

Stake wondered if Bright had heard about the sexually transmitted disease in the course of pursuing Jin Haa prostitutes, and then he remembered the unusually large number of patients waiting to be seen in little Vein Rhi, a sight he would expect more in a city like Di Noon. Had the plague that Henderson described to him reached even that hamlet?

"Upper crust women used to take very good care that their hands looked beautiful, to show that they didn't have to do menial work. It became such an obsession that eventually they began treating their hands with a solution that crystallizes them and makes them immobile, white as alabaster. It's an erotic image to Ha Jiin men; they have a fetish for it. So common women will dye their hands white or wear gloves to affect that look. Men will even put on white rubber gloves themselves to masturbate with, or else in Di Noon sex shops they'll buy porcelain hands to use for that purpose."

"Jeesh. They can have the hands all they want; it's those tight little blue bums I'm interested in."

"What was it you wanted to discuss, Mr. Bright? Besides the local fauna."

Bright gave an apologetic smile, and shifted restlessly in his seat. "With the Ha Jiin and even the Jin Haa hating the Earth Colonies so much now, it should come as no surprise to you that I'm public enemy number one around here." He flicked his chin to direct Stake's attention to another table, where a KeeZee who looked towering even seated was sawing into a huge yubo steak. Sensing Stake's eyes on him, the alien looked up and glared with three little black eyes, his massive jaws working under a thin layer of gray-black skin. When Stake faced Bright again, the businessman explained, "My bodyguard. There's been some anti-EC terrorist activity, you know. I don't trust anybody blue right now."

"Maybe you'd better stay away from the native girls, then. There's a saying to the effect that the women of Sinan have the bodies of children and hearts like hundred year-old swords. Your assassin might be wearing white rubber gloves and nothing else."

"I'll bear that in mind."

"I hate to say it, but I can understand the bad feelings. The little glitch in your process has really set off a firestorm."

"Do you think I don't know that pretty fucking well by now? Christ, I stand to lose a fortune paying restitution to the Ha Jiin and Jin Haa. I'm pushing the EC government to take some of the financial burden, and I'm sure they'll make a gesture to make themselves look good, but I'm ruined for the rest of my life. My people are doing their best to figure out what went wrong and how to shut the process down. They haven't had any more success than the blasting Jin Haa exorcists their clerics send to Bluetown. You can demolish the buildings one by one, of course, and spend a thousand years on it. But you can't bomb the town flat for the same reason bombing was limited in the Blue War—the volatile gas in their burial tunnels. That could send an underground fire through even more of their territory than Bluetown has covered, and burn down the jungles in the bargain. You could try corrosives, but again, you'd have to spend years melting building by building. My crew and the EC teams have tried poisons on the living cells of the advancing line, thinking maybe they could spread them from the air. The smart matter hasn't reacted to them. My Simulacrum Systems lab rats did a better job designing this stuff than any of us thought. It has a life all of its own, and it's shaking us off like fleas."

"And your computers can't be linked to the smart matter again, and reprogram it? Feed a virus into it? If not to destroy what's already taken form, at least to stop any more from spreading?"

"We've been doing that. Nothing has taken, yet. This thing has its program, corrupted by a virus though it may already be, and it won't pay attention to anything else we tell it." The waitress brought their drinks but Bright dismissed her with their menus still untouched. "Mr. Stake, have you had any luck in investigating those three bodies that were found? Who they were, and why my stuff cloned them in particular?"

"I haven't gotten far yet. I've been a little side-tracked."

"Look, keep at it, and I promise to supplement what Henderson is paying you."

"I'm not a scientist, Mr. Bright."

"Maybe that's a good thing. Like I said in Gale's meeting, I'm willing to look at new resources, here. Fresh perspectives." Bright glanced around him before continuing in a lower voice. "There's something else you might be able to find out about. I'm wondering if the Earth Colonies folks themselves purposely hijacked my technology so they could turn Sinan into a massive new Earth colony quickly, forcing the Jin Haa and Ha Jiin both into a subservient position, obliterating their boundaries—meanwhile setting me up as the fall guy. The scapegoat."

"Frankly, that sounds a bit on the paranoid side, Mr. Bright."

"But not impossible? Think about it a bit. And remember the war you yourself fought in, right? You remember what that was really all about."

Stake stared down into his beer to avoid taking on Bright's too perfect good looks. If he pursued the angle Bright was postulating, he felt he'd be wading into this mess far over his head. "I can't promise to look into that, Mr. Bright, but if in the course of my investigation I come across any information that suggests such a thing, I'll try to clue you in."

"Ah, dung," Bright sighed, then sipped his drink. "Why should a private eye from Punktown stand beside me? With all this hell coming down, I can't even buy a friend."

"I didn't say I wasn't sympathetic to your situation, Mr. Bright."

"If I do find out they've used me and my technology like that, they'll see a whole new firestorm from me, I guarantee it. They're underestimating me, if that's the case. I'll take on the whole blasting Earth Colonies government if I have to. What more do I have to lose at this point?" The businessman smirked wearily. "That's why I take the risk of getting myself stabbed to death by some little blue prostie."

"Well, if you do keep pursuing the local fauna, I'd keep your KeeZee, over there, in the same room with you."

"That sounds a little too kinky even for my tastes, Mr. Stake."

CHAPTER ELEVEN
BEWITCHED

WHILE STAKE FLEW his borrowed Harbinger toward Bluetown the next morning, he reflected on last night's conversation with David Bright, and the businessman's theory about the active involvement of the Earth Colonies government in the Bluetown debacle. Might it be true, and if so, might that more than anything else account for the failure to halt the city's progress? But Stake had another thought now that Bright had infected him with paranoia.

Stake's body was a skilled artist when it came to replicating another's appearance, sometimes even to the point of imitating freckles and moles, but he found that his understanding of his subjects' personalities often didn't extend much farther than their skin. David Bright, for instance, seemed distraught and anxious enough, but what if it were all an act? Despite his protests to the contrary in Gale's meeting room, what if he did have something to gain from the development of Bluetown? What if the condo project had only been a front? Might Bright even have teamed with the Earth

Colonies in unleashing Bluetown, and his offer to pay Stake to investigate was just a smokescreen to obscure his own role in that plan?

Sinon gas was so highly valued by the colonies. If the Ha Jiin and Jin Haa nations could be destabilized, with the colonies coming in to save the day at the last minute—after borders had been paved over and the land altered beyond recognition—might they at last have access to the far richer quantities of sinon gas the Ha Jiin territories had to offer?

Well, Stake figured it wouldn't make sense for Bright to put it in his head about the colonies being involved, if he himself were working in conjunction with them on such a project. Unless, that is, the deal had gone sour, Bright was squirming under his role of whipping boy, and he was now feeling vengeful toward his former bedfellows.

These possibilities didn't so much make Stake feel closer to an answer as they made it harder for him to pick out the right destination on the horizon.

Not so, with Bluetown itself. He had been on this world for four years straight, and despite his long absence since that time, he was familiar enough with the way things should look that he still couldn't assimilate the way they looked now. It was just as disturbing as stepping outside to find the moon now filled a tenth of the visible sky, and was getting larger still. Looming taller than the low forested mountains it inched toward, Bluetown looked exactly like what it was—the horizon of another world superimposed over this one.

As Stake got closer to the edge of the city, his wrist comp sounded and he took the call. He almost winced to see Thi Gonh's face there. Even so, he was surprised that her eyes should have lost most of their swelling so soon, and her bruises had shrunk but darkened a deeper shade of purple. Whatever salves or such the doctor had given her had obviously done a lot of good.

"Thi, my God, I've been worrying about you. I called last night but you didn't answer."

"Sorry, so sorry, Ga Noh. I am resting so much."

"I understand. How do you feel? Are you in pain? Did they check you for a concussion, ruptured organs, broken bones?"

"Broken bones." She gave a snort like a humorless laugh. "You broke bones of my husband. You make crack in his face." She touched her cheek. "You make crack in his foot."

"Foot? You mean his leg, his knee?"

"Yes, yes, knee. Very bad crack in knee."

"I'm sorry." But he wasn't. He was quite satisfied. Or maybe not satisfied enough.

"No sorry."

"You were yelling for me to stop."

"I was afraid! Afraid he hurt *you*, Ga Noh! I need tell you... you need understand... I do not love my husband."

"He's a monster. A cowardly little bully, and he doesn't deserve you. Has he ever beaten you before?"

"No. First time. But yell to me every day. Yell bad words, call me bad names, call me girl who fuck for money. Always. Now crazy, crazy because Ga Noh is here."

"It was your cousin Nhot who told him we had lunch together, wasn't it?"

Thi hesitated a moment. "Yes. Nhot always very jealous to me, jealous to everyone. It is her way, from child to now. Smile outside, inside hate. Maybe she hate herself too much."

"I can understand why. Your own flesh and blood; I can't believe it. Who is she to concern herself with her cousin's business?"

"Here, person's business is family's business. Whole family. That is why I call Ga Noh."

"What do you mean?"

She hesitated again, drawing in breath. "Nhot's father—my uncle—is boss of family now my father is die. Uncle very unhappy I see you again. Uncle fought you in war. Uncle shame of me when I not kill three Earth men; shame of talk call me Earth Lover. Shame of me for many years now. Now, more shame again. Nhot told him so much, so much."

"Mean-spirited little…"

"Uncle say I make all Vein Rhi people look bad to my family. Uncle say I need tell police make my husband free again."

"*What?* What are you saying? Your own uncle wants you to drop the charges against your husband, after what he did to you? He wants you to let that bastard go so he can kill you next time around? Did your uncle see what he did to your face?"

"Yes. But uncle afraid people talk about family. Uncle want husband and me to be same before."

"No, that's insane, Thi, insane! You can't let him go unpunished for this, and you sure as hell can't go back to living with him! He's dangerous!"

"Husband cry and cry to police, so sorry hit wife. Husband promise not hit me again."

"And you believe that? He isn't sorry—he's just afraid to be sent to prison! Can't you understand that, Thi? Or do you really love this guy, after all?"

"No! No love him, I swear! But understand… for Ha Jiin, men are boss, not women. My uncle is boss. My husband is boss. I must be listen to brother of father. Respect uncle, respect husband. Not what I like. But what I need do."

"I can't believe you, Thi. I can't believe your cousin, your uncle, or especially you." He was almost shaking with frustration, and worked distractedly at the Harbinger's controls as he crossed Bluetown's creeping border and began to decrease his altitude.

"Listen, Ga Noh, please, please. Today, I go police and make husband free. Before I let husband free, I like see Ga Noh one time more. Okay? Please."

"What for? What good will that do now? You saw me once and it got you beaten. And now you're letting that animal out of his cage to kill you, either tomorrow or next month or next year. What good would it do us to see each other one last time?" He was almost raging.

"Ga Noh not want to see me one time more?"

He could hear the broken edge in her voice. She was almost in tears. So fragile, so brittle now, the Earth Killer. Stake forced the rage—and a pain strong as rejection—down as much as he could manage. "Of course I want to see you. But I want you to think about this. Think very carefully."

"Ga Noh can not come to Vein Rhi, please," she told him. "I am afraid people talk and my uncle hear."

"Okay, look, I'm flying into Bluetown right now. I'm here to meet with Captain Yengun. I'll be here for an hour or two, I figure. So I'm fairly close to you. Do you want to meet me in Bluetown when I'm finished?"

"Yes, I like."

"Then you can start coming out this way now, if you want. When you reach the city, call me back. I'll get in my helicar and raise it high enough into the sky that you can get a sense of where I'm at. Sound okay?"

"Yes, okay."

"And then when you get here, you and I can talk more about this."

"Okay—I come to Blue City now, and call soon."

"Be careful, Thi."

"Ga Noh careful, too. Blue City no good. Very no good." With that, her image blinked out.

"*Fuck,*" Stake hissed, slamming the heel of one hand on the control console. "Her own family. Her own blasting family."

STAKE SAW THERE were eight of them, some sitting on the curb and a few pacing around cradling their assault engines. They watched him lower the Harbinger to the middle of the street, then climb out. Yengun was one of those sitting on the curb, and Stake noted that they had been eating—all of them except for a wizened little woman, who was staring at the newcomer with apprehension bordering on outright fear. Yengun rose to come forward and meet Stake halfway.

"Packed a picnic lunch?" Stake said, gesturing toward several lacquered woven baskets resting between the soldiers. They studied the Earther warily themselves.

"You are welcome to join us if you like. My wife makes meals for me and my men, when we are out on patrol."

"That's nice of her." Stake could sense a pride, an affection, in Yengun's words. He hoped so. He hoped he was kind to his wife—never beat her. "I'm not hungry, actually, but thanks anyway." Stake glanced around. "I didn't see your transport when I was coming in."

"We came on foot. Fortunately the witch's village is close to here. Well—it isn't fortunate for her village. It is now having to be evacuated as the city moves closer. But the witch will not ride in our vehicle. During the Blue War, I understand, a Colonial Forces tank came through her village, and in the fighting two of her nephews and a number of her neighbors were killed."

Stake glanced at the woman again. "I hope my presence doesn't agitate her too much."

"I tried to let her know you were coming, but I do not know how much she comprehends. She seems even more disoriented than the first time she brought us here. Her family told us that her dreams make her afraid to sleep."

"Tell her that she might feel better after she talks to me about them. Tell her she can unburden her dreams on me."

"And who are you to unburden the dreams on, after that?"

Stake held the Ha Jiin's gaze. "That remains to be seen, I guess."

Two of the men helped the old woman to her feet. A young soldier Stake heard addressed as Nha seemed to be wiping her mouth with a napkin, but then he realized the cloth was stained with blood from her nostrils. He was shocked at the purple veins that stood out along her temples, fat and thick as worms. He did not know that they were more pronounced than they had been the last time she had accompanied these men to Bluetown.

Hin Yengun approached the elderly villager slowly, with Stake trailing a step behind. Yengun spoke to her in their own language. The Earther didn't catch much more than the respectful title of "aunt" that preceded the captain's words. The woman's eyes, dull and glassy, moved back and forth between the faces of the two men. At last, Yengun turned to Stake and nodded. "She is ready to go inside," he said. "And she took your offer quite literally. She says that after today, the dreams will belong to you."

"That's what I'm getting paid for," Stake said.

The rest of the men stood, wiping their hands on their trousers, fruit rinds scattered around their boots. Nha and another soldier would accompany them inside. The other four soldiers would stand watch in the street, forsaken as it was.

They entered through one of the gaping windows, Nha and the other soldier pretty much passing the old witch through the opening into the hands of Yengun and Stake. As the two soldiers followed, Stake turned to Yengun and asked, "Did you know Thi Gonh's family has pressured her into dropping charges against her husband? Can't he be detained and charged despite what she wants?"

"I suggest you let her handle it the way she wishes, Mr. Stake. Maybe it is better for you this way. It is less likely now that you will have problems about the incident yourself."

"It's not me I'm worried about."

Yengun looked at him closely. "I admire your concern for her."

"Is that why you're helping me? Because I protected her when she was a war criminal?"

Yengun grimaced, as if the idea were absurd. "I simply want to know whose remains those are, and how the Blue City could clone them. If we know that, we may understand the Blue City itself better—and then, maybe find a way to stop it."

Again Stake noticed the raised scar on Yengun's cheek. These scars were meant to represent family members lost during the Blue War, but why should Yengun's scar be only half the normal length? He was about to bring it up when the Ha Jiin faced him directly once more.

"You still love her," Yengun stated.

"Yes."

The officer's hard mouth suggested the faintest of smiles. "I told you my people are romantic, poetic, and that is why some still love the Earth Killer turned Earth Lover. I think you are that way, too."

"I think you're right."

"The war burned our love, you and I," Yengun said. "But it could not destroy it." Before Stake could ask him what that bit of poetry was all about, the captain started off down the murky blue hallway. "Come."

They proceeded into the cavernous room, the two soldiers using the lights on their guns to illuminate it. They all watched as the tiny woman moved ahead of them to stand at the very edge of one of the three openings in the floor. She muttered something, and appeared to be trembling. They waited. Stake was ready to lunge forward and catch her arms if she started to topple forward. Her nearness to the pit and her shaking were making him nervous. And then, she started to speak.

"What's she saying?" Stake whispered.

"She says she remembers her dreams. She sees three of the devils with white faces."

"Huh," Stake said.

"But they are not warriors."

Stake frowned. "What? Is she sure? Ask her if they wear camouflaged uniforms, carry guns."

"If she will hear me," Yengun said, but he addressed the witch in their tongue. She answered him back in a cracked, distant voice. "No," Yengun reported. "They do not wear jungle patterns. Yes, they carry guns—small guns in pouches, she says."

"No heavy arms?"

"Apparently not." The woman said more. Yengun translated, "She says the devils did not come from an egg."

"An egg?" Had she not been the one to lead Yengun to the clones in the first place, Stake might have dismissed her impressions as delirium.

"She sees them standing in a ray of light."

Stake pondered a moment. He was distracted, and so when the old woman started moving he jolted, afraid he'd be too late to catch her, but she was turning away from the pit and shuffling toward one of the large room's barren walls, mumbling to herself as she went.

Yengun said, "They did not come here in an egg. They rode a ray of light. They were here, and then gone, and then here again."

The woman had reached the wall and ran her hands over the coral-like material, as far above her head as she could reach. She slapped it with both palms. Stake moved closer to watch her face in the beams of the flashlights. She was babbling with more animation, slapping the wall again. Then she whirled around and said something to Yengun. He responded by digging a pad and a pen from a pocket in the leg of his uniform. He handed them over to her, and she scribbled in an unsteady hand. When she was finished, she shoved the pad back into the captain's hands.

"What is it?" Stake moved beside him, and saw what appeared to be characters that were not from the Ha Jiin alphabet. An S and an M. Yengun handed him the pad for Stake to pore over. As he was doing so, the old woman stepped toward him with an irritable grunt and roughly turned the pad around in his hands. Not SM. It was a W and an S instead.

"She must have seen that symbol on the wall," Yengun observed.

"Yes. I think you're right. I think she's seeing the room that corresponds with this one—in Punktown." Stake looked up at the Ha Jiin officer. "The three people didn't come to Sinan in an egg. A pod—a transdimensional pod, like I came here in. Like the soldiers used to come here in. They came in a ray of light instead."

"But what would that be? The only way your people can come to Sinan is in the pods."

Stake returned his gaze to the witch, trying to fathom what these dreams might be saying to her. He saw that she was staring at his alien face in apprehension again, quaking. Was he reminding her of the soldiers who had come to her village in their powerful machine, killed her neighbors and nephews? Or was he reminding her more of the people she had seen in her latest visions?

She let out an abrupt cry and backed away. "Ga Noh!" she screeched, pointing at his face. "Ga Noh!"

Nha rushed forward, put an arm around her to steady and comfort her. Turned her to face away from the shapeshifter.

"Please don't do that," Yengun told Stake.

"Sorry." He touched his own face, if it could be called his own face, and felt the disturbing contours of wrinkles and distended veins.

Outside the building they heard a terrific boom, like an explosion. The sound was still rumbling, a deep thunder, as Stake and Yengun rushed from the room and to the nearest of the hallway's windows. The other two men supported the witch on either side, following more slowly.

"Christ," Stake said.

Above and between the buildings on the opposite side of the street, he could see that a distant skyscraper had toppled. Its vast weight had crushed the fronts of surrounding buildings, but they managed to uphold it at an angle. A great blue cloud of pulverized coral began to billow upwards, and within moments they could no longer see the fallen building. The last of the thunder reverberated off down the branching streets.

"Are they starting to demolish some of these buildings?" Stake asked Yengun, hoping he hadn't just witnessed an act of terrorism.

"The buildings here have foundations appropriate for your Punktown, not necessarily for this terrain. Our own science teams have concern over this, and it is one of the reasons we try to discourage refugees. What are called friction piles are to be anchored in soil, and bearing piles are to rest on rock, but if the conditions here are not duplicated along with the buildings, some of them collapse from the strain of the ground beneath them."

"If only they'd all fall down on their own, huh?" Stake murmured.

"At least my world is rejecting some of them," Yengun said.

STAKE HAD OFFERED to take Yengun and the elderly seer to her village, but she would have none of the flying machine and none of the Ga Noh. Stake had watched the party move off down the street and disappear around a corner. Then he was alone, and waiting for Thi. Before leaving him, though, Yengun had advised him to wait inside his helicar, lest some dangerous animal or squatters come along. Stake had told him he would, but he did not, stood leaning against the vehicle with his mind picking among the detritus of the old woman's visions.

His wrist comp blipped. He saw it was Thi. She told him she was in Bluetown now, and he told her to watch for his vehicle. He entered the Harbinger, lifted it high enough above the surrounding buildings for her to see as she approached. Within fifteen minutes he saw a hoverbike nearing below. When it came to a halt in the street beneath him, he lowered the craft again to come to a rest beside her. She swung herself off the bike, he stepped out of the helicar, and they met each other between.

"God." Stake touched her face lightly, wagging his head. Even though she looked better than she had at the clinic, the bruises made him cringe inside with empathetic pain. "How did he do this to you? He punched you?"

"No. I was shower my body, and husband came to me with knife. He pull me out of shower, pull me to sit at table, not let me wear clothes. Yell, yell to me, point knife to my face, and then hold my hair, here." She reached behind her head and gathered her long hair in her fist. "Make my head hit table again, again. Walk around and around table, yell to me more, then hold my hair again and hit head to table very much. Here."

She felt at the bruises on her forehead. So it was the force of these blows, as he slammed her head against the table edge, that had caused the swelling of her eyes. Stake wondered if she'd suffered a concussion that the doctor's no doubt limited equipment hadn't been able to scan. She touched herself under her jaw; he could tell from her expression that the bruise there was tender. "I hit my chin on table one time."

"I didn't hit him enough with the stick," Stake muttered. "Not nearly enough." He managed to get past the replay of the fight in his mind to ask, "What was he doing driving those animals into town when I came? Helping some neighbors?"

"They my yubo, from my farm. Move them to Vein Rhi. Every day let yubo outside to eat, then bring inside again."

"So he beats you, leaves you there at the table bruised and naked, and goes to do some chores like it's just another day for… what's his name?"

"Hin, same-same Yengun, soldier you talk to."

"No, he isn't same-same as Yengun. Not at all."

"I meaning name only."

"I know what you mean. So who was the girl who sat beside you in the doctor's office?"

"Name is Twi. Niece of mine, very good girl, only fifteen year. Twi love me so much. I teach Twi shoot, shoot gun like aunt."

"Thank God at least one of your family had compassion for you." Stake touched the side of her face again, this time letting his hand linger there. She reached up, placed her hand over his. They shifted their bodies closer, eyes locked together. And then, their mouths came together, too.

Their tongues slid over and around each other. Moist sounds, and a tiny moan from her. Stake sucked at her plump lower lip and reluctantly let it go as she pulled away slowly to look up at his eyes again. She was smiling softly. "Ga Noh," she said. "Long time ago kiss me, same as now."

His heart was rumbling in echoes like those of the fallen building. "Thi, I've never stopped thinking about you all these years. I used to be so afraid that you didn't really feel anything for me, that you were only using me back then so I'd keep the other soldiers away from you. Then when you came to Punktown to fight those men for me, I knew that you did care for me somehow. Maybe not the same way I care for you, but—"

"Same as Ga Noh," she cut him off, eyes dark with the intensity of her earnestness. "I care you same-same you care to me." Her smile widened. "I think you put magic inside me. Magic make me crazy." She touched his face this time. "Ga Noh is gentle. Feel pain of me. Here." She touched her fingertip to his forehead. He understood, then, that the semblance of bruises were manifesting on his skin there, like a saint's stigmata.

Arms still around her back, Stake pressed her small body closer to his and kissed the bruises on her own forehead. "What happened to you, Thi? What happened to the Earth Killer?"

"No Earth Killer, remember? Earth Lover now."

"No, I mean, how can a soldier who earned that name sit there and let her husband bang her skull into the table and not lift a finger to defend herself?"

"You said word—husband. I obey husband. Respect to husband. Have to, Ga Noh. Have to."

He let her go and took a step back, the fury spreading through him like heat from a furnace again. "You don't *have* to. You *choose* to." Just because he was attracted to the woman for being of another culture didn't mean that he had to love everything about that culture. He found Ha Jiin women's devotion and loyalty to their men was, at the same time, one of their best and worst qualities. Depending on the man in question, he supposed. "I don't understand why a strong and intelligent woman like you would marry a man like this in the first place."

"I was Earth Lover. People point to me, laugh to me, some hating me. Men too shy marry me. Who else have me?" And she added, with a bitter curling of her lips, "And who else have Hin?"

"I would have you," Stake said simply. It made her eyes snap back to his. "Come to Punktown with me. Right now. I'll leave this place and its problems for better minds to solve."

"Ga Noh." She shook her head slowly. "I can not."

"Why? You said you cared about me, the same way I care about you."

"True—I swear. Never forget you before. Never forget you tomorrow. But your ban ta is *marry*."

Ban ta—your lover. Why was she still calling herself that, then? "So get a divorce."

"No divorce. I understand, my uncle say no. Only uncle of mine give to me divorce. Boss of family."

"That's your choice, Thi, only your choice. Let me talk to this uncle of yours. Is he more concerned with the family honor and saving face than he is about whether or not his brother's daughter gets beaten to death, or stabbed in the shower?"

"It is my people. I am Ha Jiin. Always Ha Jiin."

"Yeah, your people. During the war both sides puts guns in the hands of women, young girls like you just out of their teens, and so this is the reward you got afterwards? They take the gun out of your hands again, give you back a broom, and tell you to mind your place?"

Thi only blinked at him, as if in her agitation she was failing to comprehend his tirade. She looked on the verge of tears.

Stake filled her silence with more of his own words. "I don't know, maybe you still love this guy, huh? You let him go free. You won't divorce him. Won't come away with the man who offers you a new life. Maybe you love that he doesn't smile at you, like you told me before. Chats with male friends but never with you. Blows his load sometimes before he's barely inside you. Wow, what a prize. You love your husband, huh?" Snarling now. "And look how jealous he got. He loves you, too, right? What a fool I was, getting between the two of you."

The tears didn't come. Her eyes hardened. She shifted back just enough of a half-step that the light reaching her eyes changed and their blackness glinted red in metallic sparks and splinters. "Ga Noh talk no good. Very no good." She turned back toward her hoverbike, and slung one leg over the seat.

Stake walked toward her, still bitter but with a desperation as he saw her ready to leave. He knew right now he was just another angry guy telling her what to do, trying to control her. "Thi, it's only because—"

Straddling the bike, she started the engine and it rose off the ground a little, bobbing slightly. She looked up at him, glaring, features pinched. "Ga Noh not believe my love."

Love. Neither of them had used the word before. Stake felt the desperation more keenly, and put a hand out to stay her wrist but she swerved the bike around in a circle to distance herself and face him again. When she did, her eyes were harder still, the eyes of the soldier she had once been. But how could she give him that look, and not the man who had beaten her?

"Hin never love me. If Ga Noh steal yubo of husband, husband angry same. I belong husband same like animal."

"Listen—"

She cut him off, voice strained. "And I never love husband, too. Marry him to be marry. He need marry, I need marry, husband talk good then so I marry. But never love before Ga Noh. Never love again. Ga Noh believe or no believe, I not care."

"But Thi, if you won't come be with me, then why did you want to see me today?"

"I want say goodbye today."

And with that, she put the bike in motion again—off down the empty street, her long hair flashing behind her like black flames streaked with red. Small with distance now, the bike turned a corner and she was gone.

WAITING FOR CAPTAIN Rick Henderson to pick up his call, Stake sat in the Harbinger and gazed off toward the building that had collapsed and was propped against its smaller neighbors, pointing at the sky like a cannon. A blue mist still hung in the air over that part of the city. On the vehicle's music system he was tuned in to a station that played very old Earth music. It was not playing at the moment, but there was a song he liked by an artist named Del Kahn, called *Paxton*. It ran in his mind louder than the music inside the car.

"Yeah, I'm goin' back to Paxton,
But why I cannot tell..."

Finally, Henderson connected and Stake lowered dead eyes to the wrist comp's screen.

"Hey, Jer," his friend said.

"Rick, I need you to arrange a pod for me."

"A pod? What do you mean?"

"Goin' back to Paxton,
Must be my favorite hell."

"I need to go back to Punktown," Stake said.

CHAPTER TWELVE
MY FAVORITE HELL

JEREMY STAKE'S BATTERED hovercar sat on the same street the next day, this time with the song *Cop Show* by Frankie Dystopia playing on the sound system.

"You think they're so real
And they're braver than most,
But they're just a bunch of actors
Chasing phantoms and ghosts."

He was staring at the building he had been staring at yesterday, except this time it stood erect, and its lights glowed against the wet gray sky.

Across the street from him, a holographic billboard opened in the air like a curtain, played a trailer for a new action movie, then folded up again and was gone. Atop the roof of one of the buildings bounced a gigantic holographic ball of flesh marbled with blue veins, representing the 150-pound sphere who was the star of the hit sitcom *Buddy Balloon*. The street itself was congested with vehicles of every stripe, from hovercars to the occasional wheeled conveyance. Higher up, helicars drifted between the city towers like gnats, these towers made from a variety of materials and in a variety of generally somber colors.

The building Stake was parked in front of wasn't all that large, however. Just five stories, but longish, with a flat roof. There was an antennae array atop the roof like a cluster of thin metal spires. The building looked blackened, scorched, along its left lower section, and all its windows—formerly with panes of invisible force—had been sealed up with metal sheets.

So this was Ginger Street, then. Longtime resident of this city though he may be, Stake was still not familiar with the whole of it. Could anyone be? Previously he had been using Punktown to orient himself in Bluetown; now he was using Bluetown to orient himself in Punktown.

A mutant less extreme than the star of *Buddy Balloon*, but unsettling enough with its face sucked inward along its midline so that it had only a single milky eye and a pinhole for a mouth, tapped on Stake's window to beg for a handout. He barely registered the being, and it moved along quickly enough. In the slum of Tin Town, mutants were so abundant that they wouldn't think to appeal to the sympathy of strangers. Stake would know; it was where he had grown up, his late mother herself a mutant. She had not possessed a gift like Stake's. Her affliction had been more fixed: her eyes spread almost to the sides of her head, their pupils as reflective as chrome, and she had no nails on her fingers or toes. If there were other marks upon her body, only Stake's father, who hadn't been a mutant, had known of them. As a boy, Stake had not found his mother's eyes eerie. They had shone at him in the dark reassuringly, like twin stars, when she had put him to bed. And his father had not found her appearance disturbing, either. He had told her she was beautiful. Stake had loved his father for that.

Stake put thoughts of his parents out of his head. Such thoughts made him feel as lost as they were—his mother's affliction having taken her early, his father maybe dead or maybe undead, submerged in his drugs. No, Stake couldn't afford to feel nebulous right now. He needed to be *here*. In fact, even now he noticed that a car had pulled up to the curb ahead of him and a man was approaching the door to the building with the antennae array on its roof. Stake slipped out of his hovercar and came up on the man from behind.

"Hello—Mr. Kabbazah?"

The man spun around, thin and with dark features that presently expressed alarm. "Please don't sneak up on me! Are you Mr. Stake?"

"Yes, I am. Sorry about that." Stake shook the property owner's hand.

"I was just going inside to put on the lights; there's still a power connection. Briefly I was renting out the offices as storage space, and for a few years I rented out the first two floors to a group of artists for studios and apartments, but I stopped last year. There's been no one renting since."

"Why is that?"

Kabbazah met Stake's eyes unhappily. "I was afraid someone would be hurt and I'd be sued. I won't lie to you, Mr. Stake; this place is a thorn in my side. I've been meaning to tear it down and just sell the plot for a while now."

"What's the problem with it?"

"We'll get to that." The man turned back to the task of unlocking the front door. "It might seem unwise of me to discourage a potential buyer, but like I say, I have to be honest. And it's not like I can hide the conditions here—they speak for themselves."

The man opened the door by punching in a key code, and Stake followed him into a dark corridor. More key punching just inside the door and a train of lights along the ceiling sputtered awake groggily. The long corridor was familiar to Stake. His gaze traveled down its left-hand side, which was even more charred on the interior.

"There was a fire?" He pointed.

Kabbazah sighed. He'd been about to lead Stake in the opposite direction. "Yes, quite a few years ago, but the structure is sound enough in that sense. I should have painted or resurfaced it, but frankly, I just can't deal with this beast. The artists said they'd paint it over for me, for a break on their rent, but they never got around to it."

"Can I go look down that end first?" Stake asked. When Kabbazah sighed again, Stake smiled apologetically and explained, "I really need to determine the structure's integrity for myself before I can consider a purchase."

"Very well." Kabbazah brushed past him to lead the way toward that familiar door. "But if I were you, I'd tear this whole building down and put up a new one instead. Though that might not affect the rift at all."

"The rift?"

"You'll see." Of the doors to individual suites or offices spaced along the hallway, Kabbazah went directly to the one Stake wanted: second to last in the row. Stake didn't have to direct him further. So the fire had begun in there. The landlord punched in a third code. It didn't take. He sighed and tried it again. A beat of hesitation, and the door slid aside with a jittery raspiness. Inside, Kabbazah tried to bring up the ceiling lights but couldn't.

"That's okay," Stake told him, pulling a tiny flashlight with a wide, powerful beam out of his jacket pocket. Kabbazah arched one eyebrow at him as Stake stepped past, sweeping the broad beam around the large room. As he moved about, a thin layer of ashy broken matter crunched under his shoes.

The windowless room had been partially stripped, but was not as barren as its corresponding room in Bluetown. There were still work counters, and some of these still had shattered equipment heaped upon them. Twisted metal wall shelves. Several cubicles containing desks buckled by intense heat, the skeletons of padded chairs scattered about the floor. He accidentally kicked a broken coffee mug from his path.

"So what was this place?"

"I was renting it to a little research group that were taking government contracts. They were young, just starting out, so they had new ideas and they came cheaper for the government."

"Research into what?"

"Quantum teleportation, mostly, as I understand it."

"Quantum teleportation has been around for a long time," Stake said. Though it was only in the past few decades that it had just about replaced the use of starcraft as the means by which citizens of the Earth Colonies could travel from world to world, it had been in use to some extent for much longer than that.

"I suppose the government wanted to find an improved process, maybe something more economical. Obviously, my tenants weren't in a position to tell me much about their work."

Stake walked across the center of the sprawling room toward a certain section of wall. He almost expected the carbonized floor to collapse under his feet to reveal three large, circular holes beneath its surface. When he reached the wall, he played his light across it. Its burnt condition had partly obliterated a large symbol there. A long crack in the wall also jagged through the symbol like a lightning bolt.

"What was the name of their outfit?" Stake asked.

"Ah, they called themselves Wonky Science."

Stake nodded. WS.

He looked about him some more, noted an air vent blown into its duct where he could imagine a ball of fire had blasted through, as if seeking its way out of the building for more oxygen to feed it. Thinking of the outside of the building made him remember the antennae on the roof, and he asked his guide about them.

"Yeah, that was their stuff. Part of their matter transmission system."

Stake turned his attention to a framework bolted into the ceiling and floor, which once might have supported the barriers of a clean room environment. Or would that have been the teleportation chamber itself? He stepped into the space. There was uneven scorching along the back wall, and for a moment his mind made him believe he saw three human shadows burnt into the wall, but they lost their shape upon further scrutiny. He stepped out of the former enclosure, approached the far left side of the room.

"Be careful that corner, over there. Shine your light." Kabbazah was pointing.

When Stake aimed his beam in the direction Kabbazah indicated, he saw that there was something moving slowly through the air. A small object with a black surface that became somewhat shiny and translucent in the torch's glare. Floating like a large soap bubble was a creature closely resembling a jellyfish, its bell black, trailing a spaghetti of bluish tendrils fine as spun glass. "Jesus," Stake whispered. It was an immature bender.

This corner was crisped midnight black, the meeting of the walls and the floor itself split with cracks. But there was more. Stake moved his beam back and forth slightly and saw that the air in the corner had a wrinkly, rippled quality, like heat shimmering above a hot road. As the jellyfish drifted through these ripples, it looked as though it were swimming in water.

"Some of their apparatus exploded, and a little rift was left there."

"What would happen if I stepped into it?" Stake envisioned being sucked into the ether, his qubits—the quantum bits of information that made up his being—scattered throughout the multiverse for all of eternity.

"One of those idiotic artist kids admitted to me that some of the others were hacking their way in here to party, and they'd stand in that corner to make themselves feel strange. It gave them a drugged sensation, though they had headaches afterwards. They told this kid they saw pictures in their heads, flashes of another planet. I evicted the whole group of them after that, and changed the key code. This warped little spot is what makes it hard for me to rent this place or sell it to a respectable buyer. That's why I suggest you have the building demolished—if that helps get rid of the effect."

"I'd have to consult someone about that," Stake murmured, stepping back a little as the tiny bender shifted direction, but it didn't seem to want to leave the vicinity of the corner. "I guess the best people to talk to about this rift would be the Wonky Science researchers themselves. Do you have their names?"

"Oh, I'd have to look that up. It's been years." The man dug a little palm comp out of his jacket's inner pocket.

"How many years?"

"Ah, it would be almost seventeen years ago, now. I've owned this place for nineteen, so yeah—seventeen years ago I rented this suite to them. And about a year after that was the mishap, and the start of all my headaches with this sorry bit of real estate." Kabbazah was obviously torn between unburdening himself of this property and unburdening his complaints about it to a sympathetic ear. He was tapping at the palm comp's miniature keys, the glow of its screen casting bluish light on his face. "I should never have rented this place out for business space, and stuck to apartments like my other properties."

Stake watched him. "No luck yet?"

"I thought I still had some names in here. But I should warn you, most of them were killed in the blast."

"Huh," Stake said. He looked over his shoulder again at the larval bender. "That creature—you ever seen a bigger version in this building?"

"No, just little ones, in this one room. They seem to come and go."

"That's good," Stake muttered. He supposed if Kabbazah had run into an adult bender, he wouldn't be standing here right now.

"Okay, here are two of them, anyway. These are the ones whose names were on the lease." The landlord tilted the screen Stake's way. He copied the first name and number into his wrist comp, though he doubted the number would still be viable after all these years. The man's name was Dink Argosax. "And the other." The landlord flicked to the number for a Timothy Leung, which Stake again took down.

Finished, Stake turned back to regard the mirage-like rippling corner. "Did the fire department see this? The Health Agency?"

"The fire was put out, the structure is legally stable, and they weren't happy with the anomaly but it didn't seem to pose any definite threat," Kabbazah said defensively.

"These things happen," Stake said.

"Hey, if the health agents condemned every building that had a definite health risk, a quarter of Punktown would be homeless."

I know a city with plenty of room they could move to, Stake thought. "The visions these artist kids were seeing," he said. "Were they of a planet with two suns? Jungles of blue vegetation?"

Kabbazah blinked at Stake warily. "Have you been speaking to other people? What sort of game are you playing here, Mr. Stake? If that really is your name."

"It's my name. I just like to do my homework, Mr. Kabbazah, before I invest my money."

"Well I suggest you leave now so I can do my homework into you. I don't mean to be rude, and I would very much like to get this property off my hands at last, but I don't want anyone being dishonest with me."

"I can understand that, sir."

The man led Stake out of the ruined business suite and sealed the door after them. As he preceded Stake through the hallway, he asked, "Are you a reporter? A health agent?"

"I'm sorry—I'm a private investigator. I tell you since you'll find that out if you look me up on the net."

"Wonderful. Wonderful. And why did you come here, then?"

"I'm investigating the remains of three bodies found on the world Sinan. After what you've shown me, I suspect that those bodies were teleported from this building, the space you rented to Wonky Science."

At the building's door, Kabbazah faced Stake again. "Why didn't you just tell me that in the beginning instead of getting my hopes up about selling this accursed place?"

"Sorry. I didn't think you'd let me in to see it."

"Well thanks for dragging me here on a rainy day like this. I hope you saw what you wanted to see."

Stake stepped out into a chilly and increasing drizzle, wishing he'd brought his porkpie hat with him, but then he'd thought he'd look too much like a private detective and not enough like a prospective property buyer. "Yes," he said to Kabbazah. "I did."

HE SAT IN a café instead of his car, munching on a falafel sandwich and drinking espresso as he watched the storm intensify through the front windows. Lightning flickered, and one bolt connected with the spire of a black tower with a tapered summit. Stake imagined that as the storm raged the veil between dimensions grew ragged, torn, and that he might glimpse Sinan's twin bluish suns if he watched long enough for a gap in the inky clouds.

Stake had called up his check on the table's ordering screen and was about to punch in his credit number when a call came over his wrist comp. He was surprised to be confronted by Colonel Dominic Gale, with his bullet-like head and strip of goatee, calling all the way from Sinan; the wonders of science. Seeing him made Stake wonder perversely how Ami Pattaya was doing. "Hello, colonel."

"Stake, I hear you're in Punktown."

"Yes, sir."

"Well I just wanted to make it known to you that I'm not putting your extradimensional commutes on my budget here. You can just take that out of the money Rick Henderson is foolish enough to pay you."

Ouch. Stake had hoped not to have to absorb that cost. He considered telling Gale that the trip was relevant to his investigation, but decided not to clue Gale in, and was glad he hadn't gotten into details with Rick, either. He trusted Henderson but he could be too honest for his own good. "As you wish, colonel," he said.

"What are you doing there, anyway? Are you finished here?"

Is that what you'd like? Stake wondered. "Some pressing personal business."

"Well, if you can't afford to zap back here then you just be advised to stay where you are, because like I said, the CF is not paying for your little personal errands."

"Understood, colonel."

Stake was tempted to ask the CF base commander about the rags of uniform and items of equipment that Yengun had seen recovered from the pits in which the clones had been formed. Yengun had said they didn't look like military uniforms, but Ami claimed the colonel had described them that way to her. Nevertheless, Stake decided not to ask Gale directly about the matter just yet. He now felt there was a good possibility that Gale knew the remains were not those of MIAs, and this would account for his lack of support in Henderson's investigation. So far he had not blocked Stake's efforts, no doubt confident that the private detective wouldn't be able to discover much, but Stake feared that if he pressed Gale now the colonel would prevent him from returning to Sinan and the CF base.

"And would you mind not doing that, for Chrissakes?" the officer growled.

"Sir?" Stake's thoughts had drifted.

"Copying me, you blasting Tin Town freak." And Gale then cut their connection.

Stake rubbed at his face with his hand, grateful that at least he hadn't been able to imitate that awful goatee.

What was he to believe now? Could it really be that Gale knew the bodies were not those of Blue War soldiers? But if he did, why wouldn't he want that fact made known? Had no one else ever thought to check the building in Punktown that corresponded to the building in Bluetown in which the trio of clones had been discovered? Was it simply due to people not being able to think of the remains as anything but the bodies of MIAs?

Still fully interfaced with his wrist comp, so that its screen spread across the desk of his mind, Stake began a net search for information on two men named Dink Argosax and Timothy Leung.

He soon found there was little to find. There were plenty of people who managed not to get wet in the net's vast ocean, but usually they were the homeless and disenfranchised, not well-educated science researchers, obviously from good homes. The limited traces of Argosax and Leung in the network could only mean that, because of their work for the government, their histories had been pared down to the barest minimum. Records of their university attendance, primarily, but there didn't seem to be much detail as to their course of studies, and there was a conspicuous absence of images of the men, even going back to their childhood, except for occasional group pictures that seemed impossible to delete because of the others in them. The one good shot of Argosax that Stake found came from an unlikely source. While attending Paxton University, Richard "Dink" Argosax had participated in an annual game competition that even Stake had seen covered on VT, called the BBB: Building the Better Booby-trap. In it, contestants entered an ultranet environment rife with dangerous flora and fauna, and were required to virtually dispatch their rivals (unless the local animal life dispatched them first) until a single victor remained, utilizing only the ingenious and insidious booby-traps that their college-educated minds could devise from the materials at hand. Argosax had won that year's competition, even beating out several students majoring in engineering, whose traps were technically more imaginative but whose strategy was apparently not up to Argosax's.

The net article featured not only a head shot of the grinning, victorious Argosax, but a little vid clip that Stake activated. Interviewed for a VT news spot, Argosax was as breathless as if he had actually returned from a grueling voyage to another world, fought its monsters with his flesh and blood body. When asked if he thought this win was an indication of his aptitude for future success, Argosax gushed, "You know it! I'm walking on the bodies of my enemies! Eat my skills—*whoo!*" And he shook his fist in the air.

Stake couldn't help smirking. He could see why Argosax was nicknamed Dink instead of Dick.

Scrawny and pale as a prisoner of war instead of a VR war hero, with a single thick eyebrow and a mop of black hair out of which protruded two ultranet jacks implanted in one side of his skull. Stake wished it wasn't an ultranet arena that he could hook Argosax up to, but a replay of his own memories, so the mighty warrior could see what combat in a real life hostile world was like, avoiding real booby-traps such as pits of stakes smeared with bender poison.

When government techs had gone editing the Wonky Science members' life histories, had this news story and vid clip been overlooked, deemed of no consequence, or had Argosax—out of pride—protected it from being deleted?

In any case, Stake lost track of Argosax altogether after graduation, as if he had just ceased to exist. Maybe lost forever in another virtual universe? But Timothy Leung was a different story.

CHAPTER THIRTEEN
AFTERSHOCKS

"THANKS, MAGNUS," TIMOTHY Leung said to the robot that had just set down a tray of coffee for his guest, Jeremy Stake. In bending close to Stake, the robot had afforded him the dubious pleasure of seeing the organic encephalon computer residing inside its transparent skull. The robot's head, upper torso, pelvis, hands, and feet were a clear honey-colored plastic as if shaped from amber. The neck, waist, arms, and legs were silvery, segmented metal. Leung had pasted a sticker that said "Somebody Kill Me" on the robot's rear and no one had made the machine any wiser. "Somebody Kill Me" was the famous catchphrase of Buddy Vrolik, the sphere-like mutant star of the sitcom *Buddy Balloon*.

Stake imagined that Leung could sympathize with Vrolik, who had to have nourishment pumped into him and waste pumped out, and be hooked up to a device that could give vocalization to his thoughts. Leung wasn't in much better condition, aside from being able to see and hear. His lips formed words but his voice, like Vrolik's, was synthesized, because there wasn't anything left of Leung's natural body below the neck. His head was fitted into a socket on something between a life support cart and a wheelchair without wheels. This could hover a little off the ground as it moved about, but presently it rested on the floor of the room he rented in a complex maintained for the elderly and disabled. There was no bed, but several chairs were provided for guests, and Stake occupied one of these.

As if being a disembodied head wasn't enough, Stake figured Leung's face to have been radically restored, as well. It just looked too smooth and didn't move quite right. He appeared even more android-like than David Bright. Stake tried not to look at the former researcher for too prolonged a stretch, though, for fear of replacing his own unnatural countenance with Leung's.

"My parents used to push me to get a cybernetic body instead of this," Leung explained, as an insectoid claw extended from his support cart to delicately dab a napkin at a spot of coffee Magnus had spilled on the tray. "But I'd only be trading one horrible state for another, so what's the difference? This way it's less like I'm trying to be something I'm not, and I can glide around and chase the nurses instead of stalking about like Magnus. The nurses feel more sorry for me this way, I think. They treat me like a baby." He gave a humorless, mechanical wink. "They wash my face, brush my hair, coo to me. I live for the day one of them unhooks me to cradle me to her breast. That would be a nice way to die, don't you think?"

Stake smiled uncomfortably and sipped his coffee. "Your parents couldn't afford to have your body regenerated?"

"Look at me, Mr. Stake. Forget regenerating—this isn't a missing arm we're talking about—I'd have to pretty much be cloned, and you know the legalities of cloning private citizens."

"Well, I'm sure it's hard for you to talk about all this again, and that's why I appreciate you seeing me, Mr. Leung."

Over their vidphones Leung had seemed very reluctant at first, but Stake had gently persisted. He had at first thought of using the same routine he had with the landlord, claiming he wanted to learn about the explosion at Wonky Science before he purchased the property, but he had decided to be up front and say that he had been hired to investigate an anomalous occurrence on Sinan that might have a connection to the ruined lab. He figured that if Leung denied him a visit, he'd just come around to the assisted living complex anyway. But here he was. Not that Leung seemed relaxed about his presence. Beneath the dry humor, Stake could feel the crackle of his discomfort. Maybe at a time like this Leung missed his limbs the most, unable to pace or fidget.

"So who is this friend of yours who hired you, Mr. Stake?"

Stake politely ignored a liquid gurgle he heard from inside a closed section of Leung's cart. "Captain Rick Henderson of the Colonial Forces, currently stationed on Sinan."

"The Colonial Forces?" That seemed to throw Leung off a little. "And what is it the Colonial Forces need to know about Wonky Science?"

"First of all, sir, what kind of work exactly was Wonky Science doing for the government?"

"You should realize I'm still not at liberty to discuss that to any great extent."

"Yes, I can appreciate that, but how about the stuff you can tell me?"

"We accepted a number of projects for them, one of which was to explore new means of teleportation that would make the Earth Colonies less beholden to the Bedbugs for assistance. They wanted a fresh perspective. We were right out of Paxton University and had innovative ideas."

"But what went wrong? How did the explosion occur?"

"I was part of a team within the team, working on a related but separate project. The team was headed by a man named Lewton Barbour. For our experiment, we were to teleport Lew to a sister lab on Earth, utilizing a new technique in scanning and duplicating atomic arrangement. What can I say? It seems we overloaded our matter transmitter, and *boom*. Lew's atoms were scattered to the void, and nearly everyone in the lab was killed."

"Was Barbour teleporting alone, or were any others going with him?" Stake asked innocently.

"Two others were to be transmitted with him," Leung replied. Was Stake just superimposing when he thought the mask-like face appeared wary at the question?

"And these three were going to Earth? Not teleporting to Sinan?"

"No, not Sinan. And Sinan is in another dimension."

"I realize that. I'm sure you've heard about what's happening on Sinan, with the city of Bluetown? What you may not know is that Bluetown is an exact replica of Punktown, in the making."

"Punktown? *What?* How can that be?"

"They don't know that, yet. But it's a fact, and another fact is that on Sinan right now there's a building that corresponds to your old research lab on Ginger Street."

"My God," Leung croaked.

"Inside the room that would be the suite for Wonky Science, three strange clones were recovered. Two were not viable, but one of them is alive, apparently healthy, though only as developed as a child of about five years old."

"Yes, yes, I heard about the clones in the news," Leung said, "but I didn't know Bluetown was Punktown, or about the place on Ginger Street."

"So this is what my friend has hired me to look into. Apparently the process that causes Bluetown to form itself regenerated human tissue it encountered in its path. And now it would seem to me that the tissues it encountered were the remains of Lewton Barbour and the other two researchers that were attempting to teleport with him."

"No, no," Leung said. He was becoming agitated, and either purposely or accidentally caused his cart to whip around a little to face away from Stake. In so doing, he bumped the serving tray and coffee slurped over the rim of Stake's cup. "I told you, they were going to Earth, not Sinan."

"Could their matter have been accidentally transferred to Sinan instead of Earth?"

"No, impossible. It's impossible. I don't know what you found on Sinan, Mr. Stake, but it can't be Lew and the others. The tissues must have come from war casualties."

"If I arranged for you to see a vid of the cloned child, do you think you might recognize his features?"

"I won't look at it!" Leung cried. "It's not one of my team—are you listening to me?"

"Okay, look, I'm not trying to upset you, Mr. Leung. Can you tell me, at least, the names of the other two people who were teleporting to Earth with Mr. Barbour? Give me a list of all the people who worked for Wonky Science, dead or alive?"

"No. Don't ask me that. I've lost track of the few survivors, and I'm not inclined to compromise their privacy. Why? So you can propose these absurd ideas to them, and dredge up their painful memories, too? Anyway, I told you, all our research is still classified information."

"I was hired by a Colonial Forces officer," Stake reminded him.

"So you say."

"I could have you talk to Captain Henderson yourself, then."

"I won't be talking to anyone else, and I don't want to talk to you anymore, either."

Stake took a last sip of coffee, rose, replaced his little brimmed hat on his head. "You aren't in the least bit curious to see this child, Mr. Leung?"

"No! It's too horrible to imagine! Why would you people have brought that thing to life?"

"It didn't need to be accelerated in any way; it was alive when it was discovered."

Leung's face gave a twitch in place of a shudder. "Horrible," he wheezed.

"I was given one other name. Dink Argosax. Do you know his whereabouts, at least?"

"I told you, I don't know, and I wouldn't tell you if I did."

Stake sighed. On the serving tray he placed one of the printed cards he carried in his wallet. "In case you change your mind."

"I never should have talked to you at all," Leung muttered.

"You were curious to know how much I knew," Stake said, moving to the door. "Call me if you get curious again."

STAKE RETURNED TO his Punktown apartment in the old Phosnoor Shipyard before calling Henderson with his report. His door was not booby-trapped and there were no Stem assassins waiting for him inside. He sat at his desk comp to call, drinking a better cup of coffee than the robotic orderly at Leung's apartment complex had served him.

Henderson listened to everything, then remarked, "It might have been better to talk about this in person."

"I'll be there in person soon; I'm leaving here tomorrow." Stake didn't explain his reason for that: if Thi's husband were to be released soon or was released already, he'd feel better being on the same planet she was on.

"Don't worry about the cost for that, Jer, I'll reimburse you right away from my own pocket."

Stake didn't argue; his own resources were limited. "Thanks."

On Stake's screen, Henderson looked far from pleased by what he had heard. "I can't believe Gale never told me about the uniform remnants or the other stuff. I'm going to see what I can find out about that—where they've got it now. Those things could definitely prove revealing."

"I've got to ask you, Rick—are you sure you want me to keep going with this, now that it looks like it isn't MIAs? It's on its way to getting messy. Maybe messy for your career."

"Blast that," Henderson grumbled, with uncharacteristic venom. "Gale has kept me in the dark. I want to put the lights on so they blind that bald-headed fuck."

"You're the boss."

When their call had ended, Stake gulped down some shrimp sushi he found in his refrigerator and hoped was still okay, and then did a net search on Lewton Barbour/Wonky Science. There wasn't much to find—certainly not about the nature of the research conducted there—other than his being directed to street atlases of Punktown on which the building on Ginger Street appeared. Stake did find an obituary listed on several sites, however. The obituary told him little more than Timothy Leung had revealed. Lewton Barbour, a twenty-three year-old researcher for Wonky Science, had perished along with most of his coworkers during the course of an experiment in which some equipment had overloaded. There was one bit of information, though, that Stake took a keen interest in.

Lewton Barbour had been survived by his wife, Persia, who had also been a Wonky Science employee.

As he had done to locate Leung, Stake next ran a net search on Persia Barbour for her current address or contact information.

Soon enough he had a number and was calling it, but if the information was correct then perhaps she was out. Stake left a simple message that he hoped would assure a return call: "Mrs. Barbour, would you please call me back? I'd like to discuss your late husband Lewton."

Stake was settling in for a comfortable night in his own flat, vegetating before his VT to take his mind off Thi as best as he was able, when his comp alerted him to an incoming call. He rushed to his desk and answered. Before him he saw a woman of about forty, and though he couldn't tell what condition her body might be in, at least her attractive features did not seem rebuilt the way Leung's had been. Large dark eyes in a small pale face, and a luxuriance of thick dark curls that Stake found quite becoming. Her expression was more leery than alluring, however.

"Yes? Do I know you?"

"No, ma'am. My name is Jeremy Stake, and I've been hired to conduct an investigation which has led me to the explosion that occurred at Wonky Science and claimed the life of your husband, Lewton."

"Hired?" she snapped. "Hired by whom? What is this about?"

"I was hired by Captain Rick Henderson, with the Colonial Forces base on Sinan."

Persia Barbour blinked at Stake once, and then her attractive face with all its dark curls was gone.

"Dung," Stake said. That had gone even less well than his visit to Timothy Leung.

He tried to call her back. She wouldn't answer. He wished he had found an address for her to go along with the number, but he hadn't, and was too tired right now to ask one of his contacts to do him the favor of tracing her number to one. Still sitting before his desk comp, Stake contemplated calling Thi next, but quickly rejected the idea. If her husband had already been released, the last thing she needed was for Stake to incense him again by calling her where she was staying. And even if he wasn't home yet, what if Nhot picked up his call, and related that information to her father later?

Stake flopped down in his bunk, bolted to the old warship's floor, and watched VT through increasingly drowsy eyes. Soon enough, the VT chattered inanely to itself.

He dreamed of the lab space rented by Wonky Science. It was charred black and in ruins, but also had three deep craters sunken into its floor. He edged closer to the nearest of these pits, a thin layer of ashy broken matter crunching under his shoes. A shard of coffee mug toppled over the rim and plunged into the amniotic fluid that filled the pits, causing ripples that momentarily obscured the naked figure curled at the bottom of the well, but when the surface grew still again he saw that the figure was himself.

He moved to another of the holes to find another copy of his own body, his own face. He rushed to look into the third hole, then jerked back in shock.

The eyes of his third clone were open, and gazing up at him helplessly.

He awoke with a start, blinking up at the bottom of the bunk above him. As his bleariness cleared, the words Yengun had translated from the old woman with PSI abilities came back to him.

"...after today, the dreams will belong to you."

CHAPTER FOURTEEN
CONDITION ORANGE

RICK HENDERSON DOUBTED that his office and quarters were bugged, but to be on the safe side he and Jeremy Stake sat in the mess hall of the Colonial Forces base to discuss in further depth Stake's quick return trip to Punktown. The last of the lunch periods had ended and they were alone in the large, sun-filled room except for a few workers cleaning distant tables. Stake had another coffee in front of him, found that he lived from one to the next, the rungs of his life's ladder. You had to have something to count on.

Henderson said, gently, "You made some good progress, Jer. For a minute there I thought you were a little too tied up with that personal business of yours."

Stake avoided his friend's eyes. "That would appear to be finished now."

Henderson obviously knew it was best not to pursue that statement, and instead said, "Do you think you came back prematurely? This Persia Barbour should be pushed some more. Maybe I should call her myself?"

"Let me try calling her again, first." The investigator downed a little more coffee. "I've been debating whether or not to fill David Bright in on what I've found."

"So you can collect the extra money he offered if you'd help him?"

Stake gave Henderson a look. "Rick, I'm not after his money. I didn't make him any promises."

"Sorry, Jer. But I think we should keep him out of this at the moment. He's too volatile."

"Maybe we could use that to our advantage, so he can press matters that might be too delicate politically for you and me to press directly."

"Still, I'd rather not align ourselves with him too much. It's not that I want to distance myself out of fear of being dragged down with him—it's just that he's an unknown quantity."

Stake recalled the question he had asked himself: if the accident with the smart matter might not be so accidental after all. He grunted, "Yeah, okay, Rick."

"Okay, now my turn to update you, Jer." Henderson slipped some photo printouts from an envelope he'd brought with him, but kept them face down on the table for the moment. "I went to Gale and told him you'd heard there was some gear and scraps of clothing found in the pits where the clones were discovered. I let him know that I'd have preferred to be made aware of this little detail, and he kept his cool the best he could and apologized for the oversight. I asked to see them, and later on he brought them to me."

"From where? The science chief told me she hadn't seen them. One would think he'd have turned them over to her, for dating and possible DNA traces."

"I don't know where he had them stashed, but anyway, I took some shots of them to show you when you got back, in case he isn't inclined to show them to you in person. This is them." Now Henderson flipped the photos over. Stake picked up the first.

The photo was of a few frayed rags of clothing, blue camouflage very leeched of color. So faded that maybe Stake could have believed Hin Yengun had been mistaken when he said the rags didn't look like uniform remnants to him—if Stake had not found out what he had in Punktown.

He examined the next photo and it didn't take him long to identify the piece of equipment it portrayed, even though Stake had never really used one of these devices himself despite his deep penetration forays. The device utilized metamaterials to reroute light rays around an individual, thus rendering a soldier invisible to his enemies (and his friends, too, unless they wore special goggles). The problem with these devices, though, had been that the red-flashing eyes of the Ha Jiin were more sensitive than those of Earth humans, and they had still been able to discern enough of an irregularity to give a soldier away at close quarters. Not to mention that the Ha Jiin began stealing the special goggles off the bodies of dead CF soldiers, and of course the invisibility devices themselves. Stake believed the simplest approach was often the best. He had stuck to conventional camouflage and the polymorphic ability he had been born with, to sometimes imitate Ha Jiin features.

Next photo. A common CF sidearm, and a magazine of bullets resting beside it. Henderson explained that the bullets were AE gel caps. These projectiles, after penetrating a subject or even bursting against them, released autolytic enzymes that set into motion a rapid, devastating self-destruction of the body's cells. They had been used during the Blue War but had since been banned due to public outcry that it was excessively cruel to make an enemy die by swiftly rotting away. The good thing about these bullets, though, was that the enzymes were always tailored to the particular race one was engaging, so that an Earth human accidentally caught in the crossfire or shot by a stolen gun loaded with such ammo would not suffer the same decomposition.

"Very good." Stake was nodding. "This is all very convincing. But it's all stuff that Gale could have dug up elsewhere. I don't buy it, Rick. This is pretty arrogant, actually. It has to be a substitution for the stuff he really found, to keep us thinking that we're dealing with MIA remains here."

"So why then, Jer? What is it Gale's hiding? Are we sure he knows about Wonky Science and their government contracts?"

"Has to be. But not just him. Maybe if he found out what I've found out, and took it to his superiors, they told him to keep a cap on it. You leaked it to the media about the clones, so now they have to let you go through the motions of an investigation, but they don't expect you to get anywhere with it. The question again, Rick, is how far do you want to push it? This could put your career on the line."

Henderson sighed, staring down at the photos scattered between them. "Brian should never have come into existence, Jer, but he did, and he's a living child, a human being. He very probably has relatives who should know about him. At the very least, he himself has a right to know who he is and where he came from, when he's old enough to comprehend it. Again, I'm glad I leaked the story. With cloning being off limits to the public, I was afraid they might use that excuse or some other to destroy him. I guess it's like you said before. The kid is my pet."

Stake smiled. "Now I remember why you're my friend, Rick."

When they had finished, like two ordinary enlisted men Henderson and Stake walked their trays up to the conveyor that would take them to be washed behind the kitchen, but one of the cleaners hustled over to intercept them. "Captain, please, let me take those," he said.

"Thank you, private." As Henderson handed his tray over, the little comp clipped to his belt chirped and he lifted it to his face. On its screen Stake saw one of Henderson's immediate assistants. "Yes, Diane?"

"Sir, I thought I should let you know that a group of Jin Haa clerics has assembled outside the front gate. It appears they're doing what the Ha Jiin clerics have done in Bluetown a number of times—chanting some kind of ritual."

"It's an exorcism, to drive out evil," he told her.

"Well, it's drawing a crowd of spectators, sir, and they're looking kind of worked up, especially the young guys."

"Okay, Diane. Be advised that we might want to announce a condition orange if things get too rowdy. Is the colonel aware of—"

Before Henderson could finish, the world burst into strobing light and blaring noise. Revolving lights spaced across the ceiling flashed orange, a klaxon was sounding, and an unexcited voice over the public address system repeated, "Condition orange. Condition orange." All this, Stake thought, to alert the sleeping, the deaf, blind, and comatose.

Henderson turned to Stake and said, "Get to your quarters and lock yourself in, Jer. I've got to reach Gale."

"All right, Rick. Be careful."

Henderson rushed off toward the mess hall doors, holding his comp up to his face again. Stake started walking after him, but when Henderson ducked out the detective changed direction and moved to a long wall comprised of floor-to-ceiling windows. These windows could be tinted opaque, but presently they weren't, and gave a fairly unobstructed view of the barrier of energy that surrounded the Colonial Forces outpost like a wall. This barrier could also be made opaque, but currently it was only tinted the soft blue color that let people know it was there, so they wouldn't walk into it. Normally, the barrier would not carry a stunning charge, but Stake knew that during a condition orange—an alert to possible aggression—the barrier would deliver a considerable shock to anyone who made contact with it.

From the windows, Stake could make out the group of clerics Henderson's assistant had mentioned. They were distant from him, beyond the energy barrier, but he knew very well what they looked like up close. During the war, he and his team had holed up for a while in a remote Ha Jiin monastery. The CF soldiers had rounded up and corralled the monks until their departure. It was during this stay, in fact, that Thi Gonh and another Ha Jiin guerilla had been captured. During this stay, that Stake and the enemy sniper had entered into an unconventional relationship behind the closed door of her makeshift cell.

Each monk wore a beautiful blue robe, a small black hat with three corners, and had a gaping hole in place of a face. As young initiates, they began smoking an incense with cancerous properties, so that their faces were eaten away over the years, a demonstration of their selfless devotion. They were essentially identical cloned soldiers of their faith, blind to the distractions and temptations of the material world, but though they no longer had lips to speak with they were still able to render their chanting. Stake could hear this chanting noise now, rising higher. A flush of gooseflesh swept over his arms. He remembered the chants of the detained monks at the monastery. He had never grown used to it. He had heard stories that, if they really wanted to, the clerics could kill a man with a certain pitch.

A mob was swelling behind and to the sides of the exorcists, excited by their presence, inspired by their eerie chants, though their own shouts and curses were mostly drowned out by reverberating intonations that seemed a combination of deep moan and floating howl. Even the klaxon inside the base had become overwhelmed by the sound. Stake saw the churning protestors, mostly young men, waving their fists and throwing objects up over the top of the barrier; fruit and whatever rubbish they could find around them. The barrier could be raised higher than the buildings within the compound, and a ceiling of energy then extended across to protect the base from air attack, though Stake supposed they didn't consider that likely.

Stake saw CF soldiers, helmeted and carrying assault engines, scrambling within the compound. A hovertank glided to a stop, blocking a little of Stake's view of the barrier, but he could see a new disturbance taking place out there. He realized it was a group of Jin Haa policemen, trying to drive the rioters back away from the wall, cracking batons made from lengths of something like bamboo across the shoulders and legs of some of the more unruly people in their path. Stake saw one bare-chested young man lash back, punching a militia man in the face. It won him a barrage of batons that drove him to his knees and elbows, with his hands laced across the top of his head to protect his skull. Other protestors, watching this, only seemed to grow more outraged and agitated. Fruit and trash started flying at the riot squad in addition to arcing over the wall.

Stake wondered if the tank would receive orders to open up on the crowd with a sound cannon or broad shock beam, either of which would be nonlethal and either of which could fire straight through the energy barrier at its current setting. He also wondered if the assembling troopers had been instructed to use only gel caps loaded with a paralyzing drug, should the need to fire arise. He imagined Gale would be concerned about not killing any Jin Haa. Not out of a moral consideration, of course, but a political one. For the meantime, the CF people were holding the fort and letting the police try to quell the uproar, but they were outnumbered. Stake feared that it would be the police who ultimately opened fire with lethal ammunition and exacerbated the political situation themselves. Stake could see them being accused of looking after the Earth base instead of their own people. Might it have been better to let the protestors get the shouting out of their systems, and not engage them this way? Stake thought the best course of action would be to appeal to the exorcists to cease the chanting meant to drive out these demons who had invaded their world from an unseen realm, and infected the land with their monstrous blue city. Then might the rabble-rousers settle down and disperse?

The two table cleaners, various kitchen workers, and other of the base's personnel had gathered along the windows by this time to gaze out as Stake was doing. Someone came beside him, almost brushing his elbow, and he recognized the person's perfume before he looked to see Ami Pattaya standing there. She smiled faintly. "Hey, shy guy. I saw you looking out. I just heard there's another protest going on outside our embassy, too."

"More monks?"

"Yeah. And more people like these." She nodded her head toward the chaos they were witnessing. "Maybe it's that awful sound that's got them so crazy." She had to raise her voice to be heard over it.

Despite the furor going on outside, Stake remained focused on the science chief. "Ami, did you ever ask the colonel to let you run tests on the gear the Ha Jiin found with the clones—to try to establish how long it was buried, and see if any DNA could be recovered?"

"No, I told you—he said there was very little stuff, and it was very nondescript."

"Could you do that anyway? Ask him if you can examine it? Where does he keep it, anyway, if not in your lab?" At no time did Stake mention the photos Henderson had shown him or their particular subject matter. He had as much as dismissed them.

"I don't know; in his quarters, I imagine."

She wasn't looking at him. Her sunny nature, as he remembered it, was clouded over. Stake still studied her. At this point he was disinclined to think she was as innocent of knowledge as she claimed. She was Gale's lover, after all. In his current frame of mind, Stake wondered if Gale might even have sent Ami to his room that time to see what the detective was about.

"Oh my God, look," she said, pointing out the window as if to distract him from his scrutiny.

The barrier had thus far kept the rioters out. Stake had seen a few people, blundering into it as they jostled each other or dodged the cracking batons, violently repelled by the transparent energy field. Hoverbikes did not ride high enough off the ground to clear the top. Now something else was coming along, however, wading through the crowd, parting them like grass. Angry policemen smacked their sticks against the legs of three giant yubos, but by then the lumbering animals had just about reached the barrier already. The single back tentacle of each was held high, and at their ends, their strange hands held a trio of Jin Haa men aloft. For a delirious moment, Stake thought it might be Thi Gonh's husband and his two friends, but it was not.

The yubos dangled the men over the top of the wall, and let go. One yubo, maybe because of the blows it was receiving, stepped too close to the barrier and its thick appendage was jolted. Stake could hear the behemoth's bellow of surprise and pain.

The three Jin Haa who dropped inside the compound hit the ground hard. One rolled onto his back, gripping a shattered ankle and crying out. The other two scrambled to their feet. Both of them were carrying something small and dark.

"Dung," Stake said, as one man cocked back his arm to hurl a grenade at several Colonial Forces men charging toward him.

They opened fire with their assault engines. The man flew back, the grenade going out of his hand behind him. At the same moment, the other man tossed his grenade beneath the stationary, floating hovertank.

The detonation under the tank barely rocked it, did not pierce its heavy armor. The dropped grenade, though, bounced toward the man gripping his ankle. He turned his head toward it in realization, then he was gone in a flare of light and a burst of obliterated flesh and bone.

This second explosion was doubly potent, as it set off the grenade in the injured man's possession. A wave of concussion rolled toward the mess hall windows, causing them to vibrate slightly against the hands and bodies of those pressed there. Ami turned her face away instinctively, as if afraid the glass would shatter, or the explosions blind her, or the flying blood splash the pane in front of her eyes.

The second, double explosion had thrown onto his back the man who had tossed his bomb under the tank. Badly wounded, he lifted his head a little, only to be shot almost point-blank by a female CF soldier who had just run up to him.

"Real ammo," Stake murmured, seeing the man's head drop back, and the puffs of misted blood from the bullet hits in his chest and neck.

The blasts had rocked the people on the other side of the barrier, as well. It was one thing to throw fruit, another to throw bombs. They began to scatter in all directions, some screaming, the militia taking advantage of the situation by chasing after them to make sure they didn't reassemble. The yubos were wheeling away from the wall, and Stake saw a teenage Jin Haa boy trip and become trampled under their massive feet.

The chanting of the monks ended. They appeared stunned, swayed as if awakened from a bout of communal sleepwalking. The klaxons inside the base changed their tone to reflect the new state of affairs. The bland voice returned to announce, "Condition red. Condition red." Full out attack.

"I'd better get to the infirmary," Ami told Stake, spinning away from the window. "They might need extra hands."

Stake watched her race off across the mess hall—as fast as her clacking high heels could take her, as if it were him she was fleeing from—before he turned again to watch the anarchy just on the other side of the glass.

THAT EVENING HE watched the VT in his room with almost the same feeling of dazed horror, feeling like a spectator to disaster all over again, except this time without the lovely and well-endowed Ami Pattaya at his elbow.

In the mess hall, Stake had been watching Ami's face, listening to her voice and gauging her demeanor, as he asked her about the fragments of uniform. The first time he had asked her about them, in his room, she had been very casual about it. This time she'd been much more tense. Stake figured that while he was back on Oasis and Henderson had asked Gale about the salvaged items, Gale had let Ami know that the two men were inquiring about them.

Ami had been right about another group of exorcists, and thus a second riot, outside the Earth Colonies embassy. The embassy did not have a barrier of energy, and a single terrorist had made it as far as the front steps of the building before detonating the five grenades strapped to his body. Sinanese people were not typically suicidal when it came to political causes, but it had been determined that the man at the embassy and the three at the military base had all been diagnosed with the deadly STD that was rampant on either side of the Neutral Zone. During some interviews of common citizens who had witnessed the embassy protest, one angry young Jin Haa man said in English, "Don't you know? The Earth devils have brought the plague with them and spread it by design, just like the Blue City! They have exhausted the gas that comes from the dead in our tunnels, and we were not dying at a rate fast enough to supply more of their precious sinon gas! And so they are killing us off to make the gas plentiful again!"

Wow, Stake thought. What a horrible thought that was.

The chief ambassador to the Jin Haa nation, Margaret Valsalva, was being interviewed all over the place. There was even footage of the embassy protest at which a huge holographic screen had opened in the air, and Valsalva's disembodied head had addressed the crowd, urging them to be peaceful and disband, assuring them that the spread of the organic city was being tackled by the finest minds the Earth Colonies could assemble.

Not feeling all that fine a mind, Stake watched as the death toll was revised through the evening, settling on a total of four dead terrorists, five policemen, and twelve citizens killed by the explosion at the embassy. Policemen injured with stones and other objects, and rioters suffering broken bones due to beatings by police, had been administered to at local hospitals, not to mention several CF soldiers injured in the explosions at their base.

The militia had erected barricades outside the embassy building and Colonial Forces base. In the case of the military compound, that meant Stake was now at the center of a barrier within a barrier—though right about now he felt he was locked outside a double barrier instead.

Finally, after hours of distraction, Rick Henderson found enough free time in the midst of the turmoil to call Stake back. "Have you seen the reason why the sudden step up in the level of protest, Jer?"

Yes. That was another aspect of the extensive VT coverage he had been soaking in. "The new development in Bluetown—yeah."

"I'm going out there in the morning to see it for myself. Make sure you're ready. I'm bringing you with me, whether Gale likes it or not."

CHAPTER FIFTEEN
THE BENEATH

BEFORE THEIR PARTY left for Bluetown, Stake asked for a suit of camouflage like the soldiers wore so he wouldn't ruin his clothes. He was given one without any problems. Good; he'd been hoping to come by a uniform by some means or other. One never knew when it might come in handy. Seeing this, David Bright asked for a uniform, too. In his case, his concern for his expensive five-piece suit was more reasonable.

Seeing the two civilians in their camouflage, Colonel Dominic Gale said to Henderson, "What the blast, Rick? Is this a tourist outing or what?"

Bright spoke up edgily before Henderson could. "This situation concerns me, colonel, in case you hadn't seen the effigies of me they're parading through the streets of two nations."

"I'm talking more about the snoop." Gale jutted his goateed chin toward Stake.

"We've been through that, Dom," Henderson said. "There's no harm in using every available resource, is there?"

"Resource," Gale snorted. He switched his hot gaze to Bright's bodyguard. The seven foot KeeZee just glowered right back at him. He was the only one in the party not wearing camouflage, his natty black suit and black turtleneck an odd match for his monkey wrench head and amber-beaded dreadlocks. The alien's sharp-cornered jacket was unfastened and Stake had glimpsed the holster of a sidearm in there, besides the pump-action shotgun he carried in his hands. Gale broke their eye contact first, turning away to board the troop transport craft that would fly them out to Bluetown.

The last person to board, running to catch up, was the outpost's science chief Ami Pattaya. Stake would have expected her to wear a short skirt and heels on even a mountain climbing expedition, but she was in camouflage herself. Still, she managed to make a fashion statement of it, her pants tight across her rear, of course, and a ponytail hanging out the back of the camouflage cap she wore. It made her look adorable, and Stake decided he needed a cap, too. He took note that Henderson and Gale were wearing them as well.

Ami wedged herself in beside Stake. Gale was up front, and glanced back at them, but the man seemed to be perpetually boiling inside his own skin and so it was hard for Stake to judge if he were any more angry to see them sitting together. When Gale turned forward again, Ami gave Stake's thigh a quick squeeze.

The flier touched down on Jin Haa land, though one wouldn't know it anymore from the way it had been transmogrified. Specifically, this was the spot upon which Bright's Simulacrum Systems team had thought to grow the condominium complex that had instead developed into Bluetown. The epicenter of the runaway process. It was also the center from which a new, secondary development was spreading.

Looking out the windows as those up front began to file out, Ami said, "You can see it's a good thing this village project was so remote. If it had been closer to Di Noon, Bluetown would already be flattening it."

"Why so remote?"

Bright heard them talking and cut in, "Their government was trying to give people the incentive to get over the war and settle closer to the border of the Neutral Zone, so it initiated this program, offering housing and land that the people could farm, and the government would split the profits from the crops with them. It was to be a kind of commune for serfs, and there would have been more of them along the border, if... well, if things had gone as planned."

The passengers toward the back were last to disembark, and Stake fumbled around as if he'd dropped something, stalling. He was relieved that Ami didn't wait for him, getting swept along with the rest. One of the last out, Stake snatched up a camouflage cap that a lingering soldier had placed on his seat while he was busy taking down his assault engine from an overhead compartment. Stake folded the cap's bill and stuck it in his back pocket.

Stepping out of the flier and looking about, the private investigator saw two incongruous trailers parked by a curb, where the Simulacrum Systems team had set up shop in their efforts to halt the city's growth. There was also a group of Colonial Forces soldiers already on the scene, assigned to protect the Simulacrum Systems personnel from disgruntled natives. The sergeant of this unit approached Gale, while David Bright went to confer with several techs who had emerged from the twin vehicles.

As Henderson came beside Stake, he said, "Well, as you can see, this is the center of Punktown itself, so Bluetown's radiating outward from the same point."

Stake shook his head, turning in a circle. "No... no it isn't. You aren't the lifetime Punktowner that I am, Rick. It's close, but we're about two blocks over from the center."

"Yeah? Are you sure you're talking about the geographical center of Punktown and not just the historical center?"

"They're one and the same: Salem Street." Stake pointed. "And that's over that way." He started off in the indicated direction, Henderson sticking with him and Ami hurrying over to make it three. They walked briskly for a fair distance, until Ami looked fidgety at leaving the others behind, but Henderson was intrigued and nodded in recognition.

"Jesus, you're right. This would be the center, wouldn't it? Salem Street."

"It's incredible, huh?" Stake said, stopping to scuff the toe of his shoe against the street. The original was surfaced with cobblestones, and the effect had been reproduced by the smart matter, looking like the blue-scaled hide of some immense slumbering dragon upon which they moved like mites. The actual Salem Street was a fairly intact remnant of the preexistent Choom town upon which the Earth colonists had superimposed Punktown, and so it retained the cobblestones and some of its brick architecture for a quaint, historical effect. Salem Street took the form of an open mall lined with upscale shops, always thronged with pedestrians but closed to vehicular traffic. Decorative trees were spaced along the sidewalks, though here the receptacles meant to hold them were empty. Here, most of the shop windows were blind blue panes of coral. Ahead, a fountain that sprayed no water.

Henderson pointed out one of the buildings facing onto the mall. "And that would be Beantown—one of my favorite coffee shops in the city."

"Looks like it's closed for the season."

"I don't get it, then. Why would Bright's process start creating Punktown at the place it did, instead of at the proper center?"

"Hey!" Gale called to them gruffly from behind, snorting like a workhorse as he strode to catch up. "Where the hell are you boys headed off to? We've got a momfuck train to catch!"

"Boys?" Stake muttered to Ami.

"That probably slipped out," she whispered. "He calls me his 'pretty boy.'"

"I didn't realize he was so, uh, affectionate."

"In his own way. But I like your way. I guess you don't like me too much anymore, though, huh?"

"I told you, it isn't that I don't like you. I've just got—other stuff on my mind."

"You men, always so serious tramping around with your scowls and your guns."

"Hey, you're out here tramping around in the same uniform with us."

"Well, boys will be boys."

Red-faced from more than just the exertion of walking, Colonel Gale led them back to where Simulacrum Systems had set up camp, and to the nearby opening of a subway kiosk. There, he turned to glower at the others, looking like the attendant of an elevator to Hell.

APPROPRIATELY, THE RECONNAISSANCE party descended into a section of subway that in Punktown was called the Blue Line.

There were eight soldiers; four up front, four in the rear, with Gale and Henderson, Stake and Ami, Bright and his bodyguard, and one Simulacrum Systems tech buffered in between. The soldiers had powerful flashlights clipped to their chests, their beams set wide to illuminate the path for the others. Stake felt like a member of a spelunking expedition. Either that, or a team of archaeologists venturing into some buried tomb.

They reached the bottom of one flight of steps, turned onto a landing and descended another. At its bottom, they stepped into a subway station with an arched ceiling, its ends vanishing into deep murk. It echoed their movements and voices eerily. Frames for video ad displays and tube schedules remained blank. Tiled walls that were supposed to be enamel smooth were instead scratchy and rough, making Stake think of a sunken ship with its interior caked in rust, and they were the fish floating through it.

Ami came to a bench near the edge of the platform and sat down on it. "Why these benches but no furniture inside the buildings up there?"

"The benches would be bolted to the platform, not mobile like furniture in your office or apartment," said the Simulacrum Systems tech. He was a young Tikki-hotto man named Cali, his head shaved to a dark stubble and his eye tendrils rippling restlessly. "They're more a part of the basic structure. That's all I can figure."

Ami stood and approached the wide trench in which the tubes would run above their repulsor tracks, resting a hand against one of the station's thick hexagonal support columns as if afraid she might topple into an abyss. She looked up and down the tunnel in both directions. "So what's the next development going to be?" she said. "I expect to see a train made from smart matter come out of the darkness at any second."

"But what would be aboard it?" Stake asked her.

"The ghosts from the Jin Haa burial tunnels, I guess."

"See here?" Cali said, calling the others to him, a bit further down the station.

When they advanced with their lights, they could see that to the left the tunnel had collapsed and debris choked off its mouth. Stake was reminded of photos he had seen of Punktown's subways after the two great earthquakes it had suffered within his lifetime. As a result of those catastrophes, some of Punktown's tube stations had been cut off and left abandoned, now serving as a home for mutants, a wayward gang of Bedbugs who called themselves the Dimensionals, and bands of rebellious robot laborers that had taken shelter down there in the aftermath of the Union War. As unsettling as this subterranean realm was, Stake figured it was infinitely safer than the one it had patterned itself after.

David Bright was looking at the ceiling, the walls, the floor, with increasing dismay but also with a kind of awe, as if he had brought all this about with god-like powers he hadn't realized he possessed. "I just can't believe this. I can't believe it."

Motioning toward the cave-in, Cali explained, "We don't understand the delay... why Bluetown didn't start replicating the lowers levels of Punktown—the Subtown district, and the subway and sewer networks—until now. The program or command for that was either in queue, or this section was meant to grow at the same rate as the city itself but got delayed by a glitch, or who knows what."

Ami said, "You've used your initiation systems in attempts to transmit new orders to the smart matter. During one of those links, might it have accessed a second map or blueprint of Punktown, other than the one that initially sparked Bluetown, and now it's adding that onto the first?"

"No, I really think it meant to get around to this all along. A stratum of living cells had to have been waiting under the floor of the calcified cells to commence this secondary process." Cali sighed. "However it came about, you can see from the structural damage that these new lower levels can't always support the upper structures, enormous as they are, the same way Punktown can. Yes, the buildings have already grown downward to produce basements—some of them multiple stories deep—and they've sent down piles to root themselves, like the originals. But these piles often have to go hundreds of feet deep, and if the smart matter encounters stone in its way that's too large to envelop, then that halts the smart matter's progress. And as tough as smart matter is, it just isn't as strong as the material these piles and other support structures would be. We've already seen some buildings up there topple for lack of support, but now that's increased as the earth gets hollowed out beneath them. Some of these skyscrapers are dropping straight down. So there's no way we're going to see an unadulterated replica of Subtown and the subways, the way we're seeing things duplicated topside."

Stake walked to the foot of an unmoving escalator, gazed up at its top where it was obstructed by more rubble—this being a mix of fragmented blue material, earth, and stone.

"But it's going to try, and try, and try," David Bright groaned. "It's going to keep trying to copy the lower levels."

"So it would seem," Cali said. "And that's almost nine hundred tube stations. In Punktown, twelve thousand subway cars transport ten million passengers every day over repulsor tracks that, if you were going to ride them all without a stop, would take you a day and a half to travel." He walked on, gesturing at the ceiling as he continued. "And let's not forget Subtown. It doesn't cover as much ground as the city above it, but it covers enough. The upper subway system is at the same level as Subtown's streets, but the secondary, lower subway system is several hundred feet below the surface, bored through granite bedrock, so I don't think Bluetown is going to manage to burrow that deep in most places. It can't penetrate the bedrock. That's something, at least."

Stake cut in, "If Bluetown's progress can be stopped by a strong enough barrier, then, has anyone thought about putting up a wall around the city to contain it?"

Gale said, "And how do you think we could achieve that? A wall strong enough to do that would have to be high, thick, and deeply rooted. Bluetown is advancing every minute. By the time you've laid down one section of wall, Bluetown would have grown past it on either side."

"This way, people," Cali told them, directing them down the other end of the tunnel. Two of the four soldiers up front wore full-head helmets with visual enhancement, plus blue camouflaged body armor. They swept their lights and guns from side to side as if cutting a swath through high grass.

Stake was still pondering the idea of blocking Bluetown, and trailing behind Gale asked, "How about an energy barrier, then? Like the one around the base?"

Gale glanced back at him as if at an addled transient begging for a handout. "Do you really think you're going to come up with something that hasn't occurred to us, Stake? Yes, you can set up a field to cut off the smart matter, if it's strong enough and penetrates the ground far enough. At least, you could until the blasting city started digging itself this deep. But you run into the same problem as a solid barrier! Even incomplete, this city is so huge that you can't just run one energy wall around it—you need to space out God knows how many individual transmission posts. How can you get all those in place, and link them up, when this thing never stops gaining ground?"

"I should think you'd at least want to cut off one part, as wide a part as you can manage, even if the city grows past the barrier on the sides. Then you cut off another part. And another. Finally you link all the parts. The wall isn't even, it isn't pretty, but..."

"Are you fucking listening to me? This city is *vast*. Think of the manpower, the energy that would need to be generated, the coordination... and listen to the sound of your idea. Do you stop a lava flow by putting a cinder block in its path here, and another one a half mile down the road, and on and on? The lava will go around it, between it. By the time you finish your raggedy wall, the lava has got where it wanted to go."

"Well, this city is vast now, but it didn't start out that way. Why wasn't a wall or barrier erected around it before it spread to these dimensions?"

Ami hastened to answer for Gale, maybe in the hopes of preventing his reddening head from exploding. "Remember, at first they didn't recognize this as Paxton, so they had no idea to what extent it was going to continue growing. The efforts in the beginning were focused on reprogramming the smart matter, trying to isolate the virus responsible, things of that nature. Shutting the process down remotely instead of containing it physically."

"Exactly," said Cali, in defense of his team.

"Thanks for bringing your friend, Rick," Gale seethed.

"I think his questions are perfectly valid, Dom."

David Bright moved up alongside Stake and whispered, "I told you, remember? I'm convinced now they don't *want* to stop this thing from reaching full size! It's their baby and they're growing it to adulthood at my expense, all innocent while I shoulder the blame."

"I still think that idea is a bit extreme."

"Do you? Did you think the Blue War was extreme? Or should we call it the Sinon Gas War? These bastards want to build here, colonize, make the Jin Haa nation part of the Earth Colonies and suck the Ha Jiin in along with them."

"By making both nations hate them?"

"By making them feel powerless, by crushing them under their treads. Except for isolated terrorist acts by extremists, and no matter how much all of this scares and upsets these people, look how resigned they are about it already! They should all of them be uniting against us... *all* of them! Instead, they're broken and beaten by this one big monster—no need for an invading army! The Earth Colonies will grow like this city is growing, grow into a whole new dimension. This isn't a city; it's a living and spreading disease. And they're just the same thing themselves."

Stake thought that Bright had reached the limits of reason, desperate with frustration. Or maybe he just didn't like contemplating the businessman's theories.

"Down here," Cali said, pointing toward an open doorway gaping blackly in the subway station's wall. The pair of armored special ops soldiers ducked through it first, their postures crouched and assault engines leveled for action.

Another flight of steps downward. The group descended, arrived at a landing, tramped down a second flight of stairs. Then a second landing, and a third flight. Treading carefully in the bobbing light from the rear soldiers' torches, Stake asked Cali, "Where is this headed? The lower level subway tunnels?"

"No—like I said, the bedrock around here won't let Bluetown work its way down far enough to complete that. This is a system of utility tunnels. I've been down here already with the CF team assigned to protect us. They cut the doors open for us along the way to give us access. Get ready, now—it gets wet from here."

The last steps were lost in black water that slurped around the legs of the first men to reach the bottom. Watching them wade ahead of him, their lights glaring off the rolling surface, Stake saw that they were immersed to their upper thighs. Ami ventured in timidly ahead of him, holding up those behind her. "Ohh," she fretted, "if it goes up to my pee-pee I'm going to die." Due to her petite size, the water did indeed rise to her groin, causing her to moan in despair. Sloshing ahead, she almost lost her balance and toppled in. Stake thrashed after her fast and, catching her arm, proceeded beside her without letting go. If Gale looked back and didn't like it, let him support her himself.

Ami cupped her free hand over her lower face and Stake did the same, but that didn't keep their eyes from burning. No one had to ask if this were really water or another fluid instead; the acidic sting in their nostrils defined it as a trapped pocket of the runoff generated by the smart matter's growth process.

They advanced through an arched utility tunnel, which opened into off-branching passageways along its length. They turned into one of these branches at Cali's instruction.

From behind her hand, close beside him, Ami asked Stake in a subdued voice, "How is your investigation coming along?"

"So-so. It would be easier if people were more helpful. So you're interested in my results?"

"Of course I am!"

"Would you like to see Brian reunited with his loved ones?"

"Well, it's not like he's someone's kidnapped child, Jeremy. These loved ones you refer to lost an adult person, with a personality and memories that can't be reshaped. This child has the same appearance, and of course he'll develop some of the same personality traits, but in the end he's another person. So I don't see finding his family as being the priority, here. I'm more interested in finding out how the smart matter could interact with his cells to regenerate him."

"You don't seem concerned about identifying him, then. But are you at least concerned about his welfare?"

"You know I am! I want to see him have a long and healthy life, wherever he ends up. Maybe Captain Henderson there and his wife can adopt him, seeing as how he named him, huh?"

"I saw how sweet you are with him."

"We're sweet with each other. He's starting to talk. He calls me 'Mee,' because he can't say Ami."

"That's why I find it hard to believe you're so indifferent about finding his blood relations. I think that's more your boyfriend talking."

"Believe what you want. And I told you when I first met you about the efforts we've made to cross-check Brian's DNA against all the Blue War combatants on file."

"I'd like to see him again."

"Why?"

"If I see him, something useful might occur to me."

She pouted. "Well then you'd better behave, and I'll think about it."

Something moved unseen below the surface, brushing the outside of Stake's knee. He might have dismissed it as his imagination, had Bright not cried out, "Fuck! What was that?" He spun around with a frightened splash. The KeeZee whipped in the same direction with his shotgun ready. In a flash of reflected torchlight, Stake spotted an albino animal that swished across the surface away from Bright before quickly submerging from view. A wide, segmented body about a foot long, outlined in a rippling fringe of many legs. Stake had only glimpsed it, but he knew these creatures from his four years on-and-off in the blue jungles. An amphibious trilobite-like arthropod with a fanged head that was not unlike the fleshless and eyeless skull of a ferret. Suddenly he was worried about the proximity of his own "pee-pee" to the inky pool.

"Keep moving, keep moving," Gale commanded.

Several more of the animals broke the surface around them and nudged their legs, but no one was bitten. Stake was afraid one of the soldiers or Bright's man might be spooked and fire into the liquid, blasting the kneecaps off one of their neighbors. Ahead, though, he could see a new flight of steps rising from the obsidian pool, and was grateful for it.

There was a doorway to the right of their exit, and as Stake came up on it the light from the soldiers in the rear of their party washed the inside of yet another tributary of this utility network. Stake glanced into the offshoot, and froze like a wary animal. At the end of the narrow corridor, where it formed a T with a cross-wise tunnel, Stake saw a thin figure standing on crooked hind legs. It was emaciated, a corpse-like blue in the stark flood of light, its ribs picked out in black stripes of shadow. A dog-like muzzle had been tearing threads of meat from the broken back of one of those trilobite creatures, which the figure held in its forepaws. It had obviously heard their approach and frozen, too, waiting for them to pass. But its eyes met Stake's, and flashed back at him redly just like the eyes of Sinanese humans.

Before Stake could warn the others, the dog-like animal dropped to all fours and plunged off into the crosswise tunnel with barely a sound, carrying its prize in its jaws. The soldiers' lights had already slipped out of the tunnel, but the animal had a natural faint biolu-minescence and Stake saw it as a ghost before it was gone.

"Oh my God," Ami said. She'd seen the thing, too.

"What's wrong, ma'am?" asked one of the soldiers behind her.

"I saw a snipe."

"Me, too," Stake said.

For decades now, there had been packs of snipes in Punktown, though no one had known where they came from originally or how they got there, only that they were not an indigenous life form. Finally, during the Blue War it had been learned that Sinan was their world of origin, though how they had ended up on Oasis before Earth colonists had first teleported to

Sinan remained a mystery. Stake thought of the rift he had seen in a corner of Wonky Science, in Punktown, and recalled speculation that the weird canine snipes knew ways of navigating such rifts, perhaps even opening them.

"There's never just one snipe," Colonel Gale said, looking back at them. "Come on; let's get where we need to be, fast."

CHAPTER SIXTEEN
TROJAN HORSE

U P THREE FLIGHTS of steps, through a door that had been cut open during Cali's earlier expedition, and the party entered a building that in its original form Stake figured was a power station, though the duplicate's gutted appearance made it hard for him to tell. They worked their way through the building, out its front door, and found themselves standing on a street in Subtown. As he took it in, Stake felt it was even eerier than Bluetown above them. At least Bluetown had an open sky. With its solid ceiling and the blackness that only their torches illuminated in jerky sweeps and flashes, it was like a city that had been swallowed under the earth in some ancient cataclysm.

As Cali had noted, the subterranean sector dubbed Subtown was not as far-reaching as Punktown proper, above it, but still encompassed a large area. Its duplicate presented the same smallish, flat-roofed tenement buildings, interspersed with manufacturing plants and office blocks built on a modest scale so as to be contained by the ceiling. The ceiling, though, was missing the complex system of pipes and conduits that the original was thick with, and of course the lamps that lent a semblance of sunlight during the day but subdued themselves at night.

They walked onward, grateful for the dry ground beneath their feet. "Two hundred munits for these shoes," David Bright grumbled. Stake was too busy resenting the squish of his socks in his own shoes to sympathize with him.

"We didn't know this was going on right below our trailers," Cali was saying. His eye tendrils swam avidly, seeing into the darkness almost as well as the helmets of the two special operatives. "Not until we saw the steam of new growth sneaking up here and there. So we scanned below us, and that's when we saw how the earth was being tunneled out down there."

"How did the Jin Haa find out?" Bright asked.

"That's what I want you to see," Cali said.

Stake's wrist comp was receiving a call, and he lifted his arm to peer at the tiny glowing screen. There, he saw the face of Thi Gonh. He did not interface his mind with the device, but he could still tell that her bruises had lessened even more since the last time he had seen her.

"Thi."

"I want see you, Ga Noh."

"I'm kind of busy. And I thought the last time was the last time, now that you've let your husband out of jail and all."

"I want see you," she said again, simply.

"I'm in Bluetown at the moment."

"I meet you there."

"You can't. I'm in the middle of something. I can't call you back to let you know when I'm finished, in case your charming spouse sees you talking to me, so you'll just have to try me again in a couple of hours."

"Okay. I call again, in couple hours."

She looked so serious. Still upset at him from their argument? In any case, it made him serious, too, when he signed off, "All right, then. Talk to you later."

Ami had peeked over his shoulder, eavesdropping. "Pretty," she said, though she didn't seem to make the connection between the face on the screen and the face Stake had imitated that time in his quarters while she'd been showering. "Old girlfriend?"

"Old enemy," he mumbled.

They turned off one street into another. At its corner, a building had been half crushed by a partial collapse of the ceiling. Stake was grateful for the support columns spaced throughout the streets, as unequal as they might be to their originals. Ahead, though, there had been an even more dramatic caving in of the ceiling, blocking off the street, but Cali kept leading them toward the wreckage. Stake understood why. A bluish haze hung in the air, churning slowly in their invading lights, and its scent was subtle but familiar. It was the gas produced by the decomposition of the Sinanese dead. The gas the Earth Colonies had named sinon.

Cali stopped to plant one foot on a block of masonry. It was not blue, but actual stone. Others in considerable numbers were mixed into a small mountain range of rubble and hard-packed reddish earth. Stake noticed something else: smears of a pasty yellow solution here and there on the heaped stone blocks and the shattered blue smart matter. Cali bent and dipped his finger in it, twisted around to hold it high for the others to see. Before he could explain it, Henderson spoke up.

"It's the stuff the Sinanese paint on their dead, to preserve them."

"There was a tomb up there." Cali pointed above their heads, and the beacons of the soldiers lifted to a yawning black hole in the ceiling, where it had given away. The thin mist of sinon gas emanated from up there. It was like staring into a void to another plane of existence—or some bleak afterlife. "Sandwiched somewhere between the basements of the buildings above, and the roof of the Subtown level. Pretty close to the roof, I'd say. Sometimes the burial tombs are fortified with stone, and sometimes they're just tunneled in the earth. This one was lined in stone, which made it heavier, and probably caused it to drop through the ceiling."

"The central tombs are supported with stone," said Stake." Or the more important ones." He knew this well. He'd been down in many of them. Killed soldiers who had taken to using the tunnels as shelter. The tunnels were like those of an ant colony, with different levels, sometimes close to the surface and sometimes quite deep. A channel so narrow it was impossible to stand in might run for a mile before it linked up to another section where the dead were stored in their niches in the walls. Sometimes the labyrinths seemed endless, and if a soldier lost or damaged his wrist scanner and contact was broken with those who might track his position, he could easily lose his way within them. Could join the population of the dead.

"The bodies dropped down, too." Ami noted, regarding a smudge of the bright yellow mineral. "But I don't see any of them now."

"Come on," said Cali. He broke off toward a building not too distant.

Before Stake followed, he looked around the base of the moraine, saw how smaller heaps of dirt had been dragged off to the sides. Stones had been piled in small cairns. He said to Ami, "Someone's been digging through this."

A rustling sound behind them caused Stake and several of the soldiers to turn around. The lights reached across the street, dimly picking out several shaggy forms lingering in the mouth of an alley. Had they been closer, the roadkill stench of the carrion trees' fruit might have given them away earlier. Seeing the nomadic plants lurking there made Stake wonder if these were the very same trees he had seen wandering into the city before, having arduously worked their way down into the lower levels. Like scavengers, they had been drawn to the taint of the dead. But why were they hanging back now? Was it their party the plants were timid about, or something else?

"Jesus," Ami whispered, as if afraid to startle the trees into advancing on them. "Do you think they've been pulling the bodies out of the rubble?"

"No," Stake said. He nudged Ami to continue following the others toward the building Cali had indicated. "It was something more sentient."

The tenement building had once had energy fields for windows, but the front door had been cut open to allow freer access. When the last of the crew had caught up, Cali said, "We found it this way. It wasn't the CF guys who burned through this."

"Wait," Gale told him. He motioned for the two special operatives to look the place up and down. Stake knew their helmets permitted them to see right through the building's walls. The ops reported that there was no one hidden inside. As soon as the reconnaissance party entered, though, they saw that the building was not really uninhabited after all.

Corpses in all states of preservation were lined up in rows on the floor with their heads touching the walls. The soldiers' sweeping lights made the shadows of their gnarled limbs move across the blue walls like the grasping arms of phantoms. Light moved in and out of skull sockets, flashed across teeth laid bare in grimaces and silent shrieks. Some of the yellow-slathered mummies were fairly well preserved, while the oldest were little more than skeletons held together by the crusted mineral solution.

The collapse of the tomb had inflicted more damage than time had, in many cases. A skull crushed here, a rib cage laid open there. Limbs horribly twisted, or torn away altogether. The next room held an even more dramatic display of the indignities suffered by the dead. It was a collection of limbs, torsos, heads, like the parts of an army of Halloween mannequins waiting to be assembled. And a third room of the tenement held another category of cadavers.

Looking down at these remains, one might have thought all of them had had their faces destroyed in the tomb's collapse into the street below. But Stake knew better, especially because this collection of bodies was dressed in blue silk robes that had fared better over the years than their flesh had. Little three-cornered hats were affixed to their scalps with pins.

"Clerics," Ami said, observing the yawning pits where these men's faces should have been, but which in life had been purposely consumed by a cancer brought about by the incense they smoked.

"This is why the clerics are in such an uproar," Cali said. "Why they led that exorcism against the CF base and the embassy."

"And those guys with the bombs just happened to come along at the same time?" Gale said. "The monks had that planned, too. Now they're not only endorsing terrorists, but working with them."

"Well, I can understand why they're upset," Ami murmured.

Gale looked up at her harshly. "You can understand why they injured some of my men with their terrorist friends?"

"I just mean I understand how this new Bluetown growth would get them more stirred up." The smart matter had already capped over the primary entrances to a number of the central tombs of the Jin Haa and Ha Jiin burial systems, but one could still get into them from areas outside the borders of Bluetown. And the basements of skyscrapers had already ruined some of the tunnels that were close to the surface, but deeper tunnels had still survived, so they had been able to relocate their dead. Yet now, with this deeper growth ensuing, the lower levels of the tombs were being threatened, as well. "This is serious stuff for them. This is holy ground."

"You think I don't know that? But does disturbing their dead accidentally justify them killing people on purpose? I don't think so."

Ami held his gaze. "I don't think so either, Dom. If a shark bit my leg off I'd understand it was hungry, but I wouldn't like that, either."

Cali had slipped into a hallway, and waited at a flight of stairs. "There's more on the second floor. In every room of this place. It's become a new mausoleum for them."

David Bright waved a hand in front of his face, cupping his other hand over his nose and mouth. "I'm not too happy about breathing this stuff," he complained, however attenuated the sinon gas was in their blazing lights. "Haven't we seen enough in here? Or do you want to bottle this up before we leave, colonel?"

Gale shifted his hot eyes to the businessman. "What's that comment supposed to mean, Mr. Bright?"

"Well, it's what you people did in the war, isn't it?" He looked to Henderson, and then even to Stake. "You came down here, set up your teleportation gear, and sucked this stuff up. Did you bring your gear with you today? There doesn't look to be a lot left, but every bit counts, right?"

"This is Jin Haa land," Gale reminded him. "We didn't steal gas from these people."

"Jin Haa, Ha Jiin, what's the difference? You bribe one people for it, kill the other people for it—either way you get what you want."

"Mr. Bright, I think you're suffering a little too much stress lately, and aren't considering your words too carefully. I know you think we're profiting from the growth of Bluetown, somehow, but ask yourself now how you think the destruction of the Jin Haa burial network is really going to benefit us—both in our relations with the Jin Haa, and in our need for sinon gas, which you keep reminding me about. You honestly think we're happy about all this?"

"I just think your plans have gotten a little out of control now."

"I think it's your paranoia that's getting out of control."

"Like to read, Mr. Stake?" Bright faced him again, giving a brittle smile. "My mother instilled a love of books in me. I read Homer in school. In the *Iliad*, do you know the name of the Greek guy who got the Trojans to drag the horse full of Greek soldiers into Troy? His name was Sinon. Funny, isn't it?"

"Huh," said Stake. He didn't find it funny to feel like one of those Greek soldiers himself, right now.

Back to Gale. "Your base is the horse full of soldiers, colonel. And I've been elected to be the piñata, full of blame. The piñata for the Jin Haa and Ha Jiin to break with their sticks."

"I think we need to get you back up-ground, Mr. Bright. I think we need to have our base's Dr. Laloo have a look at you."

"Fuck you, Gale. Fuck... *you*."

"Sir," one of the special ops men spoke up suddenly, his voice issuing from his helmet's speaker, "there's someone com—"

A banshee flew into Stake's skull. He thought he might be crying out, himself, but his voice was overwhelmed by the other, and it dropped him to hands and knees. He felt Ami bump his hip as she fell, too. He imagined she was also screaming. The banshee's cry wasn't really shrill, however, something to break glass. It sounded more like a man moaning deeply through a long, echoing metal tube, with a wavering, vibratory quality. The vibration formed an undercurrent like a cicada's buzz. That was the layer of the attack that felt most like something high-pitched. That was the part that corkscrewed a hole into Stake's skull so the thicker, deeper layer's molten copper could be poured inside.

Stake was on his belly now, and reaching out his hand for an assault engine on the floor in front of him. It lay beside one of the two special operatives. The man was sprawled across the legs of the mummified clerics, his helmet tilted toward Stake. Red liquid and gobs of meat or brain slid down the inside of his faceplate.

His fingers clawed at the fallen weapon, but the sound was filling his skull to the bursting point. Any moment now, he expected to end up like the special operative, whose helmet's enhanced hearing had worked very much to his disadvantage.

There was a shotgun blast, but Stake didn't hear it. He only knew about it when the banshee vanished from his skull, and he slowly rolled over onto his back to look up and see the KeeZee standing there in a wide stance, unfazed by the aural attack, his shotgun smoking in his hands. Stake's head turned slightly—an agonizing undertaking—and he saw that a new cleric had been added to the ranks of the dead. This one, though, was not mummified, and a ragged wound had been blown through his chest. The monk sagged against the far wall, near the open doorway he had stepped through moments earlier. Wisps of black vapor escaped from his chest along with his flowing blood. It was not sinon gas, but a related phenomenon, and occurred only when a Sinan person had their heart laid open. Much had been made by those who hated the Sinanese about the black fog in their hearts.

Stake got back onto hands and knees shakily. Gale was on his feet already, and helped Ami up. She fell against his chest, whimpering, clamping her palms over her ears.

Henderson was crouched near the dead Jin Haa monk, and groaned, "Oh God, no."

"That's great," David Bright said to his bodyguard, wiping tears off his cheeks with both palms. "Oh, that's blasting great. As if they don't hate me enough! Now a man under my employ has murdered an allied holy man!"

"What was your man supposed to do?" Gale panted. "He probably saved our lives. Did you see this?" With his toe he nudged the shoulder of the second special ops man. His faceplate, too, revealed nothing but a sheet of running gore flecked with shards of skull. "That fucker just killed two of my men, so to hell with him."

"What a mess," Henderson murmured. "What a goddamned mess."

"Is there anyone here who doubts that this was an act of self-defense?" Gale demanded. "Rick?"

Henderson hung his head, but shook it side to side. "There was nothing else we could do."

Cali of Simulacrum Systems held up empty hands like a man being taken prisoner, to show there was no protest from him.

"God, it hurts, Dom, it hurts," Ami was sobbing. "We need to go have Dr. Laloo check us out... we need to get out of here."

"I'll take that as agreement," Gale said, turning from his lover to the hired investigator. "What about you, Stake? Are you going to make a fuss about this?"

Stake was massaging his ears, just for the need to do something to them. His hearing was muffled as if a bomb had gone off too close by, and an aching pressure persisted. "This doesn't involve me," he mumbled.

"You're involved. Your friend is paying you to be involved."

"Not in this."

"What does that mean, that you're going to go to the newshounds with this? Huh? If that's what you have in mind, don't forget to tell them how you almost had your brain boiled by your toilet-faced friend over there."

"I didn't say I was going to talk to anyone about this. I won't. I realize that he might have been trying to kill us. Might. Or maybe he was just trying to disable us, and what happened inside your boys' helmets was unforeseen. My unit captured a monastery once, with ten monks in it, and they never tried to use their chants to hurt us." Stake didn't mention, though, that he himself had been reaching for a gun when they'd been under attack just now.

"Devil's advocate, huh?"

"I just like to look at things from all sides."

"Well, why don't we all look at the bigger picture here. Yes, what just happened is a major scoop of shit in the punch bowl. If the Jin Haa find out what we did, it could be the final straw to break relations between us and them. There goes our access to sinon gas—right, Mr. Bright? Poor, poor Earth Colonies. True. But poor, poor Jin Haa, too." Gale was pacing between them now, working himself up. "What these ungrateful asswipes seem to forget, lately, is that they didn't win the Blue War by themselves, not by a long shot. We won it for them. And we're what really keeps the Ha Jiin from pouring in on all sides of their tiny-ass country and reclaiming it. If the Earth Colonies ever pulled out of this dimension, the Jin Haa would be screwed. So it's not just for our benefit as members of the Earth Colonies that we keep this incident from reaching the

Jin Haa. It's for their own good, as well, whether they could appreciate that fact or not!"

Bright was unsteady on his feet, and the KeeZee reached out to help hold him up. Stake expected Bright to shake him off, resume his tirade, but the businessman seemed persuaded by the colonel's viewpoint. "Just don't you be pinning this on me later, Gale, when you need a scapegoat again."

"Maybe this will put your mind at ease, Mr. Bright. Put us both on the same level of responsibility." Gale stooped down and picked up the AE-95 Sturm assault engine that Stake had been straining to reach. "Just to show you I'm willing to put my money where my mouth is."

Blue plasma rounds ate only organic matter, and might leave behind a pile of smoking clothing. Green plasma was less particular, and it was two of these projectiles that Colonel Gale fired into the dead Jin Haa monk. Perversely, he fired them right into the spiraling cavern that was all the cleric had for a face. The gel capsules burst, and Gale stepped back as a glowing green matter like liquid fire spread quickly to blanket the cleric's entire body. It outlined his form, but then that form began to shrink away, the limbs receding, the head dropping from its neck to fall into the lap, to melt and merge with the rest of the diminishing pool. When the last of the flickering green glow was gone, all that remained of the holy man was a charred place like a lingering shadow.

"God help us," Henderson said.

"God help that bastard," one of the surviving Colonial Forces men spat.

"Remember," Gale said to the others. It sounded like a threat, and he turned to them with the bulky assault engine gripped in both fists. "This is for the good of us all. Now let's get the blast out of this hell hole, before more of these fanatics come along and complicate things more."

Before they left, carrying their own two dead men with them, Stake saw Gale smudging the charred area

with his heel, trying to make it look less like the outline of a person.

CHAPTER SEVENTEEN
ENTANGLED PAIRS

STAKE TOOK A call as he piloted his helicar back toward Bluetown, only an hour after he and the reconnaissance party headed by Gale had returned from it. On his wrist comp's screen he saw the hairless head of Thi's cousin, Nhot, her cheeks bunched with a smile and eyes thin slits like some jovial female Buddha.

"Hello, Mr. Stake—sorry if I'm disturbing you."

"Hello, Nhot. How did you get my number?"

"Sorry, but I found it on my computer; I let my cousin use it whenever she likes."

"That was very… industrious of you."

"Mr. Stake, I'm concerned about my cousin's welfare. I overheard her call you to say she wanted to come meet you in the Blue City. She just left here on her bike. Mr. Stake, I just don't think that's a good idea! Her husband is out of prison right now, and yes, he is timid at the moment because of his arrest, but I don't think it would take much for him to become angry again. I'm just worried that he may hurt Thi!"

"That worries me, too. But I think Thi can make her own decisions."

"But she's so stubborn! She isn't thinking clearly. Who will protect her when you return to your own world?"

"It would be nice if your father protected her. Since he's the head of the family, I think Thi's husband might be cowed if your father put some pressure on him."

"My father is getting old now and he's not in good health, so he can only do so much."

"Well, thank God at least Thi has you looking out for her best interest. Like when you called her husband to let him know I'd had lunch with Thi. I guess you were just trying to save her from herself."

The blue Buddha looked a little less benevolent now. "What are you saying? I didn't tell her husband about that! And yes, we are trying to save Thi from herself! You have to understand, Mr. Stake, that even if Thi left her husband—which would be disgraceful in the eyes of her people—she could never be with you."

"Your father wouldn't have me in the family, huh?"

"Well, he did fight against you not so long ago, of course."

"I realize you and your father have the family honor in mind, Nhot, but you know what? I have a cousin who's a lesbian. That's not a problem for most of my people, but I know that it would be for most of yours…"

"Yes." A tighter smile now. "It would."

"Anyway, I'd never tell my cousin that what she was doing was wrong—not that it is. I'd never judge her. I'd never act against my own flesh and blood."

"You would if you were Ha Jiin."

"No—not even then. Because in the end, this isn't about being a Ha Jiin or an Earther or anything else. It's about being a malicious, jealous little troll. And you can tell your father that he doesn't deserve to have me in his family, just like he doesn't deserve to have Thi in his family. Now I'll thank you to never fucking call me again."

Nhot opened her mouth, and for the first time Stake expected that she would vent her true venom, no longer hidden behind her apple-cheeked grin, but he banished her image from his screen before it could come. He temporarily blocked the number.

He seethed. He knew that he hadn't made things any easier for Thi, just now, but wasn't her personal situation bad enough already? Thi would never dare to put her uncle's daughter in her place, apparently. Sometimes Stake took on these dirty jobs for other people, even when they didn't pay him for it.

If he heard that the uncle wanted to punish Thi for his impudence, then Stake thought he'd show the former Ha Jiin captain what a Blue War Two would be like.

SINCE THE HELICAR was faster and Stake wanted to minimize the driving Thi would have to do on her hoverbike, he told her to meet him at the periphery of Bluetown on its Ha Jiin side. Approaching it, he saw the massive blooms of steam coming off the creeping edge of new growth, where the fast-multiplying cells bled off their liquid component in the process of calcifying like coral. A coral reef in the form of a city. Not just any city, though, he thought. *His* city.

To him, the great white columns of steam looked like the mushroom clouds of an attack on the city, burning up its edge instead of laying it down, as if Bluetown's growth were a film of consumption played in reverse. Destruction, construction. Was there a difference, here?

The wind was blowing the steam in another direction, fortunately, and his view of the streets below was clear. He saw a pack of refugee children, as Hin

Yengun would call them, chasing after a ball. They paused from their play to shield their eyes and squint up at him. Thinking of Yengun made Stake wonder if the security captain would see him nearing the border he patrolled, and come to meet him. He hoped not. Nothing against the man, but he wanted to meet one Ha Jiin only.

He spotted her. She waved up at him. As he started down toward Thi, he magnified her on one of his console screens. She was wearing a sleeveless top and matching pants of a coarse, almost metallic green-brown material, her hat with its floppy brim and a scarf around her lower face to protect her from sun and dust, respectively. He recognized her eyes despite her disguise.

Stake brought the craft to the ground and climbed out. "Hey," he said in greeting, still not sure how things would be between them after the last time they had met in this city. "Let's see if we can get your bike in the back. I don't want to leave it here."

"We leave car, maybe? Ga Noh ride on bike with me?"

As much as he liked the idea of riding behind her, his front pressed to her back, his hands on her waist, her hair streaming in his face, he said, "I'm afraid some refugees might do something to my car if I leave it unattended."

"Mm, yes... I see. Okay." She swung off the bike, and together they managed to fit it inside the Harbinger. As they did so, not looking at him, Thi asked, "Where you like go with me?"

"As I was coming in, I saw some new buildings just along the edge, here, that I recognize from Punktown. I think it's possible the neighborhood I grew up in has started to form. It would be in that direction." He pointed into the gulfs of the city. "Want to go have a look?"

"Okay. I like to see." She smiled faintly. Was she afraid of him? The idea made him sick inside. She was afraid enough of other men, these days—her husband, her uncle—without that. So Stake put his hand on her arm gently to direct her into the car.

"Come on, then. Let's see if we can find us Tin Town."

As STAKE LOWERED the helicar into a neighborhood made hallucinatory by its combination of aching familiarity and glaring transfiguration, Stake said to Thi, "Your cousin called me while you were riding out here."

"Oh!" she said. She looked confused.

"She overheard your call. She knows that you were coming to meet me. I wasn't very careful about what I said to her. I'm afraid it might make things more difficult for you."

"Nhot very no good."

"Well if I looked like that scabby-headed little monster, I suppose I'd be nasty, too. Remind me never to look at her too long, unless it's close to October thirty-first." He was exaggerating, but it felt good anyway. "I'm just afraid she might tell your husband we're meeting."

"No worry, please. Husband afraid police now. And uncle very angry at Nhot, say to Nhot no more talk to husband. Uncle angry at me, but not want husband hurt me again."

"But will your husband know where you were going? When you get back, will he—"

"Ga Noh." Before they could step out of the craft, she put a hand on his arm. "Please. Today, no talk husband, okay? No talk anything husband."

Her beseeching face was like a child's. He smiled, reassuring her. "Okay."

They disembarked, Thi bringing along a canvas bag with a shoulder strap. Seeing Stake notice it, she explained, "I brought food for Ga Noh."

"Ahh, a picnic, huh? Very nice."

The breeze had changed a little—though the air was so hot, Stake couldn't tell there even was a breeze except by the movement of the steam—and a mist surrounded them as if they had stepped into his memories, distorted and decayed. They walked together until the Harbinger vanished behind them. Stake directed her attention to an apartment building lurking in the fog and said, "That's the last place I knew my father to be living before I lost track of him. Or before he lost track of himself."

Thi apparently couldn't think of anything to say, but sensing his emotion, she took his hand and squeezed it while they continued on.

There was a continuous background noise of crunching static. Stake envisioned a wave of army ants feasting on the jungle. He pictured them more as the nanomites used in surgery and industry, though; implacable machine-animals with exoskeletons of chemically inert diamond, that couldn't be reasoned with or deterred now that they were one with their programming. But this crackling was the sound of the coralline cells, kamikazes sacrificing their seconds-long lives to add their minute skeletons to the greater cause—living just long enough to split into clones of themselves, each one bequeathing memory-encoded molecules filled with this great city in its entirety. And why shouldn't that be? Didn't Stake's parents exist in every one of his cells, figuratively and literally?

He took Thi around a corner, down a narrower street. "There," he said, indicating another tenement house ahead. "That's the last place we lived while my mother was alive." They drew closer until they stood on the opposite curb, and he pointed. "We were there on the third floor. By then she was very sick, and would sit at that window every day watching the people and vehicles go by." Now, that and every window in the modest, unremarkable building were sightless slabs of coral.

They crossed the street and Stake mounted the front steps, laid both hands on the sealed front doors. Behind him, down the steps, Thi said, "What kind gun you have? Maybe we cut inside?"

"I don't have a beam gun or any other kind of gun. They won't let me, here."

"No?"

Stake turned away from the double doors, came down the steps to take Thi's hand and tug her along. "Come on. If we can't go inside, we can at least go up top."

Behind the building, in an alley, a fire escape zigzagged its way to the flat roof. Stake mounted it ahead of her. The steps did not clang metallically as he remembered, but they supported their weight. "I used to go up here with a friend sometimes, and we'd throw stuff at other friends in the street. Or hide with a Zub we stole from my dad. A couple times I even sat up here with my dad. He'd sit up here for hours, the days after my mom died, but I left him alone. I thought he needed that."

Together they moved to the waist-high safety wall that surrounded the roof like a battlement, passing a mock utility shed, a row of three mock exhaust fans under vented domes, and the sealed staircase to the top floor. At the low barrier, Stake gestured toward a structure in the distance. "Jesus, look. I went to school in that building, there."

The building in question was still forming, so that it presented a cross section, as if exposed through partial demolition. Waste fluid ran down from floor to floor like champagne poured over a tower of wedding glasses.

"Ga Noh learn things with medicine?" Thi motioned with her hand as if injecting an invisible syringe into her temple. "I hear about."

Memory-encoded molecules, like the virus-tainted education each generation of smart matter cells passed on to the next. "No," Stake told her, "I never had that. It's mostly banned in Punktown, to preserve the jobs of educators and make sure that kids have social interaction with real teachers and other children, in a classroom setting. Sometimes wealthy people will have their kids learn that way, or by computer interface, to keep them away from all the school violence, but by law even they can only do that for a few years, spaced throughout their kids' total education." He shielded his eyes from the paired suns as they peeked through a tear in the drifting canopy of mist. Still staring at the bisected school, he went on, "I wish I could have learned that way, because someone once said, 'Hell is other people,' and it's true. That's why I feel like this gift of mine is hell, sometimes. It's like I'm possessed by every face I've ever assumed, crowded inside me. You would think that in a school of almost entirely mutants, kids would be less mocking and cruel to each other, but that wasn't the case. They were cruel, maybe out of self-loathing. There was another student with a condition like mine, but much worse. It got to the point where his face was changing features constantly—even when he was asleep—in this boiling blur of flesh, so that you couldn't ever see just one face, though you'd think you might recognize one of them for a second. You might think you saw yourself in there. But he couldn't see himself in there anymore, I guess, because one day he just put a bullet into his skull to kill all those faces at once." He nodded, as if he were watching a number of scenes played out all at once in the school's dissected rooms. "Yeah—Tin Town. This is why I escaped to the military, when I was old enough. To get away from all this self-loathing. But I didn't get far, huh? I escaped to Sinan. And now, here on Sinan, I find my home again."

Thi was leaning against the barrier, looking up at his face. She took his chin and turned it toward her. She saw his tears streaming. Stake met her gaze, and within moments he saw fat tears pop from her own eyes and roll down her cheeks. It was, essentially, the first time he had ever seen anyone imitate *his* face. He was sure she understood only a portion of his words, but she understood his feelings precisely. He didn't think he'd ever known such a moment of pure empathy with another being.

He took her face in turn, in both hands, and then they were kissing. Passion came quickly; the slippery dance of tongues, the holding of each other's heads. He squeezed one of her small breasts, feeling its engorged nipple in his palm through the material of her blouse, while she ran her hands under his shirt to slide up the skin of his back.

Thi pulled away from him, looking to left and right. At first he thought she was alarmed at some arrival, but she was surveying their prospects with blatant anxiousness. The floor of coral was too rough, so she simply leaned over the railing and looked over her shoulder at him, her eyes shining with fever. Stake pulled down her pants, and fitted himself behind her. She was small, and winced once, but he drew out her moisture and went in again more smoothly. Then, holding her waist, he began thrusting long and deep, mounting in rhythm quickly until his front slapped against the small hard balls of her buttocks. She grunted, looked out over the new city and then back at him again.

"Ga Noh is beautiful now," she panted. "Beautiful."

He knew why. He had been taking on her appearance unconsciously. Consciously, he had only been thinking: *Eleven years. Eleven years…*

"You have magic on me. Magic, I can not keep away." She reached back awkwardly, took one of his hands off her narrow waist and placed it at the back of her head. At her prompting, he took a handful of her hair, heavy black silk, but he only held it taut without pulling on it. "Oh," she panted, "fuck me." Her eyes shone back at him like red glass lit from within. "Ban ta likes Ga Noh strong... strong."

Ban ta: your lover. And he understood the rest, too, slapping his pale olive skin harder and harder against her blue skin, as if he might achieve the ultimate mimicry and meld with her body in a reverse mitosis.

HER ARMS HAD become abraded against the blue coral, so they had both removed their clothing and laid it down on the roof and made do with that. Sitting on the puddled clothing now, Stake tolerated the wall as he leaned against it with Thi leaning in turn against him. Through her back, could she feel his heartbeat easing from a gallop to a trot? When atop her, he had felt her chest pounding against his own, the two organs seeming desperate to escape their rib cages to reach each other. Her mysterious Ha Jiin heart, which if it were to be cut open would give up a black fog like sinon gas. For eleven years, it had seemed to him that a black cloud had hidden her heart from him on the outside, as well. When he had lain upon her, his face inches from hers, he had asked, "Are you doing this because you feel sorry for me?"

"No," she said huskily. "Because I feel sorry me."

Now, with their bodies still damp with sweat, Thi reached for his porkpie hat and placed it atop his head. "There. Ga Noh is ready go home."

"I don't think they'd let me on the base wearing only this. What about when you go home, Thi? What's going to be waiting for you?"

"I said, please, no talk husband today. Please. I be okay, I swear."

"If you say so."

"Hungry now? I have food I make."

"Oh yeah, great, I forgot about that. Something to drink would be nice, before I die of heat prostration."

Thi went onto hands and knees to retrieve her canvas bag. Enjoying the view, Stake reached between her legs from behind to tug gently on a tuft of her unruly hair. She looked back at him with a crooked smile, and a shadow slid across her flesh. Stake looked up, expecting to see a fresh cloud of steam blocking the intense glare of the binary stars.

Above them floated something of the size and general form of a parachute, and it eclipsed the sky so that the double suns glowed grayish through a black membrane with an oily iridescence, their light making it more translucent. From this bell hung a ring of long, ropy arms, bluish and also translucent, with a nest of shorter pitch-black tentacles squirming at the center.

Bender, Stake thought, even as one of the longer tendrils—their insubstantial-looking flesh full of paralyzing venom—lashed out at his naked body like a whip. He shot to his feet and threw himself to one side, evading the first tentacle but not a second, which encircled his leg like a lasso. Stake was jerked aloft and upside-down, his hat falling away and arms thrashing. But they didn't thrash for long, as the stunning toxins entered his bloodstream.

Thi had also thrown herself forward, gone into a shoulder roll toward the pouch she had been reaching for. She came up in a squat beside it, in the same motion having removed two items. In her left hand, a long knife she had brought to cut fruit and bread. In her right, a dull gray handgun.

Stiffening, Stake still managed to look up toward the bender's underside. Another blue limb had coiled around one of his arms, and a third slithered around his neck but he could no longer feel their touch. They were lifting him toward the black tendrils, which seemed to writhe more excitedly in anticipation. It was the black tendrils that delivered enzymes to begin the breakdown of tissues for digestion.

Through the bender's dark membrane, three darker floating shapes were silhouetted. Stake knew what they were: a smaller, spherical life form called a blastula. Symbiotically, these orange-sized creatures fed off the emanations of larger extradimensionals—their life force, some would say. In return, through a primitive telepathic connection, the little vampires served as sensory organs and guides to the benders in dimensions where they might otherwise be blind and disoriented. Always three blastulas, and Stake could see them more plainly hovering like satellites above a second bender that was drifting toward the tenement building as if it were a silent ghost galleon.

Stake's eyelids could not close, but he could still see. He could still hear, too. He heard a loud, sharp crack. Above him, as he was drawn upward, he saw one of the silhouetted blastulas burst and vanish. Then another. A third cracking sound—a third bullet zipping straight through the diaphanous canopy overhead—and the last guide creature was gone.

He could no longer turn his eyeballs, but peripherally he saw a figure spring into the air like a big cat taking down a gazelle. A blur of naked blue skin, and a silvery flash of metal in an arc. Silvery flash. Silver... glowing through the sudden darkness.

GLEAMING METALLIC EYES spaced wider than they should be in a human—maybe the eyes of some predatory cat, stealing toward him in the dark as he lay under the covers of his bed, the blanket tucked in so tight across him that he could not move his arms, his whole body. Even his head on his pillow was immobile as he watched the disembodied eyes float nearer.

His heart beat faster, but a soft voice came out of the gloom to reassure him. "Don't worry, honey," it said, "I'm watching over you. I'm protecting you." Just above him now, the glow of her eyes illuminated enough of her face for Stake to recognize his mother. He felt her hand, with its fingers lacking nails, alight cool upon his feverish forehead. "You'll be fine soon, my love."

But then Stake realized he was standing outside his body, as if astral projecting, and he saw his mother bent over his younger self. The child's face was illuminated by the gentle radiance from her eyes, as well, and so Stake could see it wasn't a younger version of himself after all. The boy turned his head on the pillow to smile at him. It was Brian, the clone found in the cloned city, and the boy said, "Don't be afraid to die. He wears the singing bracelet. Necromancy lullaby... I can't go back to sleep now."

A sudden burst of light into the room. Squinting, Stake turned toward a door held open by a small, silhouetted female figure. A new voice intruding into the darkness.

"Ga Noh—awake now."

It WAS HER tugging on his arms to get his shirt on that brought him back to her. His trousers were already on, as were her own clothes. Stake could move his head a little, and he saw that Thi was wearing his wrist comp.

His skull was filled with pain so intense that his vision was black and rippling around the edges, and he was shivering with fever. Through the ripples, he noticed several lengths of severed blue tentacles strewn across the roof; snakes hacked from the medusa.

He turned his head a little more, saw black smoke rising from a gelatinous mound on the roof of a neighboring building. The mound flickered with green fire. A second column of smoke rose from the street below, from where the other of the two giant jellyfish had sunk from view. Thi saw him looking that way, and scooped something up to show him.

"I have two kind," she explained, holding the clip of solid projectiles with which she had killed the blastulas. She had switched it, obviously, with a magazine of plasma rounds, the only real way to bring down a bender. "I give gun to Ga Noh." She patted his deep trouser pocket, a heaviness inside tugging at the material. She pushed the spare magazine into his other pocket. "You say to me have no gun. You need gun on Sinan."

"You need the gun," he croaked.

"I have bigger gun," she assured him. "They come my farm to hunt animals, I always shoot them." She pantomimed firing a rifle toward the bender's smoldering carcass.

"You need it," he insisted. "What if your husband tries to hurt you again?"

Thi held up her empty hands, fingers bent a little like iron claws. "Need no gun."

Stake tried on a half-paralyzed smile. "I remember you now," he rasped. "You're the Earth Killer."

"You talk crazy," she scolded like a fussing mother, fastening his shirt. "Poison inside. Sometime animal poison inside head for year and year. Sometime monks like poison—drink wine with animal poison inside so monks can talk to ghosts and look to future."

"I know," he rasped. In the monastery his soldiers had captured, he had seen bottles of sacred wine—forbidden to the general public—in which bender larvae had been pickled like anatomical specimens. None of his men had dared try it.

"You not fly car now." She tapped his wrist comp. "I see name your friend on computer: Henderson. I call him already. Soon he come here, take you home, okay?"

"Okay. Thanks, Thi."

"Before, in war, Ga Noh protect me from soldiers. Now, I protect you. Always."

He let her prop him up in a sitting position against the roof's barrier. Moving made the pain in his head worse, and he winced. "Just protect yourself in the future," he managed, "and I'll be happy."

"Who that face Ga Noh have now?" She touched his cheek.

"What?" He reached up to feel his own features, was surprised to find that he had transformed while he'd been delirious. Some mutants with his affliction could take on the faces of others simply by thinking about them—whether purposely or spontaneously—but he had always needed to be looking at a person or picture to accomplish his own shapeshifting.

His eyes were not as far apart as they should have been to really do the trick, and he knew their pupils would not be reflective as chrome, but he understood whose face he was imitating at that moment.

CHAPTER EIGHTEEN
GOLDEN FLEECE

THE MESSAGE ON Stake's wrist comp read: "THE PERSON YOU ARE TRYING TO REACH HAS BLOCKED YOUR NUMBER. FURTHER ATTEMPTS TO CONTACT THIS PERSON MAY RESULT IN YOU BEING REPORTED TO THE LAW ENFORCEMENT AGENCY APPROPRIATE TO YOUR LOCATION."

"Thank you and fuck you," Stake murmured. So Persia Barbour had tired of the messages he had left her. Well, he'd just try her from someone else's phone next time. In the meantime, he tapped in the number for Timothy Leung, still hoping to persuade him into further cooperation, and maybe into persuading Persia Barbour for him. The number rang a moment, and then the following message appeared on Stake's screen: "THE PERSON YOU ARE TRYING TO REACH…"

"Dung," Stake hissed, and disconnected.

"Uh-oh," said a child's voice.

Stake looked up to see Brian standing in the door to the examination room. Ami Pattaya was behind the boy, and urged him into the room. She smiled at the detective, but then frowned when she saw the livid pink burns around his neck, one arm, and one leg, as he sat on the edge of the examination table in just a pair of plaid flannel boxer shorts.

"Boo-boo!" Brian said, pointing to the wound that made it look like Stake had survived an attempted lynching.

"Isn't he cute?" Ami said. "So are you." She tugged on the cuff of his underwear, then touched his poisoned arm gingerly. "God, that thing could have killed you! You were very lucky, Jeremy."

"I was lucky I had my friend with me."

"Mm." She narrowed her eyes at him. "So I heard. Some Ha Jiin assassin you knew during the war?"

The Colonial Forces base's chief medical officer, Dr. Laloo, appeared from an adjoining room and complained, "Maybe you can persuade the investigator to let me filter the toxins from his body. He seems to think he's had a mystical experience, and will have more of them if he lets that stuff remain in his system. I told him if he wants to hallucinate, he should just buy some purple vortex or another illegal drug like a regular junkie."

"Jeremy," Ami scolded, "is that true? Don't be foolish!"

"The monks use bender poison to induce visions, and I think there might be something to that."

"The monks also smoke incense that makes their faces rot into huge holes; are you going to start doing that, too?"

Stake looked back to Brian. The way the boy was staring at him was so much like the delusion he had had while the bender was attacking him that a wave of gooseflesh flowed down his arms. "You are a cutie, Brian, aren't you?" he said. Stake lifted the arm that wore his wrist comp—"Say cheese!"—and captured a still of the boy in the little computer's memory.

A pleasant young black man named Bernard, whom Stake had seen about before, trailed after Ami into the examination room. Stake understood him to be Ami's main assistant in the science department. Before he lowered his arm, he snapped a few quick pictures of Bernard, too, to add to his growing file. Later he would sort them alphabetically. He had face files going back years. Not all those faces were still alive, though he could give them fresh life at any time. Necromancy: Brian had said it in Stake's delirium.

"He has a fever," the Choom doctor grumbled, poking about the room as if he had turned to other business and was waiting for Stake to leave. "But if he doesn't want the poison out of him, he can just deal with it." He faced Stake and tossed him a bottle of pain pills. "Here. For the headaches. I hope they're illuminating."

Ami placed a palm on Stake's forehead. "Jeremy," she sighed.

Stake smiled past her at Bernard. "She's got quite the maternal instincts, huh, Bernard?"

"She's a very nice person," her assistant replied.

"Thanks, cutie. At least Bernard still appreciates me." Ami pouted, dropping her hand.

"He's just brown-nosing the boss," Stake teased. He slipped off the edge of the table, ruffled Brian's hair, and reached for his pants.

"Well, I just wanted to come by and make sure you're okay. I'm taking Brian around the base for a change of scene and a little exercise; they won't let me take him past the wall, though. Care to come with us, if you're not busy?"

"Sure. Let me finish getting dressed."

"Do you realize you're starting to look like Brian again? Or at least, kind of what Brian would look like as an adult?"

As an adult, Stake thought.

* * *

BERNARD LEFT THEM to tend to work-related matters as they began their walk around the Colonial Forces base. Brian held onto one of Ami's hands, and reached over to take Stake's hand as well. Stake looked down at him, the boy smiling up at the investigator in return.

"He's so affectionate," Ami said, proud as a mother.

"I think you're helping instill that in him."

She smiled at Stake, then, too. "Thanks. I'd like to think that."

They ended up in the mess hall and ordered themselves ice cream. Much of their subsequent conversation revolved around Ami's revelation that she was an army brat who in her youth had traveled from colony to colony, base to base, and whose father had in fact helped her secure her current position here on Sinan. "So I know how you feel," she told Stake. "Seems like I'm a bit of a war veteran, myself. Sometimes I felt like I didn't have a home anymore."

"I know what you mean, too," he muttered.

"Yeah, you see? I was lonely through my childhood, especially being a mutant, and I'm sure you were, too. You change faces, I change partners, just trying to find out where we really belong. I think we're more alike than you realize."

"Your ice cream is melting," Stake said.

When they'd finished they worked their way back to the medical unit that Brian called home. Just outside its entrance, they heard a commotion within. Ami glanced at Stake before leading the way through. They found that Dr. Laloo had himself a new patient now—an agitated, swearing David Bright. His shirt was off, and his expensive slacks spattered with the blood that twined down his right arm. Laloo was tending to the injury, while a young male nurse passed him implements and Bright's KeeZee bodyguard loomed in the background, watching over the doctor's efforts and the newcomers with its three unblinking, distrustful eyes.

"What happened?" Ami asked.

Bright looked up and raved, "You see this? Huh?" His wild eyes went to Stake. "One of Argos's robots did this to me! I wasn't even going to hit the bastard—all I did was poke him in the chest with my finger!"

"*Whose* robots?"

Ami looked to Stake. "Argos is one of the business owners who arrived this morning. A group of them have come to assess the threat to their Sinan investments from the spread of Bluetown, especially now that it's growing belowground, too."

"The bone isn't broken," Laloo said, "but its claws lacerated his skin."

"Why were you poking his chest?" Stake asked.

"Because the fucker was poking me about Bluetown, bitching to me about how it's threatening his own damn business. Good! *Good!* I hope I ruin him. Let all these wankers go down in flames with me!"

"Argos... Argos," Stake said to himself, as if he were trying to recall where he'd heard the name, though he actually knew it well.

"Argos built the ship the Argonauts sailed on, looking for the Golden Fleece," said the well-read Bright. "Let the fucker's Golden Fleece burn to ash."

Thinking that Stake was unfamiliar with the name, Ami explained, "He's the biggest supplier of sinon gas in the colonies. I should say, pretty much the only supplier of sinon gas in the colonies. He's got a monopoly on it."

"Because he's in bed with the chief ambassador here, that bitch Valsalva," Bright fumed. "Not literally, but who knows about that, either? Wouldn't put it past either of them."

Stake was nodding thoughtfully. "I see his gas freighters just about every day where I'm living now. Seen him in the news a thousand times, too."

"Well, I'm going to sue that rich monopolizing fuck," Bright said. "Trust me! He thinks I'm ruining his business? I haven't begun to ruin his business!"

Laloo looked over Bright's shoulder and asked Stake, "So how are you feeling? Any more delirium? Mystical visions?"

"Unless I'm just imagining all this, then no. Not yet, at least."

Bright looked to Stake again. "And while I'm at it, I'm going to fire that traitorous fuck Cali, him and the whole Simulacrum Systems team. What was Cali doing here just now? I didn't send him here. Why did I see him outside the officers' lounge talking with Gale? You see, Stake? I swear this Bluetown virus is no accident! I don't trust Cali or any of them now. They're done—*finished!*"

"Please try to stay calm, Mr. Bright," Laloo advised him. "I'm sure the colonel was only conferring with your man about the ongoing efforts to stop the city's growth."

"They can confer with my ass, the both of them."

"Where is Argos now?" Stake asked.

"They were still down in the lounge—the officers' dining room, whatever they call it. All the stuffed suits who crossed over to check on their business ventures came here to tour the base, so Gale could reassure them there's still a strong security force in place. Yeah, I'm real reassured, myself. What about my business venture, huh? Who's looking out for me? I tagged along with them and I saw the hate in the eyes of even the ones who didn't openly accuse me. But when Argos started in, I couldn't hold back anymore, and that's when his machine grabbed me. Maybe the other one would have come after me, too, if my KeeZee hadn't jumped in. Good thing Argos called them off or my boy would have had them apart in seconds."

Stake turned to Ami and said, "I'd like to take a walk down to the officers' mess, if you don't mind."

"Hungry again so soon, huh?"

"Sure, and why should I have to eat in the mess hall? I was a corporal once, remember?"

"We're going to leave Brian here, right?"

"What? No. Mr. Bright said there's a tour today. So Brian gets the full tour, too."

THE PARTY WAS breaking up in the hallway outside the officers' dining room, and a diverse party it was. Stake didn't know which individual to look at first. Besides Colonel Dominic Gale, Captain Rick Henderson, and chief ambassador to the Jin Haa nation, Margaret Valsalva—whom Stake knew only from VT—there were two human males in five-piece suits, one female in a somewhat more feminine but still severe pant suit, a Jin Haa cleric, and two robots. The robots were almost exactly the same model as the one Timothy Leung had named Magnus, with chrome-bright segmented neck, waist section, and flexible arms and legs, but the head, chest, pelvic section and hands and feet were of a green plastic as clear as hard candy, instead of honey colored. Their bio-engineered brain masses could be viewed through their transparent green skulls but Stake found himself looking instead at their sharp-fingered hands, for traces of blood.

Stake couldn't be sure, for the cleric's lack of a face, but he felt the Jin Haa sensed their approach first, though the twin robots were the first to turn their heads, and Gale the first to speak.

"Well, look at this happy little family."

"I thought I'd take Brian for a walk," Ami said, and Stake was embarrassed for her at the bright nervousness in her tone, "and I figured maybe our guests might like to meet him."

"And why did you figure that, exactly, Ami?"

Before she could speak, one of the business-suited men grinned and said, "This isn't the little boy who was cloned by Bright's process, is it? Oh my Lord... look at him! It's uncanny!"

"Uncanny," echoed the other business-suited man.

Rick Henderson stepped in for introductions. "Everyone, you've met our science chief, Ami Pattaya. The boy—as you guessed, Mr. Shabo—is the clone we're calling Brian. And this gentleman is a friend of mine I brought in to help with identifying Brian and the other two cloned remains: Jeremy Stake. Jeremy and I served together in the Blue War."

"And with whom are you affiliated, Mr. Stake?" asked the second businessman. "Some government agency, or..."

"I'm a hired investigator."

"Oh, really? You mean, as in private eye? Oh how quaint!"

"That's why I became one. It seemed the quaint thing to do."

Henderson hastened to resume the introductions. "Jeremy, this is Richard Argos, the owner of the aptly named corporation Argos, which as you probably know processes and supplies sinon gas, with branches on Earth, Oasis, and other worlds. And here we have Penelope Godfrey, vice-president of operations for the Greenview Corporation. They're a lumber company."

"The view is more blue than green here," Stake said, "though neither, once the trees are cut down."

"We replant new trees constantly, Mr. Stake," Godfrey said icily.

"A little humor—forgive me."

"And this gentleman," Henderson went on, gesturing toward the man who had exclaimed over Brian, his face a ruddy red and his snow white hair rising from his head like a dollop of whipped cream right down to the single curl at the top, a style popular among business types of late, "is Hassan Shabo, owner of Shabo Bio-comestibles."

"Ah," Stake said, "bio-comestibles. You manufacture deadstock." He was familiar with these operations from a case he had worked on last year, the one that had got very ugly and inspired Thi Gonh to travel to Punktown to lend him support. Deadstock, as they were nicknamed, were bio-engineered meat animals such as cows, pigs, chickens, Kalian glebbi, and so on, but grown without heads, usually without limbs, often without any bones or internal organs, not to mention fur or feathers. Stake didn't mind eating them, but he sure hadn't enjoyed seeing the pathetic creatures in their living state—if it could be called living. He knew it was better than raising and slaughtering natural animals with brains that could register fear and pain, but shooting a child who was in a coma as opposed to a child who was normal and active would still be monstrous to him.

"Yes," Shabo said, "that's right—our specialty being Sinan's yubos. We're not only introducing yubo meat to the Earth Colonies, but selling the Jin Haa people themselves yubo meat that's produced as deadstock instead of raised in the conventional sense, to show them it can be a more affordable and practical process. I'm hoping to open a plant here next year, which will also provide a lot of Jin Haa citizens with employment. And did you know we supply all the meat that you folks eat here at the Colonial Forces base and the Earth Colonies embassy? Speaking of which, you just missed a very tasty dinner, Mr. Stake. Is that S-t-e-a-k?"

"Afraid not." Stake was impressed, if that were the word, with how readily businessmen like Shabo leapt into their spiel, as if every set of ears might be attached to a potential investor.

"There were two other visitors representing their businesses," Henderson said, "but I'm afraid you just missed them. Have you met Margaret Valsalva before?"

"Can't say that I have." Stake shook her hand.

"Thanks for coming to Sinan to help us all out with this mystery, Mr. Stake. We'll rest more easily when we know what this poor child's name really is. The other two who weren't resurrected, as well."

"And this," Henderson indicated the Jin Haa cleric, "is Abbot Hoo, one of the most esteemed religious leaders of the Jin Haa nation."

Instead of the traditional blue robes that most Sinan clerics wore, Abbot Hoo's were a shimmering orange, as if to defiantly identify himself as a Jin Haa. There was another article on his person that set him apart from the common cleric: around his neck, what appeared to be a woman's fur stole, which lifted its head to blink at Stake suspiciously. In his service days, they had called these limbless animals worm sloths, and Stake recalled hearing their slow rustle outside the windows of barracks and the cheap Di Noon hotels he had stayed in during R&R excursions, as the animals slowly and sinuously made their way up the outer walls—their gummy undersides adhering them to the surface—in search of night insects they caught with long, similarly sticky tongues. Stake had seen them turned into pocketbooks, with their tails sewn to their snouts to form a shoulder strap, but never worn as a living accessory. He noted the glistening mucus that smeared the abbot's neck, like the lubrication of a hangman's noose.

"Honored," he said, bowing a little, his eyes drawn irresistibly to the spiraling orifice that was what the holy man had in lieu of a face, like a portal to a lightless afterlife. The monk nodded his head, upon which rested the usual little three-cornered hat, and Stake heard the faintest of wheezes from within that crater-like visage.

"The abbot works closely with me, Mr. Stake," Argos explained, "to insure that our gas-collecting processes within the Jin Haa burial systems are always done with respect, and without disturbing the bodies or the tunnels they're entombed in."

As striking a figure as Hoo was, and as menacing as were the similarly silent robots, it was Argos who most commanded Stake's attention. Richard Argos was young for a mogul, not yet forty, and looked almost unnaturally fit, skin tanned and smooth, body as burly and muscled as a movie gladiator's. Too perfect; Stake figured it for the work of drugs, or even body implants, rather than hard work in a gym. His head was shaved bald, proudly displaying its bumpy contours as if they were lumps won in street brawls. He had two ports in the right side of his skull, doubtlessly for serious immersion in the ultranet, but nothing was plugged into them just now. Argos's eyebrows were as thread thin and arched as those of a drag queen.

"That's very considerate. Very respectful," Stake muttered absentmindedly, staring at Argos's eyebrows. He was feeling a bit of fever again, a little pain focused at the bridge of his nose.

"And speaking of the tombs, you served beside our Captain Henderson, eh? As a deep penetration operative?"

"Yes..."

"Well, then I have to thank you! My company, of course, started up during the Blue War, and so you and the others who helped set up those first gas-siphoning apparatuses in the Ha Jiin tunnels were, in a way, working for me." Argos's broadest smile yet.

That concept so repelled Stake that for a moment he was at a loss for words. Margaret Valsalva broke in just then to announce, "Everyone, we'll be heading back to the embassy shortly."

"It was nice to meet you, Mr. Stake." Argos shook his hand with a crushing grip, then the businessman turned to shake hands with Ami. "My dear. A pleasure, as always." Finally, he smiled down at Brian and pinched his plump cheek. "You are the adorable one, aren't you?"

Seeing Argos pinch Brian's cheek made Stake's flush of fever intensify. A wave of nausea rolled over in his gut.

Argos linked Penelope Godfrey's arm flirtatiously, speaking close to her ear, as the party began to drift off down the hall, chattering amongst itself. The robot bodyguards turned their candy green heads in unison to look back at Stake with dead silvery eyes.

As soon as Argos had moved away from Stake and Ami, Colonel Gale swept in on them like an eagle, and hissed to the science chief, "What were you thinking parading the kid in front of the investors like that? They're spooked enough by what's going on without meeting this eerie little fucker." Ami started to speak up, but Gale cut her off with, "We'll discuss this more, later." He then turned to Stake, took his arm none too gently, and pulled him a few steps aside. "And you. Where do you get off acting so superior to these people, smart mouth?"

"What do you mean? I'm the epitome of courtesy."

Gale spoke through his teeth. Stake found himself woozily watching his strip of goatee as he said, "I heard about your incident with the bender and your Ha Jiin traitor. Is the poison getting to you? Or maybe it's her. She must be one incredible fuck, to mess up your mind like this after all these years. Maybe I should have a go at her myself sometime, huh?"

Stake's mind, and eyes, sharpened. "I wouldn't try that if I were you."

"Oh, and is that a threat?"

"Sound advice. I don't think your chances of surviving an encounter with that person would be too good."

"I see. But you've survived her, huh? I guess it must be that charming personality of yours."

Stake wanted to say that Ami Pattaya seemed to find him charming enough, but he held his tongue.

"Coming, colonel?" Henderson asked from a bit down the hall.

Gale glared at Stake for a final beat before clomping off to join the others. Stake shifted his eyes to Argos, and called, "It was nice to meet you, Dink."

Richard Argos stopped in his tracks, his back broad, bald head glowing in the overhead lights. He turned to face Stake slowly, smiling oddly. Then he walked back in Stake's direction. Over his shoulder he asked, "Can I catch up with you others in five minutes?"

"Take your time, Mr. Argos," Valsalva said. The others were still chatting. "We'll wait."

As Argos approached, Stake said to Ami, "Why don't you take Brian back to the lab? Sorry about Gale."

"So am I," she said. "Very sorry about Gale." She steered Brian off down the hall in the opposite direction.

Argos stepped close to Stake, still wearing the strange smile. "Excuse me, detective, what did you call me?"

"Sorry, I didn't mean to speak with such familiarity."

"And how did you come to be familiar with that nickname?"

"As we were talking, I remembered that you won the BBB competition, oh, about eighteen years ago. I've always enjoyed following that on VT."

"You have quite the memory. So from that you recognized me? Personally, I think I look a lot different than I did back in college."

"You surely do, but come on... you're the gas magnate Richard Argos! I've seen a lot of articles about you over the past seventeen years or so. I know you used to call yourself Dink Argosax. But you've sort of reinvented yourself since those days, haven't you?"

"We're always evolving, Mr. Stake, aren't we? Who wants to stand in one place and stagnate? You have to know when to adapt to new opportunities. For instance, if David Bright had any kind of vision he'd be turning this disaster to his advantage. Look at that kid. Bright's stumbled on a new technique of cloning human cells, and all he's doing is lamenting about his stupid little construction outfit."

"You've adapted pretty nicely, though—from a young researcher for Wonky Science, to the owner of the most important supplier of sinon gas in the colonies."

Argos cocked his head a little, showing that funny smile again. "And where did you get *that* name?"

"From one of the articles I read. I can't remember where, exactly." Stake kept glancing down the hall at the others, and he knew he must appear suspiciously fidgety and evasive, but he was doing his best not to lock onto Argos's face. He had, however, stolen some shots of it with his wrist comp, while lifting his arm to rub at his lips.

"Really? I can't remember reading about Wonky Science in any particular article about me, either."

"Well, there was that mishap at Wonky Science, I remember. Researchers killed. Others injured. Were you hurt, yourself?"

"I'm afraid I can absolutely not discuss that subject at all, Mr. Stake. Honestly. If you know anything about that, then you know we were government contractors. I have to maintain an oath of silence."

"Sorry to hear that. It's an interesting topic."

"And you're an interesting man. Captain Henderson must feel you're one important private dick, in fact, to have introduced all of us to you like that."

"Rick understands me. He could tell I'd want to know who everybody was."

"Know us for what? I thought you were here to look into dead people."

"Well, what I've been finding is people who've been reborn as new people."

"Hm."

Glancing again at the others engaged in conversation, Stake noted how Abbot Hoo and the two robots faced toward Argos and himself. Though their postures were erect, the robots looked ready to bolt to their master's defense at the slightest provocation. Stake nodded toward them as he asked Argos, "The other investors don't have personal bodyguards?"

"They're not in the same position I am. As cooperative as most of the Jin Haa have been, there are still those who resent my company, especially in the current climate. Death threats are common."

"David Bright has his own bodyguard, too, for the same reason. I understand your bodyguards and his even had a bit of a run-in with each other, during dinner."

"Do you know Bright? Seen him lately? The man has absolutely lost it."

"He's absolutely lost his shirt. He's under tremendous stress."

"That's big business for ya; if you're gonna cry, then don't play with the big boys."

"Is Hoo something of a bodyguard to you, too, being the buffer between your operation and the Jin Haa?"

Argos looked down the hall at the holy man. "He's a controversial figure, so much so that there are even other Jin Haa clerics who would like to see him dead for working with us. But they're living in the dark ages, like all the Ha Jiin clerics. You have to adapt to the times."

"Sort of like how the land is adapting to the times."

"Hey, I'm as upset about Bluetown as anybody; don't lump me together with that ass Bright just because I'm on Sinan to make a living. His out of control monstrosity threatens to cut me off at the knees! Anyway, yeah, my friend Hoo is trying to calm the rest of his kind—mediate not only between us and the clerics, but us and the common people. He's appealing to the other powerful abbots to remain level-headed through all this."

"It's funny, though, that a man of his position would still align himself with an Earther, seeing how this Earth Colonies project has run so amuck. I mean, what do he and his followers get from essentially selling their ancestors' souls, as they think of sinon gas, to outsiders as product? Do they see a cut of the money?"

"Well, the clerics and the politicians are in a close relationship. A man with no face might not have a lot of desire for money, but a politician with two faces does." Argos smiled at his own cleverness. "And face or no face, every man likes power, Mr. Stake. That's what attracts these mystical types to the order. Tapping into that celestial power."

"Still seems like a big sell-out for someone who's devoted enough to let his face rot away."

"I don't pretend to know everything that goes on in Hoo's head. Let's face it—pardon the pun—they're aliens."

"Well, I can understand why some of his own kind would be upset enough to want to see him come to harm. Do your robots look after him, too?"

"It's not like me and Hoo are roommates, Mr. Stake—ours is a platonic relationship. No, the robots are wholly mine. These monks have their own bag of tricks to protect themselves. They can make sounds that'll have your brain oozing out of your ears, and a lot of them have developed PSI powers through sheer force of will. You see his pet, there?"

Both men looked. As if it understood their words, the worm sloth lifted its head again and ran its tongue over one of its huge eyes. Stake had the unsettling sense that, telepathically linked with the creature as the cleric was, he could to some extent see through those eyes. "Yeah," he said. "They can get into the minds of animals. Some say, even people."

Argos kept his voice low. "Right. They're scary buggers, and I wouldn't want to tangle with one of them. Especially one of Hoo's rank."

"Richard," called Ambassador Valsalva, "I'm sorry, but we're about ready to leave now."

Argos shook Stake's hand again, his grip even more punishing than before. "It was nice chit-chatting with you, Mr. Stake. Glad you enjoyed watching me win the Better Booby-trap competition all those years ago."

"Like I say, that's always been fun to follow. Did you know that as deep penetration operatives, Captain Henderson and I were trained to rig actual booby-traps in the jungle?"

"Well, then—maybe we'll just have to test our skills against each other sometime." Argos gave Stake a mock military salute, and then strode powerfully off down the hallway to rejoin the others.

"We already are," Stake mumbled.

CHAPTER NINETEEN
CAMOUFLAGE

IN HIS ROOM within the Colonial Forces base, Jeremy Stake again examined the handgun that Thi Gonh had stuffed into his trouser pocket while he'd been unconscious, and the two clips of solid projectiles and green plasma rounds respectively. He paced the room while getting a feel for the pistol, pointing it here and there.

The handgun's entire surface was an odd, pale glossy gray, and he recognized the type of weapon this was. Like the device that Colonel Gale had shown Henderson—supposedly recovered with the three Bluetown clones—that could render a soldier invisible by rerouting light rays, the gun's composition used metamaterials to screen itself from weapons scanners such as those at the Colonial Forces base. It was an illegal weapon, and expensive, and Stake figured Thi must have acquired it from a serious black market dealer. From having followed news stories and articles about Sinan over the years, he was aware there was a powerful Ha Jiin crime lord called Don Tengu, and he supposed Tengu's people might be able to supply such

275

a sophisticated weapon to a simple Ha Jiin farm owner. But why would she even need one with this quality? Maybe this was one of the weapons she had acquired before coming to Punktown to aid Stake last year when she'd learned that his life was at risk from dangerous enemies. He'd always figured she'd bought the sniper rifle she had used at that time from a Punktown weapons dealer. Now he wasn't so sure.

Thoughts of the invisibility cloak returned Stake to the subject of the equipment and uniform fragments Gale claimed had been recovered, compared with what Captain Yengun had seen. So Stake put away his new handgun, and turned his attention to two other instruments instead. One was his wrist comp, brimming with files. The other was Rick Henderson's own hand phone, which he had let Stake borrow within the past half hour.

The captain had offered to try Persia Barbour himself this time. Stake had said no—there was someone else he wanted her to meet.

PERSIA BARBOUR DID not pick up her call, but since he was using Henderson's phone he was not blocked and found he could leave a message, so he started.

"Mrs. Barbour, my name is Jeremy Stake. We spoke before—sort of. As I was trying to tell you, I'm a private investigator hired by Captain Rick Henderson of the Colonial Forces to look into a very strange matter on the planet Sinan, where the remains of three—"

Persia Barbour came on, cutting him off as she snapped, "Who are you? You're not the same man who called me before."

"I'm a mutant, Mrs. Barbour. I suffer a condition known as *Caro turbida*. It means 'confused flesh.' I can take on the appearance of other people. I had originally planned to show you a photograph of a little boy when I called you next, or even try to have the boy himself beside me. But then I thought it would be better if I adopted this boy's appearance myself. Since he's a child of about five years old in development, I can't match his proportions exactly. What you're seeing is the best I can do. But I figured, maybe the combination of his face and my face would give a kind of representation of what this child would look like as an adult."

"Oh my God," the woman choked, putting the fingertips of both hands to her lips.

"So you tell *me*, Mrs. Barbour—who am I? Who am I to you? Because I know I look like one of the three people who died in that teleporter accident at Wonky Science, and there's a one-in-three chance that right now I look like your late husband Lewton Barbour."

She looked away and gasped a sob. But she didn't disconnect.

"So it is. It is him."

"I saw it on VT," she got out shakily. "I saw the clone. I've seen pictures of my husband as a child, but I didn't recognize him at first. But then I thought, Sinan…"

"We'll get to the Sinan part. So you already knew the clone was of your husband, but you didn't come forward to identify him?"

Persia turned her eyes back to the screen gingerly, as if afraid what she'd see there were her husband's remains as they had appeared when they'd been rotting under the Ha Jiin soil, before the living pseudopod of Bluetown had slithered along. "How can you do this to me?" she managed.

"How can you let this situation remain unresolved?"

"Do you really want me to cut you off, Mr. Stake?"

"You can't do that. Now I know the identity of one of the clones found in Bluetown. It's your responsibility to tell me the names of the other two so we can put this matter to rest—and decide what the best future for this child could be."

"I won't talk about it anymore."

"Look, Mrs. Barbour…"

"I won't talk on the phone! If you want to discuss it, all right, but not like this! You're on Sinan? Well you'll have to come to Punktown."

"I believe this is a safe channel."

"Dung. There's no such thing. Come to see me in Punktown; it's the only way."

Christ, Stake thought, Mrs. Henderson was going to wonder what her husband was doing with all their money on Sinan. "All right… all right. Where and when?"

"I have your number. I'll call you again in two days. Will you be here by then?"

"I'll do my best."

"Then get moving. Two days."

She was gone. Only when her image blinked out did Stake realize a headache had crept up from behind to tackle him. His hand went to his forehead involuntarily. Maybe, without knowing it, his touch compressed a certain single nerve just enough, a button under his skin, because that was when the movie began playing behind his eyes.

He was on hands and knees, crawling behind another man through tall blue grass, rubbery blades with knife edges, wet with condensation. He was able to see in the dark through his special goggles, his helmet camouflaged like the uniform of the man ahead of him. The man stopped, held up a hand, and Stake halted with his hands inches from the other man's boots. This soldier got to his feet but kept low as he ducked behind a thick black tree trunk caught in a web of blue lianas. One liana hanging down from the tree's branches swept across Stake's face when he peeked up over the top of the grass. For a moment, he swept his hand at it frantically, for some reason thinking it was the stinging tentacle of a hovering jellyfish.

He saw the other soldier at the tree, leaning around its wrinkled flank slowly to see what lay on the other side.

A whoosh, like a bird of prey swooping down through the air, an owl that had been patiently waiting to launch its attack, ready to seize with sharp talons. Stake never saw what made the whooshing sound, but he did see that his companion still squatted at the base of the tree. If he hadn't been looking through his goggles, he might not have noticed that the man no longer had a head. The body gently tumbled backwards, dropped out of sight into the grass as if submerging into blue water.

A thump as something dropped into the grass closer to Stake, and it rolled until it came to a stop just in front of him. He parted the tall blades with his hands, and looked down at a severed head. Its helmet had been knocked away when the booby-trap was sprung, helping Stake to identify the features. The face was unnatural in a way that was hard to put a finger on, as though this were the head of a very realistic mannequin.

It was the disembodied head of Timothy Leung. But without being hooked up to its life support, the eyes did not follow him, the lips did not move. Well, only for a second or two did the eyes turn up toward him. Only for a second did the lips part to speak, before they went still and the unuttered words were gone like a wisp of black smoke.

"AMI," STAKE SAID into his wrist comp, "care to grab some dinner, off the base for a breath of fresh air? Away from your boyfriend's loving gaze?"

"Yeah," she said from the minuscule screen, "great idea. Especially the away from my boyfriend part. He just left the lab and my ears are still bleeding from him yelling at me about Brian. Bernard actually came into the room, afraid he might hurt me."

"I'm sure I've said this before, but it bears saying again—I don't know what you see in that wanker."

"Army brat, Jer. I can't get away from Daddy, I guess."

"Well, you can for dinner, at least. But would you mind meeting me there? I have some things to do first. I was thinking the restaurant in the Cobalt Temple Hotel."

"Are you crazy? Expensive!"

"Hey, it's my friend's money, so I'm being generous. Meet me in an hour? I'll phone in a reservation."

"Okay, why not? Sounds romantic." She narrowed her lids and spread a slow smile.

"Great—see you there."

ON THE SCIENCE lab monitor, Ami Pattaya's striking brown-skinned face, with its vaguely Asian eyes, lost none of its appeal despite the billed camouflage cap into which she had apparently bundled all her silky black hair. She narrowed her lids with a slow, sensuous smile. "Hey, cutie," she said to her primary assistant, Bernard. "Can I ask you a dumb question?"

Bernard smiled back at her through her own screen, which he didn't know was much smaller. "You're going to the Cobalt Temple in *fatigues?*"

"I haven't left yet. Listen, I know this is going to sound stupid, but with all the chaos going on I can't remember where the Bluetown artifacts were put away the last time. Not the ones Dom showed Henderson; I mean the real ones. Did Dom take those back, or did we keep them in the lab?"

"They were in the usual place, last I knew."

Ami hesitated a beat or two. "The lab."

"Right."

"Do me a favor, hon?"

"Say again? There's a lot of static—I can barely hear you."

"Really? Must be a glitch in the system." Ami spoke a bit more loudly. The science chief moved her arm, bearing a wrist comp, a bit further away from a cheap multipurpose scanning device that rested on the edge of the bed. Its field, as presently adjusted, was disrupting the vidphone image with snow and distorting the audio as well, garbling her voice. "Can you bring the stuff to me? I'm in Jeremy Stake's quarters, and I want him to have a look at it but I'm afraid Dom might walk in on us in the lab if we check it out there."

Several tense seconds, as Ami waited for a puzzled Bernard to say something like, "But Ami, you know I don't have access to that cabinet," or to ask her for a password. Instead, though he still look concerned, the young tech said, "Um, aren't you afraid he's listening in on us right now? You told me you thought he was tapping your calls sometimes."

"Good, let him listen in—I've been wanting to break up with that rat-faced son of a bitch anyway. He isn't half the man I am."

Bernard chuckled uncomfortably. "You're the boss. But I hope he doesn't blame me if he catches us. Remember, I'm just following orders."

"Right, soldier, so get that stuff over here on the double."

BASED ON THE number Ami had related, Bernard found the investigator's assigned room readily enough, buzzed outside, and Ami promptly cracked the door to lean out a little bit. "Hey, cutie," she whispered, extending a hand for the specimen box he carried.

"I switched the stuff to a new box," he said, "in case someone saw me in the halls."

"I can see that; good thinking. Thanks, hon." She drew the box inside.

"Are you sure this is a good idea?" he whispered back at her. "Gale told you not to talk to the private eye or Captain Henderson about these pieces."

"Things have changed, Bernard. This has all got way too big now for us to keep buried. Trust me, okay? I'll see you in the morning."

"Okay... you know best."

She blew a kiss at the tech through the crack as the door closed between them.

JEREMY STAKE REMOVED the camouflaged cap he had stolen from the troop craft before the descent into Bluetown's underground, and no long silky hair spilled out of it. Still wearing the camouflage fatigues he had kept from that day, he shut off the battered old hand scanner he'd used on many a prior case, to mask his voice during vidphone calls. He then turned his attention to the specimen box he had set down on the mattress of his narrow bed.

As soon as he opened it, and even before he removed each item and spaced them on his blanket, he could see the artifacts bore no relation to the military equipment that Gale had shown Henderson while Stake was back in Punktown.

Scraps of clothing, yes, but the tatters of one or more black jumpsuits rather than blue-camouflaged military uniforms. Three mismatched boots; again, not standard military issue. And two identical bracelets. Stake turned one of them in his hands. They were of pale blue metal, but otherwise looked like the black ID bracelet that Gale had sent a soldier to give Stake upon his arrival at the base, and which Stake had declined wearing, not wanting his movements to be tracked. But Stake now opened this bracelet and clasped it on his right wrist. He wondered if he could use the little comp on his left wrist to interface with the bracelets and tap into their contents; they had to be programmed with information that would identify two of the three clones, whether Persia Barbour followed through with their rendezvous in two days or not.

He smiled, not without bitterness, to know unequivocally that Ami had been helping to obstruct his investigation all along. But he had finally come to that certainty even before he'd opened the specimen box, anyway—just as he was now one hundred percent certain that David Bright was not faking his dismay about Bluetown, and not intentionally responsible for its virus. He had to cut Ami some slack, though. She worked for Gale, and slept with Gale. And she no doubt hadn't seen any great harm in keeping the authentic salvaged gear hidden—aside from standing in the way of locating Brian's loved ones. Stake was sure she had studied the bracelets, probably even accessed their data. Which meant she might have known Brian was Lewton Barbour for some time now.

Stake had taken a chance about whether or not Bernard would also be aware of the gear, but he was Ami's assistant, after all. If it had turned out that Bernard didn't know about it, Stake would have had Ami stammer something about being even more befuddled from all the chaos than she'd thought, and to never mind—she'd tell him later.

The question now was what to do with the gear. He wanted to give Henderson a look at it, but he didn't dare keep it long. When Bernard saw Ami in the lab tomorrow, he would very likely bring up the matter. Before then, Stake figured it best to have replaced it, especially should Gale come looking for it. He further decided that tonight, when he met Ami at the Cobalt Temple, he should admit to her what he'd done before Bernard could talk to her. She wouldn't like it, but he suspected she was less in sympathy with Gale lately than she had been before. Stake would treat her to an extra nice dinner. Afterwards, maybe a drink or two as they watched a little karaoke in the bar off the lobby. Maybe they could even splurge on a room in the hotel for a single night. Stake just hoped they didn't run into Bright, lest he launch into another rant about Argos.

Stake used his wrist comp to take still shots of every item, and then he replaced them in the container. All except the bracelet secured to his right wrist—he was hesitant to return it. Might he compromise, and hang onto just this one piece so he could show it to Rick, and so that he might peek into it or even copy its contents into his wrist comp?

Stake kept the bracelet on after all, on impulse more than anything else, and called Bernard again—remembering at the last moment to activate the disrupting scanner again and return his cap to his head. What would Bernard have thought of Ami with short, bristly dark hair?

"Cutie, sorry to bother you, but could you come back here to take this stuff and put it away again for the night? We've had our look, and now we're heading out for the Cobalt Temple."

"So how much did you tell your friend?" Bernard asked, sounding a little jealous. Why shouldn't he be in love with the lovely but lonely Ami like everyone else?

Stake as Ami gave Bernard a mischievous smile. "Sometimes I wonder how much *you* know, Bernard. Maybe you've learned some things that even I haven't."

"What? I know next to nothing. You won't tell me, so who else is going to?"

"Well, I don't want to underestimate you. You're such an inquisitive little boy." So, it probably wouldn't be worth the effort to dig the young tech about Wonky Science. Stake's meeting with Persia Barbour would be soon enough. In the meantime, he'd be late if he didn't hurry, and he needed to lose his date's appearance before he got there.

At least, until he was in bed with her at the hotel, and mirrored her face again. When all other sorts of love failed, people could at least love themselves. Try to, anyway.

CHAPTER TWENTY
SMOKE

At the entrance to the Cobalt Temple's lounge, a stunning Jin Haa hostess—taller and curvier than was typical, though the curves might have been surgically enhanced—smiled at Stake as he stepped out of the hotel's restaurant in order to take a call on his wrist comp. He did not smile back at her, lest he further anger Ami Pattaya, who was angry enough after what he had revealed to her over dinner. It looked like they wouldn't be sharing a hotel room tonight, after all.

It was Rick Henderson, calling Stake back. After Stake had requested the check, he had phoned Henderson and left a message, asking him to meet him at the Cobalt Temple to hear about the latest development in the case. Better there, in the event that there might be people listening in on them at the CF headquarters. Henderson told Stake he was on his way, would be there in a few minutes. Stake lowered his arm and turned toward Ami, taking her by the elbow to guide her over to a white leather love seat discreetly screened by the fronds of potted blue plants, away from the hostess and the karaoke blasting out of the bar. Easily as striking as the hostess in a similarly clingy dress, the science chief plunked herself down, arms crossed, pouting like a sulky child.

"Rick is going to hear it from me," she fumed. "He's as at fault in this as you are, for hiring you in the first place and letting you use your unethical methods."

Stake settled beside her. "Was it ethical to deceive him, a Colonial Forces officer in charge of an investigation, by keeping vital information a secret?"

"I was following the orders of a senior Colonial Forces officer."

"You act like you care about Brian, but all this time you knew the truth about him."

"What benefit is it, really, to reunite a five year-old child with his forty year-old wife? What's she going to do, adopt her husband? He doesn't know her. He'd benefit just as much from being adopted by a caring stranger. So don't you dare make it sound like I don't care about that boy!"

"Was there anything in the two ID bracelets besides personal information? Anything about why they were teleporting to Sinan?"

"Aside from the identification data for Lewton Barbour and another person named Kiyoshi Nihei, they were mostly transmitters, for the teleportation scans to home in on when it was time to bring them back again. The transmissions were extremely powerful, as I guess they'd have to be to beam back to the source of the teleportation. Not that it's such a big deal now, when we can send vidphone calls back and forth from Oasis to Sinan like it's just the planet next door."

"But nothing about the nature of the mission?"

"I suppose these Wonky scientists just wanted to develop a new process for extradimensional teleportation, like that Leung guy told you, right? So we wouldn't have to be so dependent on the technology of the Bedbugs."

"Ami, I've had another episode with the bender poison, but in the first one I saw Brian and he said something like, 'he wears the singing bracelet.' I think that's significant."

"Well, I'll tell you, it was a covert type of project, you know, so the data was encrypted; I suppose in case they got captured by the locals or whatever. The encryption's been hard to crack, but it also appears to be corrupted—either through time, or maybe even corrupted during the teleportation process. So there could be more on the bracelets, but there's also the matter of the third one. Assuming, as I think we must, that all three people who teleported were wearing these things, we're still missing one of them."

"The Ha Jiin did the initial excavation of the pits, but they've let our people look some more, correct?"

"Yes, and the ground was scanned pretty carefully, Jeremy. But a lot of time had gone by. The smart matter might have dragged some of this stuff along as it advanced, displacing it widely. Or animals could have dismembered the bodies, taking more bits of gear and the missing bracelet along with them. They may even have been stripped of weapons and equipment, if some Ha Jiin people encountered them. We don't know if they arrived dead, or were killed once they got there."

"Has Argos been asked to try to read the bracelets?"

"Yes. He's the one who came in and helped me get out of them as much as I have. But he said it was another of the Wonky people who programmed the bracelets, and she'd be more adept at sorting them out."

"She? Would that be Barbour's wife, Persia?"

"Yes. And I don't know, but listening to Argos it sounds like she hasn't wanted to become involved."

Stake didn't trust Ami enough to tell her about the meeting in Punktown he had planned with Lewton Barbour's widow. He hated not trusting her. It was why he had resisted believing she was involved in matters to this extent—a critical failing on his part. Not prudent, not professional. Still, he liked her, and not just the crossed legs exposed by the provocative dress she had chosen for their date. At another time... if he hadn't again encountered Thi Gonh... who could say what he might have felt toward her?

Ami sat up and craned her neck, gazing toward the lobby's front wall of glass, facing out upon one of Di Noon's more upscale streets, dazzling with the light of night traffic. "Is that them?" she asked. "I think a CF vehicle just pulled up."

Stake rose from the love seat. "Come on," he said, heading across the expansive lobby for the front doors. There were two conventional doors flanking two revolving doors in the center. As Stake strode toward them, he could see that Ami was right: a pair of soldiers in camouflage had climbed out of a CF helicar along with Captain Rick Henderson. The Harbinger lifted out of sight, so that the driver might park it elsewhere, while Henderson and his bodyguards headed for the doors themselves. Through the glass, Henderson spotted Stake and waved. And through the glass, Stake saw a large thin animal come bounding out of the darkness. A second dog-like creature leaped onto the hood of a hoverlimo idling at the curb, and then launched itself into the air.

"Jesus," Stake hissed, recognizing the animals at once, but it was Ami who said it first.

"Snipes!" she cried.

The first snipe, skeletal and hairless, a cadaverous blue, sprang onto one of the two bodyguards from behind, turning its head sideways to clamp its jaws on the back of his neck. He went down with the creature atop him. The man was carrying a Sturm AE-93 assault engine, but it was pinned under his own weight.

Stake bolted. It was relatively cool tonight and he wore an open button-up shirt over his T-shirt. Hidden by the outer shirt's tail, tucked into the rear of his waistband, was the scan-resistant pistol Thi had given him. As he moved, he pulled the gun out of hiding.

While the first snipe shook its head madly from side to side, jaws still locked on the back of the downed soldier's neck, Henderson wheeled around and was able to draw his own holstered pistol a moment before the dog that had leapt from the limo's hood hurled itself into his arms. Together, they fell backwards into one of the two automated revolving doors.

Stake saw a third snipe appear on the broad sidewalk outside the hotel. It had seemed to crawl out from under another hoverlimo with opaque windows that was stopped in the street. Then he noticed a door of the limo was partly open, and a fourth snipe slipped directly out of the luxury vehicle, hit the pavement with its red-glowing eyes already fixed on Henderson's second bodyguard, who had also whipped around to confront the attack. Before the car door closed, and with the snipe out of the way, Stake caught a glimpse of shimmering orange silk within.

He had planned to rush outside, but skidded to a stop and turned toward the revolving doors, in which Henderson had become trapped with one of the eerie blue canines. He had to have dropped his pistol, because he had the animal's scrawny throat in both hands, not so much trying to strangle it as hold the snapping jaws away from him, but the creature was thrashing violently and Stake didn't know how much longer Henderson could maintain his grip on it before it grabbed the captain by the throat instead. Flecks of blood had spattered the glass of the revolving doors, and snipe blood was neither red nor liquid once it hit the air.

The second bodyguard had decided on his assault engine's shotgun mode, and a blast from it sent the third snipe flying back through the air, folded and broken. A cloud of black smoke bloomed, and more smoke streamed from the shattered body that hit the sidewalk. Snipe blood when exposed to air was not unlike sinon gas, but was more like the black wisps from a Sinanese person's heart when riven. A haze spread like a spurt of octopus ink unfurling underwater.

The soldier didn't get off a second shot, however, before the fourth snipe threw itself onto him, fastening its jaws on his face. Man and dog barreled into one of the conventional doors with such momentum that they both crashed to the floor of the lobby beyond. Muffled, hysterical cries as the man tried to scream. The snipe did not make a sound, not even a growl, silent as an avenging ghost.

Henderson and the snipe he'd been holding off had spilled out of the revolving door together. Somehow the captain managed to remain on his feet, even though the snipe had latched itself onto one of his forearms and snapped its whole body like a whip as it tore into it. The snipe had already badly clawed his arms and neck with its forepaws and kicked at him with its lower legs, ripping his clothing and flesh. Under such an attack, he had no longer been able to hold onto the thing's neck.

A short distance away, Stake stopped, braced his whole body, and fired two quick shots from the pistol's clip of solid rounds. The bullets hit the creature in its chest, black smoke puffing from two neat holes. The snipe released Henderson at last and flopped wildly on the floor like a fish out of water. Even so, its jaws still gripped the man's severed left hand.

This time Stake aimed at the head. His first shot missed, whined off the floor, due to the animal's convulsions, but his third and fourth bullets hit it in the shoulder and temple respectively and the snipe went still, its jaws widening impossibly in death and giving one last quiver. Finally, the captain's hand had dropped free.

Outside, the first snipe raised its head from the neck of the soldier who'd gone down on his face. He wasn't moving. The snipe's muzzle right up to its eyes was slathered in dripping blood. It curled its lips at Stake.

Henderson, weaving dazedly, compressing his left wrist with his right hand, looked over at Ami and cried, "Don't!"

In being driven through one of the side doors, the other bodyguard had lost hold of his Sturm and it had skittered across the lobby's marble floor. Ami had darted forward to retrieve it. Hearing Henderson's cry, the snipe that had hold of the soldier's face lifted its eyes to the officer. Then it was letting go of the dying man, and lunging.

Stake whirled toward the animal, but Ami had deftly scooped up the gun, raised, and discharged it in one motion. Thunder and recoil; she was almost blown off her high heels. The buckshot caught the snipe in the hindquarters, so that it hit the floor and skidded toward Henderson, giving off a weird, piercing howl of agony and rage. Stake followed it with his pistol and fired three times. By the time the snipe had come to a stop, it was dead and largely obscured in whorls of noxious black gas.

Stake looked to Ami in surprise. *Army brat*, he thought.

He looked back toward the first snipe, but it was gone, its victim's blood pooling across the sidewalk. The hotel had a uniformed Jin Haa doorman, whom the snipes had oddly overlooked. He knelt by the body, while pedestrians timidly hung back at a distance.

Henderson slumped, crumpled. Stake saw him just as he fell, rushed to catch him too late. The captain hit the marble hard. While hunkered down beside his friend, now compressing the man's wrist himself to staunch the heavy flow of blood, Stake heard the clatter of nails on the floor behind him. Jerking around, he realized too late that the first snipe had not run off into the night. It had entered one of the revolving doors, below the level of its glass, and was now inside the lobby. Now charging toward Ami Pattaya... leaping into the air, jaws already spread wide like those of a striking snake.

It caught her by the throat, and her eyes went wide. They locked with Stake's eyes for one terrible second of shared comprehension. Her finger contracted on the assault engine's trigger and a burst of shotgun pellets shattered a basin holding huge glossy fronds. She dropped the bulky weapon after that. She dropped, too. Stake couldn't see her face, only her spasmodic legs as the snipe braced itself over her, shaking its head side to side. One of her pretty shoes was kicked off.

Stake let go of his friend's arm to aim his pistol with both hands, and fired. He hit the animal high enough in the back that the bullet would hopefully not pass through and hit Ami, unless it should be deflected off bone. The snipe released her to raise its head with a howl. The next slug struck it in the eye and punched out the other side of its head. With black smoke billowing out both eye sockets, the snipe flopped to one side and Stake was rushing to the small brown woman, who lay spreadeagled on the cold marble. Unmoving.

He crouched low, a hand flat on her belly. Her eyes were still wide, as if frozen in that moment of comprehension, but they no longer locked with Stake's. Blood poured from her savaged, gaping throat.

Stake glanced toward the front windows. The limo at the curb was still there, but the one that had stopped in the street was gone.

The doorman darted over, came to a stop above Stake. Numbly, the detective looked up at the Jin Haa and said, "Call the Colonial Forces base. Colonel Dominic Gale."

Then he looked down at Ami again, and realized he was holding her hand.

STAKE WAS SITTING on the love seat where he had sat with Ami not an hour before, cupping his head in both hands, when Colonel Gale finally came striding over to talk to him alone. Lifting his head, Stake saw that Gale's hands were stained in Ami Pattaya's blood, as were his own. And shouldn't that be the case, he thought? Hadn't they both involved her to the point of putting her in the direct path of danger?

Before Stake had half risen, Gale seized him by the front of his shirt, hoisted him to his feet, and threw him sideways to the floor. He didn't resist, even when Gale brought his boot up into his gut.

"Colonel!" one of his men said, starting forward, but Gale gave him a look that stopped him in his tracks.

Gale reached down to where Stake had openly left his gun on the cushion beside him, plucked it up and turned it in his fist. "Nice piece, Stake. And illegal as all fuck. Have you had this on my base? Huh? I could put you in a cell for this!"

"I'm sorry about Ami," Stake croaked, not looking up.

"What was she even doing here with you, huh?" The officer's voice was shaking. "Yeah... don't tell me, I don't want to know. What an idiot that little whore was! Look where it got her!"

Through gritted teeth Stake said, "Snipes in the middle of Di Noon, Gale. What does that mean to you? They were a weapon. They came out of a big white hoverlimo. Someone was trying to kill one or all of us. Rick, Ami, me..."

"Terrorists, I know. They use the clerics to control the snipes."

"Not terrorists, and not just any cleric. It was an assassination, and the cleric was Abbot Hoo."

"Shut your mouth! You know what you're saying? Hoo is a friend to the colonies—it's because of him we can harvest sinon! You've caused enough trouble without talking that dung. Listen good, Stake. If your friend Henderson dies, too, then he won't be able to protect you anymore, will he? In the meantime, I'm keeping your gun, and you're off the base for good, no matter if Henderson makes it or not. You'll never set foot on it again, you fucking understand me?"

Stake lifted his head to watch as the colonel clomped away, then from under him he slid out his left arm, which he had not so much tucked there to protect his belly as to hide the blue bracelet he still wore around his wrist.

CHAPTER TWENTY-ONE
CROSSING OVER

SALEM STREET WAS a fairly intact remnant of the pre-existent Choom town upon which the Earth colonists had superimposed Punktown, and so it retained the cobblestones and some of its brick architecture for a quaint, historical effect. Salem Street took the form of an open mall lined with upscale shops, always thronged with pedestrians but closed to vehicular traffic. Decorative trees were spaced along the sidewalks, and a fountain sprayed water into a pool upon which children floated seaworthy-looking pieces of trash.

Jeremy Stake sat on a bench, watching the children and remembering how mere days ago he had walked upon a blue-toned replica of these cobblestoned streets, bereft of all the people who poured into and out of the bright little shops. It was odd that instead of the Bluetown version seeming haunted and unnatural, now the original was the alien landscape, and these many people seemed to him like a population of ghosts. He felt invisible to them, an outsider, a mere observer, but one of the pedestrians detached herself from the crowd and approached him uncertainly.

"Are you... Mr. Stake?" she asked. She was a petite, attractive woman of about forty, with a small pale face and a luxuriance of thick dark curls. Sunglasses hid what Stake remembered as large dark eyes. She was expensively attired, and carried a shopping bag, though Stake took it to be a prop.

"Hello, Mrs. Barbour. Thanks for meeting with me."

"If it wasn't for that awful lime green shirt you said you'd be wearing, I wouldn't have known you. Who are you supposed to look like now?"

"Marlon Brando, an actor from the Twentieth Century. The way he looked in a film called *On the Waterfront*. I like it a lot." Stake didn't elaborate that his face had even cleverly copied the way the character's eyes were puffy with scar tissue from his boxing days, though it had only been makeup trickery in that ancient film—nothing like Stake's own trickery. "I've been dying for a coffee but I wanted to wait until you got here."

"Well—I'm here." She glanced around nervously.

Stake rose. "Good. Let's go over there." He pointed to a café that a sign identified as Beantown. "It's one of my friend Rick Henderson's favorite coffee shops in the city."

THEY SAT AT a little table in a corner. The atmosphere was warm and richly scented, as Punktown's moneyed minority lined up at the counter to order expensive concoctions or browsed the gift displays. Over the sound system came a female singing in Arabic; Stake recognized it as a Twenty-First Century recording from Natacha Atlas. It was indeed an afternoon for ghosts from the past. The bass-heavy Middle-Eastern beat resonated in his chest.

"Why are you so afraid, Mrs. Barbour?" he asked her bluntly. "And of whom?"

"The government, of course—for one. The work we were doing for them would have caused some controversy had it come to light. But more than them, I'm concerned about another person I used to work with at Wonky Science. Another who survived the mishap."

"Dink Argosax," Stake said. "Or these days, Richard Argos."

For a few seconds he couldn't read her face, and she hadn't removed her dark glasses, but her mouth was tight. "Tell me everything you know, Mr. Stake. Then I'll do the same."

He did so, culminating in the attack two days ago in the lobby of the Cobalt Temple. Hearing this part, Persia Barbour looked even paler than before. She fidgeted with her now empty coffee mug, pushing it about with her fingertips like a planchette on a Ouija board. "I'm sure it was Hoo," Stake said. "But Hoo acting on Argos's behalf. When we spoke, Argos could see I'm standing on his tail, and Henderson made trouble by hiring me. Ami, well, she was either just in the wrong place or else that was Gale's contribution—revenge on his unfaithful girlfriend for getting too close to me in more ways than one. But I don't know if Gale is in quite that deep with Argos and Hoo, and he seemed genuinely shaken up by what happened, so if Ami was an intentional target then maybe it's because Argos thought she looked too chummy with me and decided to eliminate her as a potential threat, too. But the question is, what is the exact threat we pose to him?"

"I'll get to that, now that it's my turn. But you see, Mr. Stake? This is why I was reluctant to speak with you before. Hearing this doesn't surprise me; I've been wary of Dink for some time. Did you know that two years ago, his wife drowned when they were vacationing together? There was some suspicion about the circumstances at the time, but with Argos's money the suspicions didn't go far. His wife was the biotech heiress, Helene Camus. So he doesn't just head Argos, now, but Camus Organics as well."

"I think I've heard of it. What do they do there?"

"A lot of research and development for other companies, but they've also released a variety of encephalon computers, for instance, and a few types of organic nanomites. It's all Dink's, with her gone. And I guess you haven't heard about Timothy, since you didn't mention it."

"Leung? Why—what do you mean?"

"His life support system crashed, and the attendants got to him too late. He's dead."

"Crashed." Stake snorted and looked about the shop, as if in search of one person who might believe such a story. "After all these years on life support, and it just happens to fail now, only days after he talked with me?"

"It didn't quite fail; they say his robot did something to it accidentally while making an adjustment, and shorted out the system. They can't look into the robot's memory, though, because it shorted out, too. Its brain was turned to mush."

"How convenient."

"Mm. Not to make you feel guilty, but I imagine after you revealed to Dink that you knew something about Wonky Science, he sent out feelers to find out how. He either learned that you talked with Timothy, by questioning staff at the complex he lived at, or else he just decided to do away with him whether you'd already talked to him or not. Looking at it now, I'm surprised Dink didn't take me and Timothy out of the picture years ago, but then again, he's been a happy man up until this Bluetown matter threatened his gas operation. Everything had been going his way. Now he's... upset. And I know Dink. He's obsessively competitive. He doesn't like to lose."

Stake massaged the center of his forehead with his fingers, as if rubbing sleep from a bleary third eye. "I saw it," he muttered. "I saw Leung die."

"What?"

He didn't relate his vision, instead asked, "You say Camus produces organic computers? Argos's body-guards are robots with encephalon computers. Maybe he was able to reprogram the brain of Leung's robot remotely, and ordered it to kill him. It had that type of system, itself."

"God... I didn't know all of that."

"Look, you should go into hiding," he told her. "Change your address."

"I'm way ahead of you. I'm staying in Miniosis now." It was Paxton's sister city, not all that distant relatively speaking, an even greater megalopolis in size though not nearly as rundown and crime-infested.

"I wouldn't rule out the government when it comes to dark deeds—I was part of some myself, when I was deep ops during the war—but I think this is all Argos. So now I want you to tell me why he feels he has to kill people over his past. What were your husband and the other two doing by teleporting to Sinan, Mrs. Barbour?"

"Well you know the background on Sinan, but let me go back to it anyway, because that's where this starts." So Persia skated over the history of the Earth Colonies' relationship with the planet Sinan, discovered by the Theta Agency research program seventeen years earlier with the aid of Bedbug transdimensional technology. The first field agents to journey there, led by a top Theta agent named Hector Tomas, had met the citizenry of the Ha Jiin nation but had also ventured into an emerging, smaller nation peopled by the Jin Haa ethnic class. Cynical critics of the forthcoming Blue War would say they couldn't tell the difference between the Ha Jiin and Jin Haa—they were reminded of the people Gulliver encountered, at war over which end of the egg to crack open—but the difference was crucial to the Earth Colonies. For one thing, the Ha Jiin tended to be religious conservatives, the Jin Haa generally more moderate. The Ha Jiin, wary and increasingly hostile toward the explorers, would not even permit Tomas's team to look in one of their burial tunnels, but the Jin Haa did. Tomas was intrigued by the bluish gas that rolled through the tunnel networks, which the Jin Haa claimed to be the spirits of their ancestors. This gas appeared to possess some remarkable qualities; for one thing, it was used to light the lamps that illuminated the sepulchers. So Tomas's crew gathered samples surreptitiously and brought them back with them when they returned to their own realm.

Shortly after this, the Earth Colonies government contracted Wonky Science.

"This is the part you don't know," Persia said. "Between the discovery of Sinan and the decision to support the Jin Haa."

"I know this much," Stake interrupted. "We wanted sinon gas, the Ha Jiin wouldn't even consider it, but the Jin Haa gave us access because we agreed to back them in the war."

"*Before* that," Persia told him sternly. "Listen. Before the colonies took that route and backed the Jin Haa, there was another plan to develop sinon gas, and that involved Wonky Science. For one thing, the colonies wanted to get people there covertly, without the Bedbugs, without even the Theta branch, who are under public scrutiny. So that was the first project: transdimensional teleportation to Sinan."

"When it went wrong and your lab caught fire, you told the press that the teleportation had been a test to send your husband and the others to Earth, using some new method. But actually, you were successful. You got your husband's team to Sinan. But how did they die there?"

"We never knew. I still don't. I suspect they arrived dead, or I don't think their bodies would have remained at that spot, unless natives discovered them there and buried them. But then, I don't think they'd have left anything like that." She pointed to the blue bracelet Stake wore on his wrist.

"What was the other part of the research, the project-within-a-project Leung hinted about?"

"That's what involved sinon gas. The government was keen to have access to it, once they'd studied its properties. But they didn't want to back a war to have it; not at first. When they realized it's a by-product of the decomposition of Sinanese bodies, they had another plan. Are you familiar with the word deadstock?"

"Very."

"Then you know it pertains to bio-engineered animal forms, mass produced as meat products, and this was something like that. Only, this idea involved bringing back tissue samples from a broad variety of Jin Haa people, dead and alive, so that a kind of Jin Haa deadstock could be developed and cloned in large numbers."

"You're saying… you mean, so they could be *killed?* And allowed to rot, to produce sinon gas?"

"Yes." Persia gave a sardonic smile. "Horrible, I know."

"Would these things at least have been without heads, like animal deadstock?"

"Boneless, maybe, but not brainless; the gas requires not just the decomposition of flesh, but the internal organs and brain."

"I can't believe they thought people wouldn't be in an uproar over something that inhumane!"

"They were going to try it and see. The idea was to make the Jin Haa deadstock at least look less than human—as I say, they'd probably have been bone-less—and to keep their brains simple and inactive."

"The Jin Haa would have been out for our blood!"

"It wouldn't have mattered. Once we had what we needed to start up the deadstock farms, we wouldn't have needed the Jin Haa or Sinan anymore."

"Jesus," Stake hissed, wagging his head. He looked away, had a thought, touched some keys on his wrist comp, and stared down at it.

"Wait, who are you calling?" Persia said, leaning forward.

"I'm not calling anyone. I have a photo of Brando in my files, and I'm staring at it to keep my lock on his features. I don't want to slip and start looking like you. Nothing personal."

She sat back. "Don't take it personal if I tell you you're starting to give me the creeps."

Without looking up, Stake said, "Okay, speaking of the creeps, this fucking unethical plan... it never started up? Because of what happened to your lab and your husband?"

"Right. Preliminary teleportation of robot probes and test animals had gone very smoothly, so my husband and two others were ready to give our process a go with human subjects."

"Who were the other two?"

"Kiyoshi Nihei and Johnny Esperanto. Nihei was a Theta agent who'd been on Tomas's team; the colonies wanted at least one Theta agent with transdimensional experience with us, and he had experience on Sinan. They felt they couldn't trust Tomas himself to agree to the project."

"I've read about Tomas. I think he'd have too much integrity to be part of that. And Esperanto?"

"A Red War veteran turned mercenary, for muscle if the team needed protection, and to help them navigate the jungle and get down into the tunnels."

"I can picture them taking the samples from corpses, but how about from live people? Was this muscle going to hold them at gunpoint while your husband took some tissue, then kill them to keep it quiet?"

"My husband had his limits to what he'd agree to, Mr. Stake. The plan was to approach rural people and gather samples in exchange for gold ingots they brought with them. They hoped they'd be back home before the authorities learned of their presence."

"But the teleportation went bad, the lab exploded, and you Wonky scientists were all but wiped out. The plan was dropped in favor of another—supporting the Jin Haa, and getting to Sinan using established technology."

"Right. Controversial, but probably still less problematic than the deadstock farm idea. Anyway, we Wonky survivors went our various ways, but Dink kept up his connection with the government. That's what led, quickly enough, to his creation of Argos."

"Did he maintain a connection with you?"

"He tried. He asked me out about a dozen times, but I declined. He always had a thing for me. In fact, Timothy—whom I did maintain a connection to—had a theory about that, but I think it may be a little overboard."

"What was it?"

"Well, knowing how competitive Dink was, and how jealous he was of Lewton being the team leader and being married to me besides, Timothy believed Dink might have sabotaged the teleportation on purpose, to kill Lewton and ruin his project, in favor of Plan B. Basically I think the idea is absurd, but then again, Dink was outside the building getting something from his car at the time of the teleportation and so he was the only one of us who wasn't killed or injured. I suffered severe burns myself, and Timothy... well, you saw him."

"Huh," said Stake. "A funny place for him to be at such an important moment. Maybe Leung wasn't being absurd."

"One thing I'm sure of—Dink's Argos company is well established now, incredibly successful, and the last thing he needs for his public image is to have Wonky Science and our Plan A to come into the spotlight. Not good for business, to be associated with an idea that ghoulish, not if we want the Jin Haa to keep working with us. If they ever learned about the deadstock idea... like you said, they'd hate us even more than the Ha Jiin ever did. So I can see Dink killing Leung and sending those snipes after you and your friends, to keep the story from reaching new ears. I can see him killing me for what I know, too, and that's why I'm frankly very afraid, Mr. Stake."

A siren whooped to life outside, and Stake saw Persia flinch. He looked out the window to see five members of a street gang go running past, but couldn't tell their race or even species because of the conical red hoods with eye holes they wore as part of their gang attire. Cars being prohibited on Salem Street, it was two hoverbikes bearing black-garbed, helmeted policemen that moments later went by in pursuit. No sector of Punktown, however moneyed, was immune to its infestation of crime and violence. Stake found himself missing the eerie serenity of Bluetown.

"So you'd been following the news about Bluetown, the clones, but were afraid to come forward."

"I figured they already knew about it themselves, but weren't letting the public know. I can see them wanting to keep you in the dark, but your friend Rick being one of them, it's odd that they've kept things from him, too."

"You should know from your own dealings with them, that when it comes to the government and military, one hand doesn't always see what the other hand is scratching. Getting back to Brian, Lewton, whatever we want to call him; you didn't want to have a say in the fate of the living clone once you realized who he was?"

"I've been concerned for him, no matter what you think, Mr. Stake, but can't you at least understand my reluctance? Yes, I'm worried about the lengths they might go to in order to hide the truth. Kill him and say he died of that plague that's rampant on Sinan. Kill him and replace him with a clone made from the remains of some MIA."

"You were his wife. You have a strong case for claiming him, giving him a home."

"You think they'd just turn him over to me like a stray kitten, a clone created under such mysterious circumstances? But besides that, Mr. Stake, a lot of time has gone by. For eight years now I've lived with my boyfriend, Joel, a very dear man. And frankly, Lewton wasn't always the best of husbands. He was greedy. He could be cruel."

"I don't know about any of that, but I do know a little boy we call Brian, who's very sweet, and he liked my friend Ami and called her 'Mee.' He's innocent, and he could grow up to be anything, Mrs. Barbour. Anybody. If someone doesn't kill him first. With Ami dead, Rick out of commission, and me banned from the base, he's short on protection right now."

"Look, I didn't say I don't want to help him, but I had another idea in mind. Lew's parents are still alive. They're good people, and they have money so they have influence. His mother is a professor at Paxton University and his dad's a surgeon. Let me contact them. I know them—they'll want that child. I do want what's best for him, Mr. Stake, and I'll do all I can but I have to protect myself. It was a risk even meeting you. For all I knew, you could have been hired by Dink himself, to flush me out."

"Henderson will back me up, if you want."

"As if I could trust a Colonial Forces officer, at this point? But I've looked into your various faces, Mr. Stake, and I haven't seen any lies in them yet, so I'll take my chances. I couldn't do anything alone before, so I'm grateful for your involvement. In fact, I'll even pay you."

"I'm already getting paid."

"Your friend is paying you to identify the clones. I'm paying you to steal the child. You need to get him off that base and into hiding until I can involve Lewton's parents and have them go public, so we can have him safely brought back here to Punktown."

"Kidnap him, from the Colonial Forces base? Christ, Mrs. Barbour."

"I know; it's dangerous. But you're already involved in this to a dangerous degree, or Dink wouldn't have set those dogs after you."

Stake sighed, glanced out the window again. "Well, maybe it's time I get out of this city, anyway. Off Oasis altogether. Start fresh somewhere new, maybe under another identity. But man, to think not too long ago I was worried about a couple of Stems trying to kill me. Now I'll have the government after my hide."

"You have lots of hides."

"All right, I'll take your money, because I'll need it. But I'll admit to you, I'd do this just for the sake of vengeance. What they did to Ami, and those two young CF troopers, and for almost killing Rick. I'll sneak Brian out of there one way or another, and find a place to stash him. I can't get him teleported off Sinan—that's too tough—so we'll have to do it legitimately once you've got his parents behind us like you say. Funny, huh? Before, the trick was to teleport your husband to Sinan. Now the trick is to teleport him back."

Persia nodded thoughtfully, lowering her eyes to Stake's hands on the table. "Cloning private citizens is illegal, of course; otherwise, even without his physical DNA, his parents could have a new clone made of him from undifferentiated cells programmed with the molecular blueprint in his ID bracelet." She tapped Stake's wristband with a nail. "But the child is already here, already made, and something has to be done with him. The public has already been following his story and shown concern. With a name and identity put to him, they'll want to see him returned to his parents as much as we do."

Stake held up a hand to make her pause. "You say his molecular blueprint is in this bracelet?"

"In one of them; I don't know if it's the one you have, precisely. But yes, a full molecular scan of each individual was programmed into his bracelet, for us back at Wonky to use in recognizing, recalling, and reassembling them on our end. I ought to know—that was my contribution to the project. I'm the one who encrypted the data and input it into them."

Stake wagged his head. "Oh my God," he breathed. "Well that's it, then. When the smart matter encountered the remains of the team, its own cellular activity prompted their cells to reproduce, but it was influenced to do this by the transmissions from the bracelets—and used their molecular blueprints to guide it."

"I suspect there's even more to it than that, Mr. Stake. The bracelets were our link between dimensions. They were transdimensional positioning devices, so that we could track the team members and collect them when the time came. So they also contain teleportation coordinates for their point of origin, in Punktown."

"Oh no," Stake said. "You're saying—they contain a map?"

"Yes. If Bluetown is Punktown, then I'm sure that's how the smart matter became infected, and went from a blueprint for a village complex to a blueprint for a whole city. The transmissions from the bracelets were powerful. They conveyed their data to the smart matter, and corrupted its original programming. From there, it's snowballed as a self-perpetuating process."

Stake steepled his fingers in front of his face and tapped them below his nose, as he felt things fall into place with an almost audible click inside him. "So this is why it began growing Punktown two blocks over from this location, instead of from the city's center. Where it started duplicating Punktown is relative to the location of Wonky Science. Though it didn't get replicated until later, for all intents Wonky Science was the true center of the blueprint." He dropped his hands. "This makes for another reason you should have come forward, then—you could have helped to stop the city from advancing!"

"Don't lay all this on me, Mr. Stake!" she hissed. "Timothy didn't even have to come forward, only talk to you, and look where it got him! I'm sorry I'm not as brave as you'd like me to be, but I'm here now, aren't I? Anyway, don't you think they already know that? Don't you think they already found the Punktown coordinates in the bracelets?"

"You encrypted them, so maybe they have and maybe they haven't; Ami didn't mention anything like that. But tell me this, Mrs. Barbour. If transmissions from the bracelets could tell the smart matter to create Punktown, could the transmissions be altered and tell the smart matter to *stop* creating Punktown?"

"I'm sure they've tried to transmit new orders to the smart matter through the computers they ignited the process with."

"You're right, they have, but not in the language the smart matter got its initial instructions from—the encrypted language you devised. If it received new orders in *that* language, maybe the smart matter would understand... and listen."

Persia Barbour removed her dark glasses at last, her eyes wide and naked. She looked like she either wished she had never agreed to meet with him, or wished she had come forward much earlier than this. Probably it was both. She said, "Then I think you'd better buy me another coffee. And if we're going to do this, I'm going to need to revise all three transmissions, not just one." She tapped his wristband again. "You're going to have to bring me the other two."

CHAPTER TWENTY-TWO
ILLUSIONS

THE LITTLE HOTEL room reminded him of those he had stayed in during the war, when he'd spent time in Di Noon on rest and recreation between assignments in the bush. It afforded just enough room to navigate around a sizable bed intended for prostitutes and their clients, a tiny bathroom, and an aquarium containing one lonely looking fish, set into the wall near the door. He made sure this was always bolted. Modest, to say the least, but the VT featured Earth Colonies programming and thus offered a wide array of channels, including a station for Ha Jiin news.

Stake sat up in bed watching this, still feeling queasy from teleporting back to Sinan—or had the bender poison been stirred up in his blood, like a sediment that settled only to be swirled into motion again? On the screen was footage of the leader of the Ha Jiin, Director Zee, participating in a parade through the capital city of Coo Lon, organized to honor those whose lives had been claimed by the mysterious sexually transmitted epidemic. Zee marched like everyone else, holding aloft a stick with a gauzy blue pennant flapping from it, representing the soul of one of the dead. Hundreds of these pennants, like a school of ghostly fish. Walking alongside Zee was his chief religious advisor, whom Stake knew was called Abbot Vonh. With his spiraling hole instead of a face, he would have been indistinguishable from any other Ha Jiin or even Jin Haa monk had his blue robes not borne gold designs of flying birds. Not only did the monks sacrifice their faces, their identities, in the strength of their beliefs, but they pinched embers of the cancerous incense between their fingers, and rubbed it into the center of their chests. After years of this, their fingers decayed until their hands were all but useless fleshy mitts, and a smaller version of the facial vortex was echoed on their chests, bared by the open V of their robes.

Abbot Vonh did not carry a pennant, his disfigured hands resting by his sides. Instead, a large bird with metallic blue feathers and a predator's keen eyes and curved black beak rode on his shoulder like a pirate's parrot, its black talons gripping his shoulder, but Stake supposed that with the discipline of these clerics the pain was of little distraction. As Stake watched him, the monk turned his faceless face toward the camera, as if staring right back at him. The bird had swiveled its head in unison. The combined effect caused the detective to shudder.

The program offered English translation, and Stake listened as the commentator reiterated the theory that was prevalent throughout both the Ha Jiin and Jin Haa lands—that the nameless plague had been brought by the Earthers. But increasingly, the consensus seemed to be that the contamination was not the result of sex tourism, as previously theorized, but very much by design. The gas reserves were being depleted. Without an increase in dead bodies, sinon gas would not be replenished in sufficient amounts for harvesting.

Until yesterday, when he'd sat over coffee with Persia Barbour, Stake might have dismissed such a claim as ignorant paranoia. Now, he wasn't willing to dismiss any possibility.

While taking in the commentary, Stake realized he'd been massaging the bridge of his nose. A moment after he became conscious of doing this, he was no longer looking at a VT screen in his cheap Di Noon hotel room.

He was in a monastery, secreted away in the heart of a jungle where every frond and blade and leaf and vine was a vivid shade of blue. He had led his men here because he was now in command of their outfit, after his two superior officers—a lieutenant and sergeant—had been eliminated by a Ha Jiin sniper. Now, they had captured the young female sniper and her wounded companion, and brought them along as prisoners to the monastery, where they planned to take shelter until another unit could rendezvous with them in a matter of days.

He was always wary of the monks, because he had heard rumors of their abilities, some almost too fanciful to take as anything but exaggeration. He had encountered them in the burial tunnels a number of times, but found that since he never made a move toward them, they did nothing but blindly gape at him with their empty faces. Still, he was cautious as he moved ahead of the rest of his squad, approaching a group of ten monks standing in a row with their backs to him.

They were running their blunted, flipper-like hands over a colorful mosaic with raised contours that they read like Braille. In a succession of panels, the mosaic told of the life of the great prophet Ben Bhi Ben, from childhood to old age. In the final panel on this wall, a flock of golden birds gripped Ben Bhi Ben's blue robes in their claws as they bore his departed spirit into the sky, toward twin suns like the staring eyes of a god, rendered on the monastery wall with glittering bits of blue crystal.

Stake narrowed his eyes, confused. Even in the midst of delusion, he understood that this was not the way it had happened. Not quite. There was one monk toward the center of the group whose blue robes were covered with a pattern of golden birds. No, Stake didn't remember that being the case on this long-ago day.

As if he could sense Stake's confusion, this monk turned around slowly. Even without features, Stake had a strong sense of the holy man contemplating him with something of befuddlement himself, as if wondering how the Earth man had been able to invade his own delusion.

Stake sensed the being's great power. It crackled in him. The Earther could swear he even saw faint flickers of violet electricity far back in the void of his face. He was afraid the monk would do something to drive him and his team out of this sacred place, or worse, so he raised one hand with spread fingers, and said, "I'm here to help you. I want to stop the Blue City. I want to stop the plague-bringer."

The cipher face regarded him for several moments more, before the cleric slowly turned back to the wall and laid his hands upon it again. The image in relief he stroked was of Ben Bhi Ben as a man in his middle years, steady with purpose, seeing his people through great adversity, guiding them toward peace.

Stake turned away, too, prepared to retrace his steps, but he found the rest of his team and the two prisoners were no longer there. He backtracked through hallways too dark for him to tell if their surfaces were covered in more relief mosaics. At last, alone, he stepped into a vast chamber, bigger than anything he had seen in a monastery before. It was something more like a warehouse, with a high ceiling and murky lighting. Along either side of this hall were dozens upon dozens of small bodies lying on slabs. At first he thought it was a great mausoleum, but the bodies appeared to be hooked up to life support systems, and there was an electronic beeping, a gurgle of fluids through tubing. Was it a hospital, then?

He crept to the foot of the nearest slab and looked down upon a small, naked figure. Its skin was blue. Slender limbs, a thatch of black pubic hair, and two tiny moles on the smooth belly near its squinted navel. One mole was pale, almost white, the other almost black. He knew those moles. They were identical to the ones on the belly of the fierce little sniper they had captured, the woman named Thi Gonh.

He moved to the next figure. It, too, had those moles on its belly. So did the third body. Stake looked across the hall, at the figures ranked along the opposite wall. Every body in this room was a reproduction, a clone from a single master. He knew them from the moles only, however, because each and every body was without a head. From the puckered stump of their necks, a few tubes and cables snaked out to connect with support units set into the walls.

Deadstock.

A thin blue mist hung in the air, growing thicker as it coiled lazily toward the ceiling, all but obscuring it. Growing increasingly anxious, Stake continued between the double rows of human deadstock. The fog became thicker, thicker, so that he could only see vague outlines of the clones. He started to run, run straight into the blue fog, until it swallowed him entirely and he saw no more.

IN ADDITION TO acquiring a hotel room, Stake had rented a hoverbike to replace the helicar he no longer had access to. The bike was dented, scraped, and so orange it almost made his eyes hurt, but at least it had a sidecar as he'd requested. At present, the sidecar was empty as Stake floated along through a street choked with many more bikes. While he rode he had activated his wrist comp, and was waiting for someone to pick up his call. After several moments, the face of Ha Jiin security captain Hin Yengun was gazing out at him from the screen.

"Mr. Stake," Yengun said, his features intense but voice polite, as usual. "So you are still here on Sinan."

"Captain, I need your help. I'll tell you more later, because it's not secure talking on an open frequency, but it's about the excavation of the pits the three clones were found in. There's something extremely important I have to find."

As the pits were on Ha Jiin territory, Yengun's commander had organized the original excavation, and passed along the findings to Gale. Stake cursed himself for not thinking earlier to meet with the commander and show him the pictures of the items Gale had displayed for Henderson; he could have proved they were bogus sooner, and asked the commander what the real items had looked like. Well, he had arrived at the truth by another route.

"Mr. Stake, my people and your people have been over that area very thoroughly. Especially your people, with scanning equipment."

"Yes, but I've been wondering if maybe your commander didn't turn over everything he found to Colonel Gale. He might have kept something that could prove the Earth Colonies were acting in a covert manner, before the war even took place."

"If he did retain such a thing, he might not be inclined to tell me, anyway. But I suppose I could try to find out."

"Another idea would be to look at the men who were hired to do the actual work. If someone found something of value, he may have pocketed it for himself."

"And if I should look into any of this, it would help you how?"

"It might help all of us, captain. You and me. The Ha Jiin and the Jin Haa. It might just stop Bluetown in its tracks."

STAKE PARKED HIS bike in front of a fast food restaurant called Burger God, part of an Earth Colonies chain and here primarily to cater to the Earth soldiers, as it was situated just down the street from the Colonial Forces base. Sitting at one of its small tables, he next called the base and via the automated menu rang through to the science division. As he had hoped, Ami Pattaya's top tech Bernard came on.

"Hi, Bernard," Stake said. "Hey, I wanted to check on how Captain Henderson is doing, but I can't get through to his number. Maybe they've got me blocked. Is there any way you could go look in on him for me?"

Bernard was looking at Stake warily, and he didn't know if that was because he blamed the detective for Ami's death, or if his request sounded suspicious. Bernard replied, "He's having his hand regenerated. I heard Colonel Gale wanted to send him back home so he could fully recover, but the captain didn't want to do that."

Stake was aware of all this. Despite what he'd said to Bernard about not being able to get through to Henderson, he had spoken with him only two days ago, when Stake had called the captain to okay the trip back home to Punktown. The idea wasn't to find out how Henderson was doing. The idea was to send Bernard out of the science lab on an errand, so that Stake might enter it in Bernard's guise.

"I'm sure the colonel would love to have Henderson off Sinan," Stake couldn't help himself from saying. "Me, too. Especially me."

"I guess. Anyway, I just saw Dr. Laloo on his way to go look in on the captain in his quarters, now that they've moved him out of the infirmary. Maybe you could call the doctor and he'd tell you how Captain Henderson is."

"Oh, yeah... okay." Stake's racing mind swerved down a new lane. "So, how's Brian doing?"

"He's all right, I suppose, but once in a while he asks for 'Mee.' Ami."

Stake winced. "The poor kid."

"I'm trying to keep him happy and distracted, so he won't miss her too much."

"You're a good guy, Bernard. So where is Brian now? Caged up in Laloo's department, or with you in the lab, or...?"

"He still sleeps in the med unit, but I have him with me for much of the day." In fact, Stake realized he could hear the distant chirps and squeals of the child playing in the background.

"Well, I wish the best for him. Thanks, Bernard. Maybe I'll try Laloo now and see if he's willing to talk to me. I guess I should have called him in the first place, but I feel more comfortable talking to you."

When Stake had finished with its vidphone feature, he looked in his wrist comp's files for some images he had captured on the sly of the Choom medical officer. Yes, Laloo. Even better.

He got up and worked his way into the Burger God's bathroom, where he closed himself inside a stall. Some acts were just too private to share.

The Burger God did good business with Jin Haa customers, too. It was bustling today, and no one seemed to notice that a different man stepped out of the bathroom stall than had entered it.

LOOKING LIKE OTHER people wasn't all that good unless you could occasionally sound like other people, too, and Stake was very adept at mimicry, through practice and maybe even an instinct related to his gift. The gruff, snappish delivery of Dr. Laloo was easy enough to imitate. Stake had noticed he sort of grumbled to himself, and so he did this as he approached the front gates of the Colonial Forces base on foot, his hoverbike still parked down the street in front of Burger God. He had only seen Laloo in surgical scrubs, but since he didn't have any he hoped it would not be out of character to wear the camouflaged fatigues he still had possession of, or the visored cap he'd pilfered. Laloo's hair was cut very close, and was graying, and the cap would hide Stake's discrepancy.

"Doctor," one of the two men posted outside, assault engine in his arms, greeted him.

Stake mumbled impatiently in return. The mumble wasn't just part of the act; portraying Chooms put his skills to the limit. Already, the muscles in his jaw ached from the stretching of his mouth back to his ears in the manner of Oasis's indigenous people. His teeth couldn't extend that far back, of course, but he kept his stretched lips closed to hide the fact.

"I didn't see you leave earlier, doc," said the other guard, as the gate's barrier of force was drawn aside to permit him entry.

"Then pay more attention—there are terrorists loose in this city!" Stake scolded him as he brushed past onto the base.

"Yes, sir," the soldier replied, cowed.

Stake was glad he was familiar with the base's layout, and made his way to the medical unit as quickly as he could, heart pounding, afraid that at any moment he'd turn a corner in the rat's maze of corridors and come face-to-face with the man he was impersonating. No one accosted him, though he nodded and grunted when passing a few of the base's personnel. Two more guards were still stationed outside the med unit, since

Brian spent the nights and part of his time in there. Stake stopped before them, patting his pockets as if in search of something. "Dung," he griped.

"Sir?" one of the men said.

"Forgot my damn ID card somewhere," Stake managed through painfully clenched teeth. A muscle in one of his cheeks was twitching. "Probably left it back in Henderson's quarters."

"I've got you, sir." The soldier leaned in close to the recognition scanner by the door, and its green light slid down his face and chest, confirming his features and ID badge. Stake was relieved, not sure whether his mimicry would have been the equal of a military scanner. As the door whisked open, the guard asked, "And how is the captain doing, doctor?"

"Coming along, coming along," Stake said, barreling into the room. The first thing he did as the door swept shut again behind him was slip a lab smock on over his camos, and exchange his military cap for a surgical hair covering. He draped a mask around his neck for good measure. Then, he leaned over a computer monitor and punched in the extension for the science lab. Once again, Stake found himself speaking with Bernard, but this time he felt confident enough not to have to distort his voice as when he'd counterfeited Ami Pattaya. "Bernard, can you please bring the boy back in here? And while you're at it, bring me the box of gear found with the clones. There's something that occurred to me that I want to look into."

"Okay, doctor. Did you happen to get a call from the detective, Jeremy Stake? He was asking me how the captain is doing."

"I don't have time for him right now. Please make it quick, Bernard, if you don't mind."

As Stake waited for Bernard to arrive, he chided himself for not going to the science department directly, lessening the chance of the real Dr. Laloo returning to the med unit before he could leave it. In the midst of this thought, his wrist comp jarred him by ringing. He looked at the caller's ID: David Bright. That was all he needed right now, listening to the next installment of the businessman's nervous breakdown. He didn't pick up.

Stake was jarred again as Bernard entered, the young black man holding Brian's hand. The child looked up at Stake without much enthusiasm; obviously Laloo wasn't his favorite person on the base. Under Bernard's other arm he carried the container Stake had requested.

"Very good, Bernard." Stake took the box from him. "You may run along and play with your test tubes now."

"Just to let you know, sir, I haven't given him his lunch yet."

Maybe we'll make a quick stop at Burger God, Stake thought. "I'll see to that, don't you worry." Stake made a shooing motion.

Bernard didn't try to hide the disapproval he felt for the man Stake imitated, his face sour as he turned and left the unit. Bernard's protectiveness toward Brian made Stake feel sorry that—if all went well—this might be the last time he would see the cloned child.

The detective leaned down to take Brian's hand, and in his own voice whispered, "Come on, my man. It's time you had a look at the world outside these walls."

THE GUARDS DIRECTLY outside the door had thought nothing of Dr. Laloo leaving the medical unit with Brian at his side, but it was the guards posted at the base's front gate who raised their eyebrows. Laloo's doppelganger waved one arm impatiently until the barrier was withdrawn. One of the guards said, "Sir, the colonel is letting you take the child off the grounds now?"

"For a brief walk, yes, if that doesn't spoil your day, private."

"Are you going to have an escort, sir?"

"Not for a fucking walk around the block. Just mind the store while I'm gone, will you?" Stake dragged Brian along a little faster, dreading that Gale himself might look out a window at any moment and see them passing through the energy barrier. He felt the guards' uncertain eyes on his back as the field closed again behind him and he pulled Brian off down the street. Even Jin Haa passing on bikes or on foot turned their heads to follow the Choom in his lab smock and the tiny Earther child, who looked around at Di Noon in bright-eyed wonder.

They made it to the battered hoverbike, waiting like a faithful horse outside the Burger God. Stake glanced in through the windows and decided it was too busy to risk taking the time to grab the child some lunch just yet. He lifted Brian into the sidecar, removed his lab coat and surgical hat, and stuffed them in beside him before straddling the machine and lifting it off the pavement.

Now they were on their way, and Stake was finally able to let the huge Choom grin relax from his face. The pain of stretched muscles was giving him a headache, and he felt alarm at the notion that one of his bender episodes might be coming on. Bad timing for that. Trying to take his mind off such thoughts, he glanced down at the blue data bracelet clamped around his right wrist, then switched his attention to the wrist comp on his left. No call had come through from Thi Gonh yet. Afraid to put Thi in danger by contacting her himself, he had asked Captain Yengun to call her instead and have her get in touch with Stake as soon as she was clear to do so. Was she unable to get out from under her husband's distrusting eye?

Again he took in the second bracelet he had removed from the base. This time, with the box still resting in the medical unit, the absence of the two bracelets was sure to be noticed. Well, with Brian stolen from the base, how much more hot water could he boil for himself? Two bracelets... one to go. But he wasn't optimistic about the odds of Yengun actually tracking it down.

Stake was well on his way through Di Noon, reassured by the distance he had put between himself and the base, when a call from Thi Gonh finally came in. By the way she didn't act surprised at his appearance, he could tell he had reverted to his own nondescript features. Her smile shone at him. "Ga Noh. I miss you."

"Thi, I have an emergency here, and I don't have anyone else to turn to." Having no choice but to hope their conversation wasn't being monitored, he skimmed over the circumstances by which the enigmatic clone had come to be in the sidecar beside him, laughing delightedly as the wind rushed in his face. "I need a place to hide him, where people aren't likely to look. Ha Jiin land would do better than Jin Haa land. I thought about asking Captain Yengun. I like the man, but I think that would be too much for him to swallow."

"Your friend, Henderson, no help you?"

"He's recovering from serious injuries, but mainly he's very dedicated to his work and he wouldn't go along with what I'm doing. In fact, I think he'd be horrified, however good my intentions. I can't involve him in this. Guess you could say I have a new employer now."

"I don't know... I can not take boy my house."

"No, not your house, of course, but do you have a friend or neighbor who you can really, really trust a hundred percent to hide the boy until I can move him someplace else?"

Thi sighed, looking distraught at the possibility of letting him down. "Maybe—I not sure. I call you again soon, very soon, okay?"

"Okay, Thi. In the meantime I'm heading out of Di Noon toward Bluetown. If you can do this, that way I'll be closer to meet with you or whoever it is you can get to help us."

"I think I know, but not sure. Maybe if you give money a little, too."

"Sure, sure, if that's what it takes."

"I call you again soon, Ga Noh, okay?"

"Okay, Thi. And Thi?" He smiled back at her belatedly. "I miss you, too."

CHAPTER TWENTY-THREE
DELUGE

STAKE WAS OUT of the city, navigating a road through the jungle on his way to Bluetown. Overhanging its borders were oversized leaves with edges like blades, serrated or razor sharp, the bayonets of two encroaching armies, all seeming to want to slice at him as he raced between them. He passed several men leading a group of yubos, but when they turned to look he saw that none of them were Thi's husband. He reminded himself he was still traversing Jin Haa soil.

Brian was getting a bit squirmy in his seat, maybe hungry besides. He was beginning to whimper, looking about more restlessly than excitedly. Stake thought of something, and produced the ID badge he had filched from Ami Pattaya. He had brought it with him in case he'd needed it to gain access within the base, but that hadn't been necessary. It bore a photo of her face. He handed it to Brian, who held it in both hands and said, "Mee."

"That's for you," Stake told him.

His wrist comp announced another call. It wasn't Thi: David Bright again. Muttering under his breath, this time Stake took it. As he had expected, the man was agitated to the point of implosion.

"Jesus, man, where were you?"

"What can I do for you, Mr. Bright? I'm sort of in the middle of something."

"I'll pay you to be in the middle of something else. Any price you ask."

"The middle of what?"

"I need you as a bodyguard. I need you to spend the night here with me until I can teleport myself the hell out of here tomorrow."

"Your KeeZee isn't bodyguard enough?"

"He would be if he was here."

"What do you mean?"

"There's a lady who works the lounge off the hotel lobby. Clean, classy—I've had her up here a few times before. I sent the KeeZee to go fetch her up here for me. That was almost two hours ago. That isn't like him at all. He wouldn't run out on me—he's a KeeZee. They're loyal as dogs."

"You think someone intercepted him?"

"To leave me defenseless in here, yes!" he hissed. "A little while ago someone tried to come in to bring me new towels but I wouldn't let them in. They want to kill me, Stake!"

"Who is 'they'?"

"Argos! Don't you get it, detective? The attack here at the Cobalt Temple, that got those people killed and Captain Henderson wounded? You think that attack was meant for you? How did they know you'd be here at that time? No—those snipes were sent for me! They knew I was staying here! But when they saw you, the people who brought those things made a last minute change of plan, to take out you and your friends instead."

"What makes you think it was Argos behind that?" It wasn't at all that Stake doubted him, only that he wanted to know how Bright had come to the same conclusion he had.

"He has Gale in his pocket! The whole of the Colonial Forces and the embassy besides! Their presence here is all about sinon gas, isn't it? And my operation has put their operation in peril. I've been making too much fuss, and now they want to shut me down and shut me up!"

"Look, Mr. Bright, I understand how desperate you must feel, but I'm honestly so deep in my own dung right now that there's nothing I can do. Not at this moment, anyway. I suggest you sit tight and try to get through to Margaret Valsalva—tell her you're afraid of another terrorist attack and insist on being given asylum at the embassy. If you take it to her like that, she'll have to act on it. The safest place for you to be right now might be in the heart of enemy territory, if you catch my meaning."

"I catch it, but I don't buy it. Valsalva is only here because of sinon gas, too. All of them."

"I don't know what else to say. My mind is a blur right now and—"

"Oh, blast you, Stake. Blast everybody! I'm on my own, totally on my own, the leper of Sinan. I thought maybe we could help each other stay afloat in the shit, but now I guess I'll be seeing you at the bottom of the pond." Bright signed off.

Stake sighed. "Fuck." Then he glanced over at Brian. "Sorry." But the boy was oblivious; seemingly pacified by the badge he clung to as he watched the approach of the mammoth blue city as if in anticipation of coming home.

FORTUNATELY THE RAIN didn't begin until Stake was well within Bluetown. He pulled the bike over to fashion a hooded parka for Brian of Dr. Laloo's lab coat before continuing on. By the time Thi called him again, darkness had fallen and the rain had gone from steady to downpour. She described a distinctive bridge to him, asked him if he knew it. Of course he did; it was the Obsidian Street Overpass. The original was an enclosed bridge based on a Ramon design and built of sturdy, black lacquered wood. Not only did vehicles swarm beneath its roof, but packed along its pedestrian walkway was a miniature shanty town of homeless shelters thrown together from every sort of scrap and material conceivable. Its replica, of course, was blue in color and devoid of both traffic and this amalgamation of shacks, tents, and lean-tos. In this part of the city, two levels of elevated highway curved and crossed above the streets below. Stake rode an exit ramp up one of these highways, and pulled his bike into the cavernous shelter of the covered bridge.

He didn't venture deeply into the tunnel, wary of its utter darkness, kept the bike near the mouth of the bridge. The rain was now of monsoon strength, blasting the roof above them like a fusillade loosed from a fleet of helicraft. His clothes were soaked and plastered to his skin, and even in this tropical climate he shivered. Despite his parka, Brian wasn't much better off. He was wet, tired, hungry, whiny, and reluctant to remain boxed in the sidecar. Stake wrung his hair out as best he could, talking to the child to soothe him. Who was going to soothe him, though? He heard an odd distant cry, and knew it was a hunting snipe calling out to another one in the street below the bridge.

Every surface of Bluetown had a porous look, and it seemed the city-in-the-making soaked up both darkness and rain, so that its presence weighed more heavily around Stake than it did in the daylight. Though he could see much less of it, it felt all the huger in the blackness, crushing him with its swollen presence. It was easy for him to imagine this was a coral city resting at the bottom of a deep-sea canyon, and he was drowning slowly in the heart of it.

Scattered here and there in the city, at street level but also in high windows, he saw tiny orange embers of light that he knew must be the campfires and lanterns of refugees. A fleeting but bolder source of light came in lightning flashes like the burst of distant bombs, that blended the silhouettes of buildings with those of the shaggy and frayed heads of tropical trees—as if the trees grew within the streets themselves, had overtaken a city of decaying ruins. Stake envisioned such a city so clearly that he couldn't tell if it were solely his imagination or the bender poison at work. He saw a city reclaimed by the forests that it had consumed to come into existence. He saw streets carpeted in moss that thrived in the shadows of skyscrapers with fronds bursting out of their windows like greenhouses run wild. Nets of lianas covered the faces of some structures in feathered leaves, wooly vines like cables were draped from buildings to bridges, from bridges to traffic signal poles. Was it a premonition of what the city would look like once it stopped growing? He found comfort in the thought that, whether Bluetown reached full size or not, the jungle might have its revenge yet.

Another detonation of thunder, this one directly overhead, made Brian begin to cry and become even more agitated. Stake had an idea, and the soft light of his wrist comp came on. He found an image of Ami Pattaya in its memory and studied it closely. He felt the almost subliminal whisper of his cells as they shuffled, realigned, seemed to shrink or expand. When he sensed the transformation was sufficient, he turned on the headlight of the bike, which he had kept off before to avoid attracting unwanted attention. He moved into the light and squatted down so Brian could see him, worrying that the alteration of his features might frighten rather than calm the child.

Brian sobbed and held his arms out, fingers reaching. Stake stood up, lifted the boy into his arms. He clung to Stake like an orphaned monkey, whimpered in the crook of his neck. Stake patted his back and rocked him side to side, not speaking so as not to break the illusion with his voice.

He didn't hear them come up behind him until they were only steps away. They had entered from the other end of the bridge, Stake realized as he whipped around. He sucked in his breath, thinking it was a pack of snipes. Three black shapes in glistening camouflaged parkas, the brief flicker of eyes floating red against black. Now that their presence was known to him, the figures moved closer until they came into the light thrown by the hoverbike's headlamp—revealing themselves to be Thi Gonh and two other Ha Jiin women.

Stake recognized one of the women to be the tall, willowy teenager with sweet eyes who had sat with Thi outside the doctor's office after Thi's beating. Her niece Twi, Stake recalled, and he remembered Thi had said she was teaching the girl to shoot like her aunt, so as to defend livestock from the attack of benders and other predators. In fact, the girl held a sniper rifle in her arms, as did the third woman, older than Thi and thickset, with her hair cut short under the hood of her parka. Thi had one of these rifles slung across her back, herself. Stake knew it as a Kalian model called a Whistler, black and with a mean, almost organic wasp-like look. Their aluminum-coated depleted uranium bullets blew through their victims with such force that the air was said to whistle through the tunnels they left.

Thi was smiling as she took in Stake cradling the boy in his arms, Brian looking up at the newcomers sleepily. She stepped closer and cupped Stake's transfigured face. "Beautiful," she said.

Stake turned his face into her palm and kissed it before she withdrew her hand. He didn't care what the other two women thought of this, but he saw them smile shyly. Thi turned to sweep her arm toward the eldest of the three. "Older sister, Yha."

"Older sister? Oh!" Stake said, and nodded his head in respect. With Thi's uncle calling the shots in the family, Stake hadn't expected Thi to have so close a blood relation still living. Then again, the uncle was a man and Yha was not. Yha bore a resemblance to Thi, now that he looked at her again, but was maybe ten to fifteen years older, her eyes and mouth gentle but also hardened around the edges. The woman nodded back at him.

"Sister is mother of Twi," Thi went on. "Farm of sister gone, too. Sister and Twi live in Blue City now."

"Really? Oh God, that's terrible. Why hasn't your uncle or Nhot taken them in, too?"

"Sister hate uncle and Nhot."

"Well, can't blame her for that."

"Sister need money from Ga Noh, a little," Thi said in a lower voice, looking embarrassed to ask.

"Well, sure, but I don't have much to spare."

"Two hundred munits? Very much for her."

"Oh, okay, that works." He dug out his wallet and counted off 200 colonial munits, handed them over. Yha examined each bill in the light as if he might be trying to pass off counterfeits, but at last she slipped them into a pocket and smiled at him. They exchanged nods again.

"Sister fight in war like me, a little," Thi explained. "Take care of baby very good."

"Right now he needs food and sleep."

Thi said something to Twi, who leaned her weapon against the bike to come forward and accept the boy into her slender arms. She bent back with the effort, but Brian wrapped his limbs around her, perhaps swayed by her soft beauty, laying his cheek against a stream of hair as long and black as Ami's had been.

"You stay with sister too, Ga Noh?"

"No. I'd like to, especially to keep off Jin Haa land, but it's not a good idea. These bracelets are tracking devices." He indicated the pale blue band around his wrist. "I don't know if they've cracked enough of their code to be able to trace them remotely—and since they can't find the third one, I'm assuming they haven't—but I don't want to take the chance of leading the Colonial Forces straight to Brian. I'm not sure, but I might head back to Di Noon and try to get Henderson on my side until Brian's family can get here to claim him."

Thi gazed off into the torrents, which were lessening in severity as the storm plodded onward. "I go home soon, before husband too angry. Husband understand I am with sister, but no like my sister."

"Are you on foot? Is your sister camped far from here?"

"Maybe good I not say. Maybe soldiers hurt you, make you say where baby is."

"Torture me? They wouldn't, but yeah, they might truth scan me, so I guess it is better if I don't know exactly where Brian is." Stake stepped close to her, wanting to touch her, wanting to put his arms around her, but mindful of the two women watching. "Are you okay?"

"Okay."

Stake asked her what she had told her husband she was doing out tonight, and she explained that she had said she was bringing supplies to her sister in the Blue City. Would he try to follow her? She laughed. At night, in the rain, with the city stalked by snipes and benders? "Right," he said, "only crazy people would be out here now." They smiled at each other. The moment was broken by a call on his wrist comp. Bright, again? Or maybe even Gale, with accusations and threats? By now there must have been a search underway for Brian, the bracelets—for a Dr. Laloo look-alike who could only be the mutant Jeremy Stake. Stake had blocked calls from the Colonial Forces base, to prevent his wrist comp and thus himself from being tracked and located, but there were always ways around such measures. Unless Stake wanted to block all calls, except for those from a few certain people, all Gale had to do was call him from a phone outside the base's frequency.

But he saw that it was Hin Yengun, and when he let the call through the security captain skipped the greetings and got straight to business. "I've found the third one," he said cryptically.

"Ah! Fantastic! God, that was quick!"

"Well there is a complication. It's not in my possession—I still need to go and retrieve it. I will tell you more later, but right now I request that you accompany me. I don't want to involve any of my men in this, but I would like someone as a second pair of eyes."

"Gladly. I'm already in Bluetown; I can meet you at the place where the clones were found."

"All right, then, in an hour."

"In case we're being monitored, if you see anyone other than me there, turn away."

"First of all, I'm an officer of national security. I would like to see your people try to harass me on Ha Jiin land. Secondly, with your gifts, Mr. Stake, how would I know if it was you or a stranger, anyway?"

"Point taken, but I'll try to be myself for the occasion."

They broke off, but just as Stake began to turn back toward Thi another call came in. With a grumble of irritation, he saw that this time it was indeed David Bright. Given Bright's agitation, he felt too guilty about ignoring him, so he let the businessman through. "Stake," he sighed.

The image on Stake's miniature screen was tipped at a giddy angle. Confused, he leaned in and allowed himself to engage with the device so that it linked directly with his brain, the screen opening up to fill his mind's eye. It became immediately apparent that Bright's tabletop computer had tumbled to the carpeted floor of his hotel room. Stake saw the leg of a chair, the corner of a bed. And there was a sound, something between a dry wheeze and a liquid gargling. He knew, even before he saw red-smeared fingers dragging an arm into the frame, that he was listening to the aspiration of blood.

"Bright!" Stake called out.

But the fingers stopped their laborious crawl through the carpet's lush fibers. And a moment later, the wheezing sound had stopped, too.

CHAPTER TWENTY-FOUR
ANALOGS

STAKE WISHED THEY could have agreed on another place to meet than the facsimile of Wonky Science, where people from the Colonial Forces base might think to look for him, but it had been easy to suggest the location where he and Yengun had met previously. It was a place they both seemed drawn to, unable to avoid, as if they had been bound there as surely as the remains of Lewton Barbour's expedition.

So Stake was wary of the vehicle that approached along an otherwise barren street, its headlights causing the diminishing rain to sparkle in their beams, until he recognized the military vehicle with oversized wheels that had transported Hin Yengun the first time he'd met him. When it pulled up alongside, Yengun gestured for Stake to bring the hoverbike around back so they could hoist it aboard rather than leave it at risk from refugees. Yengun barked at a man who had ridden beside him to help with the bike. This man wore a short-sleeved shirt left unbuttoned to reveal his thin, almost concave chest, and had a wad of stained gauze taped over one ear. With an unenthusiastic expression, he jumped down from the vehicle to lend a hand. Stake said to Yengun, "I thought I was going to be your second set of eyes."

"This gentleman is named Honrei. You may call him Henry, if you like; it's what he likes, and he speaks English well. Henry has been to this building before. In fact, he is one of the men that my commander gathered to drain and excavate the three holes the clones took form in."

"And so I take it Henry found something? Something he didn't mention earlier?"

"He mentioned it, but only to his boss—a man known as Don Tengu."

Henry glanced up at the name, looking more miserable than ever. They had the bike stowed now and climbed aboard Yengun's vehicle to take seats. "I've heard of Don Tengu," Stake said. "He runs a major black market operation."

Yengun put them in motion, his eyes cutting into the night as intensely as the headlights. "It embarrasses me, as an officer in service to my country, that my commander is very... shall I say, lax about Don Tengu's movements across the Neutral Zone. It disgraces all of us in national security—disgraces my *people*. I've been too lax, myself, in not having reported my commander's activities or opposed him before. Now, it infuriates me to think he handed this job over to a team of men on Tengu's payroll, and that this might have prevented the Blue City from being halted sooner."

"Captain," Stake goaded him gently, "tell me what this guy did with the bracelet."

"What did you do with it, Henry?" Yengun snapped. Stake took in the bloodied bandage over Henry's ear again. Stake admired the captain, but this and Gale's experiences as a captive during the war reminded him why he had always been ready to put a round through his own head before letting himself be captured by the enemy.

"I gave it to Don Tengu," Henry grumbled. "I didn't think it was much!"

"But you thought it was enough to hide and not turn over to the Earth people!" To Stake, Yengun said, "He probably would have kept it for himself if he'd thought it was really of value. He hid a handgun that he found at the site, too, and gave that to Tengu also—hoping to win his favor, knowing that he collects them besides selling them illegally to any farmer, teenager, or drug addict who can afford them."

"So where is it we're going now?" Stake asked, though he knew the answer already.

"I've never visited Don Tengu at his place of abode before," Yengun said. "Henry is going to introduce me."

THEY WAITED OUTSIDE a metal wall adorned with rust art, like the wall that encircled the town of Vein Rhi, except that instead of country life and religious imagery the chemical corrosion had rendered lithe nude figures like water sprites cavorting around a pool, men firing rifles and handguns, tangles of bodies that might be orgies or heaps of victims. Razor wire topped the wall, and there had been two guards posted behind the barred gate. One of them, carrying a shotgun, had gone to report the arrival of these unexpected guests. The other, carrying a full-sized Sturm AE-95 assault engine, remained to glower at the men through the bars like a warder.

Stake glanced around him while they waited. They were on the outskirts of Coo Lon, the capital city of the Ha Jiin nation. He had dozed off while riding, but a peek at his wrist comp had told him it was past midnight by the time they arrived, and the rain had stopped altogether. Night insects trilled in the saturated brush that sprouted thickly between expensive walled homes. Did living in this suburb afford Don Tengu a facade of respectability, or was he merely keen to stay that much closer to the Neutral Zone, it being the bridge between his two client bases?

The man with the shotgun returned, and spoke to Henry in their native language. "Don Tengu will see us," Yengun said to Stake, as the guard worked to unbolt the iron door.

The three men were ushered inside the compound, and a man carrying a scanning wand came forward to pass it around them in search of weapons. It beeped when it circled Yengun, and he handed over his sidearm grimly. Satisfied, their guide led them past a built-in swimming pool, its interior surfaces beautifully tiled with colorful mosaics. Around the pool, even at this hour, frolicked what very well might have been the models for the rust art naiads. Tiny, slippery smooth figures in bikinis, some eschewing tops to reveal their breasts, either natural and slight or grotesquely bulbous from surgical enhancement. From their exaggerated beauty and the quality of their voices, Stake began to catch on that they were not women but young men transformed by synthetic hormones, even before he spotted one of the nymphs emerging naked from the pool, water dripping off a shy penis. A lady-boy squirming on the knee of a drunken man with a pistol in a shoulder harness licked his lips at Stake as he walked past.

Inside, they navigated through close hallways, passing smoky rooms in which loud-voiced men appeared to be drinking and gambling, or soberly sorting through black market merchandise. Finally, their guide conducted them into a room in which sprawled heavy lacquered furniture with velvety cushions. A man lounged in a throne-like chair, cigarette drooping from his hand, watching a film that played within a vidtank covering the whole of the far wall. Though Stake could tell it was a very old movie, made before VT technology, the vid-tank cleverly extrapolated to make everything appear three-dimensional. There was already one guard stationed in the room, and the new guard joined him by the door as the man in the chair sprang up to greet his guests with a sunny grin. He was short but uncommonly muscular, wearing a black polo shirt too small for his body in order to show off his chest and arms, and tight black jeans that revealed he had neglected to work his lower body. His head was shaved to a warrior's stubble, eyes gleaming and hungrily alert. Stake was already sneaking wrist comp picture grabs of the man called Don Tengu.

"Well, Henry," Tengu said in accomplished English, "who are these guests you've surprised me with?"

"Sorry to come unannounced," Yengun spoke up, polite but firm, "and at such a late hour, but it's a matter of great importance. It's about the Blue City—something that concerns us all. Yourself included."

"It is a troubling situation, isn't it? Or perhaps not. It would normally take generations for a city of that size to be built, and a world as relatively untamed as ours to become so civilized. Now, it's practically happening overnight! Resourceful people with vision will know how to turn this to their advantage. I can think of certain possibilities myself!" Yengun began to reply, perhaps to protest, but Tengu stepped nearer and extended his hand to Stake. "I'm already familiar with you, Captain Yengun, though we've never been formally introduced, but who is your Earth friend, here? I've only rarely had visitors from the Earth Colonies in my home, sorry to say."

Stake shook his hand. "I'm Jeremy Stake, a private investigator from Oasis. I was commissioned to help look into the identities of the three clones found in Blue-town."

Yengun resumed, "It has come to my attention that the men who excavated that site were employees of yours, this man Henry among them."

"Well, I do allow my employees to make money on the side in any manner they choose. Isn't that right, Henry? And by the way, are you all right? You look like you've been injured." Don Tengu gestured at his man's bandaged ear.

Henry could only nod and grunt something unintelligible. Stake thought he looked like he might pass out from terror more than pain, at any moment.

"It has also come to my attention," Yengun said, "that certain items found at the excavation were not given to the Earth Colonies authorities, but to you instead. It is greatly important that these items be returned. Again, this is a matter of national security."

"Again, that's a matter of perspective. I think it's all quite exciting. When I watch the news and see the latest developments of the Blue City, I feel like a colonist on a brand new world, filled with opportunities. That's the way your people feel each time they conquer a new world, isn't it, Mr. Stake? That's how they felt when they first came to Sinan, I suppose? The proud conquistadors?"

"I wouldn't know, Mr. Tengu—I was born on Oasis." To avoid duplicating Don Tengu's appearance, Stake kept looking past him, following the action of the VT film. Noticing this, Tengu glanced over his shoulder.

"I collect gangster movies, Mr. Stake. Twentieth Century Earth gangster movies are my favorite. You can learn from them! Educational… yes." He snorted. "That's why my men call me Don Tengu, after the Mafia don in *The Godfather*."

"I see. Well, some people call me Don Quixote," Stake said. Tengu smiled warily, recognizing the use of wit but not catching its meaning, and probably feeling the remark was at his expense. Not wanting to alienate the man, Stake quickly changed course. "I'm an admirer of Brando myself."

"Ahh—a chameleon, that one."

Huh, Stake thought. Did Tengu know something about him, and wanted him to know he knew, or was he being too wary himself?

Tengu approached the vidtank and waved an arm toward it, as if he were a director presenting his film at a press screening. "This is one of my favorite movies, called *Afraid to Die*. I can watch it again and again. It's a Japanese yakuza movie from the year nineteen-sixty, directed by Yasuzo Masumura and starring the great literary figure, Yukio Mishima. Mishima had the script written for him, with the requirements that he play a gangster, wear a black leather jacket, and die in the film. Oh, and what a death scene he has! At the end of the film he is trying to escape his criminal life, and has changed into a brilliant white jacket, but he is shot and runs in place on an escalator, unable to get anywhere, unable to escape his destiny... until he dies there."

Stake liked the crazy, screechy, discordant jazz score he was hearing, distracting as it was. "Seems like a nice blend of cheesy and artsy."

"Yes! And so is the dialogue. My favorite line is when Takeo's girlfriend—Takeo is Mishima's character—says to him, 'You call yourself a man?' And Takeo says to her, 'Me? Nah, I'm a yakuza!'" Tengu barked a laugh and walked away from the VT. "I love that!"

Stake had the sense that Yengun was letting him run with the ball. At a bit of a loss but trying to be courteous, he asked, "So you feel a connection with Takeo?"

"Him, and Mishima. I'm a body builder like he was, for one thing." Tengu stopped to flex one arm, bunching thick muscles. "Impressive, huh? A lot of work, making myself big and hard like this. Like Mishima, I used to be small and scrawny. A complex man, a fascinating man. But you might think I am patterning myself after him, or after some phantom gangster on this screen. What would that make me, though? A phantom of a phantom?"

Tengu touched a key on his VT's remote to put it on pause. Mishima was frozen in a wild-eyed expression that reminded Stake the author had died by ritual suicide, disemboweled and then beheaded by his male lover.

Tengu was pacing like a leopard in a cage. His tone was growing harder, his voice rising. "This is the arrogance of the Earth people. You would feel I identify with Mishima because he has slanted eyes like I do, and emulate him because he is an Earth man. You say of the races you meet on other worlds, 'They look like Earth people. They look like humans.' I have heard it said that we Sinanese, in our realm of existence, are an analog of a certain nation of Earth people. This is the height of arrogance—dismissing us as an entire world of mere shadows! Just some alternate version, a distorted reflection of one small group of your kind! But look at yourselves compared to us. We here on Sinan all have the same color, the same basic religion—we are whole, undiluted, pure! We are not in physical and cultural disharmony like you! That is why we opposed the Jin Haa in their desire to break from us, and it never would have been successful had the Earth people not interfered." He glared at Yengun. "You are too proud to take my gifts, as your commander does... yes, I have heard about you. You disapprove of me. But I am as much a patriot as yourself!"

"Really? While I was fighting the Jin Haa and the Earth people, you were building your empire on military contraband. Without the war, you never would have thrived."

"If your yubo dies while plowing the field, you must make the most of it and cut it into steaks. This is all I did. But do you understand my meaning, captain? Ben Bhi Ben told us that it is those who dwell on the other side of the veil who are the illusions. You!" He pointed to Stake. "Him!" He pointed to Mishima. "You are the ghosts, not I! I am not Mishima's analog... if anything, he is mine!"

"I didn't realize you were so spiritual, in addition to being a patriot," Yengun said.

Stake wanted to shush him. Tengu's wild mood swings made him nervous; they still needed to get something from this man, and had to treat him carefully. But Tengu's mood swung back again, and he smiled as he replied to Yengun, "Gangsters are always ironically religious. Would you like to see just how devout I am?" He turned to one of the guards and gave an order in his own tongue.

Moments later, a strange figure was escorted into the room. Stake suppressed a gasp. He had seen Sinanese clerics many times and so he was used to the yawning hole where a face should be, the lesser hole in the center of the chest, the fingerless mitt-like hands. The figure wore blue robes and the typical little three-cornered hat. But this cleric didn't reach the guard's shoulder, and Stake figured him to be a boy of about ten years. He had heard of such things, but had never actually seen it before this. A living icon. More so in the past than now, rich men had used them to attract the favor of the gods and bring them prosperity. Even then, it had been an illegal practice to fashion such a being—and they were created in early childhood, sometimes from one's own offspring—but ownership of one indicated a person's status and power. Stake had also heard that these blighted individuals, something between a prisoner and a pet, might even be taken to bed. Again, communion with them was thought to put one in touch with celestial forces.

The child was barefoot, and around one of its ankles was clasped a familiar blue band.

Stake glanced at Yengun. He could tell the captain had spotted it, too.

"You asked me if I came into possession of anything found by my men in those pits. Yes, as a matter of fact, Henry did bring me a few things, to demonstrate his loyalty—knowing my love of the unique, the singular. There was this." From atop a cabinet containing stacks of vid disks in their jewel boxes, Tengu picked up a for-midable-looking handgun. It was a black cannon of a revolver, with an eight-inch barrel and a translucent grip of red plastic. Stake recognized it as an old, classic Decimator .340. If it had indeed been found alongside the three clones, and thus belonged to a member of Lewton Barbour's party, Stake figured its owner to have been the hired mercenary Johnny Esperanto. Tengu resumed his pacing, letting the gun hang at the end of his arm. "My favorite weapon, now—oh, does it pack a punch! And of course there was that." He pointed the pistol at the living icon's ankle as he paced past. "A trin-ket that I gave to my good luck charm as a gift from another world. Now, I don't know which of these items you gentlemen might have in mind, but if it were your commander who had come here to ask them of me, I would have given them both gladly and asked for noth-ing in return." Tengu quit pacing directly in front of Yengun, challengingly. "But since you have come to see me alone, unannounced, I must assume your com-mander knows nothing of this. Therefore, I don't think he'd object if I demanded a price of fifty-thousand colo-nial munits for whichever of these two toys you desire."

Stake saw the muscles stir in Yengun's tight jaw. "Neither of us have such an amount."

"I see. That's a shame. Perhaps you should go tell your commander about all this, then, and see what he says about it."

"I suppose I'll have to do that." Stake didn't believe Yengun; felt he was merely calling the crime lord's bluff. "But I don't think he'd be happy to hear that you withheld these items from the colonists' investigation."

"I suspect your commander will remember, more clearly than yourself, with which people his loyalties should lie. In any case, until such time as he might discuss this with me, I'll wish you gentlemen a good night. It was an unexpected pleasure, especially having a visitor from the ghost world some call Earth." He chuckled, making it sound like a joke, as he switched the Decimator to his left hand so he could shake Stake's hand again with his right.

Yengun took Henry's arm, to bring him along as he and Stake were led to the door by the guard who'd brought them in. Seeing this, Don Tengu called after them, "Henry, why don't you remain here, since you're home already?"

"But he doesn't actually live here, does he?" Yengun said, looking back, not letting go of his prisoner. "I'll see him safely home."

Stake knew that Yengun had probably just saved the traitorous Henry's life. But they still left behind the blind and mute avatar, prisoner and pet, and as Stake followed Yengun and Henry out of the room he glanced back at the child, strangely reminded of Brian.

"He's vile," Stake said in a low voice as he, Yengun and Henry walked away from the iron gate that had just banged shut behind them, like the drawbridge of a castle.

"I can not believe my commander would deal with this scum. All his talk. A criminal who sells drugs and guns to people on both sides of the Neutral Zone, a *patriot?* He questions *my* loyalties? He's so confused with his love and hate of your people, he'd make a better Jin Haa than a Ha Jiin."

"That poor child he keeps."

"Yes."

"So what are we going to do now? Scrape up the money? Maybe if I talk to Persia Barbour—"

"No." Yengun stared straight ahead as he marched toward his parked vehicle.

"No? Are you really going to talk to your commander, then?"

"I have a different message to send my commander," Yengun said through his teeth.

CHAPTER TWENTY-FIVE
AFRAID TO DIE

DURING THE RIDE from Coo Lon to the small town where Hin Yengun made his home, someone calling from a payphone at the Cobalt Temple Hotel tried to reach Stake, rousing him from another half doze. Blearily, he looked and saw that whoever it was had not set the call to block Stake's preview feature, so he checked to see whose face was gazing into the screen before they could see his own. When he saw that it was Captain Rick Henderson, he hesitated out of dread but then accepted the call. "Hey, Rick. You up and around now?"

"Hey yourself! Where the hell are you, Jeremy?"

"I don't actually know at the moment. I'm on the move."

"You don't know, huh? And I suppose you don't know where Brian is either, huh?"

"Rick..."

"You took him, didn't you? You were going back to Punktown to talk to Persia Barbour—is this something you cooked up together?"

"We should be careful about what we say."

"Jeremy, what the fuck, man? I hired you to find the kid's identity, and it looks like you've done that—thanks. But I did not hire you to do *this!* You're fired, okay? I want to know where Brian is, and then I want you off Sinan."

"You don't trust my judgment, Rick?"

"You aren't here to judge, just to do your job! What the hell are you thinking? You're a kidnapper now! Gale wants to nail your head to a wall! Are you trying to drag me down with you?"

"I'm sorry if any of this hurts your career, Rick."

"Don't try to pull that on me. I'm not just worried about myself, here—I'm worried about that kid."

"Believe me, I have his best interest at heart. I'm doing the best thing that can be done for him."

"That isn't for you to determine!" Henderson shouted. Stake had never seen his friend even remotely this angry at him. Or at anyone else, for that matter. "And on top of all this, you stole some things from the lab—items found with the bodies. That makes it not only kidnapping, but espionage!"

"It's the real gear that was found at the dig, not the bogus stuff Gale showed you, and it might put a stop to Bluetown if it's in the right hands."

"It *was* in the right hands! Do you think the Earth Colonies and Colonial Forces don't want to see Bluetown stopped as much as you and I?"

"They do, but they're at cross-purposes with themselves by trying to keep the past buried. You're not in their confidence, Rick. It's not me you should be screaming at, but them."

"Well right now I choose to scream at you!"

"Hold that thought for a second. You're at the Cobalt Temple. So that means you must know what happened to Bright."

"And so how do *you* know something happened to Bright?"

"He tried to call me but died before he could speak."

"I'm surprised he could even manage to do that, from the shape he was in. So you knew about him, and you were going to let the authorities know about it... when?"

"I've been busy."

"I can see that!"

"So how did Bright die, Rick?"

"His KeeZee tore him to pieces, that's how. Bright managed to shoot the thing, but the damage was done."

"His KeeZee? He'd called me earlier and told me his KeeZee had gone missing for two hours."

"Well, I guess it came back to attack him, then."

"Attack him why?"

"Paid to do so. You know how many people wanted to see harm come to Bright. Jin Haa and Ha Jiin alike!"

"And not just them, but our own people, Rick. I have in mind one very vindictive person in particular. I doubt the KeeZee did that to him. I'll bet if an autopsy was done on the KeeZee, you'd see he died hours before Bright, and then his body was brought back to Bright's room."

"And who brought that giant fucking corpse back to Bright's room, then—room service?"

"I don't know how it was accomplished, but Bright trusted the KeeZee. You know how loyal they are. That's why people use them for security. That's why the KeeZee had to be taken out before anyone could get close to Bright. Jesus, Rick, next you'll be telling me you think it was terrorists behind the snipe attack on you and me."

"So who do you think was behind it?"

Stake sighed, feeling wearier than ever. "I think we've said enough for the moment."

"We haven't even begun to talk about this, Jeremy!"

"You're right, but I have to go now." Behind the controls, Yengun was nodding and pointing down the narrow, puddled street ahead of them. They were nearing their destination.

"Jeremy, you listen…"

"Sorry, captain, but I guess I've gone AWOL."

Stake broke the connection, and Hin Yengun pulled to a stop in front of a house that wasn't much bigger than the burly vehicle, surrounded by a wall. Decorative bits of colored glass were embedded in its concrete, and along the top, the bases of broken bottles were set like jagged fangs.

"This is my home," the Ha Jiin said.

THEY HAD BEEN quiet, hoping not to wake Yengun's two young sons at this early morning hour, but finally his wife shuffled into the kitchen in faded flowered pajamas, her long hair in disarray around her face. She was no doubt surprised to see the two men going through her makeup supplies at the kitchen table, but Stake was surprised, too. He nodded to the woman awkwardly. She, in turn, looked uneasy not only to find a man of Earth blood in her home, but about how she must appear to him.

The left side of the woman's delicate face looked like wax that had melted only to solidify again. Her left hand was missing at the wrist, as well, ending in a withered stump.

To break the moment, Yengun said something to her in their language and she turned away, busied herself. "I told her to make us a little meal," Yengun explained. "She doesn't speak English."

"I see."

Yengun raised his eyes to him. "I know what you're thinking. You're remembering that I told you my wife is very beautiful. I tell everyone my wife is beautiful, because it is true. She is beautiful in my memory... but not only that. The other half of her face—I challenge any woman to match its beauty with the whole of her face. And her smooth body, under my hands, is a marvel from the gods. She is like my nation: damaged by war, but its beauty persisting."

"It happened in the war?"

"Of course. She was spattered by a shell from a plasma mortar."

"Was it fired by the Jin Haa, or Colonial Forces?"

Yengun's eyes narrowed to knifepoints. "Will it ease your guilt if I tell you it was the Jin Haa?"

Stake might have said to the man that there were many Jin Haa women who had been wounded in the war, as well—but then, they weren't this man's beloved wife. Now, at last he understood the half scar on one of Yengun's cheeks. A full-length ritual scar would indicate the loss of a loved one. This one, abbreviated, appropriately signified a lesser if still permanent kind of damage. "I'm sorry," Stake said.

"I'm not asking you to apologize." Yengun returned to picking through the makeup items, but Stake could see he was still seething. That he was ever seething at the harm that had come to his woman, even after these long years.

She set plates of fruit and cups of chilled water in front of them, then sat at the table herself. Stake smiled across at her while he said to Yengun, "I told you a little about my family when I first met you, but I didn't tell you my mother was a mutation. She had her own disfigurements. But my father, who was not a mutant, would always tell her she was beautiful, too."

The wife made an inarticulate cry and turned her face away, squeezing shut her good eye. Yengun looked first to her, then to Stake. "Please!" he said.

"Oh my God, I'm sorry," Stake said, turning away as well. He touched the left side of his face, felt the skin there, hard and twisted as if with thick scar tissue. "I'm so sorry."

But Yengun murmured, "I understand. You were empathizing with her." He had leaned over to stroke the back of his wife's head. He spoke in his native tongue, and Stake heard the term "Ga Noh."

"Please ask her to forgive me for stealing her foundation," Stake said, holding up a jar of the blue pigment she used to cover the discolorations of her scars. "I promise not to use her eyeliner."

Yengun translated to his wife. She still kept her face averted shyly, but Stake heard her titter.

He unscrewed the lid of the jar, smelled the familiar scent of the foundation he had used many times during the war, to tint his skin before assuming the appearance of a Ha Jiin in his deep penetration forays. He had never expected to use it again, to embark on another such foray, just as dangerous. It might cost him his life. But what else was there to do for a soldier who no longer had a war to fight in? And he was sure that Captain Hin Yengun felt the same.

THE BOTTOM LEVEL Ha Jiin gangster who called himself Henry was in different clothes and had apparently changed the bandage over his ear as well. It was without stains, but he cupped a hand against the side of his head anyway, moaning and staggering with agony. The two guards behind the gate watched him come, saw him slump against the bars and cling to them to keep from falling. One guard laughed and the other asked him a question in their language. All Henry did was groan in reply and slip a little further down the bars. The one who'd laughed came forward to unlock the gate.

Henry lurched inside a few steps, then dropped to his hands and knees between the two men. One of them said something in a mocking tone, and kicked him lightly in the thigh. No doubt they found it amusing that, after betraying their boss to the security captain, he would dare to come back here alone seeking asylum. No doubt they were urging him to get to his feet so that they might take him to see the boss himself.

Henry heard the barest cough of sound, followed quickly by another. He felt a wet mist across the back of his neck, and one of the two collapsing guards fell against him on the way down. He pushed him off, and when the man hit the ground he saw that the guard was missing the front of his skull above his stunned eyes.

No longer evidencing signs of pain, Henry rose quickly to stand beside Hin Yengun, who had appeared from around the side of the metal wall and slipped through the open gate, wearing black clothing and carrying a pistol with an internal silencing feature. It was not his issued sidearm, but a Don Tengu special—untraceable—bought on the black market a few years back.

Wearing the face he'd borrowed from Henry and the makeup he'd borrowed from Yengun's wife, Jeremy Stake looked again at the two dead guards and felt a twinge of revulsion, maybe even guilt. He had sneaked up on and killed his fair share of Ha Jiin soldiers in his deep ops forays, but the intervening eleven years had left him more changed than he'd realized. He tried to bear in mind that there was a bigger picture here. And he tried to keep in his head the image of that child—the living idol.

Drawing the pistol that Yengun had given him—a big Panzer automatic also with a silencing system—Stake helped drag the two bodies into the shadows of the wall. Yengun took the less bloody of the two men's rain ponchos and slipped it on, in a hurried attempt at disguise for himself. Then, Yengun motioned for Stake to follow him toward the house, going not only on memory but on the detailed directions he had elicited from the real Henry.

Inside they sensed the house in slumber, as if the air were more humid and dense with the exhalations of sleeping men. Stake heard someone cough in a room nearby. They stole their way into a hallway, its various doorways covered by a variety of means: beaded curtains, velvet drapes, and—at its end—a heavy wooden door lacquered to match the furniture within Don Tengu's private quarters. There was snoring behind a velvet curtain, and through one of the beaded curtains the murmur of a VT with volume turned low, its bluish light glowing in a darkened room. Stake hoped that those who'd been watching it, in whatever numbers, had all lapsed into drink-induced dreams.

Yengun met Stake's eyes for a moment, and then tried the handle of Tengu's door. It was unlocked. He eased the door open, slipped in like smoke, Stake's Panzer nosing its way in behind the security officer.

The huge VT was still playing in here, too, though the sound was muted. This movie was a disk of Tikki-hotto porn, in which one man, one woman and one transsexual lay with their three-dimensional bodies and worm-like eye tendrils entangled and writhing. The woman shifted around to pour her tendrils into the shemale's mouth, while the man's eyes started reaching for her presented posterior.

Stake eased the door shut behind him with a soft click.

Don Tengu lay in a pool of disheveled silk sheets, wearing only black silk boxer shorts. Against one wall of his chamber was a sort of three-sided crib that Stake had wondered about during his first visit, earlier tonight. Now, upon its velvet cushion he saw the living icon curled in sleep, still in his blue robes but with the tricorn hat removed from his shaven head. A wheeze came from deep within the child's well of a face.

Around one ankle he wore the blue metal data bracelet.

It would have been easier to just unclasp the bracelet, and if the child awoke in the process he wouldn't be able to call out in alarm anyway. But both men had discussed this, and were in agreement: the child was coming with them. Turned over to a monastery, at least he could live the rest of his life among similar beings. Stake thought that was a somewhat better option than shooting the poor creature to relieve it of its miserable condition, but he knew he wasn't capable of doing that anyway.

He moved toward its little bed, thinking to lift the child into his arms. Yengun was keeping his pistol trained on the dozing Tengu. Neither realized that the door to an adjacent bathroom had opened until they heard the shrill, startled cry behind them.

Yengun spun around to point his gun at the figure in the doorway, a nude little nymph, blue and smooth and barely male, with long sweaty hair hanging about its wide-eyed face. The ladyboy began backing into the bathroom again, holding up his hands and begging for his life in the Ha Jiin tongue.

Stake had taken his eyes off Tengu, and looked back to see him rolling off the side of the bed, landing on his feet in a clattering spill of video disks that he had knocked down in retrieving the Decimator .340 from atop their storage cabinet. Stake's finger was microns away from depressing the trigger of his Panzer, and peripherally he saw Yengun jerking his gun back toward Tengu also, but the crime boss had extended his arm to aim the oversized revolver at the child in its crib. The boy had sat up on his cushion, startled awake, but turned his head from side to side blindly.

"I'll kill him!" Tengu cried. "You want that, captain? Huh?"

"You won't kill your good luck charm," Yengun said with icy calm.

"We don't want a big mess here," Stake said. "Just let us take the boy and you can keep the damn gun."

"Henry? What are you, an undercover cop?" Stake figured Tengu had learned the term "undercover cop" from the movies.

"I'm not Henry. It's me, Jeremy Stake again."

"What the blast?" Tengu snarled.

They heard the sound of the bathroom door snicking shut. Was there a phone in there that the ladyboy might use to awaken the others, or a weapon he might use to come blazing through the door? Neither Stake nor Yengun were inclined to take their guns off Tengu to go in there and find out.

Tengu was inching sideways closer to the crib. Yengun gave the child an order; Stake could tell by the way it turned its head suddenly in his direction and looked poised to stand up. But Tengu barked an order at it, too, and the child remained frozen, indecisive with uncomprehending fear.

"You want to die over this child and that blasting bracelet?" Stake said.

"You want to shoot me, huh? Go ahead and shoot me." Tengu thumped his bare chest with his free hand, eyes wild and bulging. "But I hope I don't get my blood on you. I have the gift that you demons have brought to my world—the plague that's ravishing Sinan. Your new microscopic army, to kill those of us you didn't exterminate with your soldiers! Yeah, that's right, I'm full to the brim with your poisons! So is every one of my men, here, and all the boy toys we keep. I forgot to thank you for your present, Mr. Stake, when you visited me before!"

"If you weren't afraid to die, you wouldn't be using that child as a hostage," Stake said.

"I just don't like to lose, Mr. Stake!"

"That's not true. You have something to live for... a cure. You know one will come along eventually, and with your money you can keep alive until it gets here."

"If you kill the boy," Yengun cut in, "we'll just kill you and take the bracelet. We still win."

Tengu was only a couple feet from the child, his muscled arm and the pistol's long barrel unwavering. "Oh, captain, I have a lot to say to your commander about you. He'll either boot you out of the service or shoot you himself!"

"He's too much a coward to face off against me."

"And are you brave enough to face off against all my men? If you kill me, you won't get out of here alive."

"Take a good look at our guns, Tengu. You should recognize their models; I bought them off one of your own dealers a while back. Both of them fire silently. Your men will go on dreaming of beautiful ladyboys while we're well on our way home."

"Am I to believe you'll leave me here alive if I surrender to you?"

"We're either going to tie you up and gag you— which you might even enjoy—or bring you along with us until we reach our vehicle, after which you are free to return here, unscathed except for your immense pride."

"All right, look, I'll strike a deal with you." The .340's muzzle was inches from the living idol's head. "You take the trinket, but leave my lucky boy here with me."

"Not a chance," Stake said.

"How about I just shoot your precious trinket, then?" Tengu shifted his weapon to point at the child's leg, half-folded under him.

"If that's worth dying for."

"I told you, I'm already dead!"

"Don't play games with us!" Yengun snapped. "I'm telling you, we only want the child! We leave here, and you can go about your filthy operations with my commander's blessings, as before!"

Slowly, Don Tengu turned to face the two men fully. Slowly, he lowered the gun that had belonged to Lewton Barbour's clandestine team. "All right, then... all right. I'm not an unreasonable man. If I were so lacking in flexibility, if I did not know when to step back from a fire, then I wouldn't be where I am today. Go, then. Take my boy. I'll just have another one made. Maybe from one of my slinky pets, here." He tipped his chin toward the closed bathroom door.

"Put your gun down," Yengun commanded.

Stake was a little surprised that Tengu obeyed him, laying the massive handgun down on the floor before he rose again, but he was too proud to raise his hands in surrender.

Stake then rushed to the crib and scooped the boy into his left arm. The child squirmed a little and gurgled deep in its throat, but Stake whispered in its ear as he backed toward the door.

"You're coming with us, just for a short walk," Yengun told the crime boss. "Quietly."

Don Tengu smiled. "I hope you sleep with your eyes open, Yengun," he purred. "And I hope you never turn your back on your family for too long."

"What did you say?" said Hin Yengun.

"I said—"

Yengun's gun coughed, and the slug drilled through the center of Don Tengu's chest, flinging his tainted blood clear across the room to spatter and streak down the glowing aquarium of lust that was his vidtank. Tengu was slammed back against the wall, slid down it into an awkward sitting position, legs splayed wide. Shaking uncontrollably, he still managed to look down in wonderment at his tunneled body and the black puffs of gas exhaled by the faltering beats of his ruptured heart. He looked up at Yengun again with a brave attempt at a movie star's smile.

"I told you," he rasped, "I wasn't... afraid." And then his head drooped low over his smoking chest, as if in death breathing in his own escaping essence.

"Jesus, Yengun!" Stake hissed.

"That was a mistake," the Ha Jiin captain said, "mentioning my family." He retrieved the Decimator from where Tengu had set it down, then nodded toward the door. "Let's get out of here."

EVEN WITH DON Tengu dead, Hin Yengun told Stake he would keep one of his men posted at his home at all times when he was away, until he thought he no longer had to fear reprisal from his commander or Tengu's men, should they ever learn he was the one who had killed the crime lord. There was the one witness, after all: the frightened prostitute who'd hidden in the bathroom.

The sky had grown light when one of Yengun's men arrived at his home—young Nha—during which time Stake had cleaned the blue pigment from his face and hands. He thanked Yengun's wife again for the use of it. Stake left the house just as he heard the two sons stirring in another room. Yengun drove him back toward Bluetown, which was so hazy and ghostly in the distance that it looked as if it were on the other side of the sky looking in.

Stake twisted around to glance at the child seated behind him in the bulky security vehicle. Yengun's wife had put his robes into a little bag for him, since he'd no doubt need them again at the monastery Yengun would be bringing him to after he dropped Stake off in Bluetown, but for now the wife had changed him into a set of clean clothing from one of her own children. The new clothing made Stake pity him twice as much as before. The boy wore shoes, also... but Stake wore his bracelet. He now had two on one wrist.

Utterly exhausted from too little rest, Stake turned to the front again and laid his head back against his seat, soon falling into a sleep more like unconsciousness. Before it came over him, however, he was remotely aware of a pain crowding the confines of his skull.

BEHIND THE BUILDING, in an alley, a fire escape zig-zagged its way to the flat roof of the last apartment building Stake had lived in while his mother was still alive. The steps did not clang metallically, as he remembered, but they supported his weight.

Atop the roof, the figure of an Earth man leaned over a large bundle. At the sound of Stake's shoes on the blue coral, the man looked up and around. He was almost unnaturally fit, skin tanned and smooth, body as burly and muscled as a movie gladiator's. His head was shaved bald, proudly displaying its bumpy contours as if they were lumps won in street brawls. He had two ports in the right side of his skull, and a bluish cable was plugged into one of them, but it trailed off into the sky and vanished as if it pierced the atmosphere and extended into space itself.

"What are you wired to?" Stake asked Richard Argos.

"The future," Argos said. "And the past."

Stake shifted his attention to the bundle in front of Argos. It appeared to be a human figure under a filthy blanket swarming with tiny insects. No, not insects—nanomites. Noticing that Stake was studying the blanket, Argos indulged him by taking hold of its edge and drawing it away as he stood up. Indeed it was a human body, that of a woman in an advanced state of putrefaction, swollen a shiny dark purple. Argos grinned, as if performing a magic trick. "Shh," he said, "it's my wife, Helene."

"What are you doing with her?" Stake took a step nearer.

"I wouldn't get too close if I were you," Argos said. "She hasn't been at all well." With a snigger, he pointed to the heavens. "I was going to build a trebuchet, and launch her the way armies used to catapult the parts of anthrax-ridden cows in the Middle Ages, but that's just too comical an image, isn't it? So I came up with something more beautiful, I think. Look."

Argos took hold of the cable socketed into his skull and began pulling at it hand over hand, so that it looked like he was climbing a rope into the air, but actually he was hauling something down from it. While he worked he said, "I'd squeeze the gas right out of the bitch herself if I could, but I should have married a Ha Jiin girl for that."

Stake looked up and almost gasped to see a dark parachute—diaphanous and iridescent—tethered to Argos by that one line, while a profusion of similar lines snaked freely. He hadn't seen the bender descend through the sky's blue haze until it was hovering just above them. Argos kept pulling it down, and Stake expected to see its arms reach for either of them, but instead the animal seemed attracted to the corpse of biotech heiress, Helene Camus. Its ring of longer blue arms began to encircle her body, lifting it up a bit so that the inner nest of shorter black tentacles could reach her plum-like flesh. The longer tentacles paralyzed their prey, though Helene Camus was well beyond that, but the black tentacles administered flesh-dissolving enzymes, and in her already putrid state the enzymes went to work rapidly. Stake clamped a hand over his nose and mouth and stared as, in what seemed only moments, the corpse was not only dissolved by the tendrils but sucked up through them like drinking straws, liquefied bones and all, until there was nothing left of the woman but a fetid slick.

Argos pulled the one connected limb from his head and released it. As if that were all that had kept the

huge animal grounded, it began to rise again like a hot
air balloon.

"Watch this!" he said, as engorged on pride as the
bender was on his wife.

Floating above the rooftop of Stake's old home, the
bender was beginning to give off what looked like the
windblown seeds of a milkweed pod. More and more
of these gauzy spores took to the air and dispersed in
every direction. The creature was giving birth to a
horde of larvae, each one contaminated by the foul
body its parent had absorbed. Each one would in turn
give birth to more poisonous offspring.

Stake felt frantic to stop them, but glanced around
helplessly. Argos was intent on watching the larvae as
they drifted away, his arms spread as if he were orches-
trating their flight or might take flight himself. Stake
moved to the low barrier wall that surrounded the
roof, and gazed down into the street below. There, he
saw a group of clerics walking in a line out of a shadowed alleyway. The robes of the foremost monk were
atypically covered in a pattern of golden birds, and
Stake recognized him from VT as Abbot Vonh, the
chief religious advisor of the Ha Jiin leader, Director
Zee.

Stake was afraid to call out to them and give himself
away to Argos, but he directed his thoughts at them,
hard, hoping the monks with their honed mental abilities would receive them.

"He's here!" Stake shouted at them, silently. He even
pointed toward Argos, though he knew they couldn't
see him. "Here!"

Abbot Vonh stopped in the middle of the street
below, and so the others stopped behind him. Slowly,
the cleric turned his head and lifted his missing face in
Stake's direction.

CHAPTER TWENTY-SIX
POW

THE GLOBAL POSITIONING feature of Stake's orange hoverbike wasn't working, but he was now familiar enough with Bluetown to know when he had passed from Ha Jiin land, into the Neutral Zone, and then into Jin Haa territory. And no sooner had he done so, than he saw a helicar lift from the roof of a building where it had been perched like a bird of prey waiting for its time to swoop. He veered into an alley too narrow for the craft to slip in and follow, but he knew it would keep pace above the rooftops, and when he emerged from the other end he saw there were now two helicars running with him above. They were Colonial Forces Harbingers—with guns he was sure were trained on him.

"Stake!" a voice rasped, cutting in through the speaker of the bike's vidphone. "Pull over and surrender yourself or we will open fire!"

He recognized the voice of Colonel Dominic Gale. He felt fairly certain that Gale meant what he said, but he thought he'd still put it to the test by taking a sharp turn into another, even narrower alleyway, so tight that he tucked in his elbows and hugged his legs close to the bike's flanks. He flinched and steadied his ride as the sidecar was torn away, banging end over end in his wake in a spray of sparks. Shooting out of the alley's mouth, he fought to control the yawing of the bike from side to side. He just about had it stabilized when a third Harbinger descended out of nowhere, directly in front of him, front guns leveled for action. Stake had to swerve to avoid colliding with it, and finally the bike went out from under him. Riderless, it jetted above the street for a bit before crashing into the side of an imitation mailbox. Behind it, Stake hit the ground in a bone-jarring roll, felt the coral's harsh texture tear his bare arms.

When he came to a stop he lay on his side, hugging his especially shredded left forearm, concerned that his wrist comp had been bashed against the pavement. Lifting his head, his hair ruffled in the wind thrown from a second descending helicar, he saw the camouflaged legs of soldiers as they appeared on either side of him like bars. "Do not *move!*" one man commanded, training an assault engine on him while another bent down to relieve him of the Panzer automatic.

From the second craft strode Colonel Gale, and he accepted the Panzer when his man offered it to him. "You keep managing to find yourself illegal weapons, I see."

"And you keep managing to take them away from me."

"That's the idea. But it's those I want, now." Gale pointed at the two metal bands on Stake's right wrist.

"You almost crashed me into a building. If I went up in a ball of flame, you might not have gotten these back in one piece."

"They survived all those years buried in the forest; I don't think a little fatal bike crash would've hurt them too much. Hand them over."

Stake hesitated the one second it took for the man who'd confiscated his gun to hunch down and remove the two data bracelets himself. "These things might stop Bluetown, Gale."

"Where'd you get the third?"

Third? Stake wondered how Gale could know these weren't the only two they'd officially found. So was he aware that Stake had spirited one of them away to Oasis?

"I want to talk to Henderson."

Gale slipped the bracelets into a pocket and sealed it. "I'm still enforcing the captain's convalescence. But you might want to contact a lawyer, Stake, because I'm having you arrested on suspicion of terrorist activities."

"Terrorist, huh? How is that?"

"Undermining the Earth Colonies investigation, impersonating Colonial Forces personnel... sounds like counter-intelligence or worse to me. You're coming from Ha Jiin land. That's where the kid is, isn't it?"

"You're the one undermining the investigation."

"I'll have you truth scanned, momfuck!" Gale bellowed, leaning down over Stake as if he were a fresh recruit who couldn't do that last push up. "I'll have every last drop of your memory squeezed onto a disk! I'm sick of your blasting games!" The colonel turned his flushed face to the men who'd disembarked from his Harbinger with him, while the third kept watch over the scene by hovering above. "Get this bag of dung into the can!"

"I need a doctor," Stake said.

"Yeah, Dr. Laloo will love to see you," Gale said, "after you used his identity to steal the clone."

"Are you just too proud to realize I'm on the same side as you, in this?" Stake asked the man. "Or are you still hoping to keep the old Wonky Science plan buried, so it doesn't embarrass the EC and your good friend Dink?" Stake grunted as he was roughly hoisted to his feet. "All those deadstock that would have been?"

"You're the only deadstock I see," growled Gale. He gestured toward his vehicle. "Toss him in!"

STAKE SAT UP on the edge of his bunk when he heard the cell's blue-tinged barrier of force become deactivated. He hoped to see Rick Henderson there in the doorway, but expected it to be Gale instead. What he didn't expect at all was Richard Argos, wearing a bright yellow five-piece suit and an equally sunny grin. He stepped into the cell with the barrier remaining open behind him, and two CF guards standing alert just outside. "Hello, Mr. Stake. I heard you were pretty banged up this morning. Feeling any better?"

"Gale won't let Captain Henderson talk to me, but he lets you in, huh? Do you want to sell me some gas, Mr. Argos? I hear you're full of it."

"Not really, not so much as I was once. The stores are a bit depleted these days."

"So I gather. What we need is another war to boost the body count. The way things are going, that might just happen."

"Now Mr. Stake, can't we be civil? I just wanted to be sure you were okay."

Stake nodded toward the guards behind the businessman. "Where are your robots?"

"They're around."

"And your pal, Abbot Hoo?"

Hands in his pockets, Argos strolled casually further into the cell. "You've been away, so I guess you haven't been following the news."

"What news?"

"Hoo's been assassinated. Can you imagine how? He was coming out of his temple when a flock of carrion birds attacked him—those blue things you see around, sort of a cross between pigeons and vultures? Tore the man to pieces right in front of the other monks. Horrible... horrible."

"Wow. And I'm sure you know what kind of people around here can influence animals in that way. So what do you think—it was Ha Jiin clerics?" Stake remembered Abbot Vonh from VT, and from his visions.

"That's actually not what I think. I'm afraid it's worse—that the more conservative Jin Haa clerics decided Hoo was too friendly with us Earth folk, and wanted him dead. This is a very, very unfortunate turn of events in an already catastrophic situation."

"Yeah... now it will be even harder for you to mine what little gas there is left."

"You're too cynical, detective. I mean, this can damage our relationship with the Jin Haa as a whole."

"I don't see where that's necessarily so bad. They'd be better off without us here, anyway. Bluetown. The plague." Bringing up the latter, Stake watched Argos's face, but gleaned no reaction.

"Ohh, I know your type, Mr. Stake. You like the idea of noble savages living close to the land, spreading their manure and all. But where do you choose to live? What you love is a fantasy, an ideal, but I'll bet all these Sinanese would choose to live in Punktown too if they could. My question is, which of these noble savages do you identify with the most? Gale seems to think you support the Ha Jiin."

"Gale still thinks he's at war. The fact is, I do support the sovereignty of the Jin Haa, but at the end of the day I don't care too much about the politics as long as people aren't killing each other and can live a decent life."

"That's what we all want, here. Peace, goodwill, and the mutually beneficial partnership my company has enjoyed with the Jin Haa people. If you can't see that, and they lose sight of that, then I have to say I despair at the ignorance that passes for moral superiority."

"Well, anyway, I'm sorry to hear about your friend, Abbot Hoo. I believe I saw him briefly at the Cobalt Temple Hotel, the night Captain Henderson was injured and Ami Pattaya was killed by a pack of snipes, but the abbot and I didn't have a chance to share a drink at the bar. And speaking of the Cobalt Temple and following the news, I am aware at least that David Bright has been killed. Ripped to pieces like a doll, I understand."

"A KeeZee can do that."

"So can a robot."

Argos stopped pacing like a condemned man to lean back against the wall, muscular arms folded over his broad chest. Stake noticed a shiny residue of contact jelly around one of the open jacks in his skull. His smile was growing less unfazed, taking on a more wary aspect. "Do you know the main reason I wanted to see you, detective? I had the most remarkable experience this morning. I was in the ultranet, attending a virtual conference in my virtual office, and I had a virtual baseball bat in my hands. I was walking around the table, expressing my dissatisfaction with my PR people about their lack of effort in this time of crisis. Did you ever see the Twentieth Century gangster film, *The Untouchables?*"

"No." But Stake was sure Don Tengu had.

"Well, I was just about to let the head of PR know exactly how dissatisfied I am. Hey, it's only VR—actual fatalities occurring in the ultranet are uncommon enough, right? But then in the middle of it all, suddenly I'm not in my office anymore. I'm standing on a roof somewhere in Punktown, talking to you about my dead wife, and she's lying there between us all bloated and wet from drowning." He made a wincing expression meant to represent personal loss. "I had on a parachute and I was trying to leap off this building to sail away from your pesky questions, but you wouldn't let me. And that's all I really remember. But so strange! So disturbing."

"Huh. Wow. Well... a glitch in the net. It happens."

"Yeah." Argos nodded slowly. "Felt so weird, though."

"You're under a lot of stress. And memories of your wife must haunt you. Do you feel guilty?"

"Guilty?"

"That she died while you were on vacation together? That you couldn't save her?"

"I feel sad about it, if that's what you mean."

"But at least she would have been pleased to know that her company Camus Organics carries on as her legacy, under your management. And talk about stress—it must be a real handful running both those corporations! The most powerful sinon gas operation, and a biotech research and development company besides."

"You have to be ambitious, have a vision."

"I have visions, too. But I lack your sense of competitiveness."

Argos narrowed his eyes. "I think you like competition more than you say. I think we're having our little booby-trap competition even as we speak."

"Can I tell you about my visions? I had a dream very similar to yours. In my dream, your wife wasn't drowned but a victim of some terrible plague, apparently, and you were helping spread her body's corruption across this whole planet."

"That's a very unflattering dream," Argos chuckled. "And why would I do that?"

"I suppose, to increase the rate of mortality in the Ha Jiin and Jin Haa both, to replenish the sinon gas in their burial systems."

"Oh, Mr. Stake, Mr. Stake. Next you'll be accusing me of selling diseased blankets to the people of Sinan, like English colonists used to give blankets infected with smallpox to Native Americans, at peace talks and the like."

"Funny you're familiar with such a concept."

"The truth of the matter is the opposite of what you're so crudely implying. Rather than spreading this terrible outbreak, my biotech firm is working to find a cure for it!"

Stake applauded. "Well, I have to hand it to you, Mr. Argos. First you'll make a fortune off those killed by the plague, then you'll make a second fortune curing it once your gas reserves have been replenished. That's what I call vision. But it's tunnel vision. It doesn't take into consideration the idea of accountability. It's so arrogant that it's self-destructive."

"And you aren't arrogant, detective? Self-destructive?"

"Reckless, maybe, yeah. But I can handle losing." He'd lost his parents. Lost Thi Gonh. Maybe even lost his sense of home. Was he really handling all of that, though? Nevertheless, he went on, "I'm not too proud to lose. I saw a man die last night for being too proud to lose."

"Ah, Mr. Stake." Argos stepped away from the wall and sighed. "You are an interesting man, I have to give you that." He motioned toward Stake's face. "And growing better looking all the time, too."

Stake understood he'd been reinventing himself to resemble his visitor, the way Dink Argosax had reinvented himself to become Richard Argos. "You're an interesting man, yourself. Not only a mass murderer, by introducing a disease to these people, but a serial killer besides. David Bright, Anthony Leung... maybe even Lewton Barbour and everyone else killed in the mishap at Wonky Science."

This time Argos wasn't smiling, his composure fractured at last. "That's just insane, now. You're more paranoid than that moron Bright was. Unless it was my dear old friend Persia who put that particular bug in your ear. If I'm as psychotic as you suggest, Mr. Stake, then why are you provoking me like this?"

"Because I want you to know I'm onto you, and that you should back off and let me do what I have to do and stop Bluetown from spreading, whether it brings the Wonky Science project to light or not."

"And who's stopping you? We all want the same thing here."

"No we don't. You want to make money. I want to help these people, not turn them into rotting deadstock for a profit."

Now it was Argos who applauded. "And people think I'm the king of gas production! But my gas supports a vast array of technology. My gas enables teleportation across space and through dimensions! It enhances the lives of countless people. All your gas is good for is a farting contest. If that's what we're competing at, then I concede. You win, detective!"

"I know what your gas company produces, Mr. Argos. But let's get back to what your wife's company produces. Organic computers, for one. Like the brains in your bodyguards. This STD results in massive neurological damage and the deterioration of the brain. I figure if one can make brains, one can also find a way to destroy them. Who knows... maybe this degeneration of the body makes corpses decay faster, huh? Produce sinon gas that much more quickly?"

"Oh, now this is a stretch, even for you."

"Maybe. But Camus has also designed organic nanomites, a microscopic life form. Just as this virus is a microscopic life form."

"Your science is wretched, Mr. Stake. There's a universe of difference between micro-surgical nanomites and a mutant strain of virus. What do you think, that I have some loyal cult of diabolical fiends helping me achieve all these plots you accuse me of?"

"No, just a group of people who like your money an awful lot. I just pray that the government isn't aware you're spreading this disease. I just pray they don't like your money that much, too."

"What's going on?" said a voice from the door. Stake looked up to see that a new figure in a camouflaged uniform had appeared beyond the threshold, and Rick Henderson had both his hands again. It was his eyes that looked ready to strangle, however. "Mr. Argos, I don't see where you have any business being in here."

"I was just concerned about your friend's welfare, captain."

"I'm sure. But if you'll excuse us, please."

"Of course." Argos shifted toward the exit as Henderson stepped inside to let him pass. "I'm sorry we have to end our conversation at such a compelling point, Mr. Stake. I divide my time between Punktown and Earth these days. Should you be deported to Punktown, perhaps I'll look you up sometime."

"And if we both get sent to prison, for our various improprieties," Stake told him, "maybe I'll look you up there."

Argos smirked. "Unlikely, since you and I dwell in different spheres—it might as well be different dimensions—but I'll keep that in mind. We'll do lunch sometime, somewhere." Argos bowed a little to Henderson on his way out. "Good day, captain."

The officer turned to Stake. "What was that all about?"

"Gale let him in."

"Well that won't be happening again. I've been pushing CF high command on Earth, and I've got absolute authority to handle all aspects of the Bluetown investigation, the clones and everything else related to it—including you. Gale has to step out of my way whether he outranks me or not. But it wasn't just my efforts that turned things around. There are some people here from Paxton. Persia Barbour, with her late husband's parents."

Stake rose from his bunk. "Thank God. That was fast."

"They have some clout. Lewton Barbour's father is a top biomech surgeon and the mother is an anthropology professor at PU. And to back them up, they've got the media behind them, shining a bright light on the proceedings. Crews from three news agencies are here, including the Punktown branch of the Earth Colonies News Network."

"Good job, Persia," Stake sighed. "I didn't know if she had the guts to go all the way."

"Well, she does look pretty spooked to me. Last I saw her, the parents and their whole retinue were at the embassy with Margaret Valsalva. Persia Barbour seems very keen on avoiding meeting Argos face-to-face. When she was told he was over here with Gale, she wouldn't come see you."

"I don't blame her for wanting to avoid him. She's in danger from him. If he doesn't know she's here, the longer it can be kept from him the better."

"You'd better concentrate on your own welfare, for the moment." Aside from their recent phone conversation, Stake had never seen Henderson look so stern with him. "You're in some serious deep dung here, Jer. The only way I can help you now is if you tell us

where you took Brian. If we can put a happy end to
the cute clone story for the media, and the Barbours
take him home to raise their son all over again, you'll
be a good guy instead of a kidnapper and the obstruc-
ter of an EC investigation. But you have to take us to
Brian *now*."

"I can't lead you to him, Rick. I have a friend caring for him. My involvement with this person puts
them in danger. I have to go and get Brian alone, and
then I'll bring him back to you. That's the only way I
can do this."

"Gale caught you coming over from the Ha Jiin side.
Brian's on Ha Jiin land, then, isn't he? Who's he with,
Jer? Who do you know over there? It isn't Thi
Gonh…"

"No names, Rick. You have to trust me, here. I'll get
the Barbours their son, but it has to be done my way."

Henderson blew the air from his cheeks. "All right,
look, let's go over to see the Barbours and talk to Margaret Valsalva. I'll have to tell them how this is going
to happen."

"Can we trust Margaret Valsalva?"

"With the ECNN cameras in her face, I'd say yes.
Everyone wants to look good on VT."

WHEN HENDERSON AND Stake arrived at the Earth
Colonies embassy, they found Chief Ambassador Margaret Valsalva had Persia Barbour and her in-laws in
her office, but there were no media people in attendance at present. Stake smiled at Persia, who nodded
back at him with a tight smile of her own. Lewton Barbour's parents were very anxious once Stake was
introduced to them.

"Are you sure the child is safe right now?" the mother asked.

"He's in good hands. The people he's with are just
waiting for me to reclaim him."

"I remember seeing him on VT spots, and I thought it was a strange and sad situation, but I never once made the connection with my son. We were told Lewton died in an attempt to teleport to Earth, not Sinan," she gave her daughter-in-law a look of restrained accusation, "and everyone has said the Sinan clones were from Blue War soldiers missing in action." Lewton Barbour's mother appeared stricken with guilt at not having recognized her son from VT, and torn as to whether to view this anomaly as her actual child reincarnated, or as a facsimile that she might love anyway in homage.

"A good thing someone leaked it to the media about the boy in the first place," Stake said, giving Henderson a quick glance to remind him that the detective wasn't the only one who had gone to extreme lengths to protect Brian, "or you might never have known your son's clone existed."

"We've been shown some vids," the father said, weary with pain and confusion himself but his eyes shining with the pride of a parent who had just seen their child take its first steps. "He's beautiful. We want him to have a normal life—in as much as that's possible—with a loving family. His *own* family. We won't leave Sinan without him."

"I'll go and get him straight away, after I make a call to arrange it." As had been their system, Stake would call Yengun first so that he might contact Thi himself, in case her husband was monitoring her. She, in turn, could let her sister know that Stake was coming to claim the boy.

"We all want what's best for this child," Margaret Valsalva said, folding her hands on her desk as if posing, should the camera crews return at that moment. Stake thought of the "Valsalva Maneuver," which was a means of forcing out the contents of one's bowels while seated on the toilet. *A good name for an espionage movie,* he thought.

Without replying to the woman, Stake turned to Henderson. "What about the ID bracelets, Rick? Did you get back the two that Gale took from me?"

"I have them," Persia spoke up, "and the one you gave me before. I've already been reprogramming it, as we discussed, to transmit new information to the smart matter in the code it understands. I'll reprogram the other two immediately. And when I arrived I spoke to a gentleman named Cali, a technician for Simulacrum Systems. He and his whole team are going to work with me on this, lending me support in doing everything we can to get the smart matter to listen to the new commands. Well, not that the bracelets commanded the smart matter in the first place—the Simulacrum equipment did that—but the positioning transmissions gave it a new schematic, so what I'm going to do is ascertain how much of the Punktown map the smart matter has reproduced, then bracket off just a little more land area and delete the rest of the map. Theoretically speaking, when the smart matter comes to the borders of this new edited blueprint, it will feel that its work is complete... and stop. Better than trying to alter the cells' nature. Even primitive cells want to follow their destiny. This way it's, 'Good job, boys—you can call it a day.'"

"Sounds like a plan."

"Well done, acquiring that third bracelet, Jer," Henderson told him. "How'd you manage it?"

"A story for another day. I have a gun, too, that belonged to Barbour's team, but I left that with another friend in case I needed it later to prove Gale was lying about the artifacts found with the clones." Not to mention that Hin Yengun had simply become enamored with the big Decimator revolver.

"I promise to look into the fact that the existence of these items was not made known to me," Margaret Valsalva said. "The colonel faces some serious questioning about how this matter was handled."

Save it for ECNN, Stake thought, remembering how chummy the ambassador had been with Argos the first time Stake had met him. He said to his old friend, "Rick, I'm going to need to borrow a helicar again. And I'm serious—I need to protect my friend, here. You have to promise me I won't be observed, tracked, or followed."

"You have my word on it."

CHAPTER TWENTY-SEVEN
WHISTLERS

STAKE KNEW WELL the place where he was to meet Thi Gonh, when Yengun called him back to relay the information. He saw it before him now as he approached in his borrowed Harbinger. The Plastech Foundries company had been shut down for many years, before even the map Bluetown was following had been generated, so Bluetown portrayed it in its sealed up state. Not only that, but the smart matter had replicated the parasitic restaurant called J. J. Redhook's Crab Cabin, which stood on legs in what had once been Plastech's cooling basin. Stake had eaten there numerous times, the silverfish-like crustaceans the restaurant served being seeded and raised in the basin itself. He saw that tropical rains had filled the basin almost to the level of its original.

As he neared the towering foundry building one of the military craft's display monitors alerted him to another presence in the air: what appeared to be a helicar tailing Stake at a closing distance. He scowled. Would Henderson break his word and send someone to track him, after all? He thought not. Maybe Gale then, acting on his own? Unlikely, at this point. He thought it might be one of the VT crews, having got wind of his errand; they would be less wary of the politics regarding Ha Jiin territory. But just as Stake was beginning to get angry, and considered flying past the rendezvous site in order to lead the other craft away, it veered off into a city chasm and left his screen. He considered opening up the monitor's range, but decided that the craft hadn't been following him after all. Maybe just tourists, anxious for a look at the infamous Bluetown.

As he curved around in a descending half-circle, Stake realized his heart was beating hard, and not out of anxiousness about retrieving Brian. Maybe it wouldn't have mattered so much if he'd let Henderson and others accompany him to the pick up. The simple fact was, he had to admit, that he wanted to meet with Thi Gonh again without his fellow Earthers looking on.

He took in the scene below, the most salient element being a yubo standing at the edge of the flooded cooling tank. It was dipping its sinuous back appendage into the water, and Stake saw it raise the limb up suddenly, grasping a squirming something-or-other in its eight-fingered hand. A number of boys and old men lay on their bellies or sat at the edge of the crab cabin's platform, trailing fishing lines into the pool. Had amphibians or some other type of animal made the basin their home, or had the Ha Jiin introduced them into the water as J. J. Redhook stocked his own tank with his giant silverfish? A fire had been built off to one side, and more of the pool's catch were cooking on a metal grill.

He hadn't noticed until now, because of their blue-on-blue colors, that plants were growing on the buildings themselves in this area. Some walls, facing the dual suns, were almost entirely covered as if with ivy. He recognized these as air plants, like terrestrial epiphytic plants, that needed no soil to root in. Instead, their airborne seeds had nestled into nooks and crannies, where their roots had taken hold. Now, fern-like shrubs exploded out of open windows, beds of spiny-leaved plants jutted up from tenement roofs, and flowers like orchids—themselves an epiphytic plant—bloomed along ledges as if growing out of window boxes. Even more amazing to Stake was that he saw women tearing handfuls of leaves from one of these types of plants and stuffing them into woven baskets. He realized it was a kind of herb he had eaten in various Sinanese soups and dishes. He was reminded of his vision of a city reclaimed by the jungle—but it wasn't only the jungle reclaiming it.

Laundry dried on lines strung like lianas between buildings. A woman with a broom swept in front of what had been an outer shed of a steelworks complex, now serving as a home. Stake understood that what he was seeing was a village, superimposed upon the city after it had superimposed itself over numerous villages—as if, impossible to remain drowned, these submerged communities were rising again to the surface.

Blue faces tilted up to watch Stake bring his vehicle in for a landing. He scanned them for the one face he sought. Just as the craft was alighting, he spotted a familiar group standing off near the peripheral structures of the steelworks. They were watching him, too. Climbing out to the street, he focused on three women who carried the wasp-like Kalian rifle known as a Whistler. A small boy with an incongruously pink face stood half-behind a tall young girl Stake knew would be Thi's teenage niece, Twi. And there was a small man standing near Thi Gonh herself. Recognizing him, and hearing the man's excited shouts, Stake strode toward them briskly.

"You! *You!*" Thi Gonh's husband screamed, jabbing his finger toward Stake before gesticulating at her again. "I knew she come here and meet you! I knew! I follow the bitch and see!"

"Calm yourself down," Stake said ominously as he came. Seeing Brian with his hands over his ears only made the dark brew bubbling in his guts more bitter.

Thi's husband Hin thrust one hand at her and snarled, "Give me that gun, bitch!"

Stake saw Thi look to him, her eyes hooded and tense. He knew that under other circumstances, she would have backed down quickly, out of respect and probably even fear. But she had another obligation—to return the child entrusted to her care—so she remained planted there between the boy and her husband without saying a word and without moving a muscle, like a POW standing firm under interrogation, even on threat of torture.

Hin looked back at the approaching Earther, and jerked his open hand at his wife more urgently. "Obey me, cunt!" He stepped closer to her and cocked back his arm, fist clenched for a blow. "Give it to me!"

"You stupid fuck," Stake said, seeing what was coming even before Thi Gonh took a single step forward and swung the butt of the Whistler up in an arc. There was a crack like a ball against a baseball bat. Hin's head shot back as if he'd taken a bullet in the forehead, and his body hit the pavement.

Still conscious but minus his two front teeth, Hin lifted his head to see that Thi's sister Yha and her daughter Twi had edged nearer to his feet and were aiming their own Whistlers down at his face. He didn't sit up one millimeter further. Thi spoke in her native language then, in a hard dark voice, and though Stake couldn't understand most of it the meaning was pretty clear.

"I apologize for dishonoring you, husband, but you have dishonored me since the day we were married. The apology I owe you is for marrying you in the first place—it was unfair to both of us, because I never loved you any more than you loved me. For becoming your wife, I am truly sorry. I will respect our ways and stand by my vows. I will care for you as a wife should. And if you ever put a finger on me again, I will kill you in an instant."

Hin stared up at the three cold-eyed women with his own eyes wide, spluttering frothy blood bubbles in exasperated terror.

Stake came to a stop, facing Thi with her husband lying between them, but ignored him as if he were of no consequence. "Please thank your sister and niece for taking care of Brian, Thi. It's time for me to take him to his family now."

"I am sorry you see that, Ga Noh."

"Don't be sorry. If I can only go on remembering you, at least I want to remember you with respect."

"Only you respect me."

Stake nodded toward her sister. "I don't think that's true. Having said that, I do think you're a fool if you stay with this worm."

"If I am wife of Ga Noh, not want me stay with you always?"

"If you were my wife, I'd treat you the way you deserve. Your loyalty is misguided, Thi. Whether it's loyalty to him, or to your culture."

"Some things we never understand each other. Please... not judge me." Her eyes finally looked moist. "Enough people judge my life. Earth Killer. Earth Lover. I am only Thi."

Yha barked an order at Hin, and jerked the barrel of her rifle to indicate he should get to his feet now. He looked like he was on the verge of muttering to himself, but thought better of it and spit some blood onto the ground instead. Thi was just turning to say something to him again herself, and Stake was turning toward Twi with Brian behind her, when a string of holes opened up in the pavement just to the right of the detective. From the holes jetted pulverized smart matter, looking like puffs of billiards chalk. Stake swung around and saw a second line of holes zigzag toward Twi and Brian. The last puff in the air was red, and Twi dropped to her side screaming, leaving Brian exposed and startled. Blood spread across Twi's pants at midthigh.

"Run, run, run!" Stake shouted, rushing toward Twi and grabbing one of her arms. With her other, she still held onto her weapon despite her wild sobbing. Half dragging Twi under his arm, Stake looked back to order Thi to scoop up Brian, but saw she already had and was running off with him in another direction, to make their attacker have to choose between two moving targets. Hin was left whirling around in circles, abandoned and disoriented, before he loped off in a third direction with his head tucked into his shoulders.

Refugees were crying out, scattering, a couple back toward the old foundry even plunging into the water of the cooling basin. Stake made it to one of the steelworks' satellite structures and ducked behind it even as a firecracker chain of projectiles strafed across the front of the little building. He flattened himself there for a moment, pushing Twi behind him, and then crouched low so he could peek around the building's corner.

A figure was racing in his direction, looking like a cross between a human and a giant ant with its green body segments connected by lengths of flexible silver cable. In one hand, the robot carried a machine pistol with a curved magazine. The barrel raised, the muzzle flashed a nova of hot gas, and the gun made a distant, soft burble. Stake pulled back just in time as bullets chewed up the edge of the building.

Stake spun toward Twi with the intention of grabbing the Kalian Whistler from her. What he saw was the teenager at the other end of the back wall, bracing herself against it to take the weight off her wounded leg. Before Stake could tell her to stop, she had the gun wedged into her shoulder and was slipping around the side of the building out of view.

"Jesus," Stake hissed, and he almost lunged after her. Instead, he peeked out from behind the chewed corner again. He thought he heard something fizz through the air, though the rifle itself was silent, and the thick central cable that passed for the robot's waist was severed. Scythed into two pieces, the automaton went down, though its legs did their best to run for a few steps more before they toppled.

The upper body was more alive than the lower, however. The head and gun lifted from the pavement. Stake almost pulled back, but the robot's skull shattered like a green lollipop, releasing an atomized spray of encephalon tissue. As the machine dropped back, truly dead this time, Stake glimpsed Yha across the way, leaning out from behind a storage shed with her Whistler shouldered.

Stake sought out Twi on the far side of the building, and this time he did take hold of her weapon. She resisted a little, her beautiful face crumpled in agony, but Stake grasped her by the wrist and directed her to put pressure on the wound in her leg. He hoped he wasn't being egotistic in thinking his experience with weapons might be better than the education Thi Gonh had passed on to the girl.

"Shh," he said to her, poking his head out and retracting it again. He didn't know if she understood him, but he said, "There's still another one of these things."

The helicar that he'd wondered about; so it had been tailing him after all. Was the second robot waiting behind the vehicle's controls for its partner to rejoin it, or had it disembarked on foot as well? Stake almost marveled at Argos's lack of discretion, but he knew the man was unused to limitations. The question was, was the target him or Brian? He supposed Argos would be happy to see either of them filled with bullets. Stake, because he was his new enemy, and maybe Brian because he was an old rival who wouldn't stay buried.

"Stay here," Stake whispered, gesturing to the girl and dropping his eyes to her bloodied pants again to determine an artery hadn't been hit. "They don't want you." Then, clutching her gun in both hands, he broke into the open and ran toward another structure, this one looking like some sort of power relay, more machine than building. He almost hoped to draw fire, so he'd know if the second robot was close by and where it might be lurking, but nothing came. He caught his breath in the relay's shadow, his eyes on the next outbuilding. This was the direction Thi had bolted in, lugging Brian in her arms. His wrist comp hadn't been damaged in his bike accident, after all, but he knew Thi didn't have a comp on her that he could contact.

A person dashed between two buildings and Stake tensed up, thinking it was Thi at first, but then recognizing it as Yha headed toward her daughter's hiding place. Good; Stake felt less guilty about having left her.

Then he heard the splutter of a machine pistol, not aimed in his direction. The other robot had discovered Thi, then, before he could. He broke cover again and sprinted toward the deceptive purr of a second discharge of automatic fire. This burst was more prolonged, as a finger kept the trigger depressed. Puffing as he ran, Stake realized a knifepoint of pain was slipping behind his left eye, probing toward the bridge of his nose.

There was a tree sitting at the edge of a parking lot ahead of him, appearing as though it had grown straight through the blue pavement, though its reek and the eerie movement of its roots identified it as a slow-moving carrion tree. The second blast of fire had ended but Stake was following its last echoes when a skeletal shape stepped out from behind the tree's trunk. Without stopping he brought the Whistler up close to his face, and a bullet struck the weapon as others hummed past his head and took a notch out of his right ear. The impact against his gun levered it hard in his arms, smashing him across the nose. Stake fell backwards, meeting the ground in what seemed a flashback of his hoverbike crash.

He couldn't raise both his head and the Whistler, so he left the latter lying across his chest and looked up through a new membrane that had grown over his eyes, gelatinous and pulsing with dark veins. The creature from the tree shadows was striding toward him. It was working at one of its limbs, which ended in a bulky smoking appendage. He heard a metallic scrape as the creature dislodged a curved section of the appendage's underside. The creature was like an insect, with sinuous silvery limbs dazzling with glints and glitter. Stake thought of insectoid surgical nanomites. He had seen a news story about a mutant strain of escaped nanomites dwelling in one of Punktown's slums; their queen was as big as a hippo when the health agents discovered her. This was an entity like that, then. It was here to see that its countless microscopic brethren dispersed their viral contamination throughout the land. It was here to destroy anyone who stood in the way of that mission—as soon as it had fitted a new curved object into the underside of its smoking hand.

A bright smacking sound. The nanomite's head came open like an egg, and damp spores of corruption blew into the air in a volcanic mist. The creature teetered, swayed, spilling cranial fluid between its dead silver eyes. Then, it crashed forward onto its face and Stake saw pickled brain matter oozing to the ground like some escaping giant ameba.

He let his head rest back on the pavement and closed his eyes, willing their new lenses away. A touch of hands made him open them again, and he recognized Thi Gonh leaning over him. Her fingers were dabbed red from examining his clipped ear, but she was smiling. "I am always saving Ga Noh."

"Yeah," he mumbled drunkenly. "Well, you said you owed me, remember?"

CHAPTER TWENTY-EIGHT
AUDIENCES

STAKE HAD A dream along the way to the capital city of
Coo Lon, which lingered at the edge of the vast Ha Jiin
territory as if to gaze wistfully and resentfully across
the Neutral Zone at its divorced counterpart of Di
Noon. When they arrived, and he awoke, Stake knew
it had been a dream instead of another bender episode.
In the dream, he had come to Sinan to find that he had
impregnated Thi Gonh during the Blue War, this genet-
ic impossibility apparently overcome by the
adaptability of his mutant cells. The blue-skinned child
Thi introduced to him, however, was only five years
old. The boy seemed to recognize him, lifting his little
arms and saying, "Mee!"

"Me?" Stake said to the dream child.

Hin Yengun, in handsome dress uniform, accompanied Stake as they were led by a party of armed guards
into the seat of the Ha Jiin government, a beautiful
palace of blue marble clouded with white and veined
with gold. They were conducted into a chamber with a
high ceiling supported by gilded columns, the ceiling a

colorful mosaic depicting more scenes from the eventful life of the prophet Ben Bhi Ben. Behind a high counter of lacquered wood sat the leader of the Ha Jiin people, Director Zee, handsome with his close-cropped head and trimmed goatee. To his right sat his top religious advisor, Abbot Vonh, in his familiar robes embroidered with golden birds. Stake had to remind himself that he had never seen the man in person before this. He wondered if he seemed just as familiar to the inscrutably faceless cleric.

There was another familiar person in attendance, whom Stake had not anticipated. Atop a velvet cushion in a high chair to Abbot Vonh's right sat what might have been a miniature version of himself. Stake knew this was the child he and Yengun had freed from Don Tengu's compound; his good luck charm. The living icon wore a brand new robe. It was covered in a design of golden birds.

To Director Zee's left stood a stunning young woman with a sweetly melodious voice, who commenced to speak in English. "Jeremy Stake, you have been summoned into the presence of the honorable Director Zee so that he might extend to you his appreciation for helping to liberate this poor child from the possession of a disgraceful criminal whom had eluded justice for too long. Had the existence of this child been known to Director Zee, he would have called that criminal to task sooner."

Stake didn't want to ask why the Ha Jiin leader had indeed not dealt with Don Tengu many years before this. It was easy to denounce the man now that his dead hands could no longer pass out money. Stake found it easier to simply nod in acknowledgment.

"And the information has come to us that you have made great efforts to halt the advance of the Blue City, efforts that it now seems will prove successful. While you may have acted more on the behalf of your own people and the Jin Haa, you have helped put a stop to one of the greatest catastrophes the Ha Jiin people have ever faced. For this, Director Zee would like to bestow upon you a token of his gratitude."

From the counter she lifted an object wrapped in a velvet cloth, which she bore before her as she stepped down from her perch and approached Stake. She turned back a flap of the cloth to reveal the handle and part of the blade of what he knew to be a short sword at least a hundred years old. These were what Ha Jiin warriors had once carried into battle, long before Sturms and Decimators, Panzers and Whisperers. Stake accepted the sword with a deep bow in the leader's direction. Director Zee gave a small smile and slight nod.

Next, Director Zee himself spoke to Yengun in their shared tongue, his voice softly modulated. At the end of this, again the young translator came bearing a swaddled sword to present to the security officer.

"Now," the woman said, having returned to the leader's side, "we are told you would like to address the honorable director, Mr. Stake?"

"Yes." Stake cleared his throat. "First of all, I would like to thank the director for this great honor; I'm very proud." He paused to let her translate this. "What I wanted to ask the director is if he would also acknowledge the assistance the war hero, Thi Gonh, lent me in my endeavor to understand and control the Blue City. She, her sister, and her sister's daughter risked their lives to protect the cloned child who was the key to this great mystery."

After she relayed all this, Director Zee spoke to the woman, and she said, "Your recommendation has been noted."

Director Zee's smile had spread somewhat. Was he amused at this request from the man who was obviously the Earth Lover's lover, or was he impressed with

Stake's devotion?

The Ha Jiin leader hadn't finished speaking through the woman yet, so she went on, "Abbot Vonh has been having troubling visions, Mr. Stake. Some of them concern the Earth business owner, Richard Argos. The abbot believes you may understand what he means by this. The abbot believes you have encountered each other in the dream realm several times."

Sort of like the original ultranet, huh? Stake thought. "I survived the sting of a bender, yes. I've had a number of strange premonitions myself. In several of these, it did seem I crossed paths with the abbot."

"As you have investigated the Blue City situation exhaustively, Director Zee would like to know what your own observations are regarding Richard Argos."

As much as he was appalled by Argos's actions, Stake didn't dare tell even Yengun about his suspicions that Argos had spread the nameless STD epidemic by design. It was a familiar theory by now, but not one that any Earther had thus far spoken in support of. Director Zee might believe the Earth Colonies government itself had been aware of Argos's activities, had even sanctioned them. And he couldn't say for sure that he didn't believe that, himself. For the same reason, he didn't want to spell out the whole of Wonky Science's Plan A, which had resulted in Lewton Barbour and his two teammates perishing on Sinan before there had ever been a Blue War. If the Ha Jiin and Jin Haa found out everything eventually, then let them do it on their own. If Earth colonists were barred from Sinan as a result of that knowledge, he washed his hands of it, as ardently as he hoped that wouldn't happen. Because if it did, he might never return to Sinan himself one day.

Instead, Stake was evasive but still very clear, he felt, when he replied, "Mr. Argos is a terrible and dangerous man. He is no friend to the Ha Jiin or even the Jin Haa people." He turned to face Abbot Vonh directly as he continued, "I return to Oasis tomorrow night, so I've arranged to meet Richard Argos for drinks this evening." He tried to screw his thoughts into the holy man's orifice of a face. Had he seen the faintest flicker of violet electricity far back in there? "At the Cobalt Temple Hotel."

"Why would you meet him socially," asked the woman, "if you feel he is so terrible a man?"

"I guess I just want to rub it in again that I see inside him. I want him to know, again, that I haven't finished with him yet. I'm sure that's why he agreed to meet me. I'm sure he isn't finished with me yet, either."

Director Zee dictated to his translator, who said in turn, "You must be very careful, then, Mr. Stake. Director Zee will say a prayer for your safety, and he wishes you a safe return to Oasis as well."

With their audience come to a close, Stake and Yengun were escorted out of the chamber. Stake threw a look back at the living idol. The boy raised one fingerless hand as either a gesture of goodbye or a benediction.

OUTSIDE THE GOVERNMENT palace, parked at a discreet distance down the street, was a small hoverbus usually rented for tourist excursions, which had brought Stake here to Coo Lon. Yengun walked him back to it. "May we never cross these swords in combat, Mr. Stake," Yengun said, carrying his wrapped award reverently.

"I'd never want to cross swords with you," Stake said. "There are limits to my courage."

When they had arrived at the bus, Yengun motioned toward Stake's bandaged right ear. "You look like you're imitating Henry again. How is your ear?"

"What?" Stake cupped a hand to it.

Yengun smiled, and gave Stake a Colonial Forces style salute. "Corporal Stake."

"Captain Yengun. Excuse me—that is, Commander Yengun."

The new commander of Ha Jiin border security, as of this very afternoon, nodded in return. Stake watched the man pivot on his heel like a soldier on parade, and march away.

Inside the hoverbus, waiting for Stake, were Persia Barbour and the crew from ECNN. The latter had been forbidden from filming the proceedings inside the palace, but had shot Stake entering and leaving the building from inside the vehicle. He showed them all his sword, and the cameraman took footage of it while Persia noted, "The more you're in the public eye, like Brian, the less likely anyone in the government or CF will dare put a finger on you."

"No longer an advocate of hiding, Mrs. Barbour?"

"I just hope that seeing the Ha Jiin make so much of you doesn't cause the Jin Haa and our own people to lose sight of all you've done for them."

"Let them hate me. With David Bright dead, someone has to be the pariah."

Persia's former in-laws had come along, as well, as had Brian and Bernard, who was sharing with Lewton Barbour's parents his knowledge of the boy's needs and behaviors.

"Our miracle boy's come amazingly far in just a matter of weeks," Bernard noted. "I've taught him something new today, detective. Want to hear it?"

"Sure."

Bernard bent low and interrupted the boy from scribbling with crayons to whisper in his ear. Brian promptly beamed up at Stake and said, "Jer-a-MEE!"

* * *

A NUMBER OF gorgeous Jin Haa women with killer cheekbones and inky hair, spaced along the bar of the Cobalt Temple lounge, smiled at Stake as he made his way past them, and he wondered if one of them were the "clean, classy" lady David Bright had favored and fatally sent his KeeZee to retrieve. At the end of the bar was a person with a rather less welcoming expression, however: Dominic Gale, with two soldiers on the stools flanking him. Though Stake could now see Richard Argos sitting alone across the room, and beckoning to him, Stake went to Gale first. The colonel had summoned him with a jerk of his goateed chin.

"Going home tomorrow, Stake?"

"Yep."

"Good."

"I'll miss you, too." The private investigator started away, but looked back to say, "How's it feel to be Argos's new bodyguard, colonel? Or should I say, his new robot? I'm sure Ami Pattaya would be proud."

"Listen, Stake. Come here," Gale snapped. When the detective had returned a few steps, Gale said in a lower, more subdued voice, "I just want you to know that no matter what gets investigated now, no matter what might come out in the media about Wonky Science and all... well, you know the rumors about the plague. The rumor that it's been spread intentionally. I just want you to know that no matter what, I wouldn't have anything to do with something like that. I wouldn't."

Stake stared at the man for a long moment, and nodded. He believed him about that much. "I've got a date with your buddy now, if you'll excuse me." He then turned away to go join Richard Argos at his table in the murkiest corner of the room. It wasn't until he seated himself opposite Argos that he saw a cable was plugged into one of the jacks in the businessman's skull, the other end attached to a small device tucked into a breast pocket of his jacket. His expensive business suit was a brilliant white.

Stake waved a hand in front of the man's face as if he might be in a trance. "Are you here with me, Mr. Argos, or in the ultranet at the moment?"

"I'm in the shallow end of the pool," Argos said amicably, lounging back in his seat. "Doing a little business. It's what you call multitasking, consolidating my time. What's the matter, detective—you can't pat your head and rub your belly at the same time? Don't worry, you have my undivided attention despite appearances."

A waitress brought them drinks: an exotic green concoction in a martini glass for Argos and a Zub beer for Stake. As if his own bright green drink reminded him of his dead twin robots, Argos said, "I'm terribly sorry to hear my two robots attacked you and your friends, Mr. Stake. It's very unfortunate that their brains were destroyed; now we won't know what terrorist might have reprogrammed them to do such a thing."

"Mm."

"It could be someone trying to frame me."

"A lot of heinous plots like that going around—yeah."

Stake repositioned himself anxiously in his seat, and glanced over his shoulder toward the entrance to the lounge as if he might spot a Ha Jiin monk lingering in the threshold. He had looked up and down the street before entering the Cobalt Temple, but had seen not a single cleric. No flock of metallic blue birds perched on the ledge of a roof, awaiting their commands. No snipe crouching with glowing eyes under a parked vehicle. As terrifying as any one of these things would have been, he was nevertheless disappointed by their absence.

"How's my dear Persia looking these days? A lovely, lovely lady. Have you thought of asking her out for a drink? She's a bit of a cold fish, I'm afraid, though I intend to look her up when I've ventured back to Oasis myself."

"You can stop trying to give me the creeps; it's not something you have to force."

"Oh boy, Mr. Stake—please remind me why I even agreed to meet with you tonight at all?"

"It's our Building the Better Booby-trap competition. No fun unless you can look your competitor in the eye."

"Sounds more like chess."

"Whatever your analogy of choice is."

"The fact of the matter is that the business I'm conducting," Argos tapped the ultranet pod in his pocket, "is a meeting with my lawyer, and I'm a bit stressed this evening with all the commotion going on, so I'd hoped we might be civil and relax a little together. Call a temporary truce, you know, like what happened at Christmas during World War One? The two enemy forces coming out of their trenches to exchange gifts before they went back to shooting each other's heads off the next day? I love that story." Argos dabbed a mock tear from his eye. Stake despised him. The man steeped in his own loathsomeness with something like glee. Stake supposed that was all a part of being so successful: celebrating your flaws until they became something exalted. "You know, just a couple of regular guys out for a few drinks?"

"You and I will never be regular guys."

"I'll drink to that!" Argos raised his glass. "And who would ever want to be?"

Argos's glass remained poised in midair, and his face took on a quizzical expression, as if a thought had occurred to him and stayed his hand halfway to his mouth. After several beats, watching the man's fixed but unseeing eyes, Stake leaned forward and said, "Mr. Argos?" He wanted to wave his hand in front of the businessman's eyes again.

The glass dropped from Argos's hand, striking the glass tabletop and shattering. Argos fell back on his cushioned seat, and through the clear table Stake saw his legs beginning to spasm and jerk. His arms were flopping, spread out to his sides, as well. A weird sound rose and fell from the man's gaping mouth, and still his eyes didn't blink.

"What is it?" Stake heard Colonel Gale call behind him, and as the detective got to his feet the officer and two soldiers came to his side. The four of them looked on as Argos's seizure rapidly intensified, and he flung his head from side to side. His arms batted at the air as if to drive off a swarm of stinging wasps.

One of Gale's men said, "Sir, I think it's his ultranet connection—we should disconnect him!"

The other soldier started forward, but Gale thrust out an arm to block his chest. In an uncommonly cool tone, the colonel said, "Don't touch him. Just call Dr. Laloo down here."

"Sir," the first soldier said, "he might not survive until Dr. Laloo gets here!"

"We don't want to make his condition any worse by acting rashly. Unless you forgot to tell me you're a field surgeon, private, you'll just do as I say."

The soldier complied, stepping aside to activate his comp. Stake glanced over at Gale, but the officer continued to watch Argos as he thrashed and wouldn't acknowledge him.

Finally, wailing uncannily as he whipped his head, Argos managed perhaps by accident to catch hold of the cable jacked into his skull, and tear it loose. It was as though his power source had been severed. The seizure immediately ceased, and as Argos's arched, rigid back settled, a wisp of bluish smoke uncoiled from the port in his shaven head.

Argos's eyes rolled like those of a man lost in the thrall of drugs, but when they found Stake the man reached a hand out to him. Stake moved in close. Argos grasped the front of his shirt, drew him lower to whisper in his ear.

"Snipes," he said. *"Snipes."*

Stake felt the hand clutching his shirt relax, and then it slipped away, Argos's arm falling limply across his chest. Stake straightened up, saw that the man's eyes were still open but seeing into a realm as devoid of anything as the ultranet was full.

Stake looked around at Gale, but the man continued to ignore his gaze, despite their complicity in what had just taken place. Instead, the Colonial Forces commander gave new orders to his underling.

"Call Dr. Laloo again, and tell him that Richard Argos is dead."

EPILOGUE
WAR HEROES

YELLING CHILDREN PRECEDED the rumbling vehicle into Vein Rhi like a scruffy vanguard, looking over their shoulders as they ran to get a sense of where exactly in town the machine was headed. With its windows tinted an opaque black on the outside, it was impossible for them to know who was inside, but it was obviously a military conveyance. It eventually ground to a halt in front of the house of Thi Gonh's cousin, Nhot, whose father and mother were also on the scene, lending a hand as Thi and her husband Hin made preparations to leave their temporary home. With the machine's arrival, they had all stopped in the middle of loading boxes into the back of a wagon harnessed to a snorting, restless yubo and another pulled by a three-wheeled motor-bike. Commander Hin Yengun and six of his patrolmen emerged from the muscular vehicle and jumped to the ground. The new border security commander was in his dress uniform, and holstered at his side was a huge Decimator .340 revolver that had once belonged to a mercenary named Johnny Esperanto.

"Sir," Yengun said to Thi's uncle, greeting him as the patriarch of the extended family, as was customary. The uncle, a former captain in the Blue War, gave a crisp but wary nod in return. Yengun then focused his attention on Thi herself. Her hair was tied back in a jaggy ponytail and her thin, yellow top and pants were smudged with the dirt of her labors. "I have come on behalf of our leader, Director Zee," Yengun announced in the Ha Jiin language, "to recognize a former war hero for their contribution to the good of the Ha Jiin people."

The uncle straightened his posture a little, but it was to Thi that the commander walked, extending to her a parcel wrapped in a velvet cloth. She wiped her hands on her legs before accepting it. A corner of the cloth was folded back to reveal the handle and part of the blade of a century-old short sword.

"Accept this token of Director Zee's appreciation for aiding in the efforts to halt the Blue City and thwart our latest enemies, but also in belated recognition of your courageous service during our civil war."

Thi nodded. She was too humble to smile in pride.

Yengun's smile signified that he was now relating his own sentiments, and not representing the chief of his nation. "We have much work ahead of us, regarding the Blue City. With the help of the Earth Colonies, some areas will be razed but most of them will have to remain, and we will make of them what we can. It is my understanding that you have decided to claim the portion of the city that once was your farm?"

"Yes, sir. We are heading there now. There are several buildings we are converting to our uses." The windows of one building had been extensive energy barriers separated by thin frames. Only the frames had been reproduced, allowing much sun and rain to enter into the various floors of this structure. Thi hoped that they could spread soil deeply enough on the floors of these rooms to build a multileveled greenhouse of sorts to grow crops in. On the ground floor of another, smaller building in which they intended to live, they planned to open a small store out of which to sell these crops—and other items trucked in from Coo Lon—to their neighbors. They were auctioning off their yubos in exchange for a small breed of comestible bird and to help fund the customization of their transformed property.

"Many families will be doing the same," Yengun said. "More and more of them will be returning to the Blue City. They will find themselves at risk from the benders and packs of snipes that have become rampant there and taken to hunting refugees. Our security forces will be taxed, and we will need to either recruit more soldiers or deputize citizens to give us assistance. I would like to reinstate your military status, Thi Gonh, and ask you to lend me your support. Your skills as a sniper would be of much use to us in ridding the city of these dangerous creatures, and in keeping the peace by discouraging two-legged predators and troublemakers."

This time Thi allowed herself a smile. "I am honored by your offer, sir, but I will be so busy working on my property..."

"Of course, but will you consider it, at least? Our crews work on a rotating basis. If you could only give me a day or two in that schedule, even that will help."

Thi looked over at her husband. He had always known of her skills as a combat sniper, but except for the killing of animals had never seen this for himself until the two robots had attacked. From his hiding place that day, he'd witnessed her dispatching the second automaton. Thi then glanced at her uncle. He was looking on with hurt pride rather than pride for his niece, since his hands held no velvet-wrapped sword of his own, but he still stood erect in an obligatory attitude of respect. Yengun followed the woman's line of sight and saw the cowed look in the two men. He next took in Nhot, with her scabrous bald head. Jeremy Stake had told him about her. Nhot met Yengun's gaze. Yengun stared at her until she was forced to avert her eyes lest they catch flame in their skull sockets.

"I will consider your offer," Thi told the commander.

"Fair enough." He backed away a step. "Fair enough. Regardless of your decision, I will be around your property from time to time, to see how you are progressing, and if there is anything I can do for you." Yengun turned to face Thi's husband and moved close to him. He leaned his head in closer, and in an intimate low tone said, "You are married to a very special woman, sir. You would be wise to count your blessings. Should you forget how fortunate you are, and so much as pluck one hair from her head, my men and I will nail you to a tree in the jungle, and every day we will visit you and take off another inch of your worthless hide." Then, grinning as if at an old friend, Yengun patted Hin's shoulder. Before he walked away Yengun heard the man's throat click as he swallowed.

Yengun returned to Thi's side, and this time leaned in close to her, too. He murmured, "There is someone in my vehicle who is waiting to see you, if you would please let yourself inside a moment."

Without explaining herself to her husband or any of the others, Thi Gonh moved toward the dusty vehicle resting there on its big wheels, stepped up onto its running board and opened one of its hatch-like doors. There was a lone Earth man sitting far back inside. He was in his neutral, "factory settings" mode, as anonymous as a crash test dummy that awaited some planned cataclysm, and yet even without his little porkpie hat Thi would have recognized him. She shut the door heavily behind her so she could go sit close to Jeremy Stake. As soon as she had done so, their arms went tightly around each other and she laid her head in the hollow of his shoulder.

Stroking her small, sleek head, Stake whispered to her, "I'm going home now." She nodded against him. "If you ever need me, you call me. I'm only a dimension away." She nodded again.

After a few hushed moments, during which he continued to stroke her hair, she began speaking to him. What she said was entirely in her own language, but he knew she was articulating to him what she needed to hear herself say. And while he only comprehended a few of the words himself, such as the last term she used, Jeremy Stake understood his former enemy perfectly well.

She said to him, "I understand now why I love you. I have many faces, too. A face for my husband, a face for my lover. Face of a patriot, face of a traitor. We have both been seen as traitors by our people, but we have always been true to ourselves, haven't we? I have heard they are proposing a name we can call this city by. They want to name it Paxton—the 'town of peace.' Some people don't like that idea and want to call it something new, but I hope that is what they call it. I want to know I am living in the same city you are living in. Walking the same streets you are walking. I will be under these twin stars, but I will also be beside you, in Punktown, my Ga Noh."

ABOUT THE AUTHOR

Jeffrey Thomas's milieu of Punktown has been the setting for other of his books, such as the novels *Everybody Scream!*, *Monstrocity*, and *Deadstock*, which is the first novel to feature *Blue War*'s protagonist, Jeremy Stake. Thomas's Punktown-based short stories are collected in *Punktown* and *Punktown: Shades of Grey* (with brother Scott Thomas). Several of these books have been translated into German, Russian, and Greek language editions. Jeremy Stake also appears in the story "In His Sights" in the first volume of *The Solaris Book of New Science Fiction*. When not visiting Punktown, Thomas resides in Massachusetts, USA.

Check out Thomas's blog, message board, and more at: *www.jeffreyethomas.com*

"The king of high-concept SF." — *The Guardian*

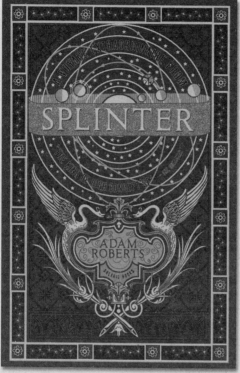

ISBN: 978-1-84416-490-5

When Hector discovers his father has channelled the family fortune into a bizarre survivalist sect who await the imminent destruction of the Earth, he is wracked by feelings of betrayal and doubt. Things change, however, the night an asteroid plummets from space and shatters the planet, leaving Hector and the remnants of the human race struggling for survival on a splinter of the Earth.

www.solarisbooks.com

 SOLARIS SCIENCE FICTION

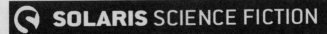